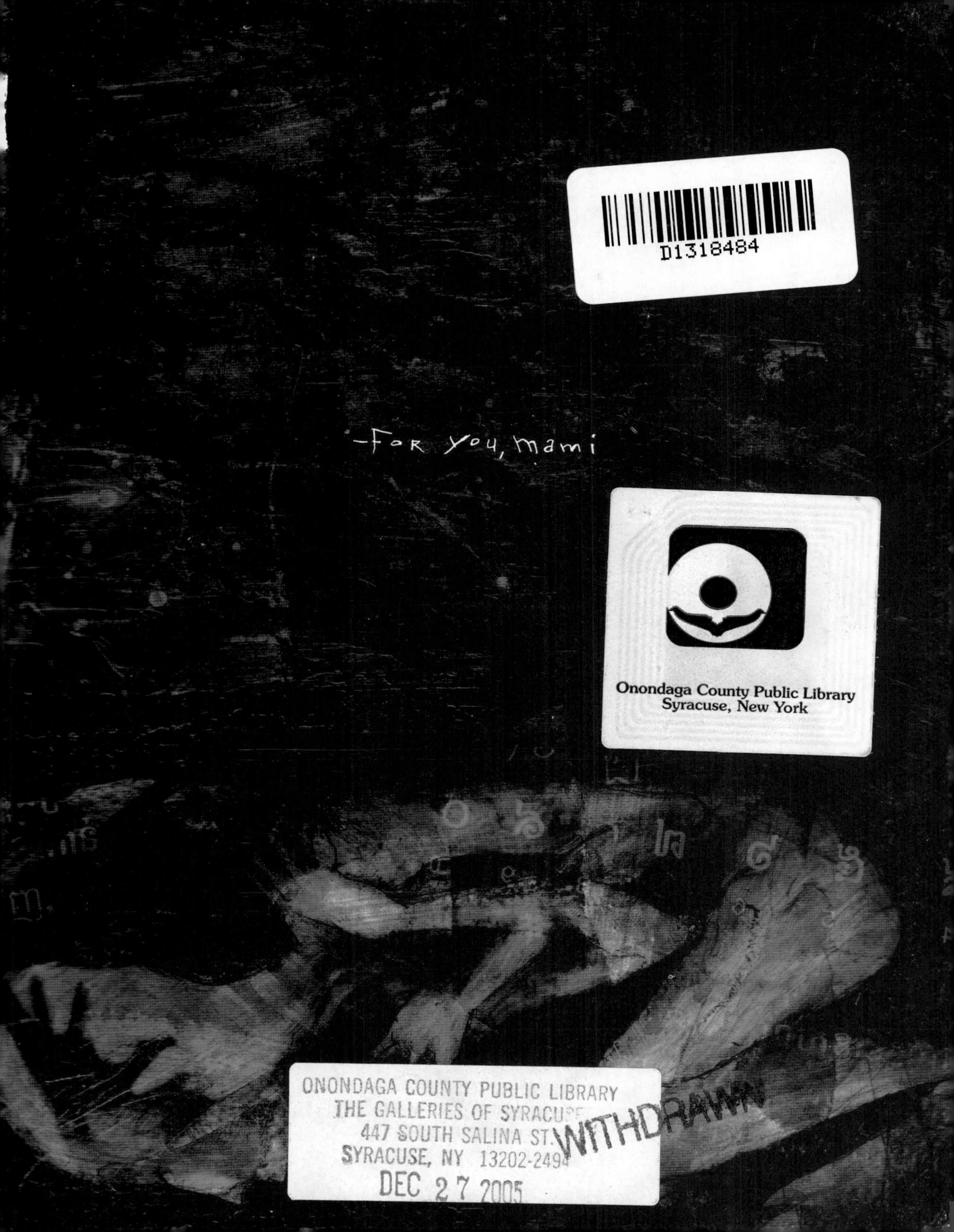
-For you, mami

Acknowledgments

For their support, advice or inspiration, I'm grateful to Gary Groth, Kim Thompson, Caroline Tse, Tony Cheng, Glenda, Suheily Natal-Nazario, Lord Jesus, Barnes & Noble, Ben of Civilized Age, Andrew Lis, Jello Biafra, Ivan Vélez, Maalox, Venus Photography, Juxtapoz Magazine, Smith & Wesson, Haroula Spyropoulos, the University of Chicago, Absolut Vodka, Carlo Rossi, High Times, the writings of Daniel Guérin, Howard Zinn & Noam Chomsky, Kinko's, Sendero Luminoso, Ill Taz, RJ Reynolds, and to my father, for showing me what kind of man not to be.

X-tra krispy thanx to Ho Che Anderson.
—get some taste and buy his stuff.

A big fuck you to the Department of (in)Human Services of Illinois
EAT SHIT AND DIE, MAGGOTS.

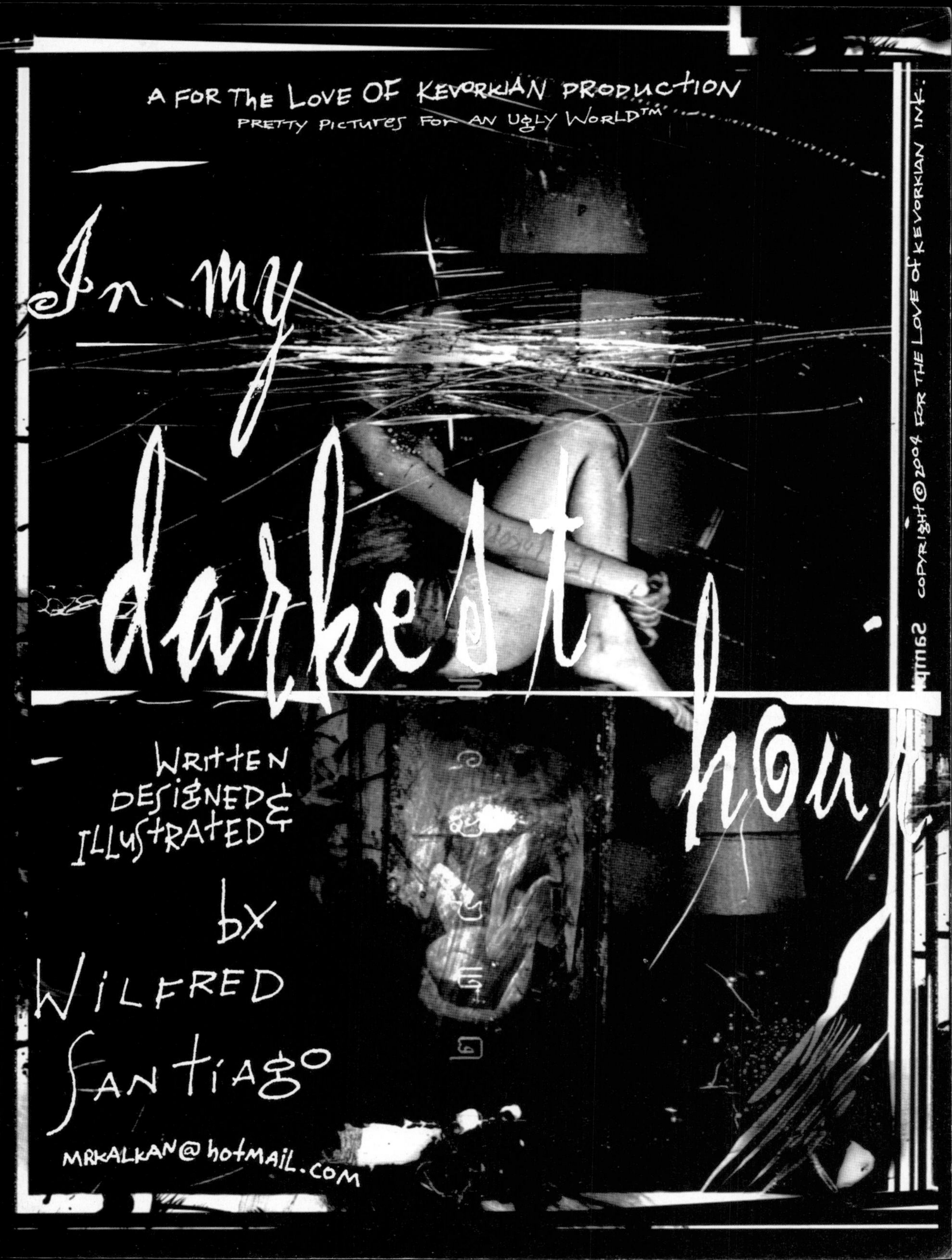
A FOR THE LOVE OF KEVORKIAN PRODUCTION
PRETTY PICTURES FOR AN UGLY WORLD™
In my darkest hour
WRITTEN DESIGNED & ILLUSTRATED
BY
WILFRED SANTIAGO
MRKALKAN@hotMAIL.COM
COPYRIGHT © 2004 FOR THE LOVE OF KEVORKIAN INK.

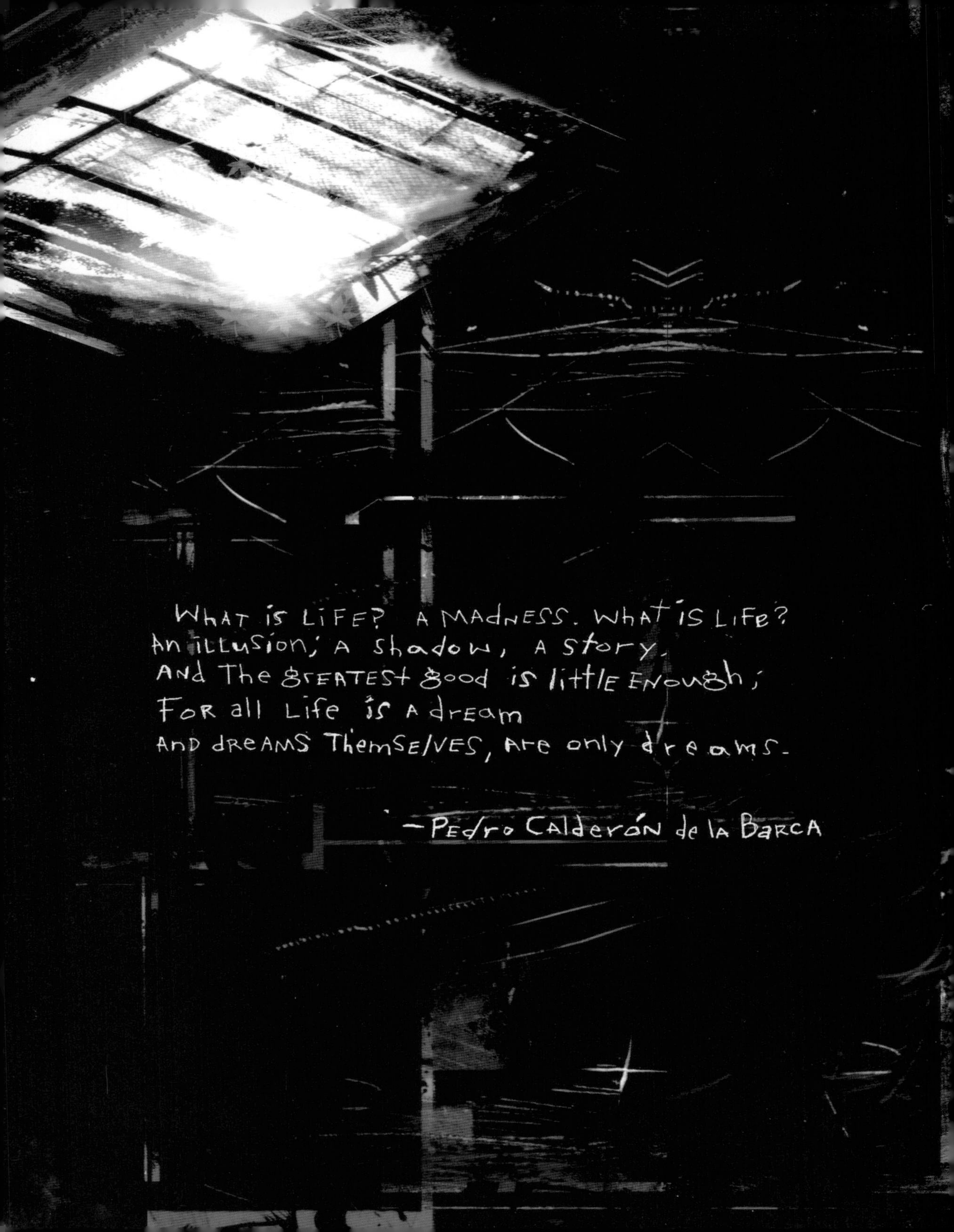
What is life? A madness. What is life?
An illusion; a shadow, a story.
And the greatest good is little enough;
For all life is a dream
And dreams themselves, are only dreams.
—Pedro Calderón de la Barca

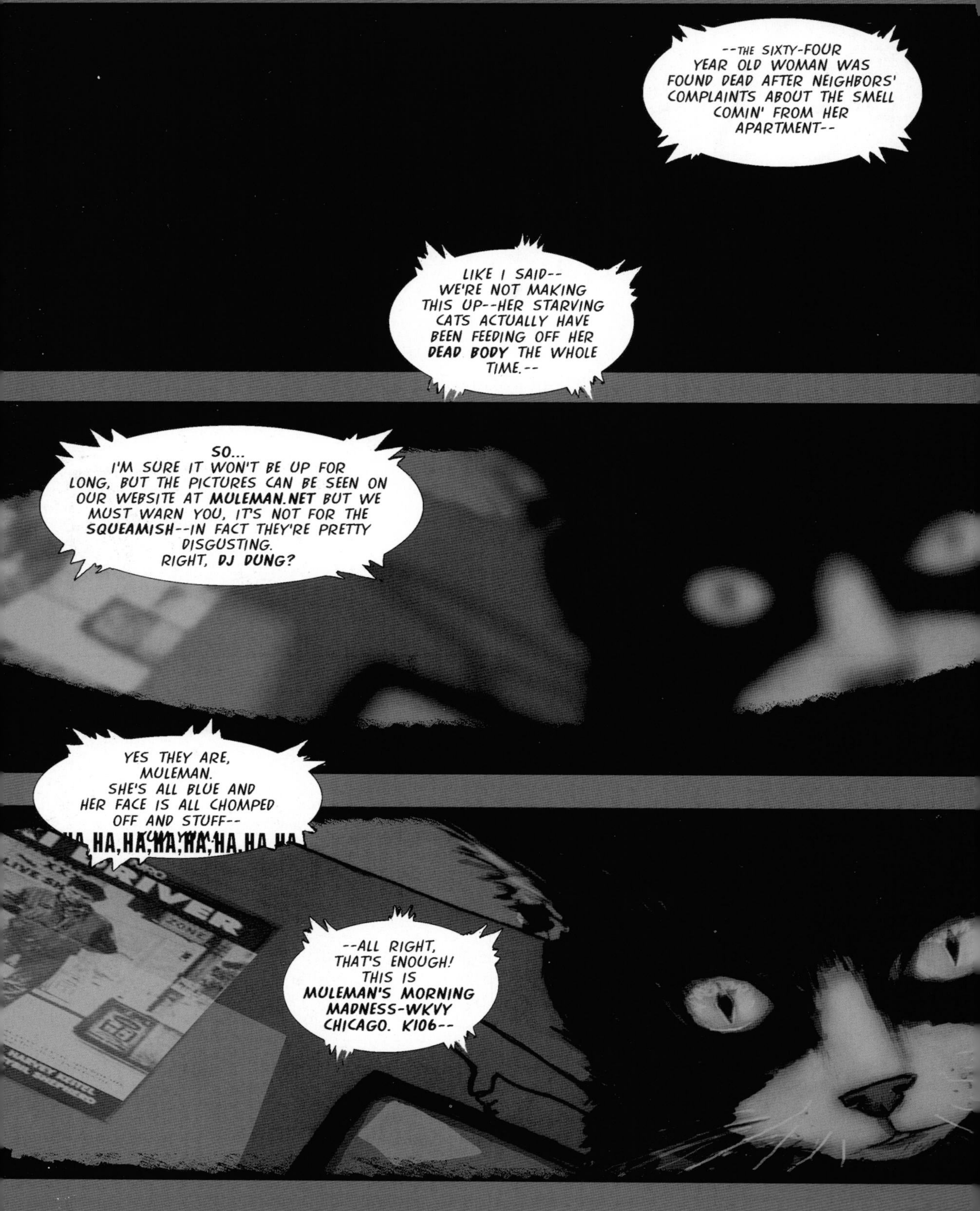
--THE SIXTY-FOUR YEAR OLD WOMAN WAS FOUND DEAD AFTER NEIGHBORS' COMPLAINTS ABOUT THE SMELL COMIN' FROM HER APARTMENT--
LIKE I SAID-- WE'RE NOT MAKING THIS UP--HER STARVING CATS ACTUALLY HAVE BEEN FEEDING OFF HER DEAD BODY THE WHOLE TIME.--
SO... I'M SURE IT WON'T BE UP FOR LONG, BUT THE PICTURES CAN BE SEEN ON OUR WEBSITE AT MULEMAN.NET BUT WE MUST WARN YOU, IT'S NOT FOR THE SQUEAMISH--IN FACT THEY'RE PRETTY DISGUSTING. RIGHT, DJ DUNG?
YES THEY ARE, MULEMAN. SHE'S ALL BLUE AND HER FACE IS ALL CHOMPED OFF AND STUFF--
HA,HA,HA,HA,HA
--ALL RIGHT, THAT'S ENOUGH! THIS IS MULEMAN'S MORNING MADNESS-WKVY CHICAGO. K106--

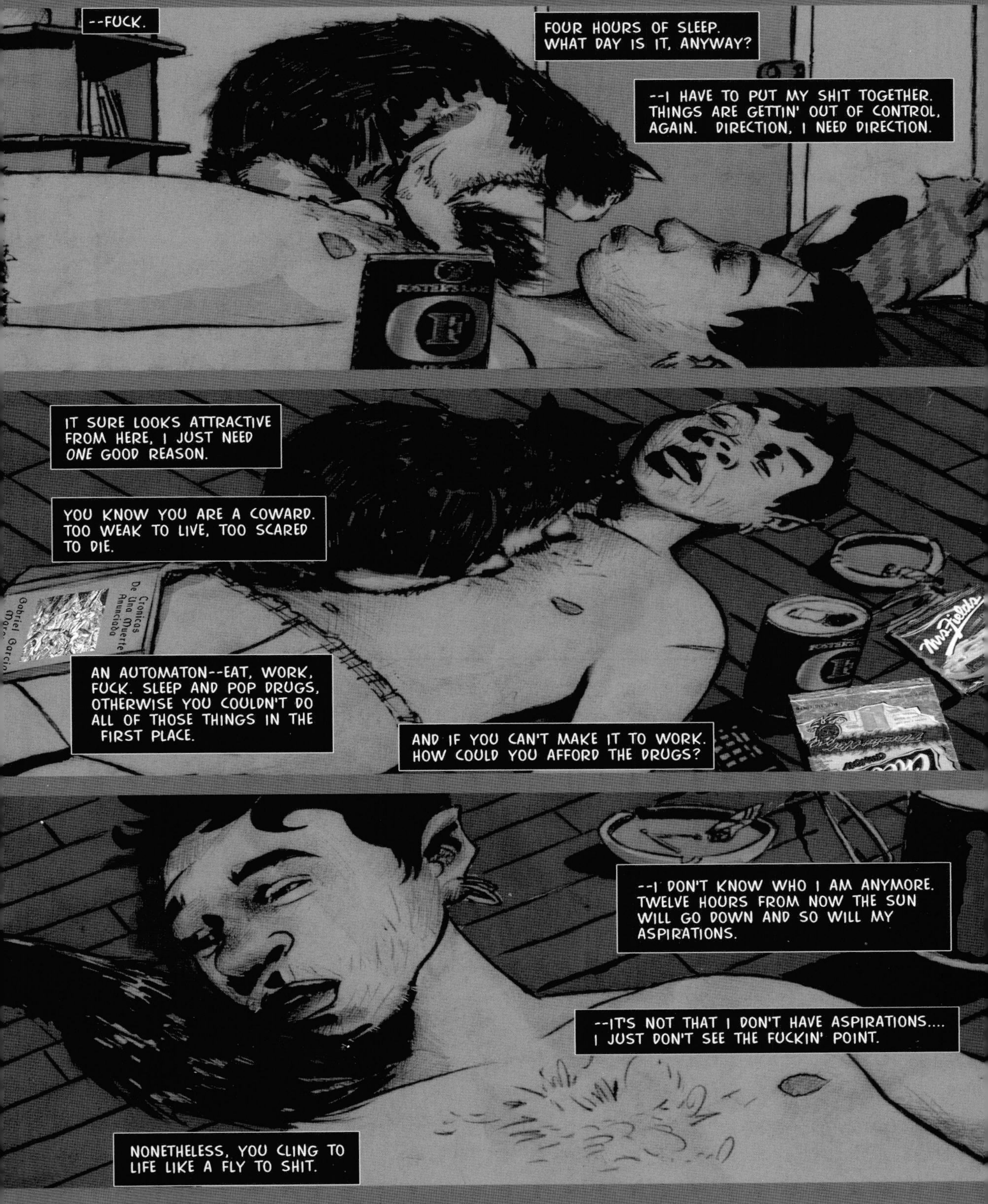
--FUCK.
FOUR HOURS OF SLEEP. WHAT DAY IS IT, ANYWAY?
--I HAVE TO PUT MY SHIT TOGETHER. THINGS ARE GETTIN' OUT OF CONTROL, AGAIN. DIRECTION, I NEED DIRECTION.
IT SURE LOOKS ATTRACTIVE FROM HERE, I JUST NEED *ONE* GOOD REASON.
YOU KNOW YOU ARE A COWARD. TOO WEAK TO LIVE, TOO SCARED TO DIE.
AN AUTOMATON--EAT, WORK, FUCK. SLEEP AND POP DRUGS, OTHERWISE YOU COULDN'T DO ALL OF THOSE THINGS IN THE FIRST PLACE.
AND IF YOU CAN'T MAKE IT TO WORK. HOW COULD YOU AFFORD THE DRUGS?
--I DON'T KNOW WHO I AM ANYMORE. TWELVE HOURS FROM NOW THE SUN WILL GO DOWN AND SO WILL MY ASPIRATIONS.
--IT'S NOT THAT I DON'T HAVE ASPIRATIONS.... I JUST DON'T SEE THE FUCKIN' POINT.
NONETHELESS, YOU CLING TO LIFE LIKE A FLY TO SHIT.

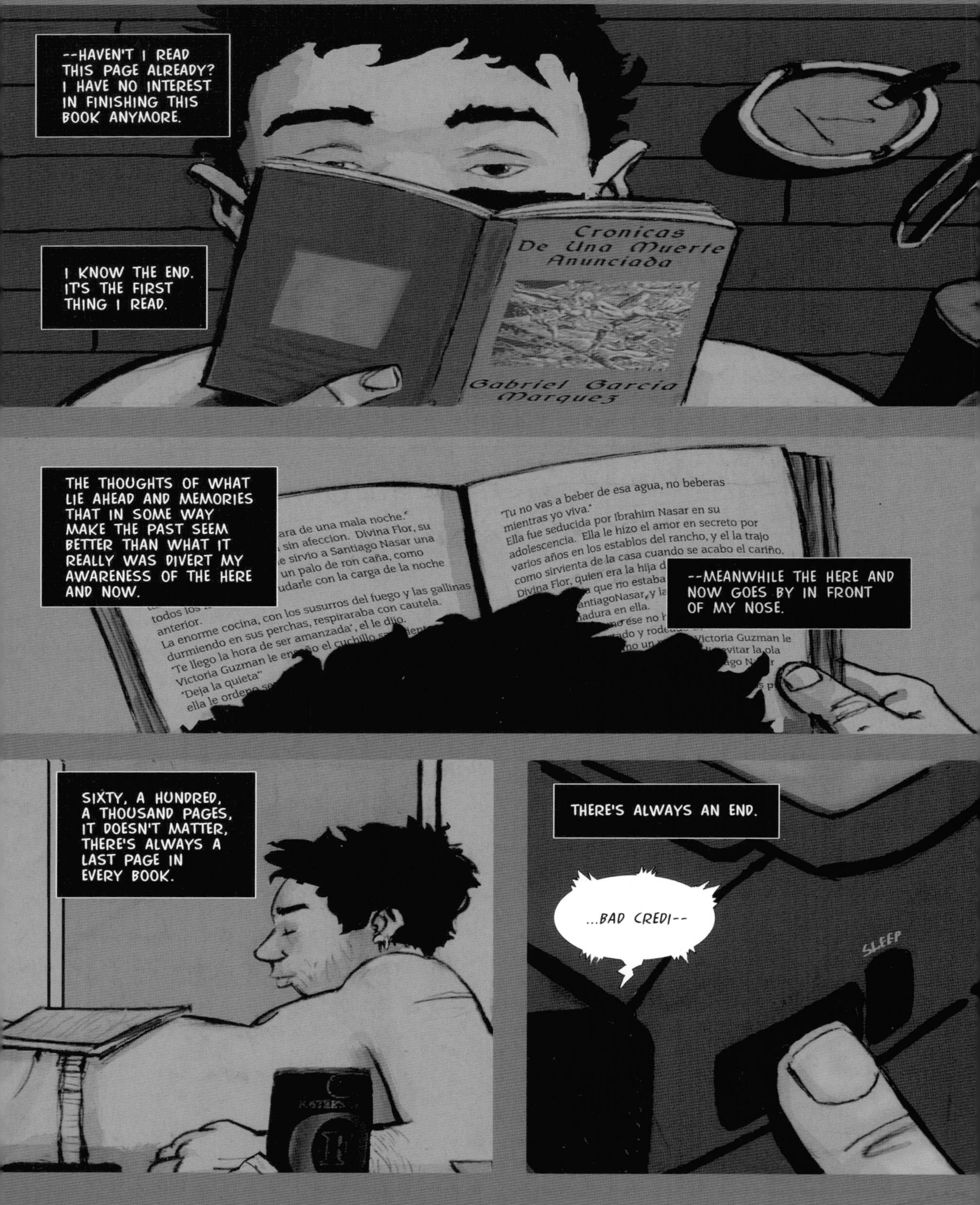
--HAVEN'T I READ THIS PAGE ALREADY? I HAVE NO INTEREST IN FINISHING THIS BOOK ANYMORE.
I KNOW THE END. IT'S THE FIRST THING I READ.
Cronicas De Una Muerte Anunciada
Gabriel Garcia Marquez
THE THOUGHTS OF WHAT LIE AHEAD AND MEMORIES THAT IN SOME WAY MAKE THE PAST SEEM BETTER THAN WHAT IT REALLY WAS DIVERT MY AWARENESS OF THE HERE AND NOW.
--MEANWHILE THE HERE AND NOW GOES BY IN FRONT OF MY NOSE.
SIXTY, A HUNDRED, A THOUSAND PAGES, IT DOESN'T MATTER, THERE'S ALWAYS A LAST PAGE IN EVERY BOOK.
THERE'S ALWAYS AN END.
...BAD CREDI--
SLEEP

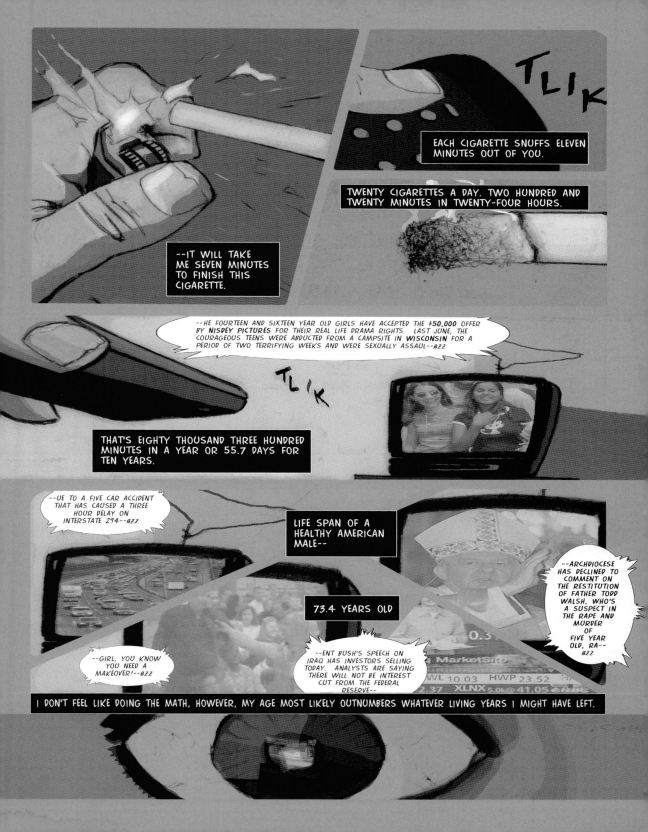

TLIK

EACH CIGARETTE SNUFFS ELEVEN MINUTES OUT OF YOU.

TWENTY CIGARETTES A DAY. TWO HUNDRED AND TWENTY MINUTES IN TWENTY-FOUR HOURS.

--IT WILL TAKE ME SEVEN MINUTES TO FINISH THIS CIGARETTE.

--HE FOURTEEN AND SIXTEEN YEAR OLD GIRLS HAVE ACCEPTED THE $50,000 OFFER BY *NISDEY PICTURES* FOR THEIR REAL LIFE DRAMA RIGHTS. LAST JUNE, THE COURAGEOUS TEENS WERE ABDUCTED FROM A CAMPSITE IN *WISCONSIN* FOR A PERIOD OF TWO TERRIFYING WEEKS AND WERE SEXUALLY ASSAUL--*BZZ*

TLIK

THAT'S EIGHTY THOUSAND THREE HUNDRED MINUTES IN A YEAR OR 55.7 DAYS FOR TEN YEARS.

--UE TO A FIVE CAR ACCIDENT THAT HAS CAUSED A THREE HOUR DELAY ON INTERSTATE 294--*BZZ*

LIFE SPAN OF A HEALTHY AMERICAN MALE--

--ARCHDIOCESE HAS DECLINED TO COMMENT ON THE RESTITUTION OF FATHER TODD WALSH, WHO'S A SUSPECT IN THE RAPE AND MURDER OF FIVE YEAR OLD, RA-- *BZZ*

73.4 YEARS OLD

--GIRL, YOU KNOW YOU NEED A MAKEOVER!--*BZZ*

--ENT BUSH'S SPEECH ON IRAQ HAS INVESTORS SELLING TODAY. ANALYSTS ARE SAYING THERE WILL NOT BE INTEREST CUT FROM THE FEDERAL RESERVE--

0.3
MarketSite
WL 10.03   HWP 23.52
2.37   XLNX 5.0k@41.05

I DON'T FEEL LIKE DOING THE MATH, HOWEVER, MY AGE MOST LIKELY OUTNUMBERS WHATEVER LIVING YEARS I MIGHT HAVE LEFT.

KLIK

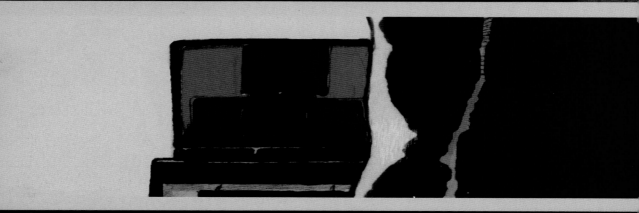

--I CAN'T STAND THIS FUCKIN' SILENCE....

PURRRRRRRRRR

IT MAKES YOU
FEEL LIKE PREY.

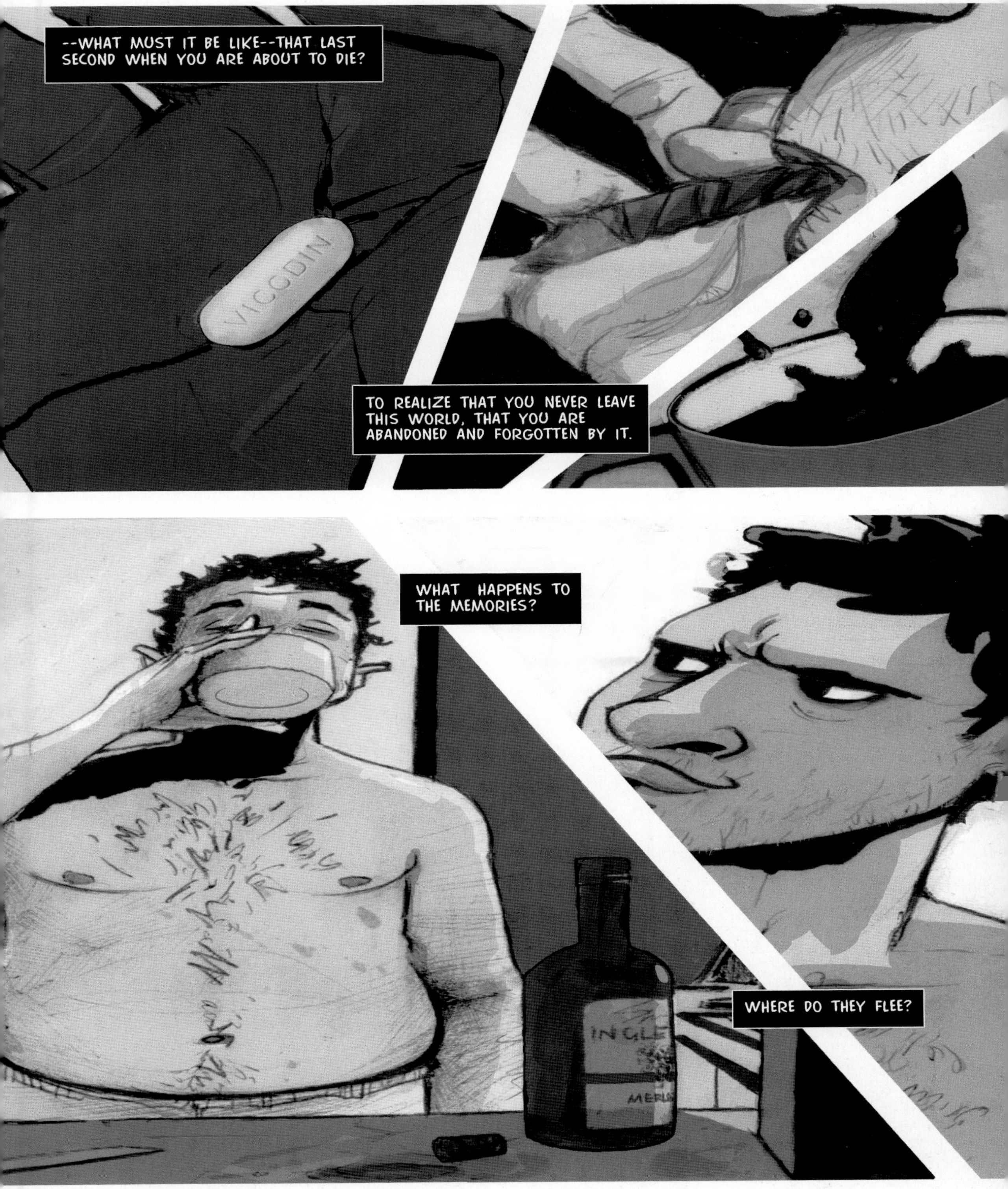
--WHAT MUST IT BE LIKE--THAT LAST SECOND WHEN YOU ARE ABOUT TO DIE?
VICODIN
TO REALIZE THAT YOU NEVER LEAVE THIS WORLD, THAT YOU ARE ABANDONED AND FORGOTTEN BY IT.
WHAT HAPPENS TO THE MEMORIES?
WHERE DO THEY FLEE?

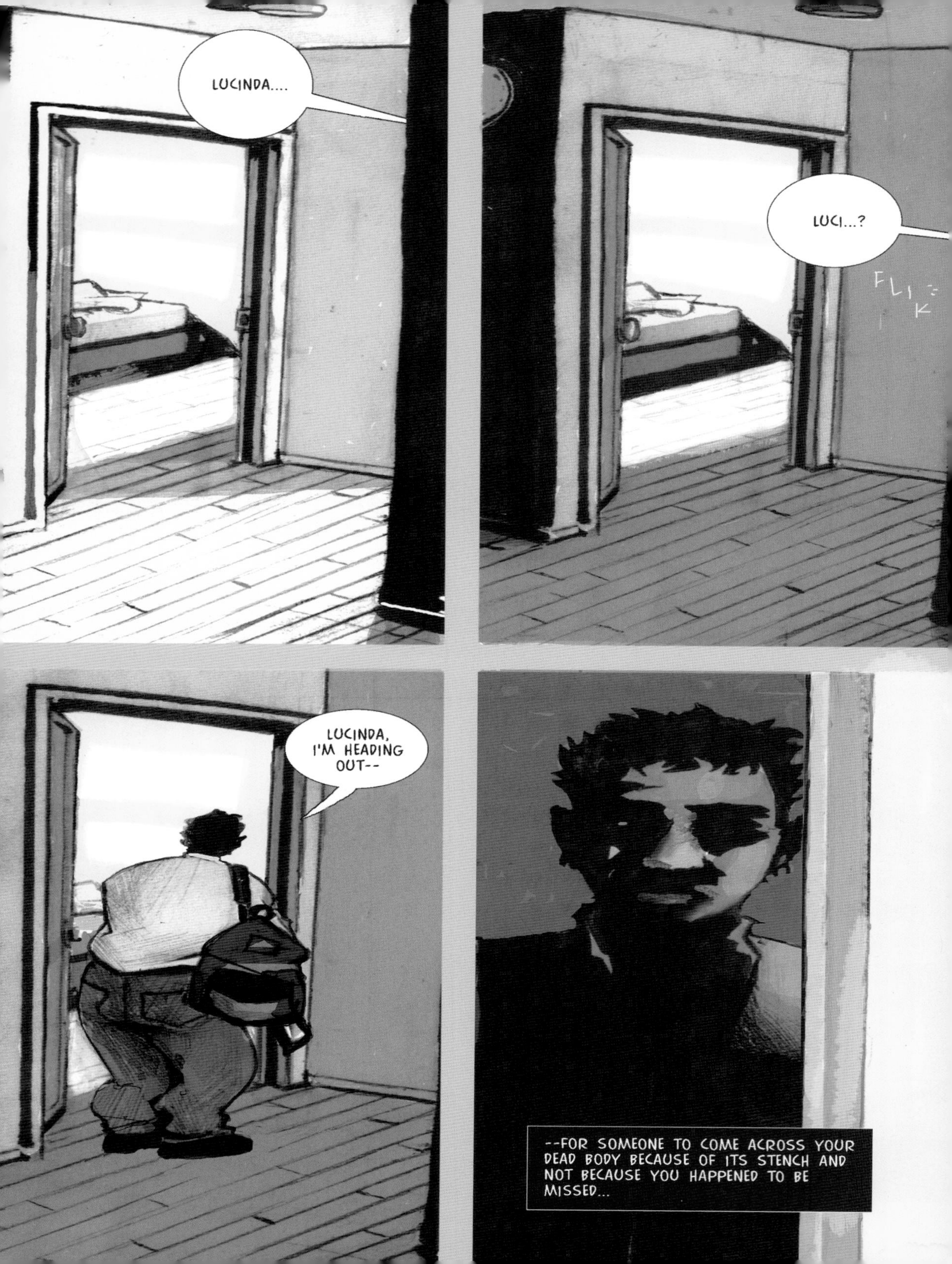
LUCINDA....
LUCI...?
LUCINDA, I'M HEADING OUT--
--FOR SOMEONE TO COME ACROSS YOUR DEAD BODY BECAUSE OF ITS STENCH AND NOT BECAUSE YOU HAPPENED TO BE MISSED...

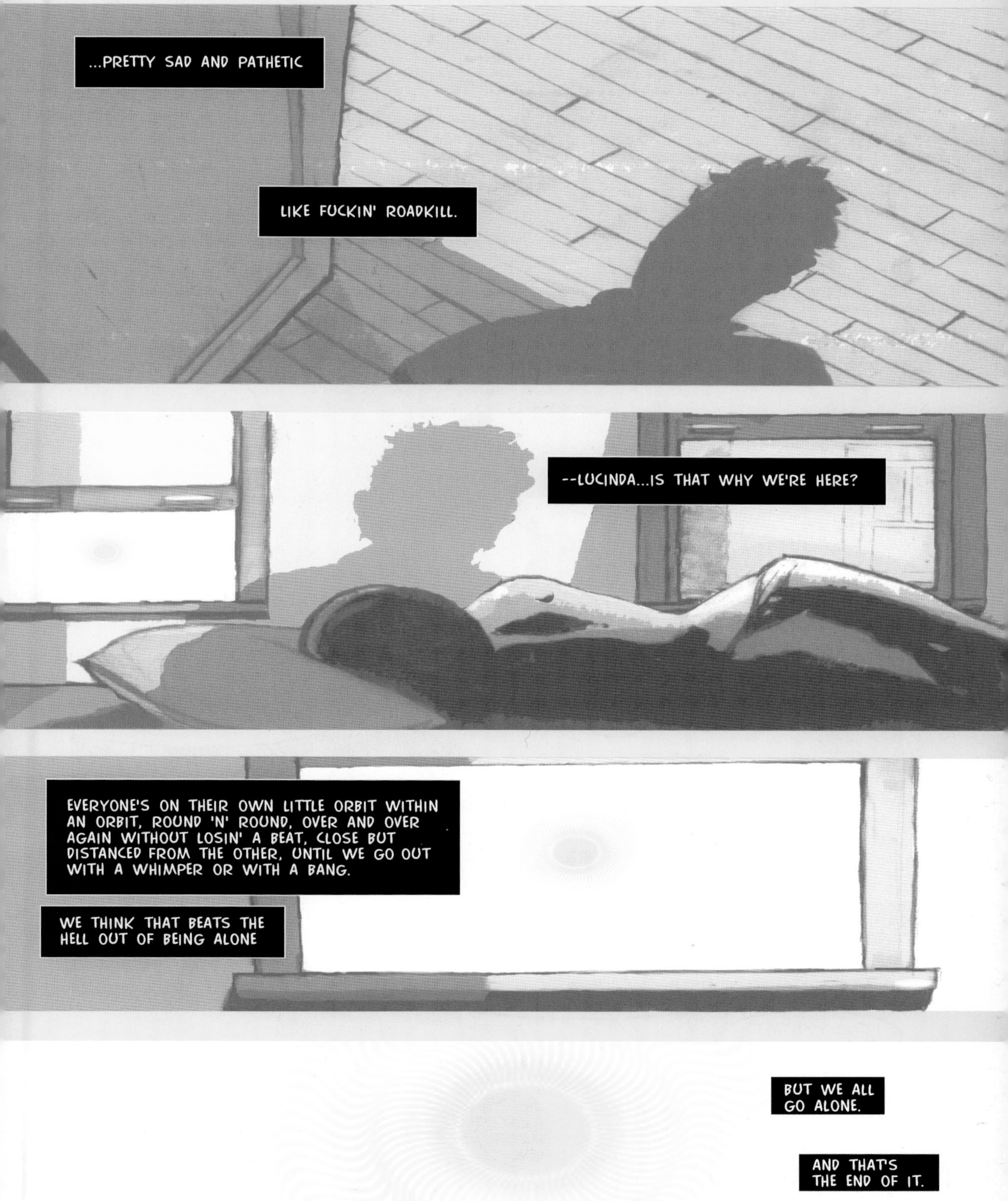
...PRETTY SAD AND PATHETIC
LIKE FUCKIN' ROADKILL.
--LUCINDA...IS THAT WHY WE'RE HERE?
EVERYONE'S ON THEIR OWN LITTLE ORBIT WITHIN AN ORBIT, ROUND 'N' ROUND, OVER AND OVER AGAIN WITHOUT LOSIN' A BEAT, CLOSE BUT DISTANCED FROM THE OTHER, UNTIL WE GO OUT WITH A WHIMPER OR WITH A BANG.
WE THINK THAT BEATS THE HELL OUT OF BEING ALONE
BUT WE ALL GO ALONE.
AND THAT'S THE END OF IT.

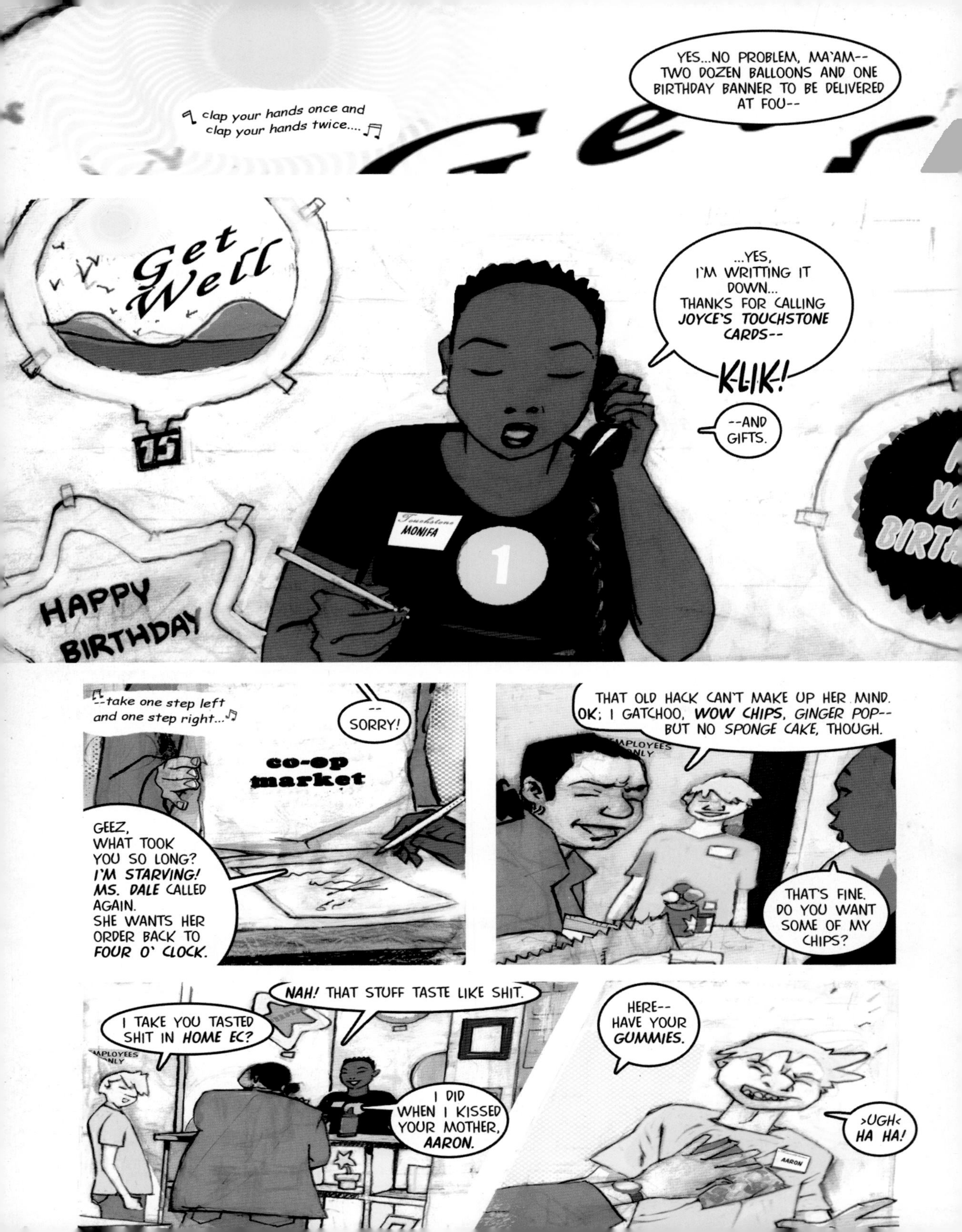
clap your hands once and clap your hands twice....
YES...NO PROBLEM, MA'AM-- TWO DOZEN BALLOONS AND ONE BIRTHDAY BANNER TO BE DELIVERED AT FOU--
Get Well
...YES, I'M WRITTING IT DOWN... THANKS FOR CALLING JOYCE'S TOUCHSTONE CARDS--
KLIK!
--AND GIFTS.
HAPPY BIRTHDAY
Touchstone MONIFA
--take one step left and one step right...
--SORRY!
co-op market
GEEZ, WHAT TOOK YOU SO LONG? I'M STARVING! MS. DALE CALLED AGAIN. SHE WANTS HER ORDER BACK TO FOUR O' CLOCK.
THAT OLD HACK CAN'T MAKE UP HER MIND. OK; I GATCHOO, WOW CHIPS, GINGER POP-- BUT NO SPONGE CAKE, THOUGH.
THAT'S FINE. DO YOU WANT SOME OF MY CHIPS?
NAH! THAT STUFF TASTE LIKE SHIT.
I TAKE YOU TASTED SHIT IN HOME EC?
I DID WHEN I KISSED YOUR MOTHER, AARON.
HERE-- HAVE YOUR GUMMIES.
>UGH< HA HA!
AARON

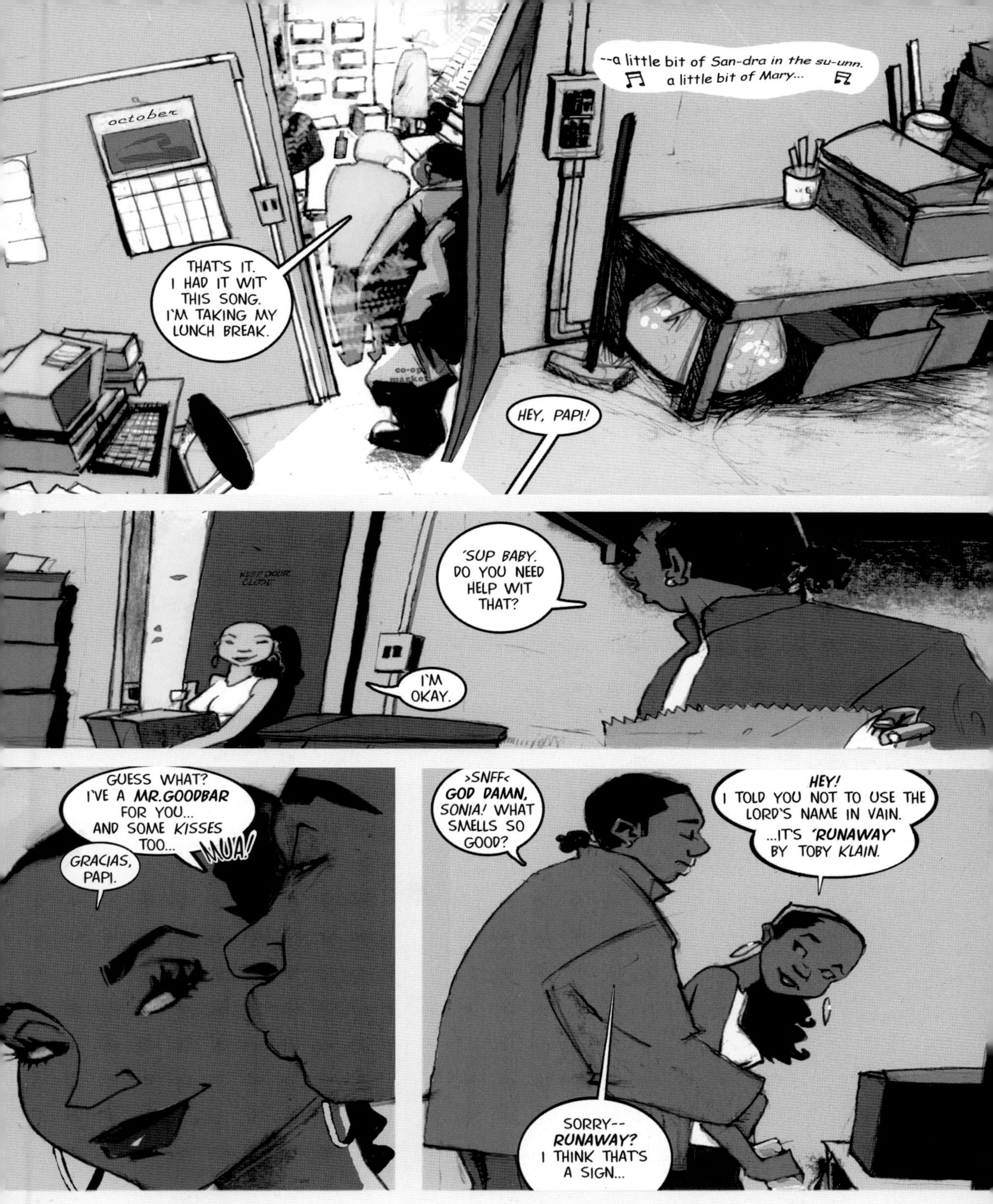
--a little bit of San-dra in the su-unn.
a little bit of Mary...
october
THAT'S IT. I HAD IT WIT THIS SONG. I'M TAKING MY LUNCH BREAK.
HEY, PAPI!
'SUP BABY. DO YOU NEED HELP WIT THAT?
I'M OKAY.
GUESS WHAT? I'VE A MR.GOODBAR FOR YOU... AND SOME KISSES TOO...
MUA!
GRACIAS, PAPI.
>SNFF< GOD DAMN, SONIA! WHAT SMELLS SO GOOD?
HEY! I TOLD YOU NOT TO USE THE LORD'S NAME IN VAIN. ...IT'S 'RUNAWAY' BY TOBY KLAIN.
SORRY-- RUNAWAY? I THINK THAT'S A SIGN...

HEE HEE! WHAT ABOUT *LUCINDA*...?

WHAT ABOUT HER? YOU SAY WHEN AND I'LL DITCH HER IN A NEW YORK MINUTE.

'SHE STILL MAD ABOUT THE PHONE BILL?

NO. WELL-- SHE'S MAD ABOUT SOMETHIN' ELSE... I DON'T KNOW WHAT'S UP. LATELY, IT'S LIKE EVERYTHIN' BOTHERS HER. MAYBE I'M GETTIN' TOO OLD OR TOO FAT FOR HER.

YOU ARE A LITTLE CHUNKY, BUT YOU STILL *A HUNK!* AND YOU ARE NOT OLD-- AGE IS NOTHING BUT A NUMBER. I BET YOU CAN GET ANY BOOTY YOU WANT.

ANYONE CAN GET '*ANY*'. IT'S *YOURS* I WANT. MARION IS ONE LUCKY NIGGA.

IT'S NOT JUST HIM, MAYBE IF YOU DIDN'T HAVE A GIRLFRIEND AND I WAS *AT LEAST* TEN YEARS OLDER...

HOLDUP! 'AGE--JUST A NUMBER' ??

I DON'T WANT YOU GOING TO JAIL.

HELL, ME NEITHER BUT... YOU *DO* KNOW WHAT A MARVELOUS ASS YOU HAVE...

YOU KEEP BRINGING ME *CHOCOLATE!* --AIN'T GETTING TOO BIG?

BELIEVE ME MAMI, EVERYTHIN' IS SWELL IN THE *GLUTEUS DEPARTMENT*-- OFF THE CHARTS AS FAR AS I'M CONCERNED.

PROBABLY GENETICS. SO I GUESS I CAN HAVE MY *MR. GOODBAR* THEN.

I'M GOIN' FOR A SMOKE.

I LIKE IT WHEN YOU SMILE, OMAR.

...YOU SHOULD SMILE MORE OFTEN.

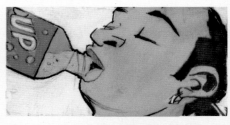

KEEP DOOR CLOSED

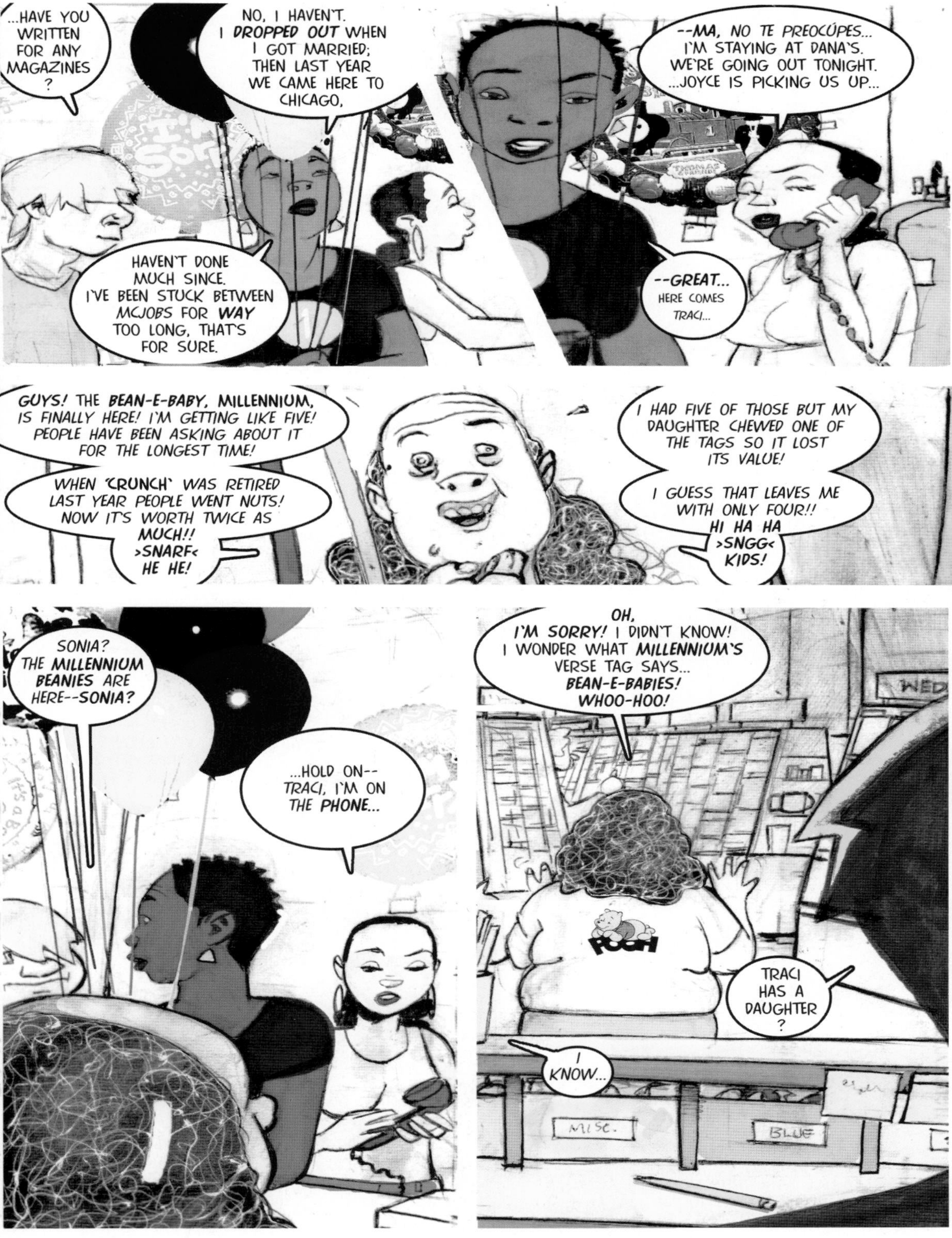
...HAVE YOU WRITTEN FOR ANY MAGAZINES ?
NO, I HAVEN'T. I DROPPED OUT WHEN I GOT MARRIED; THEN LAST YEAR WE CAME HERE TO CHICAGO,
HAVEN'T DONE MUCH SINCE. I'VE BEEN STUCK BETWEEN MCJOBS FOR WAY TOO LONG, THAT'S FOR SURE.
--MA, NO TE PREOCÚPES... I'M STAYING AT DANA'S. WE'RE GOING OUT TONIGHT. ...JOYCE IS PICKING US UP...
--GREAT... HERE COMES TRACI...
GUYS! THE BEAN-E-BABY, MILLENNIUM, IS FINALLY HERE! I'M GETTING LIKE FIVE! PEOPLE HAVE BEEN ASKING ABOUT IT FOR THE LONGEST TIME!
WHEN 'CRUNCH' WAS RETIRED LAST YEAR PEOPLE WENT NUTS! NOW IT'S WORTH TWICE AS MUCH!! >SNARF< HE HE!
I HAD FIVE OF THOSE BUT MY DAUGHTER CHEWED ONE OF THE TAGS SO IT LOST ITS VALUE!
I GUESS THAT LEAVES ME WITH ONLY FOUR!! HI HA HA >SNGG< KIDS!
SONIA? THE MILLENNIUM BEANIES ARE HERE--SONIA?
...HOLD ON-- TRACI, I'M ON THE PHONE...
OH, I'M SORRY! I DIDN'T KNOW! I WONDER WHAT MILLENNIUM'S VERSE TAG SAYS... BEAN-E-BABIES! WHOO-HOO!
TRACI HAS A DAUGHTER ?
I KNOW...
POOH
MISC.
BLUE

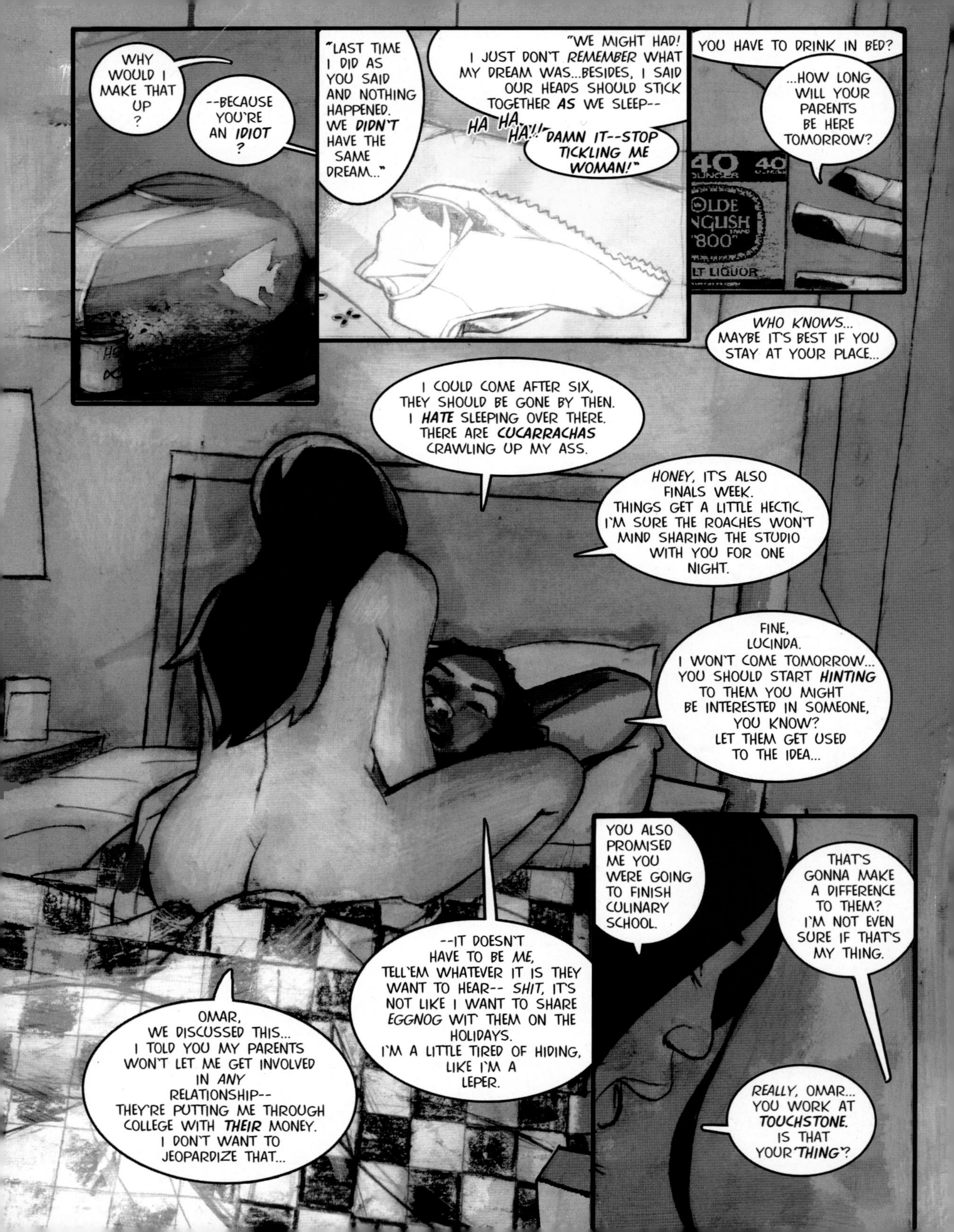
WHY WOULD I MAKE THAT UP ?
--BECAUSE YOU'RE AN IDIOT ?
"LAST TIME I DID AS YOU SAID AND NOTHING HAPPENED. WE DIDN'T HAVE THE SAME DREAM..."
"WE MIGHT HAD! I JUST DON'T REMEMBER WHAT MY DREAM WAS...BESIDES, I SAID OUR HEADS SHOULD STICK TOGETHER AS WE SLEEP--
HA HA HA!!
DAMN IT--STOP TICKLING ME WOMAN!"
YOU HAVE TO DRINK IN BED?
...HOW LONG WILL YOUR PARENTS BE HERE TOMORROW?
OLDE ENGLISH "800"
WHO KNOWS... MAYBE IT'S BEST IF YOU STAY AT YOUR PLACE...
I COULD COME AFTER SIX, THEY SHOULD BE GONE BY THEN. I HATE SLEEPING OVER THERE. THERE ARE CUCARRACHAS CRAWLING UP MY ASS.
HONEY, IT'S ALSO FINALS WEEK. THINGS GET A LITTLE HECTIC. I'M SURE THE ROACHES WON'T MIND SHARING THE STUDIO WITH YOU FOR ONE NIGHT.
FINE, LUCINDA. I WON'T COME TOMORROW... YOU SHOULD START HINTING TO THEM YOU MIGHT BE INTERESTED IN SOMEONE, YOU KNOW? LET THEM GET USED TO THE IDEA...
OMAR, WE DISCUSSED THIS... I TOLD YOU MY PARENTS WON'T LET ME GET INVOLVED IN ANY RELATIONSHIP-- THEY'RE PUTTING ME THROUGH COLLEGE WITH THEIR MONEY. I DON'T WANT TO JEOPARDIZE THAT...
--IT DOESN'T HAVE TO BE ME, TELL'EM WHATEVER IT IS THEY WANT TO HEAR-- SHIT, IT'S NOT LIKE I WANT TO SHARE EGGNOG WIT' THEM ON THE HOLIDAYS. I'M A LITTLE TIRED OF HIDING, LIKE I'M A LEPER.
YOU ALSO PROMISED ME YOU WERE GOING TO FINISH CULINARY SCHOOL.
THAT'S GONNA MAKE A DIFFERENCE TO THEM? I'M NOT EVEN SURE IF THAT'S MY THING.
REALLY, OMAR... YOU WORK AT TOUCHSTONE. IS THAT YOUR 'THING'?

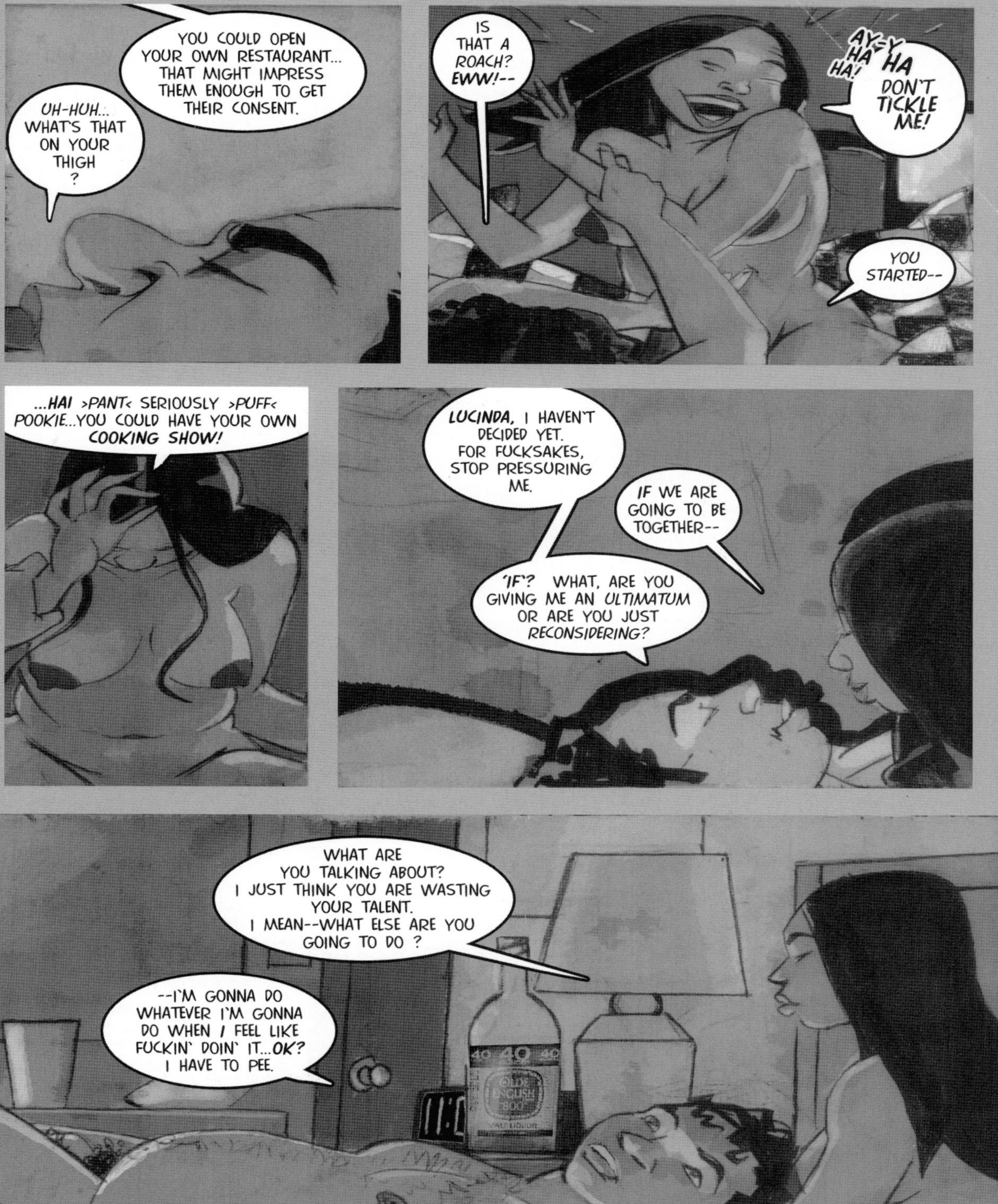
YOU COULD OPEN YOUR OWN RESTAURANT... THAT MIGHT IMPRESS THEM ENOUGH TO GET THEIR CONSENT.
UH-HUH... WHAT'S THAT ON YOUR THIGH ?
IS THAT A ROACH? EWW!--
AY-Y HA HA! HA DON'T TICKLE ME!
YOU STARTED--
...HAI >PANT< SERIOUSLY >PUFF< POOKIE...YOU COULD HAVE YOUR OWN COOKING SHOW!
LUCINDA, I HAVEN'T DECIDED YET. FOR FUCKSAKES, STOP PRESSURING ME.
IF WE ARE GOING TO BE TOGETHER--
'IF'? WHAT, ARE YOU GIVING ME AN ULTIMATUM OR ARE YOU JUST RECONSIDERING?
WHAT ARE YOU TALKING ABOUT? I JUST THINK YOU ARE WASTING YOUR TALENT. I MEAN--WHAT ELSE ARE YOU GOING TO DO ?
--I'M GONNA DO WHATEVER I'M GONNA DO WHEN I FEEL LIKE FUCKIN' DOIN' IT...OK? I HAVE TO PEE.

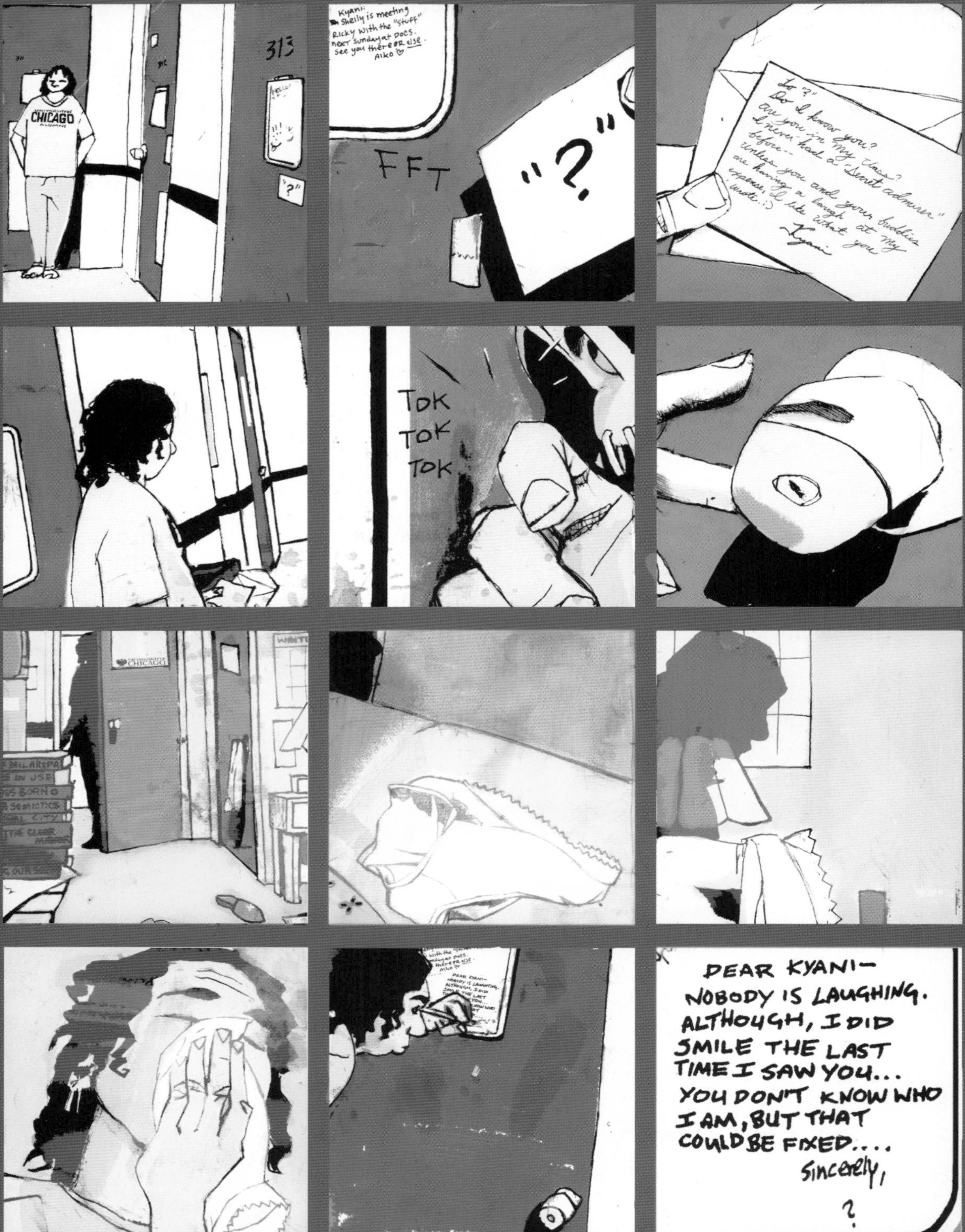
313
"?"
Kyani:
Shelly is meeting
Ricky with the "stuff"
next Sunday at Docs.
See you there OR else.
Aiko
FFT
"?"
To "?"
Do I know you?
Are you in my class?
I never had a "Secret admirer"
before--
Unless you and your buddies
are having a laugh at my
expense, I like what you
wrote..:)
Kyani
TOK
TOK
TOK
DEAR KYANI—
NOBODY IS LAUGHING.
ALTHOUGH, I DID
SMILE THE LAST
TIME I SAW YOU...
YOU DON'T KNOW WHO
I AM, BUT THAT
COULD BE FIXED....
Sincerely,
?

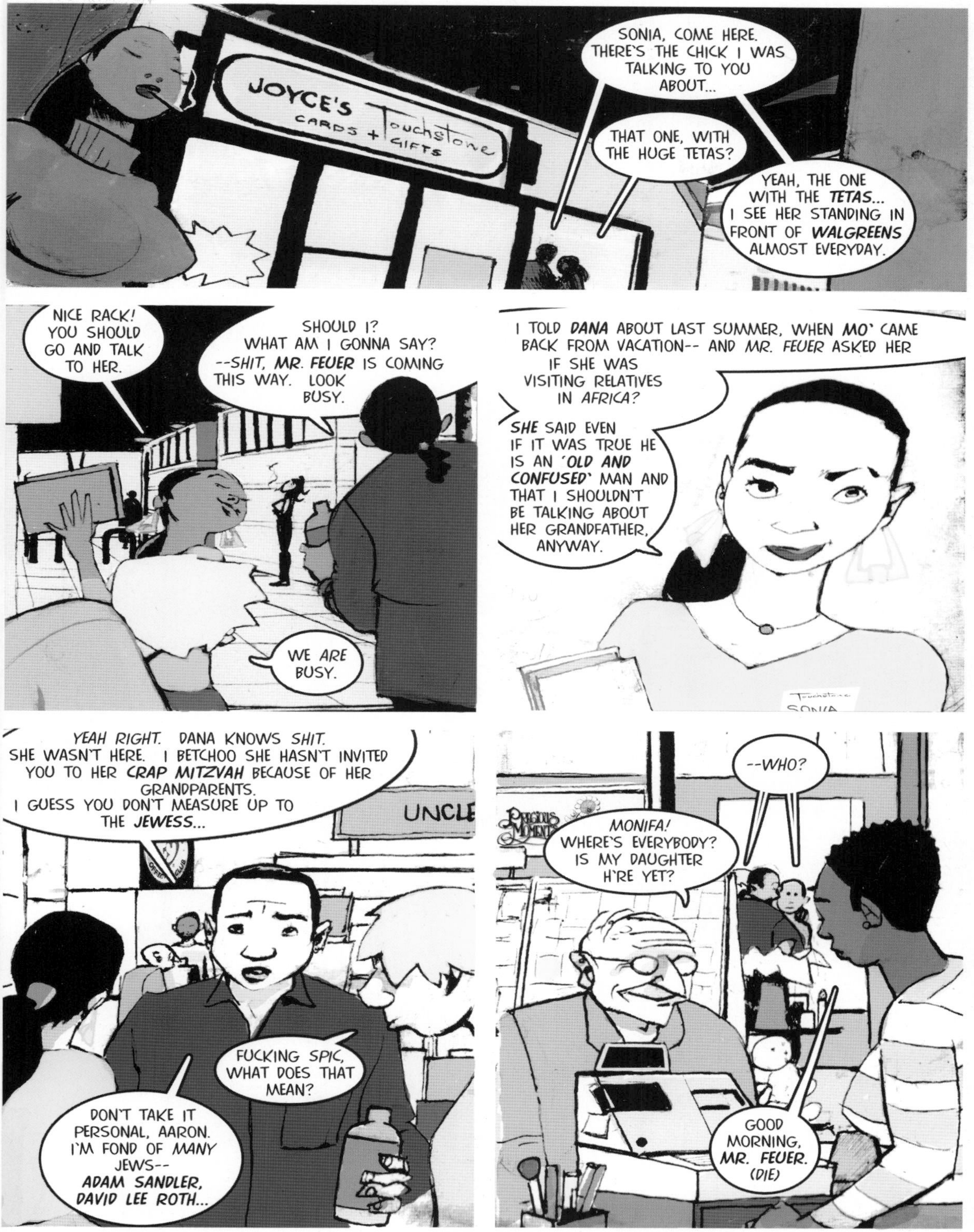
JOYCE'S Touchstone CARDS + GIFTS
SONIA, COME HERE. THERE'S THE CHICK I WAS TALKING TO YOU ABOUT...
THAT ONE, WITH THE HUGE TETAS?
YEAH, THE ONE WITH THE TETAS... I SEE HER STANDING IN FRONT OF WALGREENS ALMOST EVERYDAY.
NICE RACK! YOU SHOULD GO AND TALK TO HER.
SHOULD I? WHAT AM I GONNA SAY? --SHIT, MR. FEUER IS COMING THIS WAY. LOOK BUSY.
WE ARE BUSY.
I TOLD DANA ABOUT LAST SUMMER, WHEN MO' CAME BACK FROM VACATION-- AND MR. FEUER ASKED HER IF SHE WAS VISITING RELATIVES IN AFRICA?
SHE SAID EVEN IF IT WAS TRUE HE IS AN 'OLD AND CONFUSED' MAN AND THAT I SHOULDN'T BE TALKING ABOUT HER GRANDFATHER, ANYWAY.
Touchstone SONIA
YEAH RIGHT. DANA KNOWS SHIT. SHE WASN'T HERE. I BETCHOO SHE HASN'T INVITED YOU TO HER CRAP MITZVAH BECAUSE OF HER GRANDPARENTS. I GUESS YOU DON'T MEASURE UP TO THE JEWESS...
UNCLE
FUCKING SPIC, WHAT DOES THAT MEAN?
DON'T TAKE IT PERSONAL, AARON. I'M FOND OF MANY JEWS-- ADAM SANDLER, DAVID LEE ROTH...
PRECIOUS MOMENTS
MONIFA! WHERE'S EVERYBODY? IS MY DAUGHTER H'RE YET?
--WHO?
GOOD MORNING, MR. FEUER. (DIE)

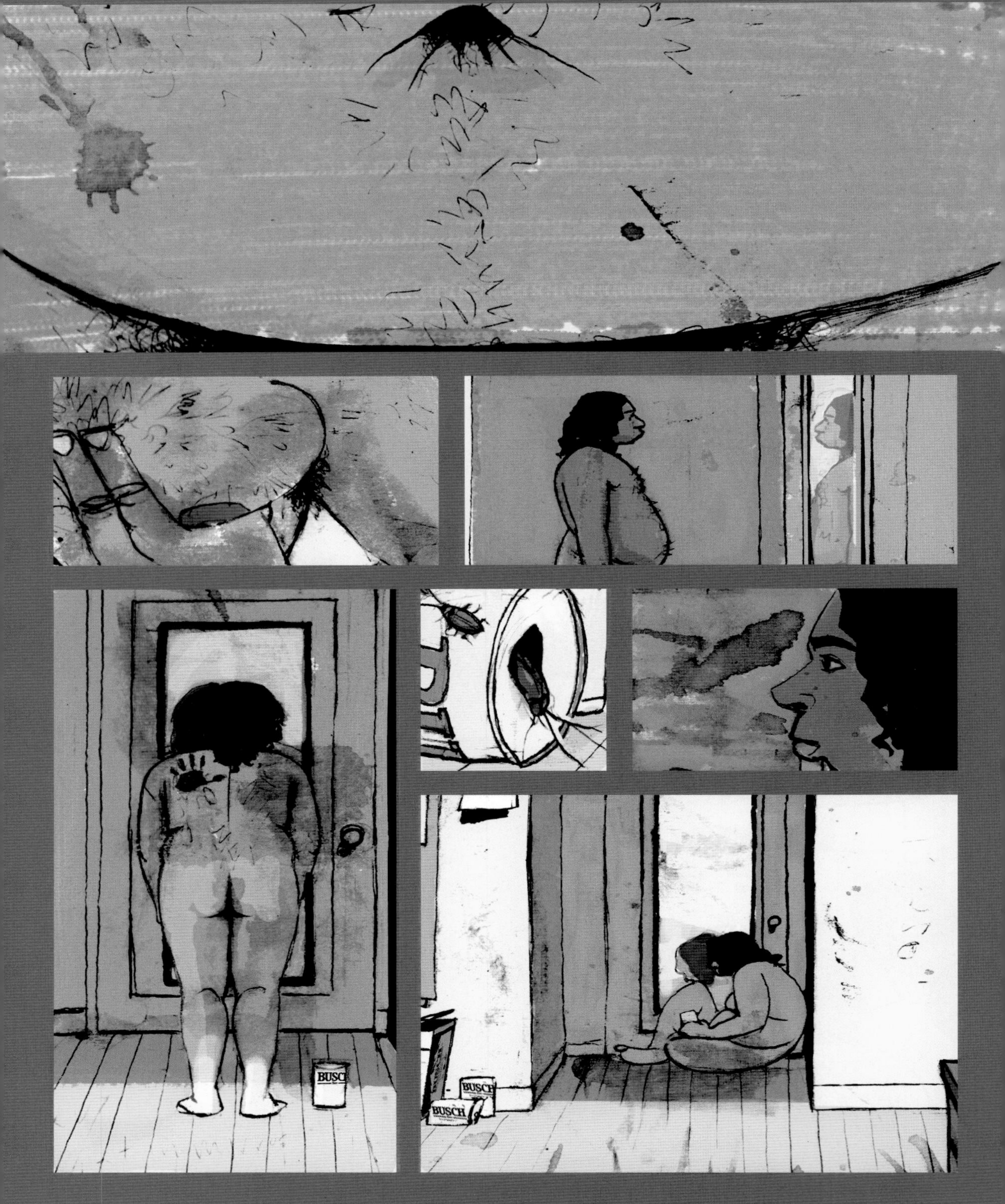
BUSCH
BUSCH
BUSCH

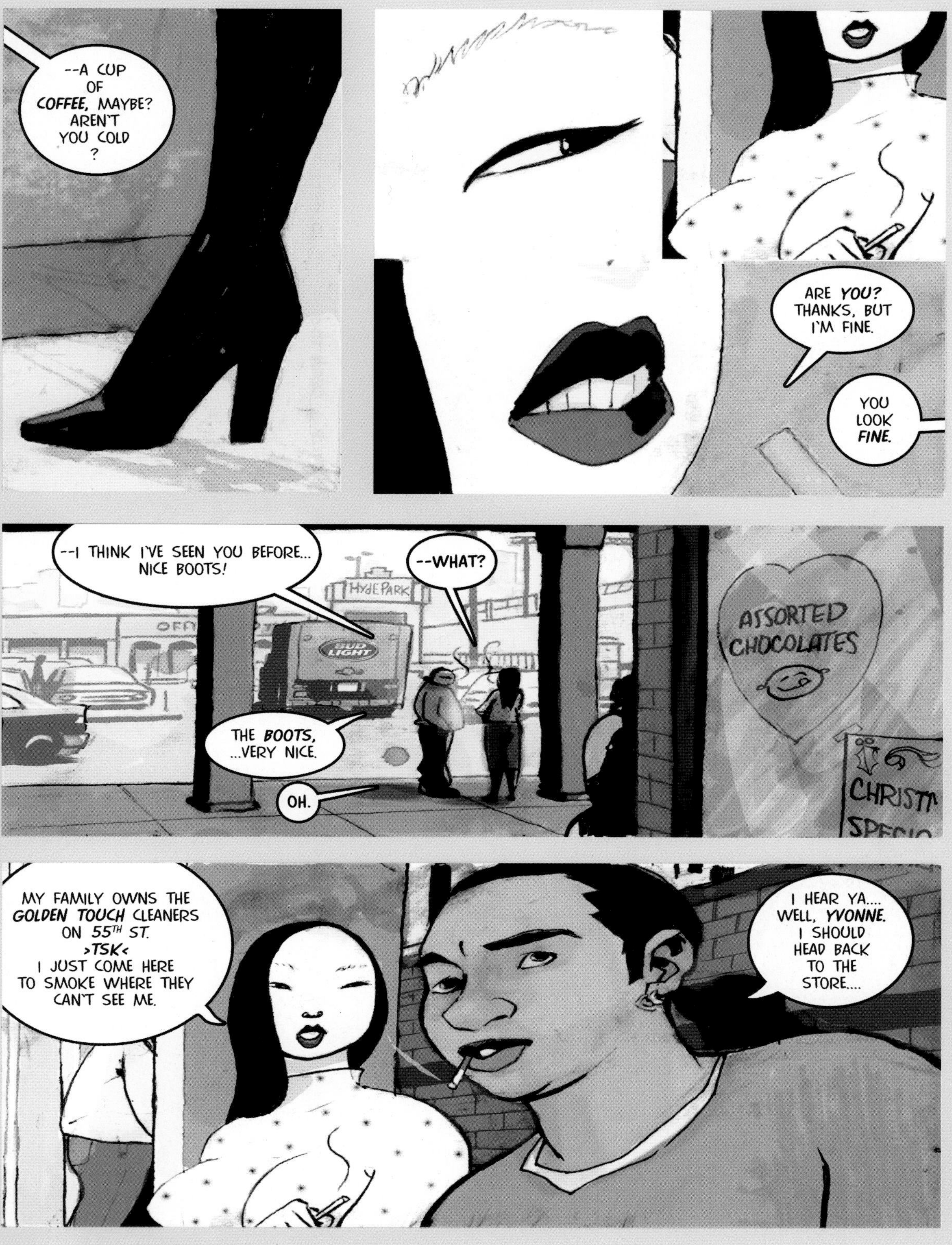
--A CUP OF COFFEE, MAYBE? AREN'T YOU COLD ?
ARE YOU? THANKS, BUT I'M FINE.
YOU LOOK FINE.
--I THINK I'VE SEEN YOU BEFORE... NICE BOOTS!
--WHAT?
HYdE PARK
BUD LIGHT
ASSORTED CHOCOLATES
THE BOOTS, ...VERY NICE.
OH.
MY FAMILY OWNS THE GOLDEN TOUCH CLEANERS ON 55TH ST. >TSK< I JUST COME HERE TO SMOKE WHERE THEY CAN'T SEE ME.
I HEAR YA.... WELL, YVONNE. I SHOULD HEAD BACK TO THE STORE....

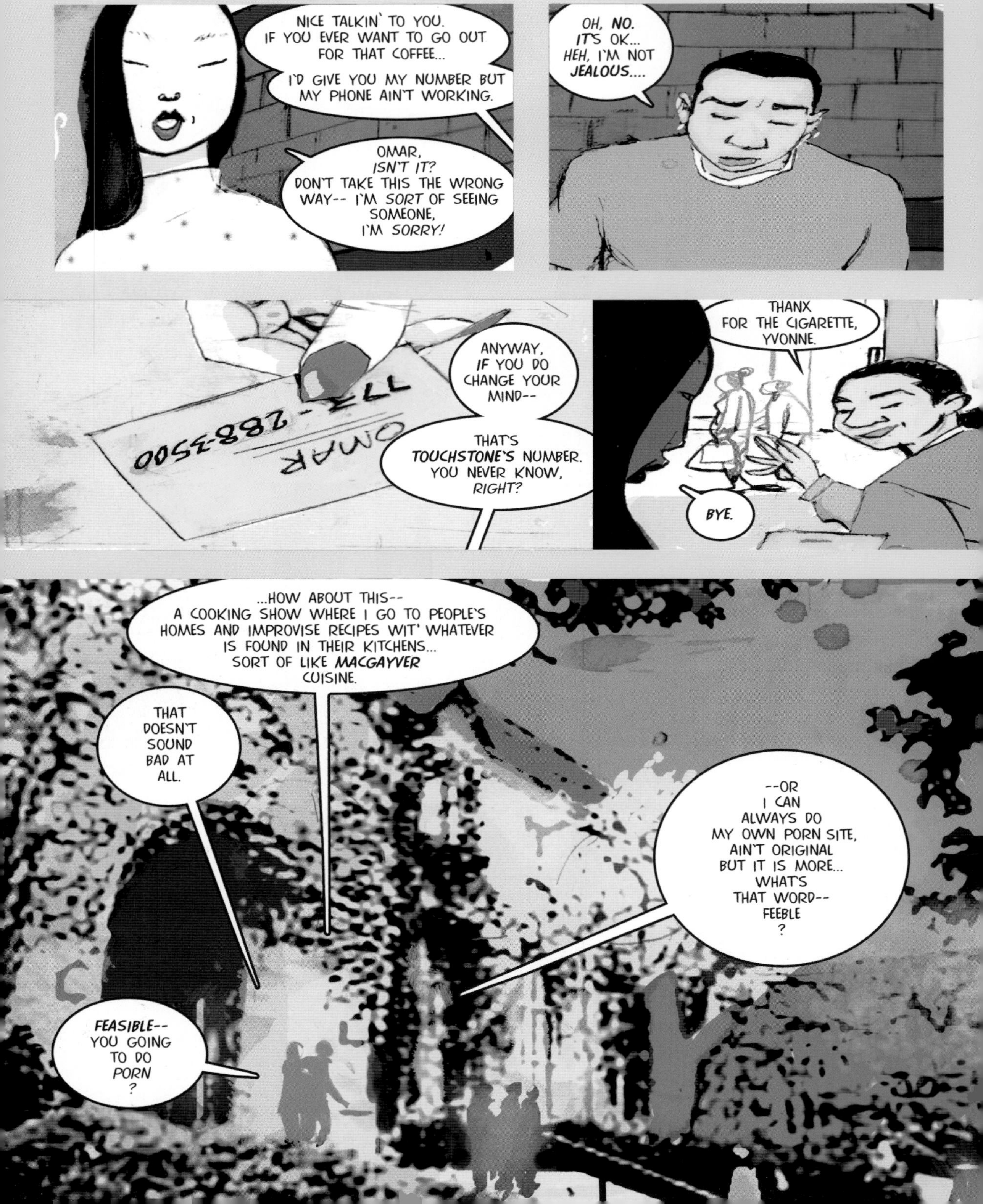
NICE TALKIN' TO YOU. IF YOU EVER WANT TO GO OUT FOR THAT COFFEE...
I'D GIVE YOU MY NUMBER BUT MY PHONE AIN'T WORKING.
OMAR, ISN'T IT? DON'T TAKE THIS THE WRONG WAY-- I'M SORT OF SEEING SOMEONE, I'M SORRY!
OH, NO. IT'S OK... HEH, I'M NOT JEALOUS....
773-288-3500
OMAR
ANYWAY, IF YOU DO CHANGE YOUR MIND--
THAT'S TOUCHSTONE'S NUMBER. YOU NEVER KNOW, RIGHT?
THANX FOR THE CIGARETTE, YVONNE.
BYE.
...HOW ABOUT THIS-- A COOKING SHOW WHERE I GO TO PEOPLE'S HOMES AND IMPROVISE RECIPES WIT' WHATEVER IS FOUND IN THEIR KITCHENS... SORT OF LIKE MACGAYVER CUISINE.
THAT DOESN'T SOUND BAD AT ALL.
--OR I CAN ALWAYS DO MY OWN PORN SITE, AIN'T ORIGINAL BUT IT IS MORE... WHAT'S THAT WORD-- FEEBLE ?
FEASIBLE-- YOU GOING TO DO PORN ?

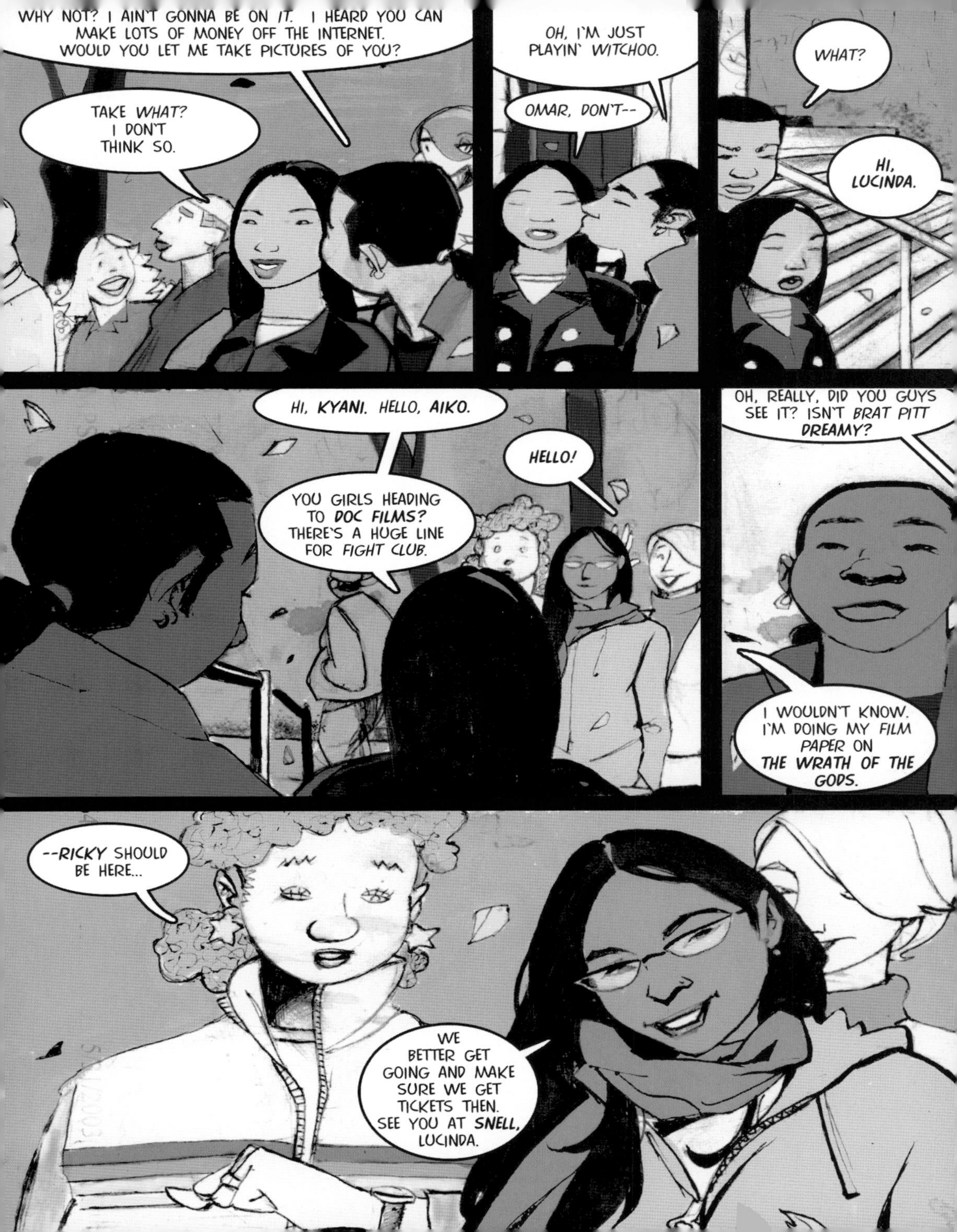
WHY NOT? I AIN'T GONNA BE ON IT. I HEARD YOU CAN MAKE LOTS OF MONEY OFF THE INTERNET. WOULD YOU LET ME TAKE PICTURES OF YOU?
TAKE WHAT? I DON'T THINK SO.
OH, I'M JUST PLAYIN' WITCHOO.
OMAR, DON'T--
WHAT?
HI, LUCINDA.
HI, KYANI. HELLO, AIKO.
HELLO!
YOU GIRLS HEADING TO DOC FILMS? THERE'S A HUGE LINE FOR FIGHT CLUB.
OH, REALLY, DID YOU GUYS SEE IT? ISN'T BRAT PITT DREAMY?
I WOULDN'T KNOW. I'M DOING MY FILM PAPER ON THE WRATH OF THE GODS.
--RICKY SHOULD BE HERE...
WE BETTER GET GOING AND MAKE SURE WE GET TICKETS THEN. SEE YOU AT SNELL, LUCINDA.

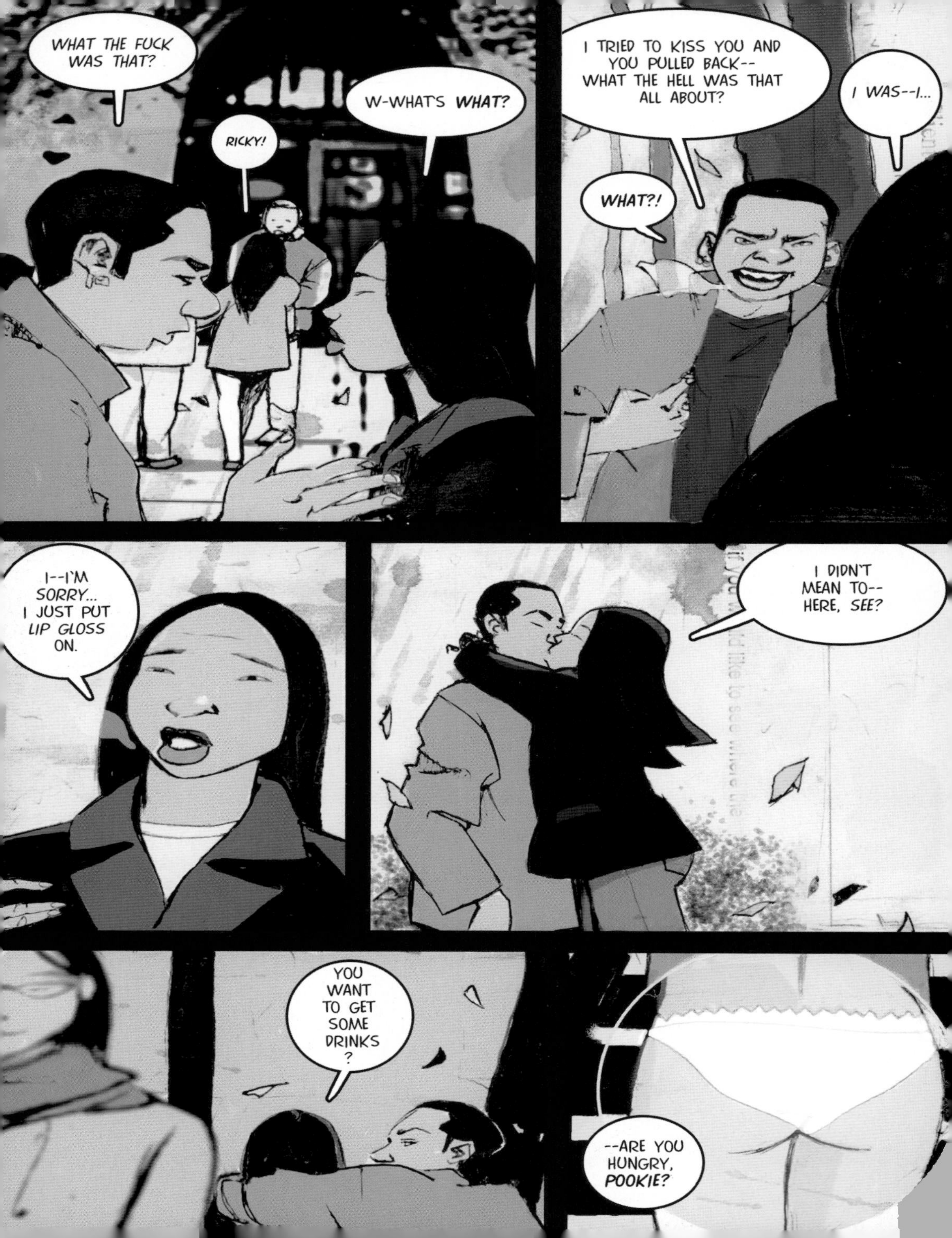
WHAT THE FUCK WAS THAT?
RICKY!
W-WHAT'S WHAT?
I TRIED TO KISS YOU AND YOU PULLED BACK-- WHAT THE HELL WAS THAT ALL ABOUT?
I WAS--I...
WHAT?!
I--I'M SORRY... I JUST PUT LIP GLOSS ON.
I DIDN'T MEAN TO-- HERE, SEE?
YOU WANT TO GET SOME DRINKS ?
--ARE YOU HUNGRY, POOKIE?

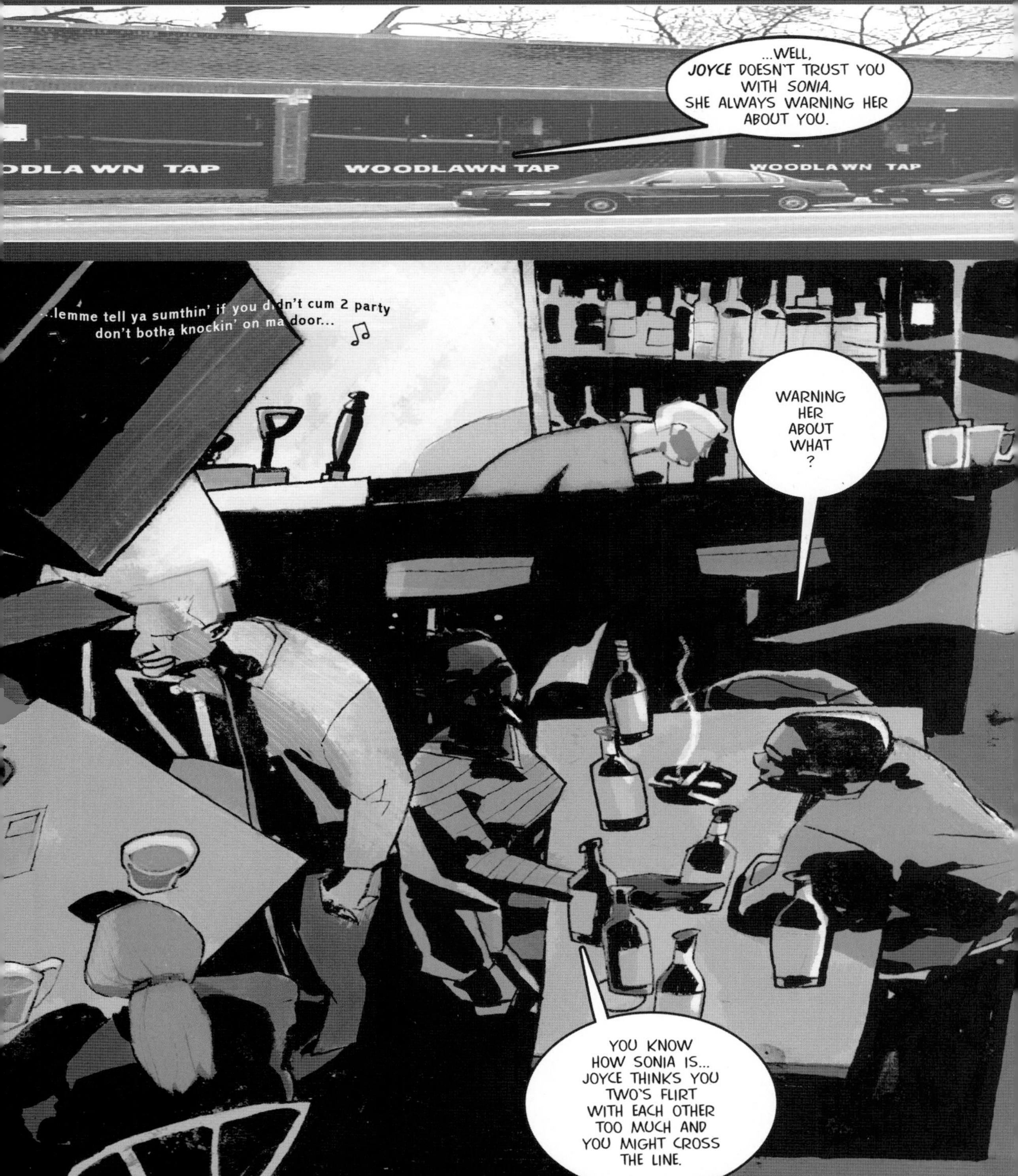
WOODLAWN TAP
WOODLAWN TAP
WOODLAWN TAP
...WELL, JOYCE DOESN'T TRUST YOU WITH SONIA. SHE ALWAYS WARNING HER ABOUT YOU.
...lemme tell ya sumthin' if you didn't cum 2 party
don't botha knockin' on ma door...
WARNING HER ABOUT WHAT ?
YOU KNOW HOW SONIA IS... JOYCE THINKS YOU TWO'S FLIRT WITH EACH OTHER TOO MUCH AND YOU MIGHT CROSS THE LINE.

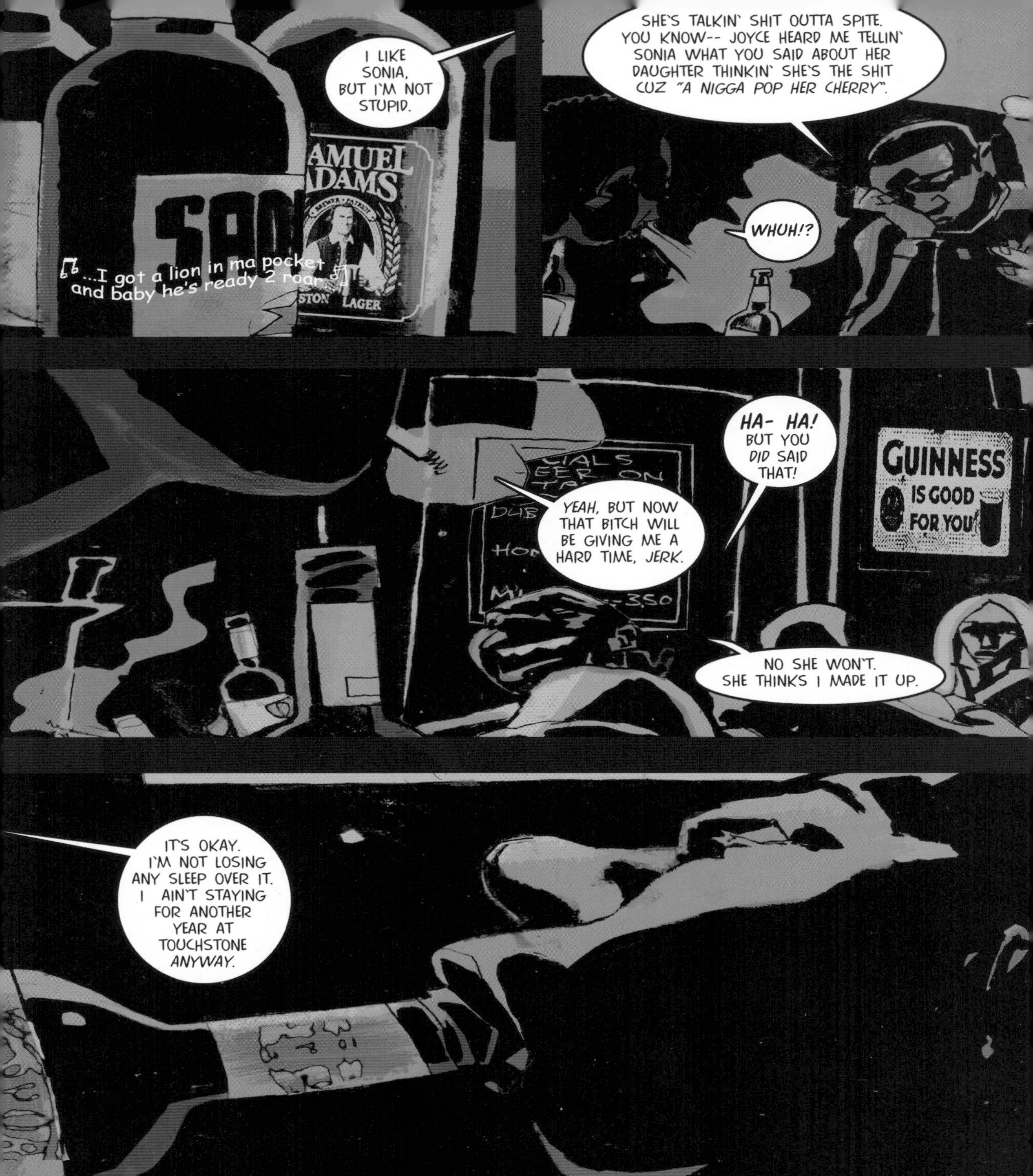
I LIKE SONIA, BUT I'M NOT STUPID.
SAMUEL ADAMS
BOSTON LAGER
...I got a lion in ma pocket and baby he's ready 2 roar
SHE'S TALKIN' SHIT OUTTA SPITE. YOU KNOW-- JOYCE HEARD ME TELLIN' SONIA WHAT YOU SAID ABOUT HER DAUGHTER THINKIN' SHE'S THE SHIT CUZ "A NIGGA POP HER CHERRY".
WHUH!?
YEAH, BUT NOW THAT BITCH WILL BE GIVING ME A HARD TIME, JERK.
HA- HA! BUT YOU DID SAID THAT!
GUINNESS IS GOOD FOR YOU
NO SHE WON'T. SHE THINKS I MADE IT UP.
IT'S OKAY. I'M NOT LOSING ANY SLEEP OVER IT. I AIN'T STAYING FOR ANOTHER YEAR AT TOUCHSTONE ANYWAY.

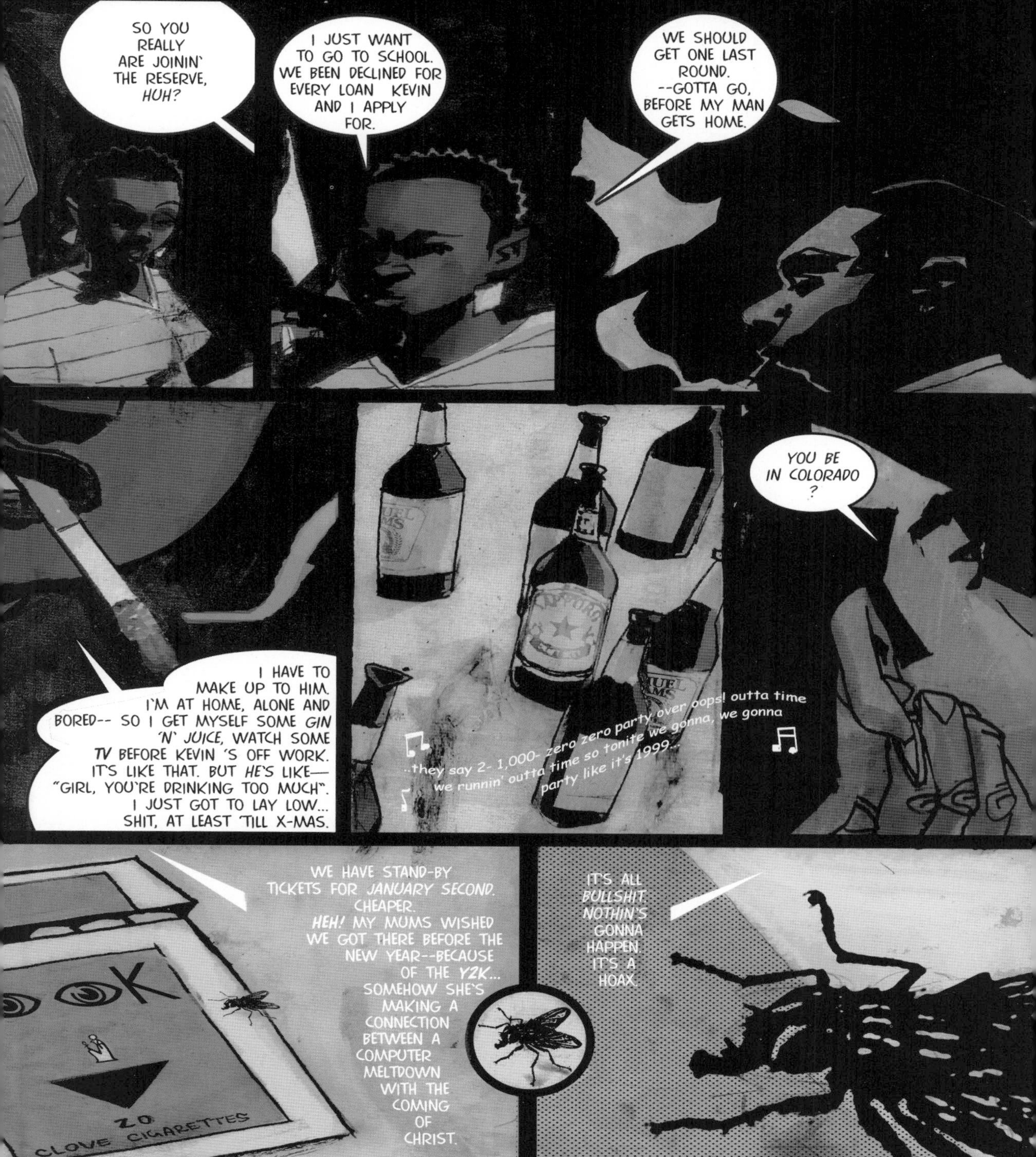
SO YOU REALLY ARE JOININ' THE RESERVE, HUH?
I JUST WANT TO GO TO SCHOOL. WE BEEN DECLINED FOR EVERY LOAN KEVIN AND I APPLY FOR.
WE SHOULD GET ONE LAST ROUND. --GOTTA GO, BEFORE MY MAN GETS HOME.
I HAVE TO MAKE UP TO HIM. I'M AT HOME, ALONE AND BORED-- SO I GET MYSELF SOME GIN 'N' JUICE, WATCH SOME TV BEFORE KEVIN 'S OFF WORK. IT'S LIKE THAT. BUT HE'S LIKE— "GIRL, YOU'RE DRINKING TOO MUCH". I JUST GOT TO LAY LOW... SHIT, AT LEAST 'TILL X-MAS.
..they say 2- 1,000- zero zero party over oops! outta time
we runnin' outta time so tonite we gonna, we gonna
party like it's 1999..
YOU BE IN COLORADO ?
WE HAVE STAND-BY TICKETS FOR JANUARY SECOND. CHEAPER. HEH! MY MUMS WISHED WE GOT THERE BEFORE THE NEW YEAR--BECAUSE OF THE Y2K... SOMEHOW SHE'S MAKING A CONNECTION BETWEEN A COMPUTER MELTDOWN WITH THE COMING OF CHRIST.
ZO
CLOVE CIGARETTES
IT'S ALL BULLSHIT. NOTHIN'S GONNA HAPPEN. IT'S A HOAX.

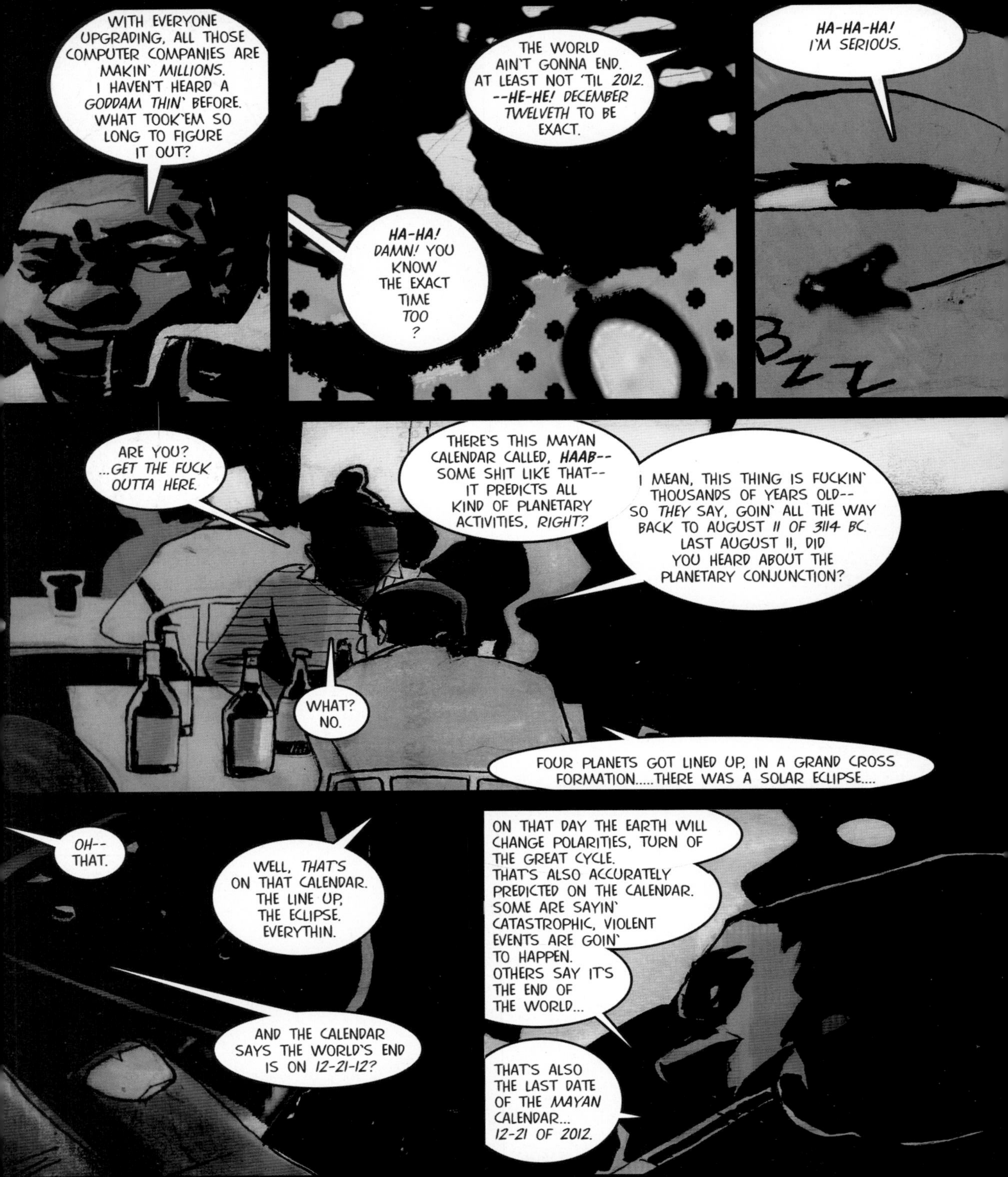
WITH EVERYONE UPGRADING, ALL THOSE COMPUTER COMPANIES ARE MAKIN' *MILLIONS.* I HAVEN'T HEARD A *GODDAM THIN'* BEFORE. WHAT TOOK'EM SO LONG TO FIGURE IT OUT?
THE WORLD AIN'T GONNA END. AT LEAST NOT 'TIL *2012.* **--HE-HE!** *DECEMBER TWELVETH* TO BE EXACT.
HA-HA! *DAMN!* YOU KNOW THE EXACT TIME *TOO* ?
HA-HA-HA! *I'M SERIOUS.*
ARE YOU? *...GET THE FUCK OUTTA HERE.*
THERE'S THIS MAYAN CALENDAR CALLED, **HAAB--** SOME SHIT LIKE THAT-- IT PREDICTS ALL KIND OF PLANETARY ACTIVITIES, *RIGHT?*
I MEAN, THIS THING IS FUCKIN' THOUSANDS OF YEARS OLD-- SO *THEY* SAY, GOIN' ALL THE WAY BACK TO AUGUST 11 OF *3114 BC.* LAST AUGUST 11, DID YOU HEARD ABOUT THE PLANETARY CONJUNCTION?
WHAT? NO.
FOUR PLANETS GOT LINED UP, IN A GRAND CROSS FORMATION.....THERE WAS A SOLAR ECLIPSE....
OH-- THAT.
WELL, *THAT'S* ON THAT CALENDAR. THE LINE UP, THE ECLIPSE. EVERYTHIN.
AND THE CALENDAR SAYS THE WORLD'S END IS ON *12-21-12?*
ON THAT DAY THE EARTH WILL CHANGE POLARITIES, TURN OF THE GREAT CYCLE. THAT'S ALSO ACCURATELY PREDICTED ON THE CALENDAR. SOME ARE SAYIN' CATASTROPHIC, VIOLENT EVENTS ARE GOIN' TO HAPPEN. OTHERS SAY IT'S THE END OF THE WORLD...
THAT'S ALSO THE LAST DATE OF THE *MAYAN* CALENDAR... *12-21 OF 2012.*
BZZ

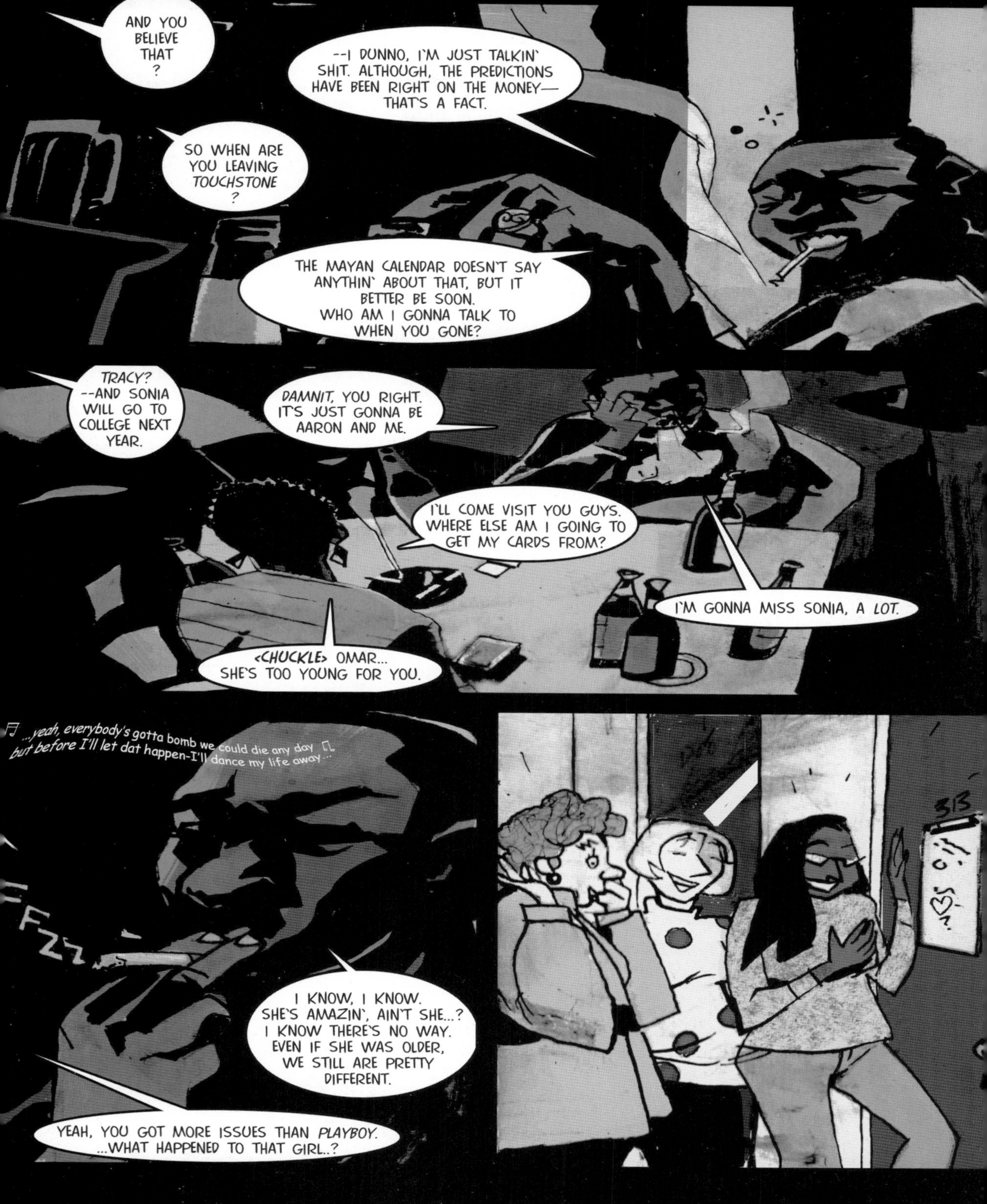
AND YOU BELIEVE THAT ?
--I DUNNO, I'M JUST TALKIN` SHIT. ALTHOUGH, THE PREDICTIONS HAVE BEEN RIGHT ON THE MONEY— THAT'S A FACT.
SO WHEN ARE YOU LEAVING *TOUCHSTONE* ?
THE MAYAN CALENDAR DOESN'T SAY ANYTHIN` ABOUT THAT, BUT IT BETTER BE SOON. WHO AM I GONNA TALK TO WHEN YOU GONE?
TRACY? --AND SONIA WILL GO TO COLLEGE NEXT YEAR.
DAMNIT, YOU RIGHT. IT'S JUST GONNA BE AARON AND ME.
I'LL COME VISIT YOU GUYS. WHERE ELSE AM I GOING TO GET MY CARDS FROM?
I'M GONNA MISS SONIA, A *LOT.*
<CHUCKLE> OMAR... SHE'S TOO YOUNG FOR YOU.
♫ ...yeah, everybody's gotta bomb we could die any day ♫ but before I'll let dat happen-I'll dance my life away...
I KNOW, I KNOW. SHE'S AMAZIN`, AIN'T SHE...? I KNOW THERE'S NO WAY. EVEN IF SHE WAS OLDER, WE STILL ARE PRETTY DIFFERENT.
YEAH, YOU GOT MORE ISSUES THAN *PLAYBOY.* ...WHAT HAPPENED TO THAT GIRL..?

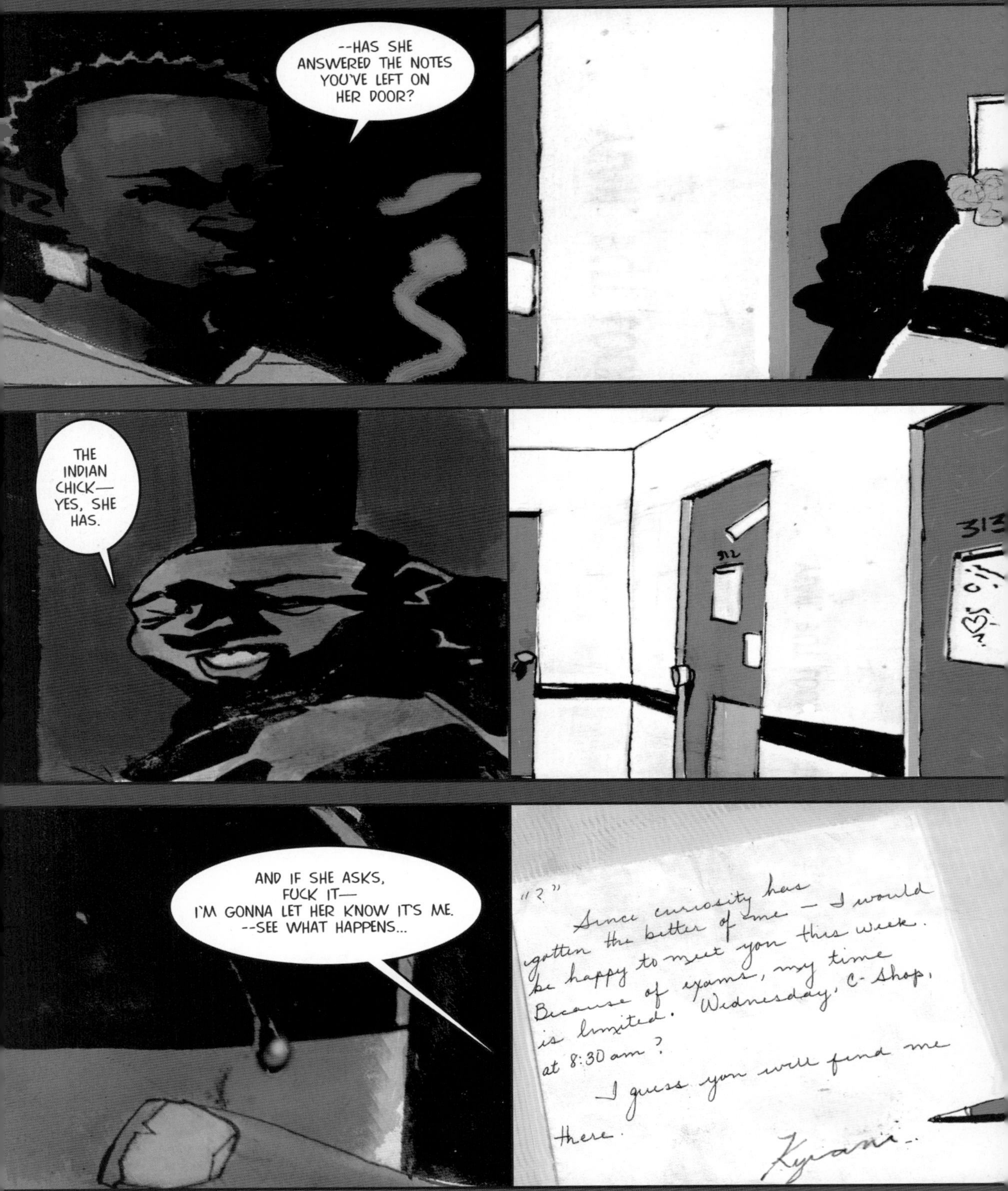
--HAS SHE ANSWERED THE NOTES YOU'VE LEFT ON HER DOOR?
THE INDIAN CHICK— YES, SHE HAS.
312
313
AND IF SHE ASKS, FUCK IT— I'M GONNA LET HER KNOW IT'S ME. --SEE WHAT HAPPENS...
"?"
Since curiosity has gotten the better of me — I would be happy to meet you this week. Because of exams, my time is limited. Wednesday, C-Shop, at 8:30 am?
I guess you will find me there.
Kyrani

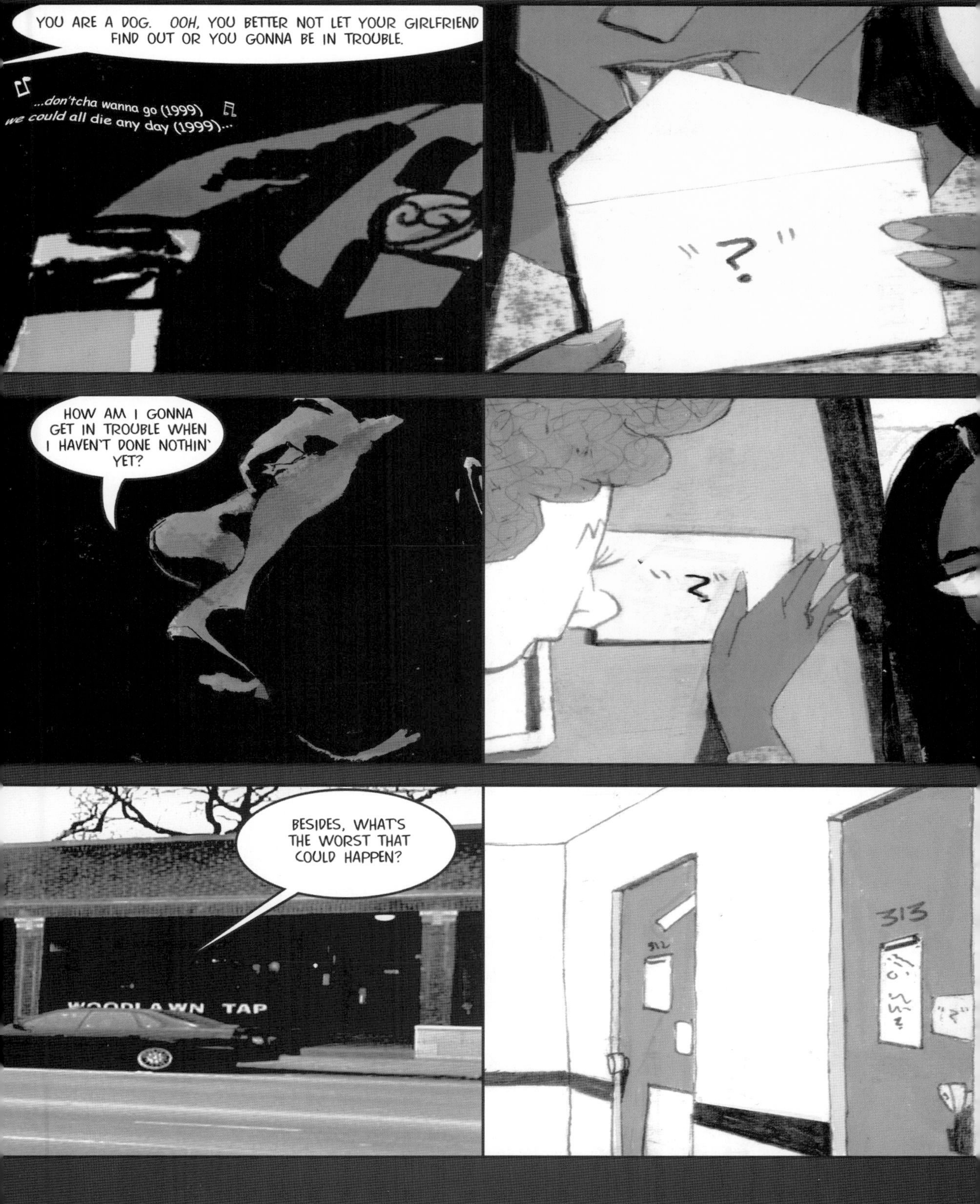
YOU ARE A DOG. OOH, YOU BETTER NOT LET YOUR GIRLFRIEND FIND OUT OR YOU GONNA BE IN TROUBLE.
...don'tcha wanna go (1999)
we could all die any day (1999)...
"?"
HOW AM I GONNA GET IN TROUBLE WHEN I HAVEN'T DONE NOTHIN' YET?
"?"
BESIDES, WHAT'S THE WORST THAT COULD HAPPEN?
WOODLAWN TAP
313
"?"

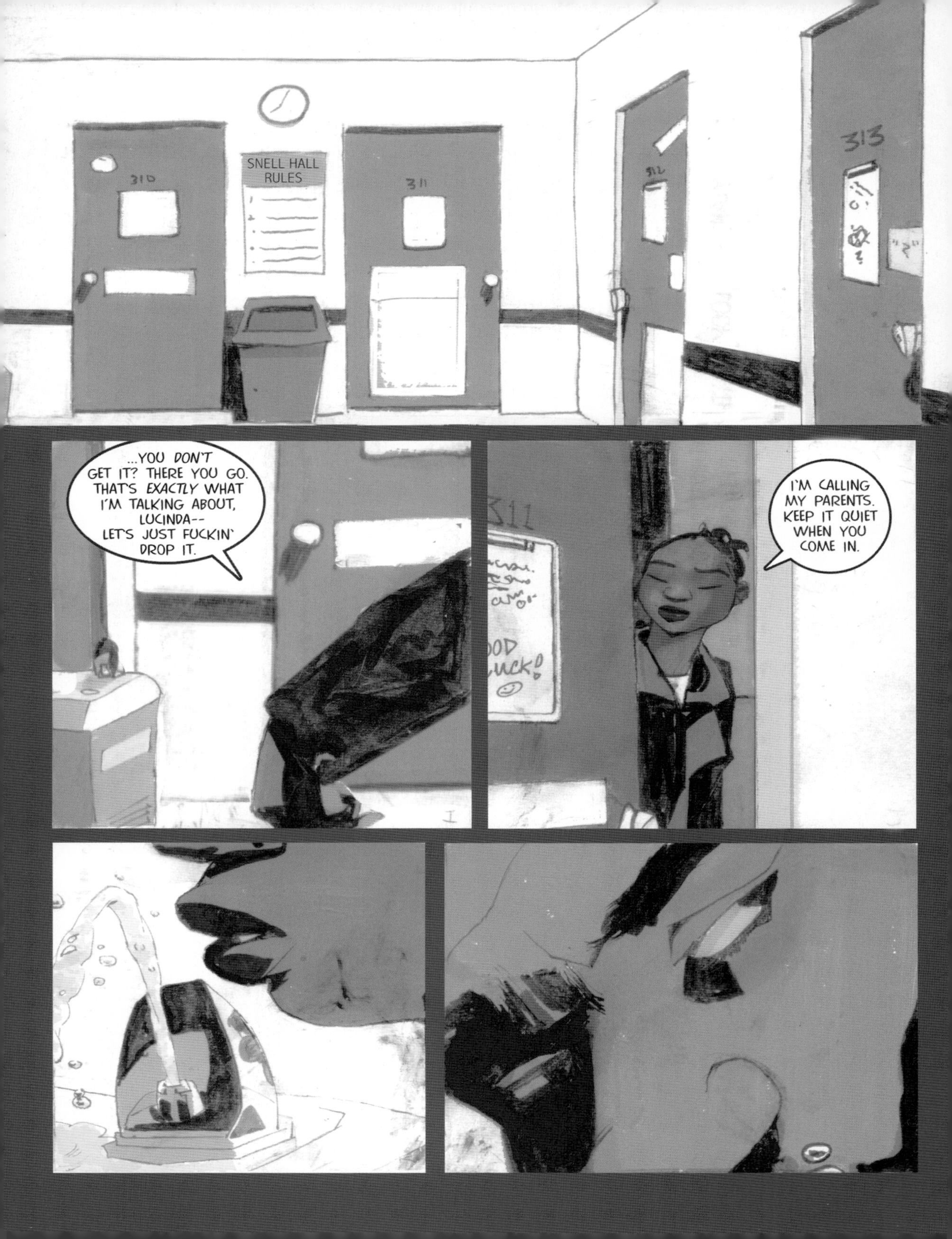
SNELL HALL RULES
310
311
312
313
...YOU DON'T GET IT? THERE YOU GO. THAT'S EXACTLY WHAT I'M TALKING ABOUT, LUCINDA-- LET'S JUST FUCKIN' DROP IT.
I'M CALLING MY PARENTS. KEEP IT QUIET WHEN YOU COME IN.

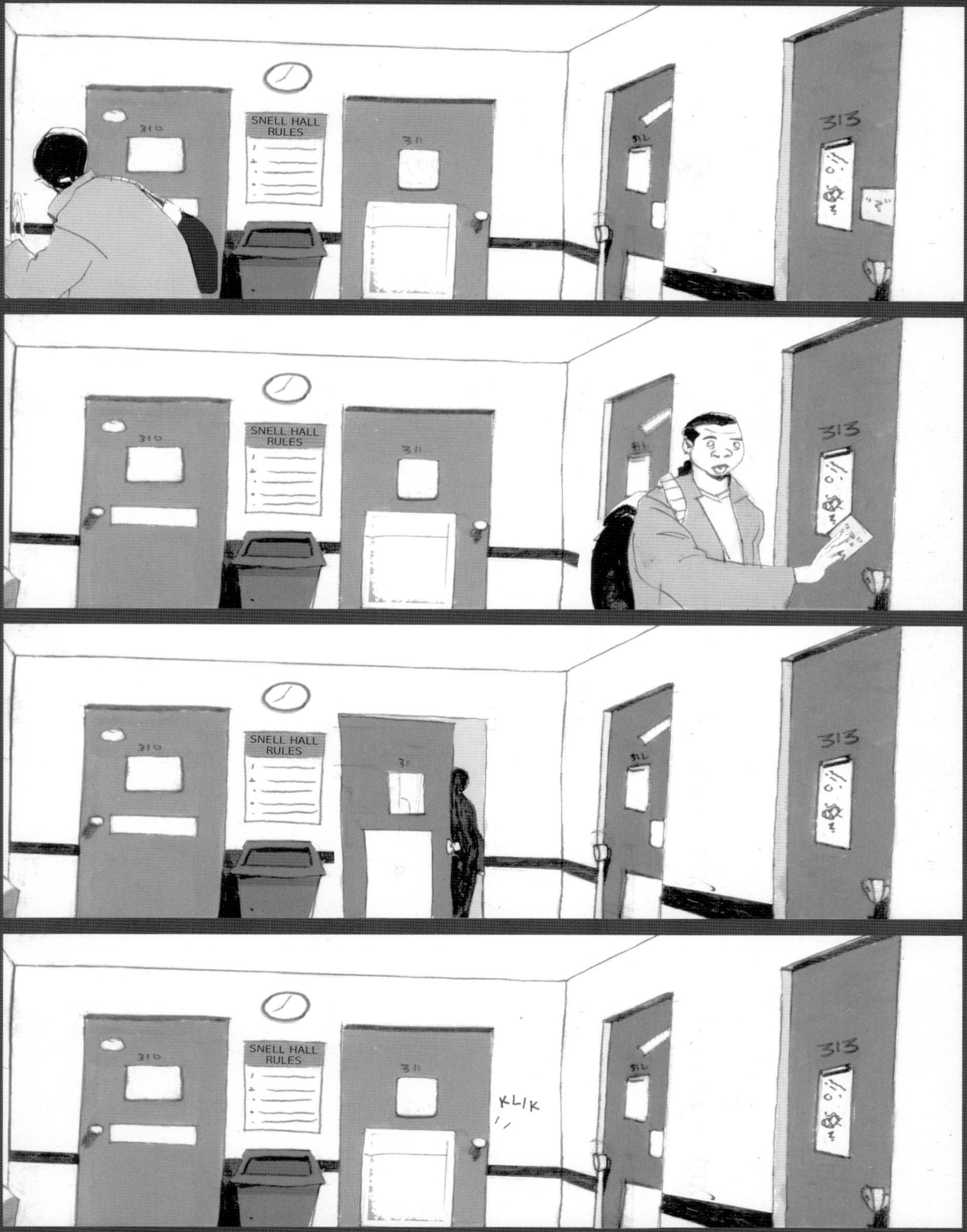
SNELL HALL RULES
310
311
312
313
SNELL HALL RULES
310
311
313
SNELL HALL RULES
310
311
312
313
SNELL HALL RULES
310
311
KLIK
312
313

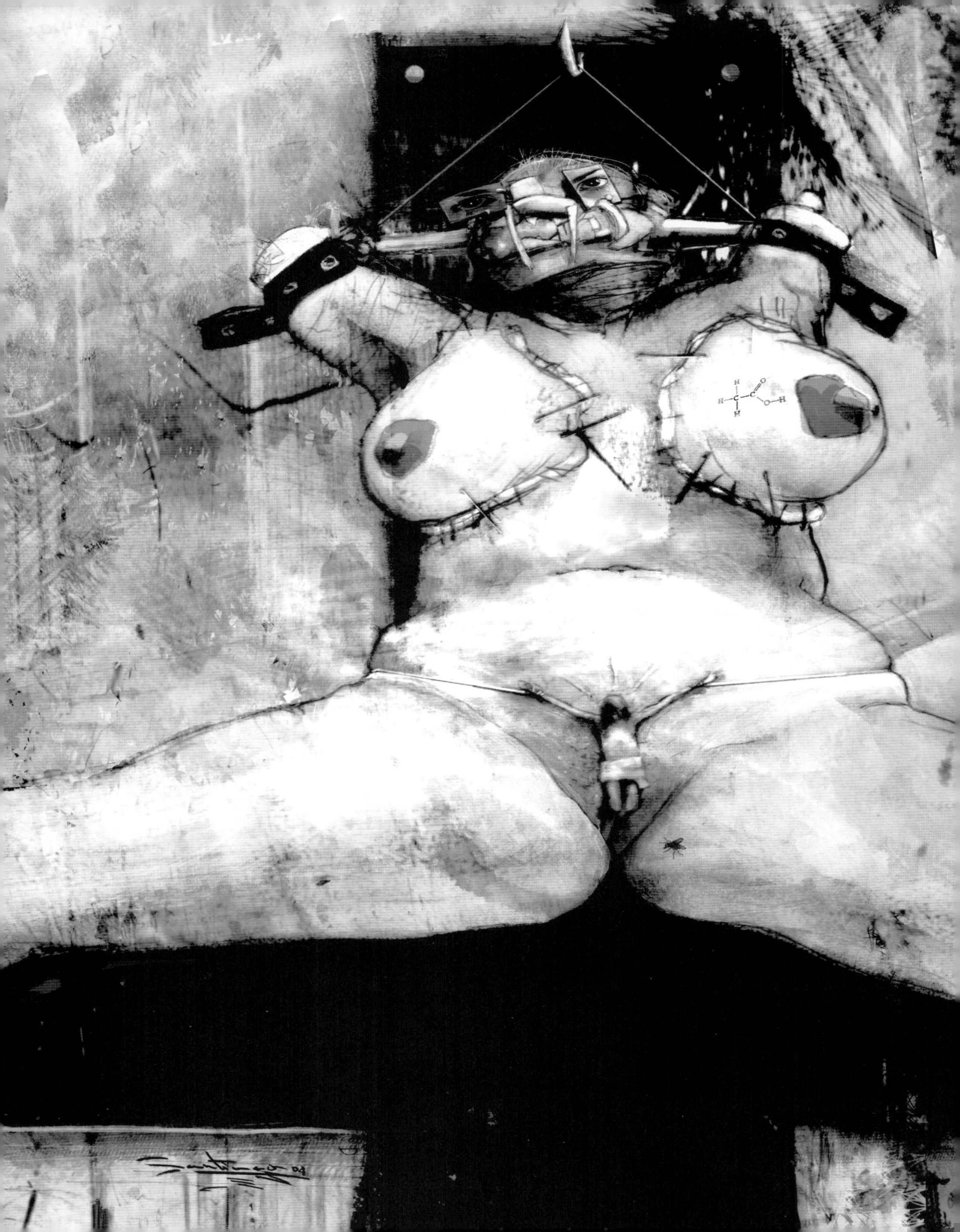

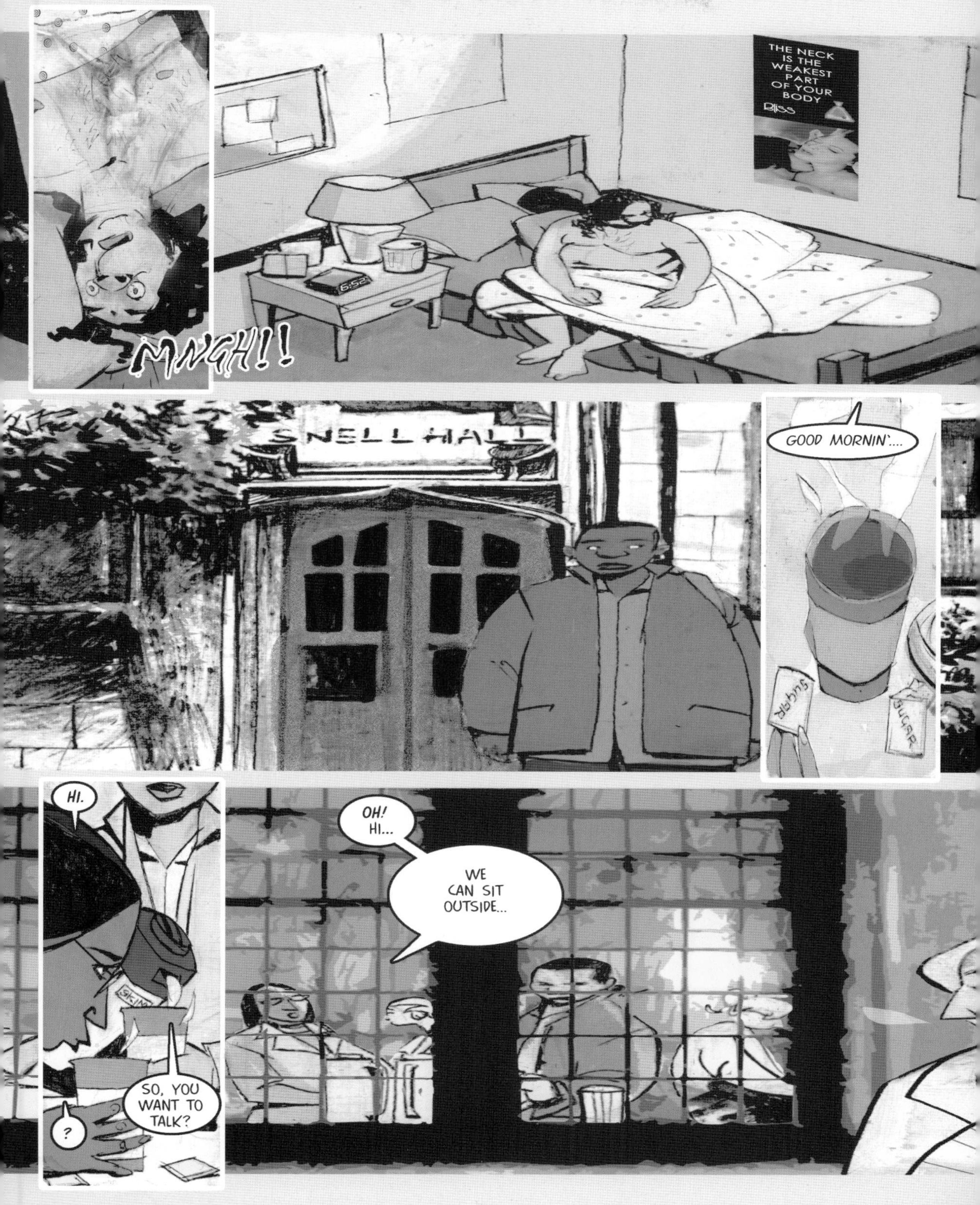
THE NECK IS THE WEAKEST PART OF YOUR BODY
MNGH!!
SNELL HALL
GOOD MORNIN'....
SUGAR
SUGAR
HI.
OH! HI...
WE CAN SIT OUTSIDE...
SO, YOU WANT TO TALK?
?

SO TELL ME OMAR, WHY ARE YOU CHOOSING TO SINGLE ME OUT FOR SUCH ATTENTION? ARE YOU SOME KIND OF PRANKSTER?

NO, NOT AT ALL... WHY DID YOU COME IF YOU THINK IT'S A JOKE?

I TOLD YOU... I WAS INTRIGUED. --BAFFLED ABOUT HOW YOU ARE "PERPLEXED BY MY BEAUTY"? WHAT DID YOU HOPE TO GET OUT OF SECRET ADMIRER NOTES, OMAR?

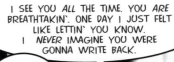

I SEE YOU *ALL* THE TIME. YOU *ARE* BREATHTAKIN'. ONE DAY I JUST FELT LIKE LETTIN' YOU KNOW. I *NEVER* IMAGINE YOU WERE GONNA WRITE BACK.

ARE YOU AND LUCINDA BREAKING UP ?

WELL--YEAH. WE TRYIN' TO STAY FRIENDS, *YOU KNOW.*

I'LL BE LEAVING FOR *SPAIN* NEXT QUARTER FOR A STUDY ABROAD PROGRAM. I AM FLATTERED, BUT RIGHT NOW I CAN PROMISE YOU ONLY MY FRIENDSHIP--

IT'S 8:45..?

I HAVE A CLASS AT NINE. TELL YOU WHAT, I'LL GIVE YOU MY EMAIL ADDRESS.

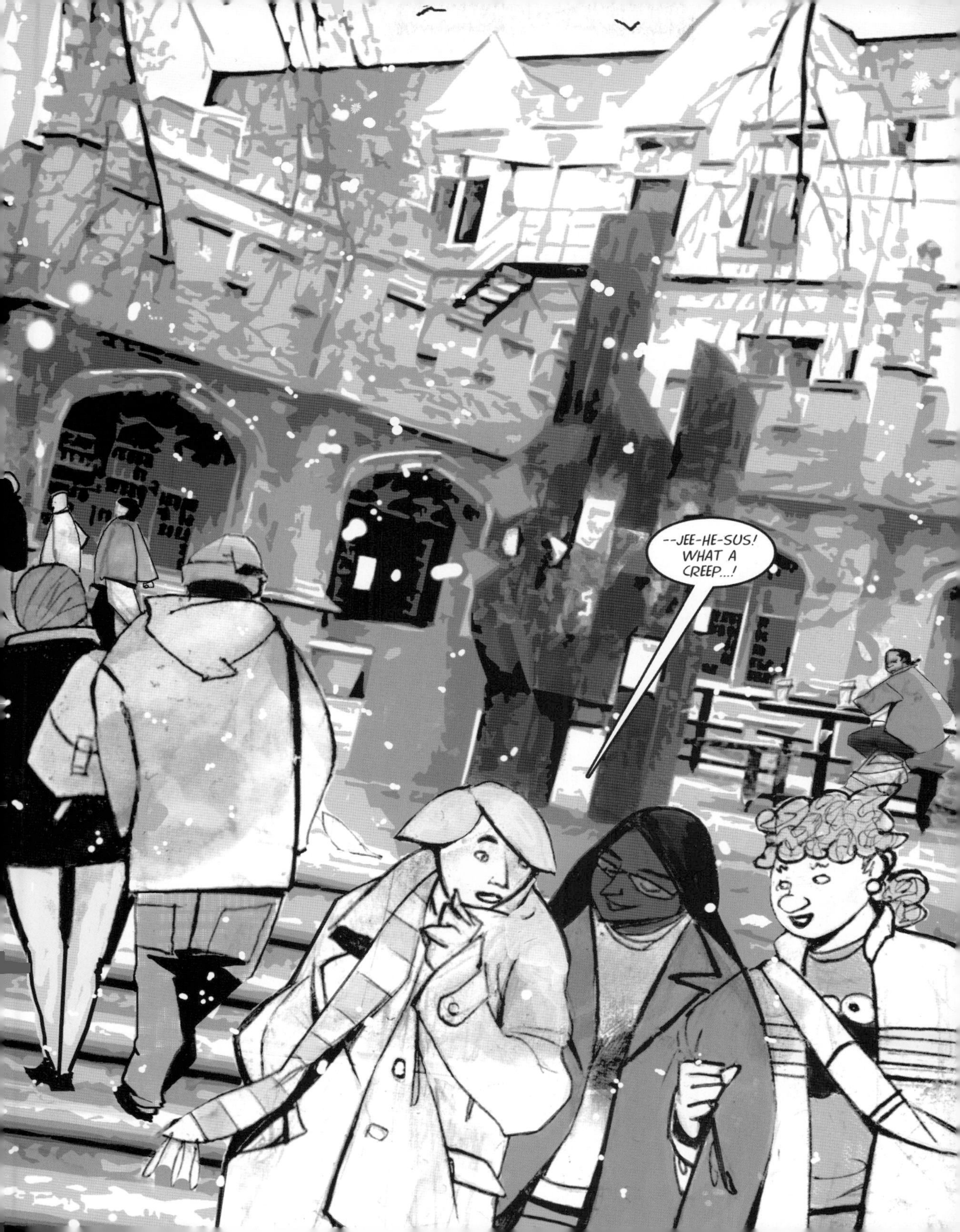
--JEE-HE-SUS! WHAT A CREEP...!

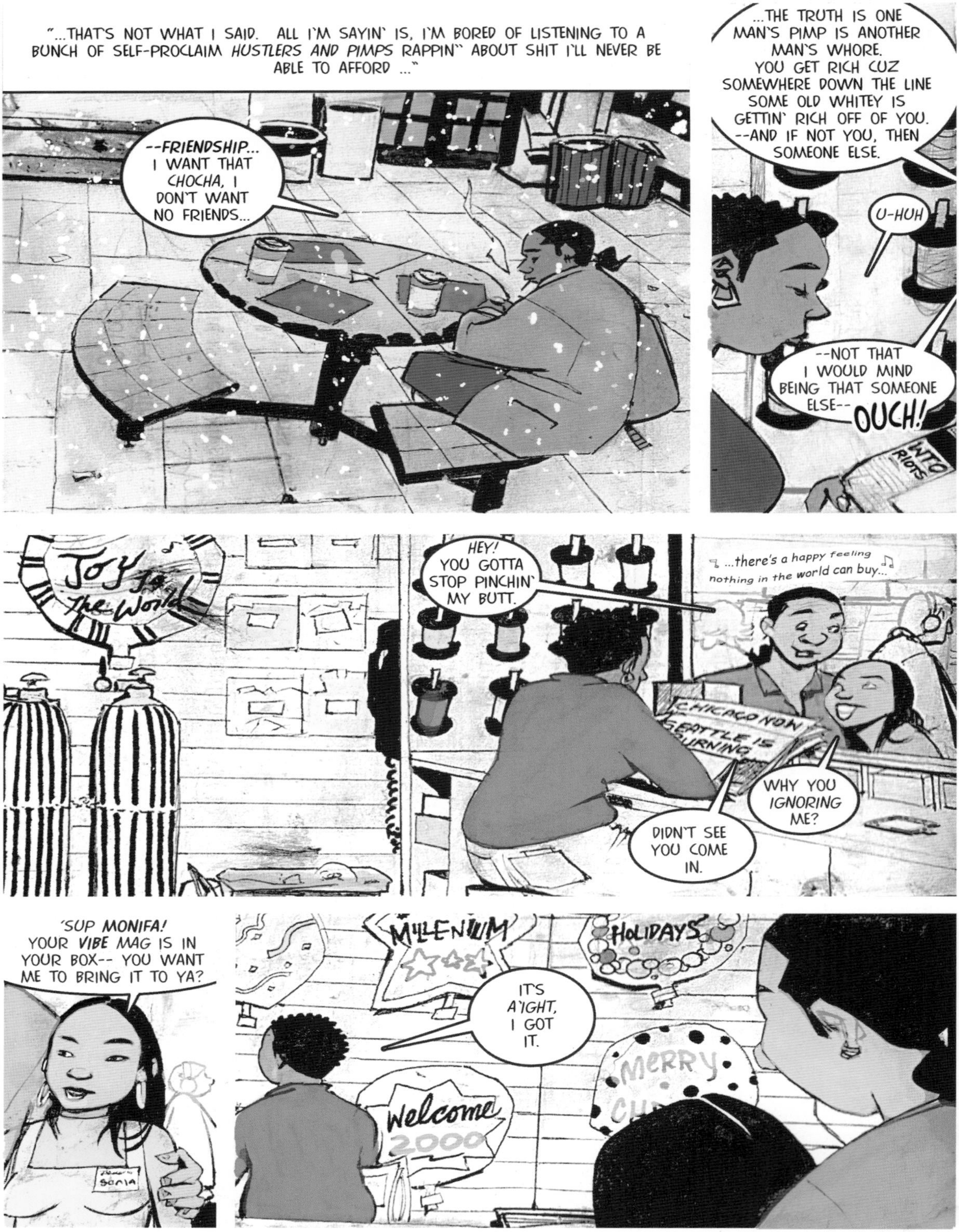
"...THAT'S NOT WHAT I SAID. ALL I'M SAYIN' IS, I'M BORED OF LISTENING TO A BUNCH OF SELF-PROCLAIM *HUSTLERS AND PIMPS* RAPPIN'' ABOUT SHIT I'LL NEVER BE ABLE TO AFFORD ..."
--FRIENDSHIP... I WANT THAT *CHOCHA*, I DON'T WANT NO FRIENDS...
...THE TRUTH IS ONE MAN'S PIMP IS ANOTHER MAN'S WHORE. YOU GET RICH CUZ SOMEWHERE DOWN THE LINE SOME OLD WHITEY IS GETTIN' RICH OFF OF YOU. --AND IF NOT YOU, THEN SOMEONE ELSE.
U-HUH
--NOT THAT I WOULD MIND BEING THAT SOMEONE ELSE-- OUCH!
WTO RIOTS
Joy to the World
HEY! YOU GOTTA STOP PINCHIN' MY BUTT.
♪ ...there's a happy feeling nothing in the world can buy... ♫
CHICAGO NOW SEATTLE IS BURNING
WHY YOU IGNORING ME?
DIDN'T SEE YOU COME IN.
'SUP **MONIFA!** YOUR ***VIBE*** **MAG** IS IN YOUR BOX-- YOU WANT ME TO BRING IT TO YA?
Sonia
MILLENIUM
HOLIDAYS
IT'S A'IGHT, I GOT IT.
Welcome 2000

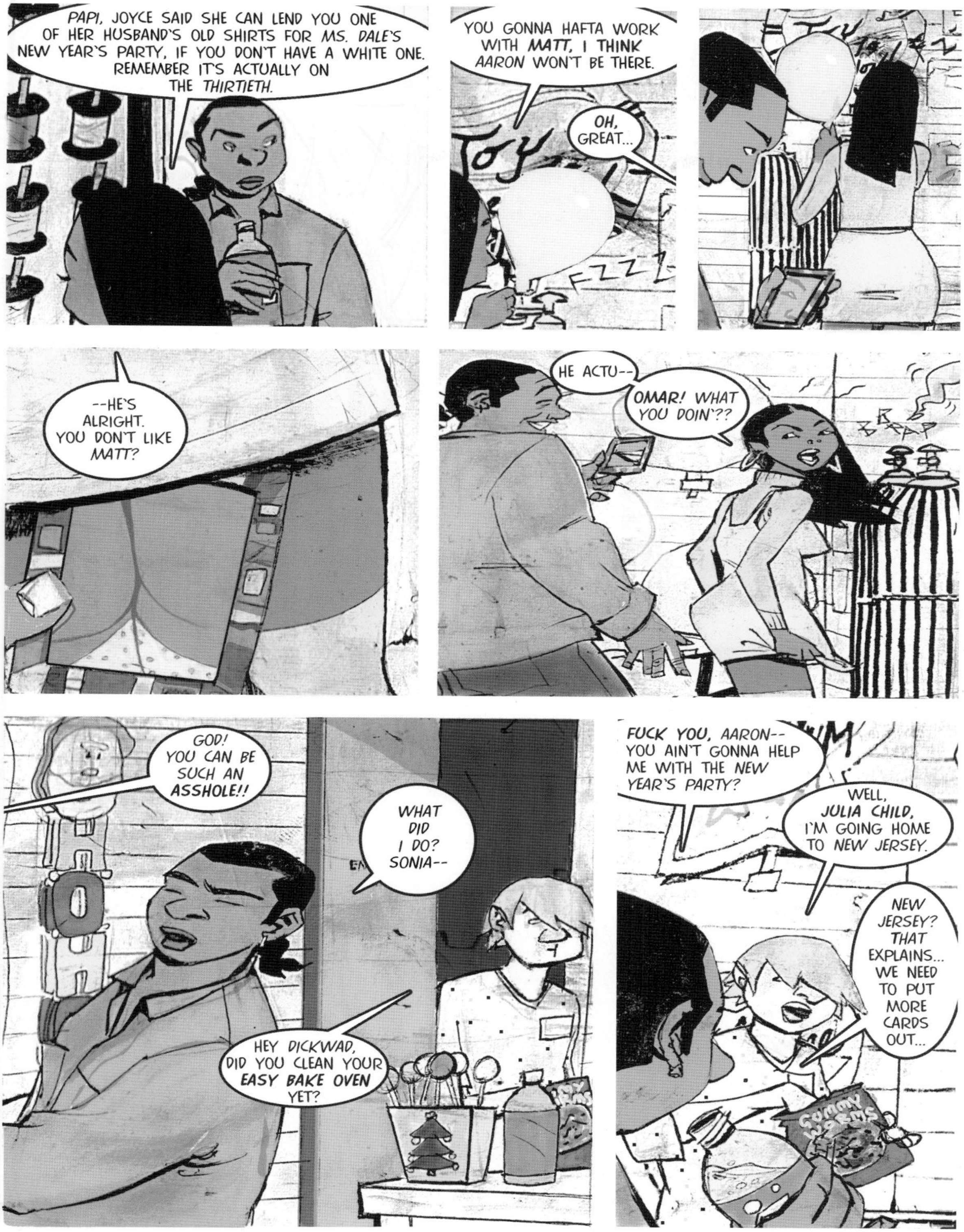
PAPI, JOYCE SAID SHE CAN LEND YOU ONE OF HER HUSBAND'S OLD SHIRTS FOR MS. DALE'S NEW YEAR'S PARTY, IF YOU DON'T HAVE A WHITE ONE. REMEMBER IT'S ACTUALLY ON THE THIRTIETH.
YOU GONNA HAFTA WORK WITH MATT, I THINK AARON WON'T BE THERE.
OH, GREAT...
--HE'S ALRIGHT. YOU DON'T LIKE MATT?
HE ACTU--
OMAR! WHAT YOU DOIN'??
GOD! YOU CAN BE SUCH AN ASSHOLE!!
WHAT DID I DO? SONIA--
HEY DICKWAD, DID YOU CLEAN YOUR EASY BAKE OVEN YET?
FUCK YOU, AARON-- YOU AIN'T GONNA HELP ME WITH THE NEW YEAR'S PARTY?
WELL, JULIA CHILD, I'M GOING HOME TO NEW JERSEY.
NEW JERSEY? THAT EXPLAINS... WE NEED TO PUT MORE CARDS OUT...

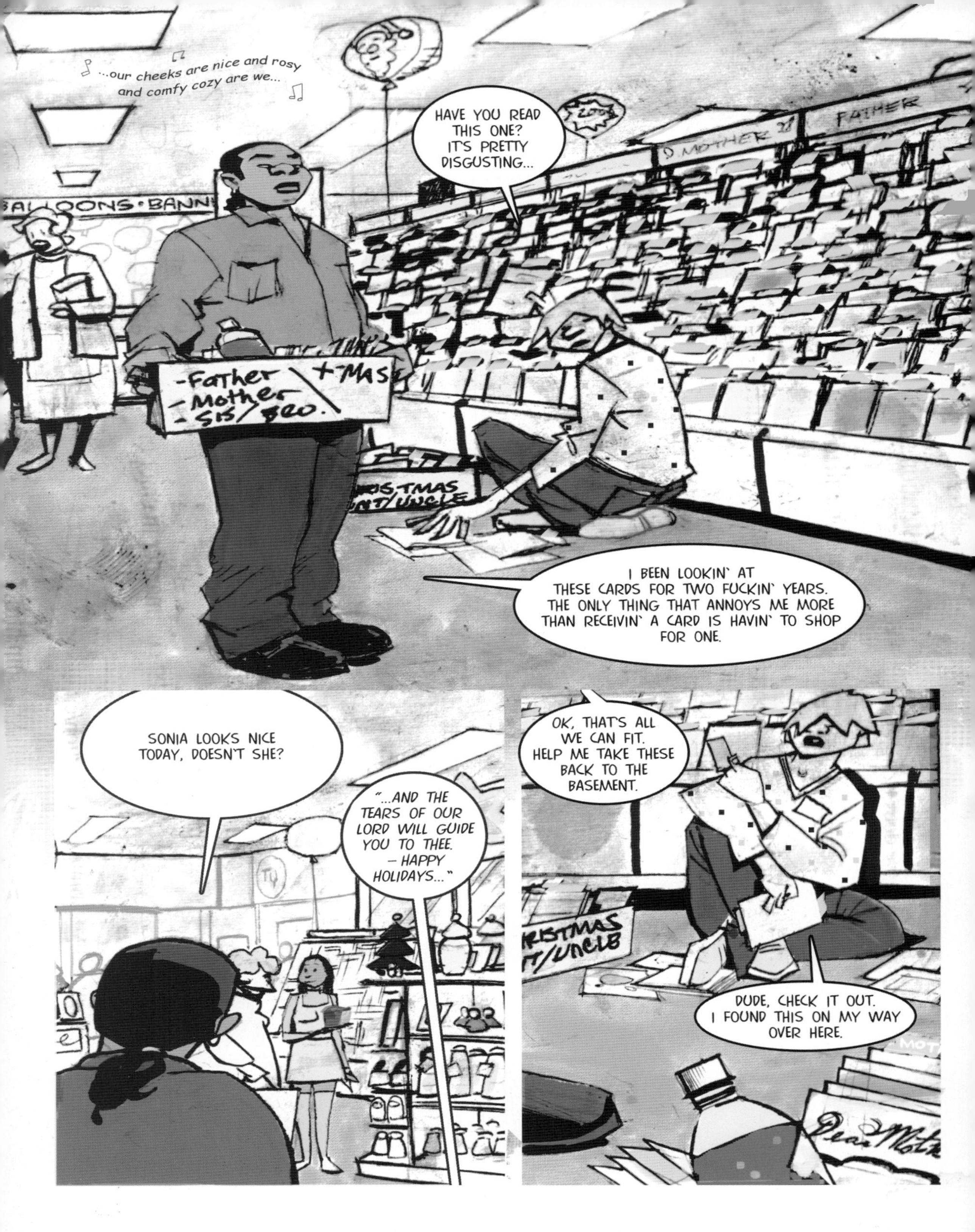
...our cheeks are nice and rosy
and comfy cozy are we...
FATHER
MOTHER
HAVE YOU READ THIS ONE? IT'S PRETTY DISGUSTING...
-Father
-Mother
-Sis/Bro.
X-Mas
I BEEN LOOKIN' AT THESE CARDS FOR TWO FUCKIN' YEARS. THE ONLY THING THAT ANNOYS ME MORE THAN RECEIVIN' A CARD IS HAVIN' TO SHOP FOR ONE.
SONIA LOOKS NICE TODAY, DOESN'T SHE?
"...AND THE TEARS OF OUR LORD WILL GUIDE YOU TO THEE. – HAPPY HOLIDAYS..."
OK, THAT'S ALL WE CAN FIT. HELP ME TAKE THESE BACK TO THE BASEMENT.
DUDE, CHECK IT OUT. I FOUND THIS ON MY WAY OVER HERE.

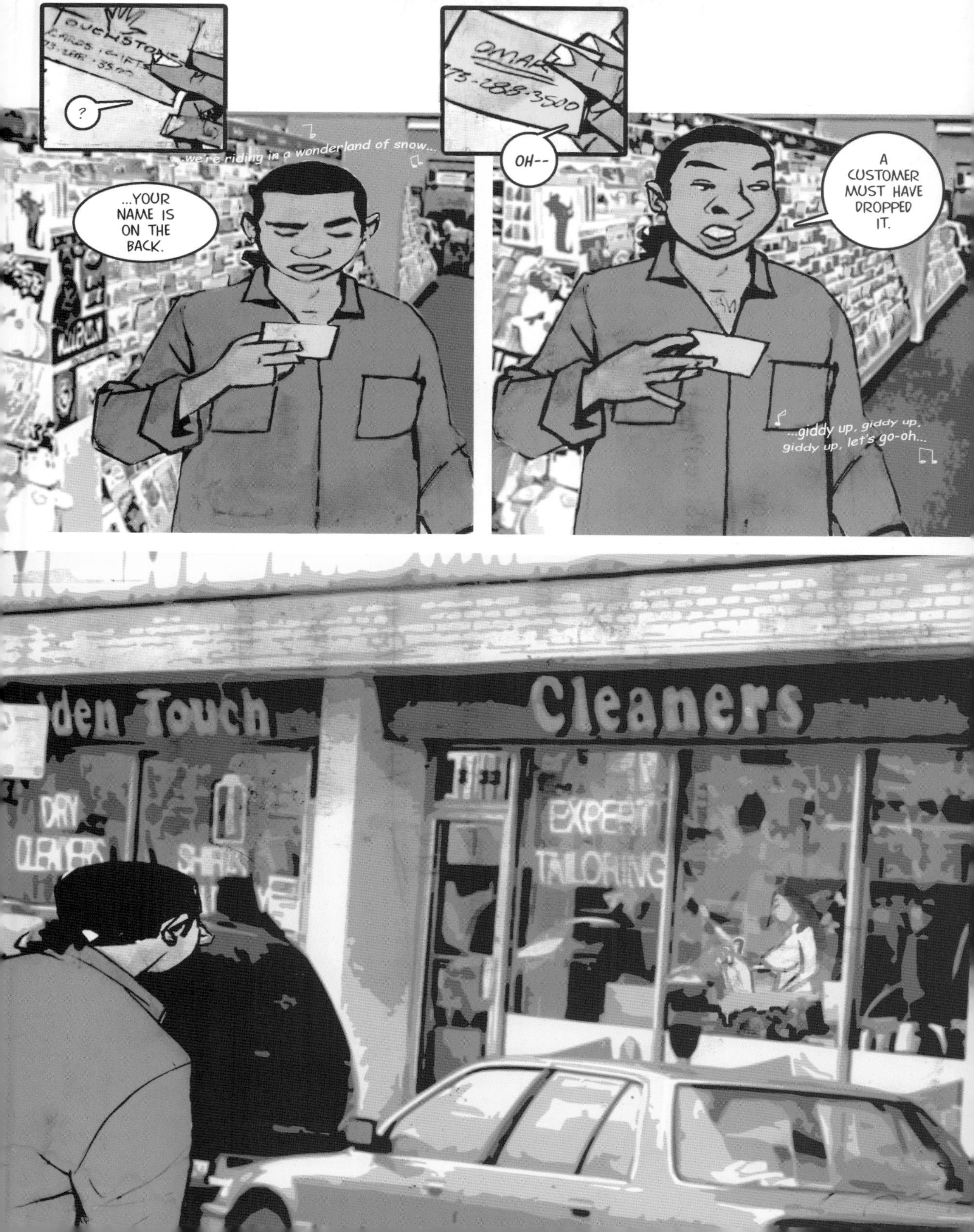
?
...we're riding in a wonderland of snow...
...YOUR NAME IS ON THE BACK.
OMAR
OH--
A CUSTOMER MUST HAVE DROPPED IT.
...giddy up, giddy up, giddy up, let's go-oh...
den Touch
Cleaners
DRY
EXPERT
TAILORING

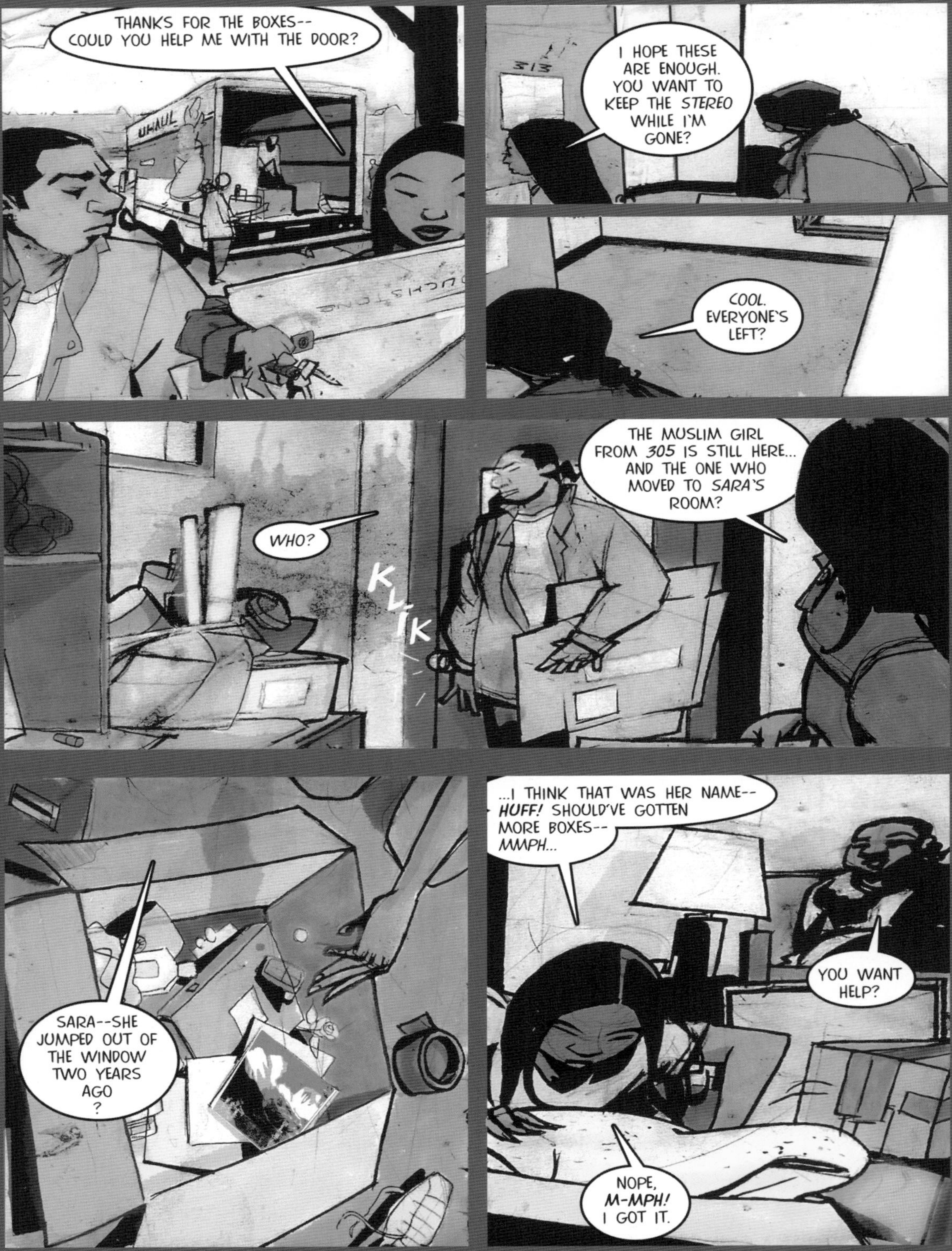
THANKS FOR THE BOXES--
COULD YOU HELP ME WITH THE DOOR?
UHAUL
I HOPE THESE ARE ENOUGH. YOU WANT TO KEEP THE STEREO WHILE I'M GONE?
313
COOL. EVERYONE'S LEFT?
WHO?
KLIK
THE MUSLIM GIRL FROM 305 IS STILL HERE... AND THE ONE WHO MOVED TO SARA'S ROOM?
SARA--SHE JUMPED OUT OF THE WINDOW TWO YEARS AGO ?
...I THINK THAT WAS HER NAME-- HUFF! SHOULD'VE GOTTEN MORE BOXES-- MMPH...
YOU WANT HELP?
NOPE, M-MPH! I GOT IT.

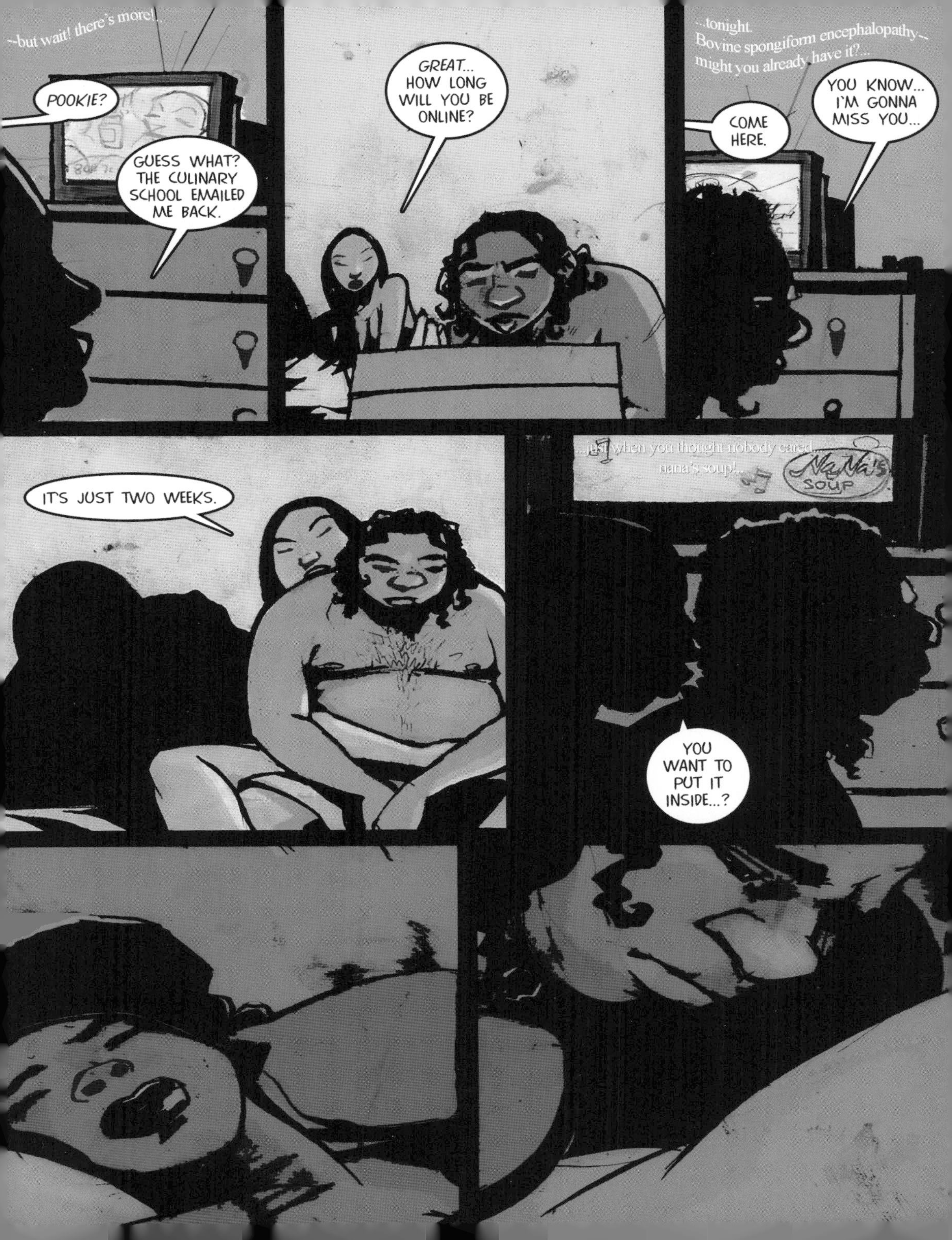
--but wait! there's more!..
POOKIE?
GUESS WHAT? THE CULINARY SCHOOL EMAILED ME BACK.
GREAT... HOW LONG WILL YOU BE ONLINE?
...tonight.
Bovine spongiform encephalopathy--
might you already have it?...
COME HERE.
YOU KNOW... I'M GONNA MISS YOU...
IT'S JUST TWO WEEKS.
...just when you thought nobody cared...
nana's soup!..
NaNa's SOUP
YOU WANT TO PUT IT INSIDE...?

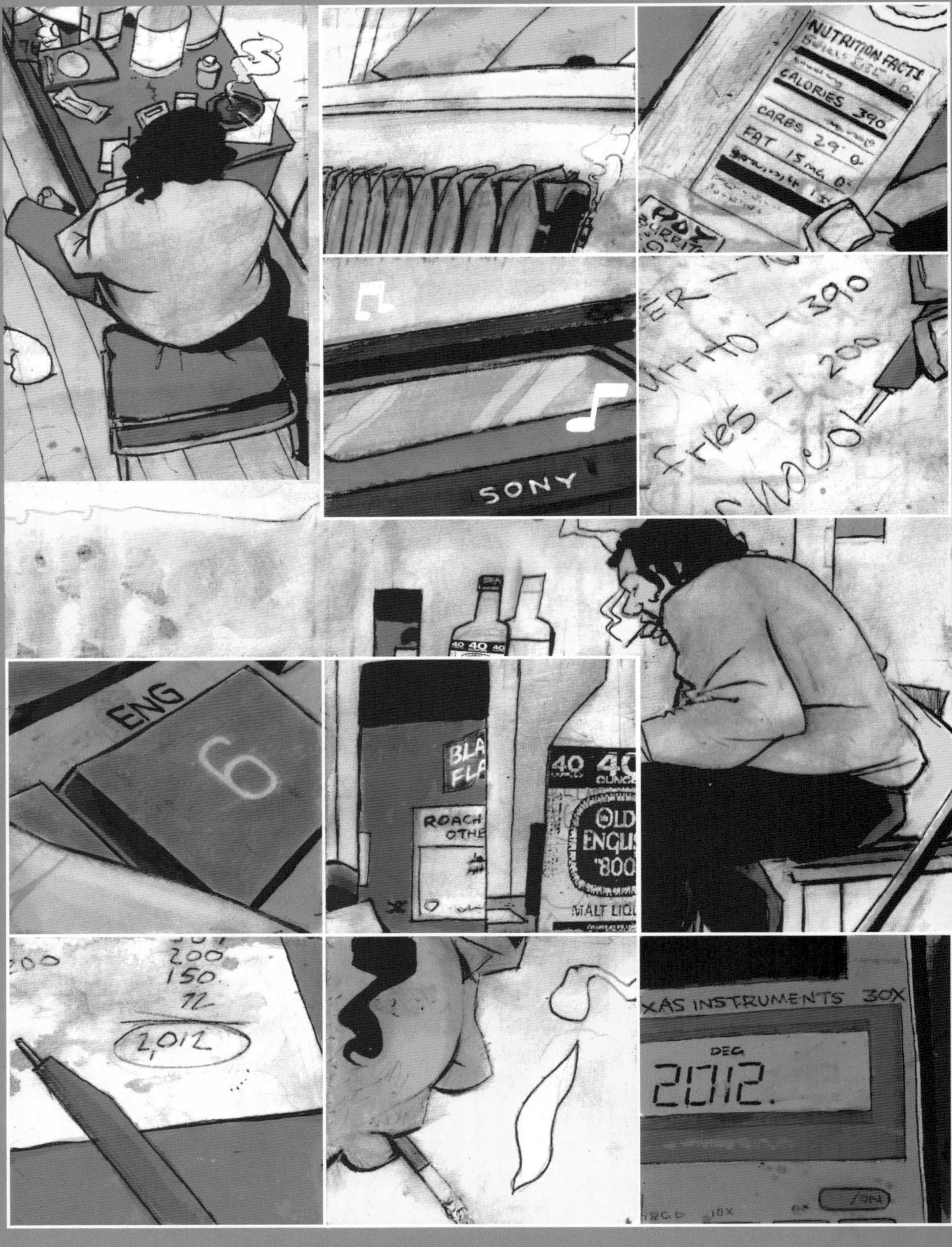
NUTRITION FACTS
CALORIES 390
CARBS
FAT
SONY
URRITO — 390
Fries — 200
ENG
BLA
FLA
ROACH
OTHE
40 40
OLD
ENGLIS
'800'
MALT LIQU
200
150
72
2,012
XAS INSTRUMENTS 30X
DEG
2012.
ON

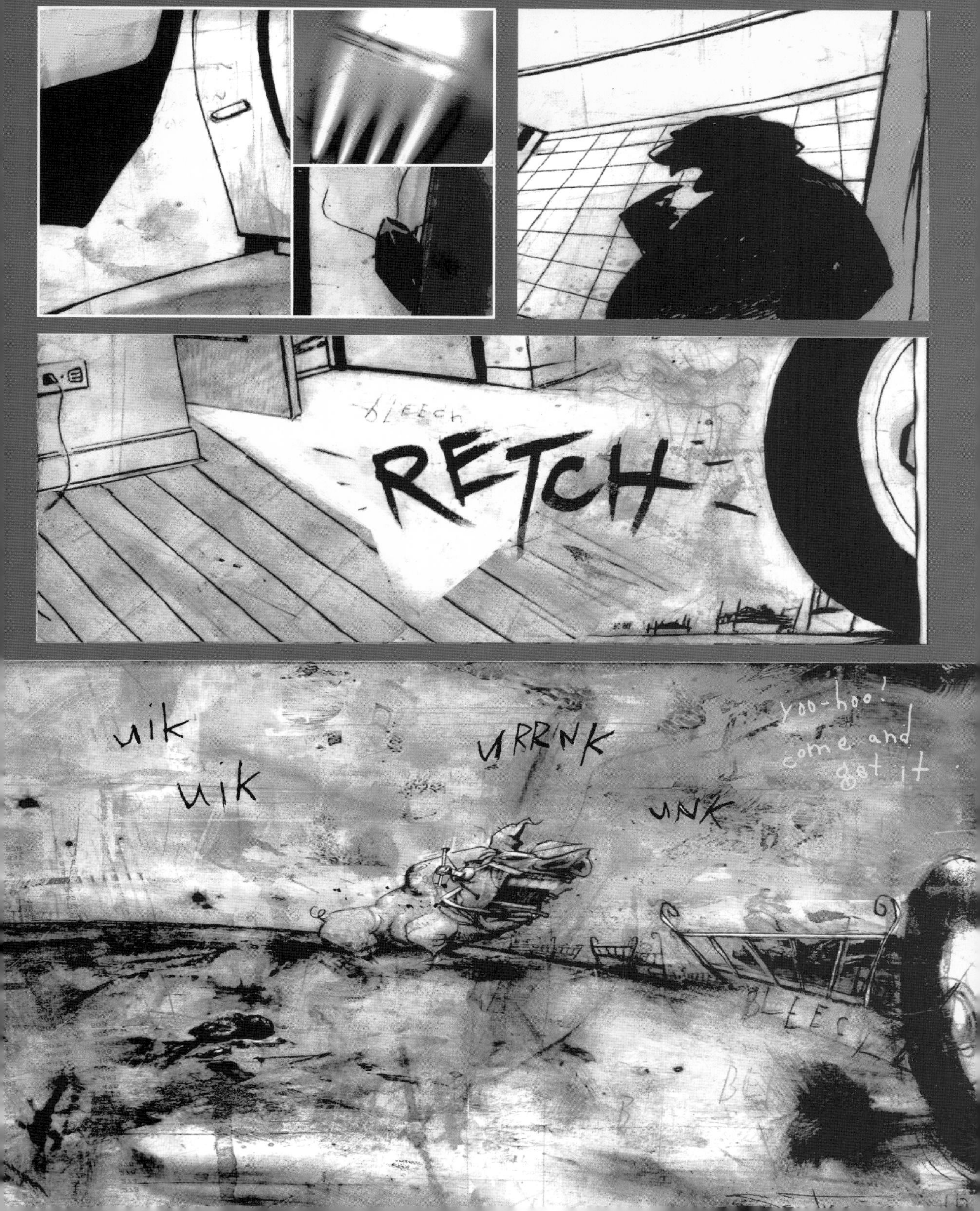
BLEECH
RETCH
uik
uik
URRNK
UNK
yoo-hoo!
come and
get it

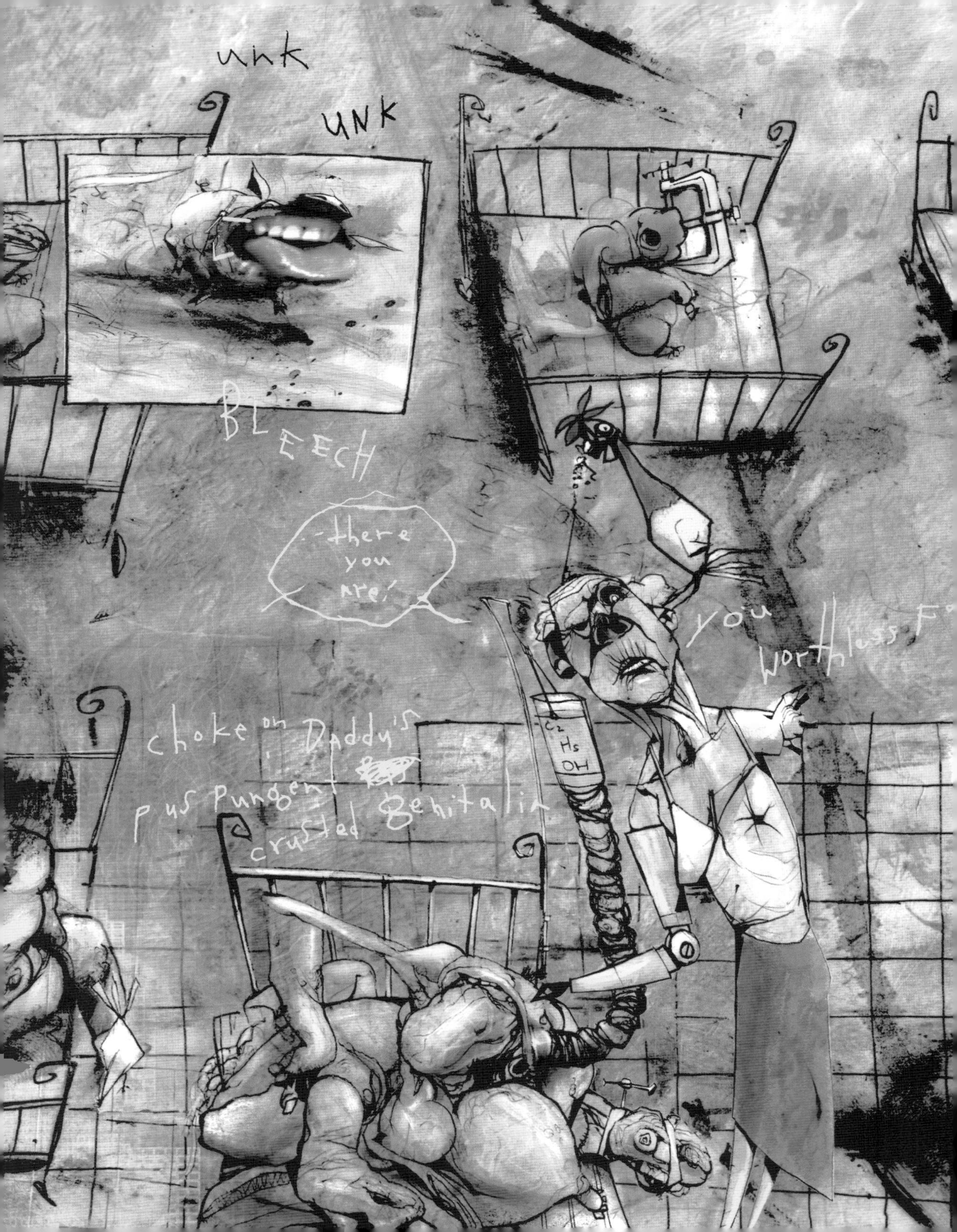
unk
UNK
BLEECH
there you are!
you worthless F
choke on Daddy's pus pungent crusted genitalia
C_2H_5OH

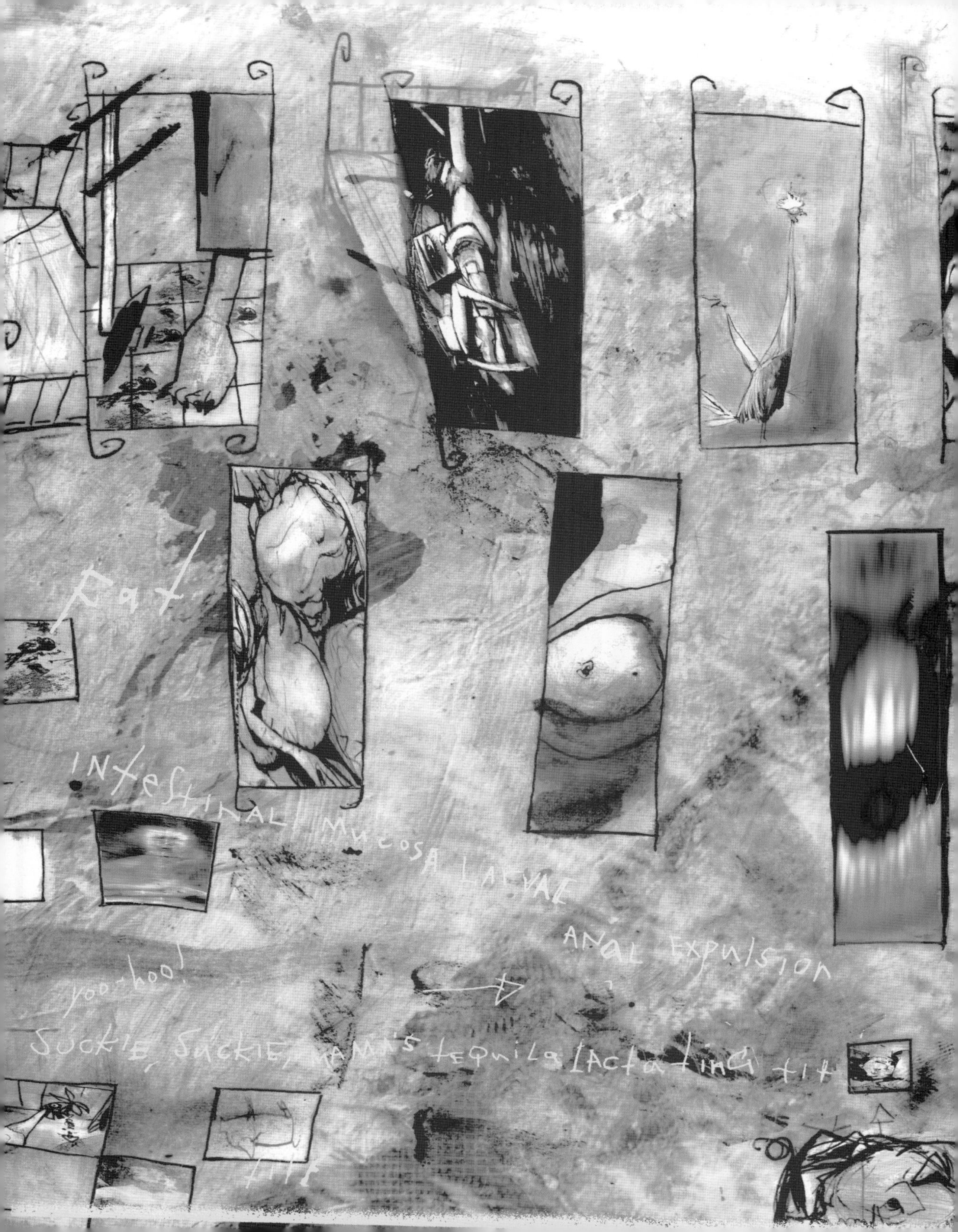
Fat
intestinal mucosa larvae
anal expulsion
yoo-hoo!
suckie, suckie, mama's tequila lactating tit

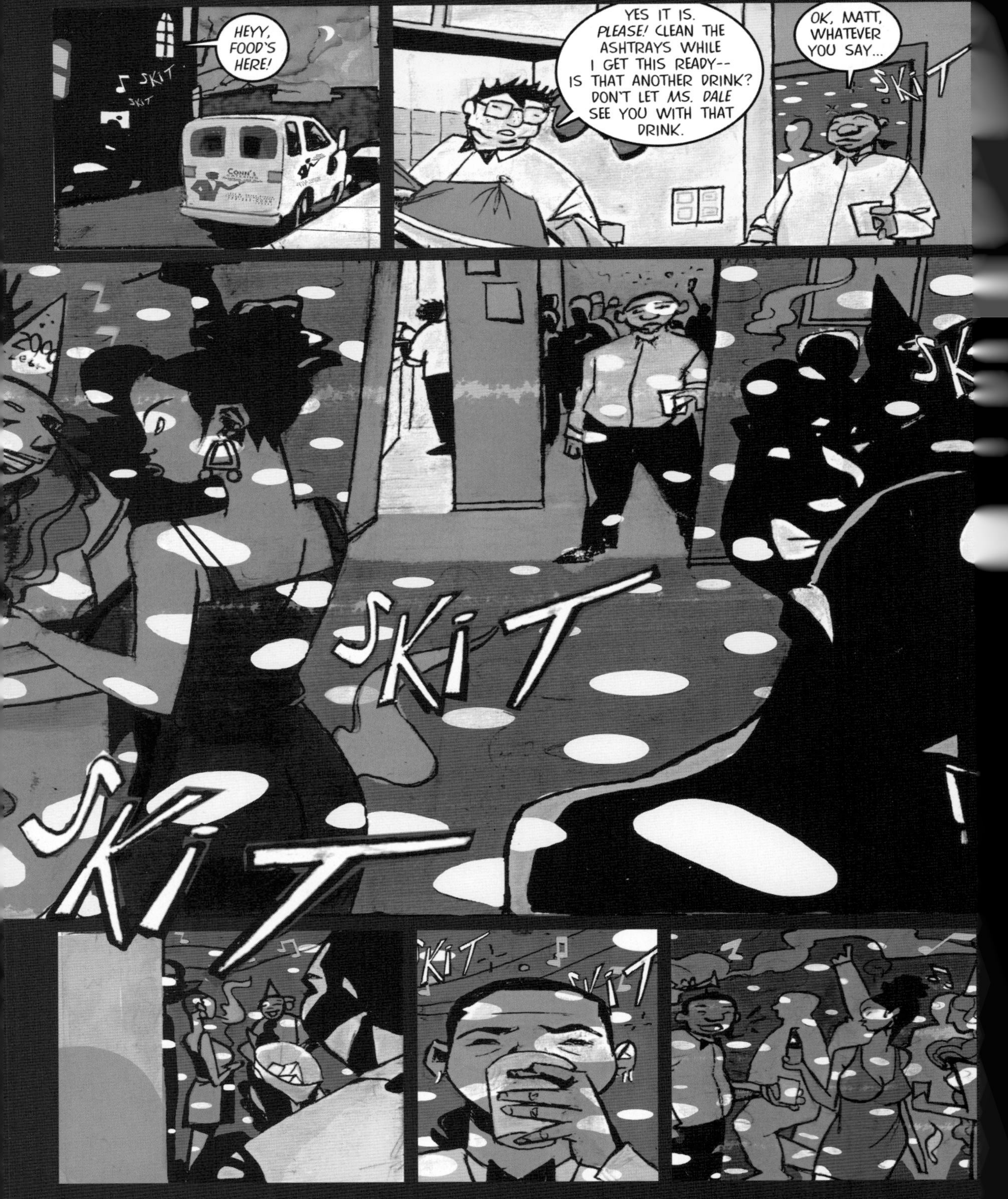
SKIT
SKIT
HEYY, FOOD'S HERE!
YES IT IS. PLEASE! CLEAN THE ASHTRAYS WHILE I GET THIS READY-- IS THAT ANOTHER DRINK? DON'T LET MS. DALE SEE YOU WITH THAT DRINK.
OK, MATT, WHATEVER YOU SAY...
SKIT
SKIT
SKIT
SKIT
SKIT
SKIT

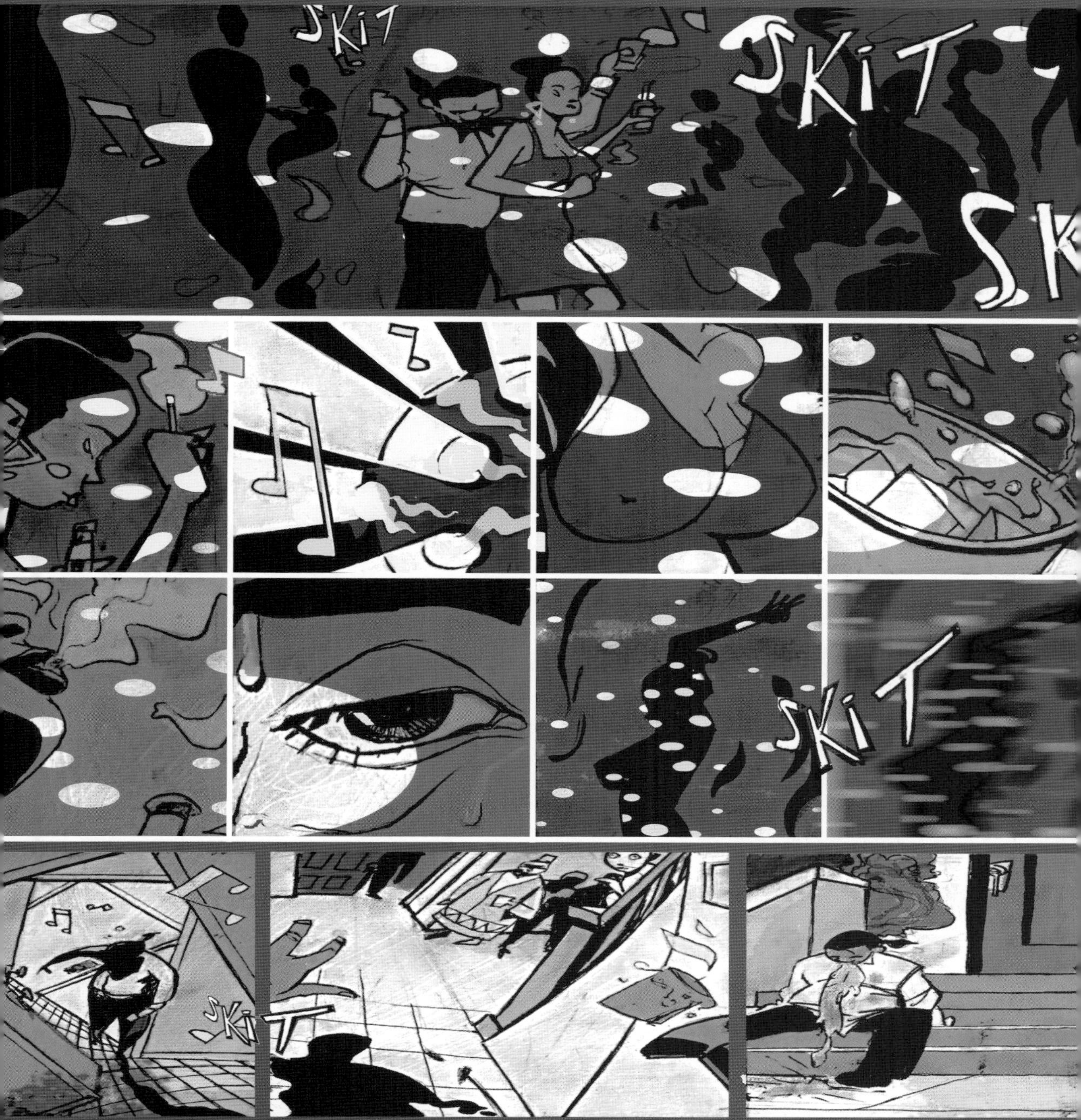
SKIT
SKIT
SK
SKIT
SKIT

"I DON'T HAVE ANY IDEA HOW I GOT HOME..."

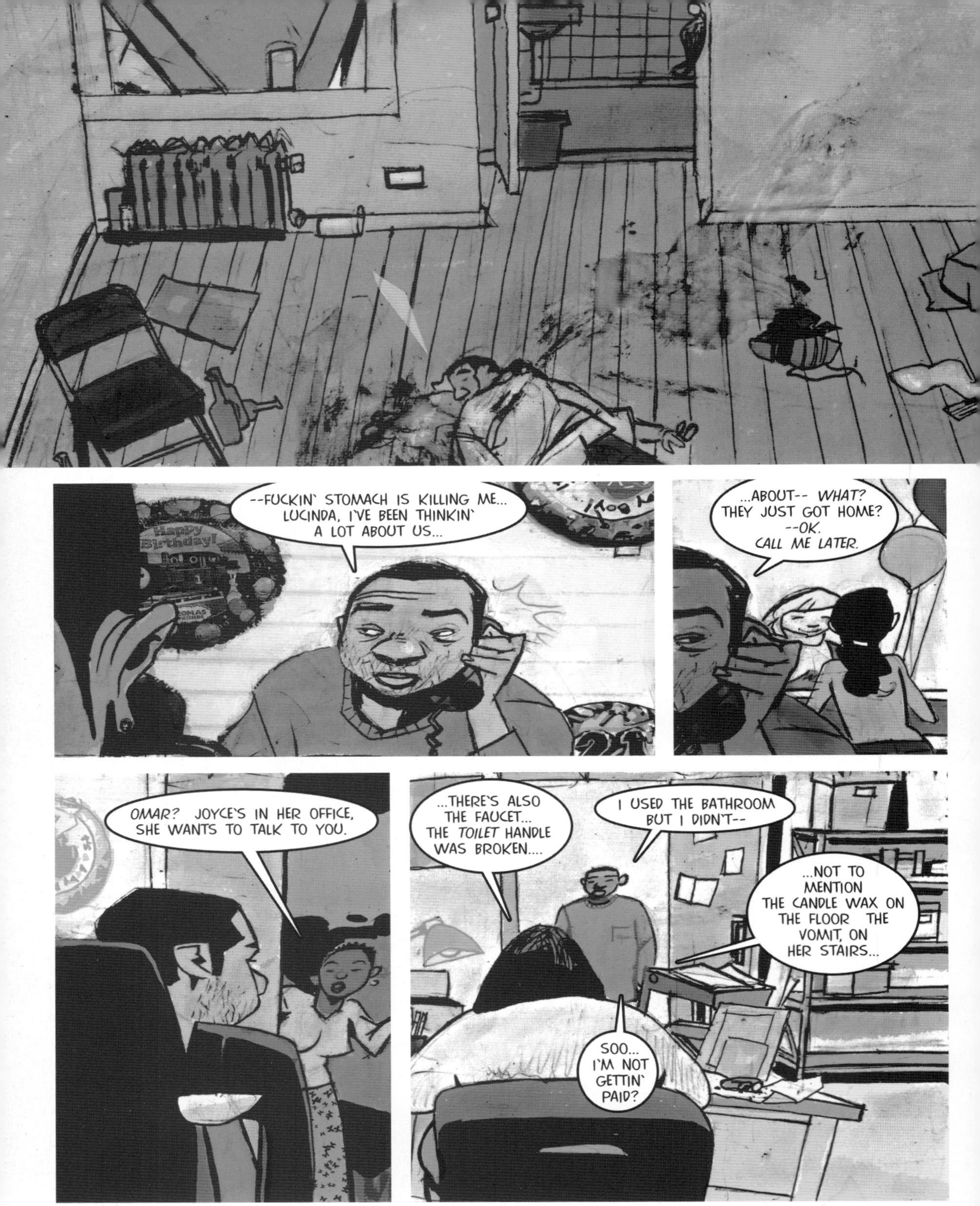
--FUCKIN` STOMACH IS KILLING ME... LUCINDA, I'VE BEEN THINKIN` A LOT ABOUT US...
...ABOUT-- WHAT? THEY JUST GOT HOME? --OK. CALL ME LATER.
OMAR? JOYCE'S IN HER OFFICE, SHE WANTS TO TALK TO YOU.
...THERE'S ALSO THE FAUCET... THE TOILET HANDLE WAS BROKEN....
I USED THE BATHROOM BUT I DIDN'T--
...NOT TO MENTION THE CANDLE WAX ON THE FLOOR THE VOMIT, ON HER STAIRS...
SOO... I'M NOT GETTIN` PAID?
Happy Birthday!

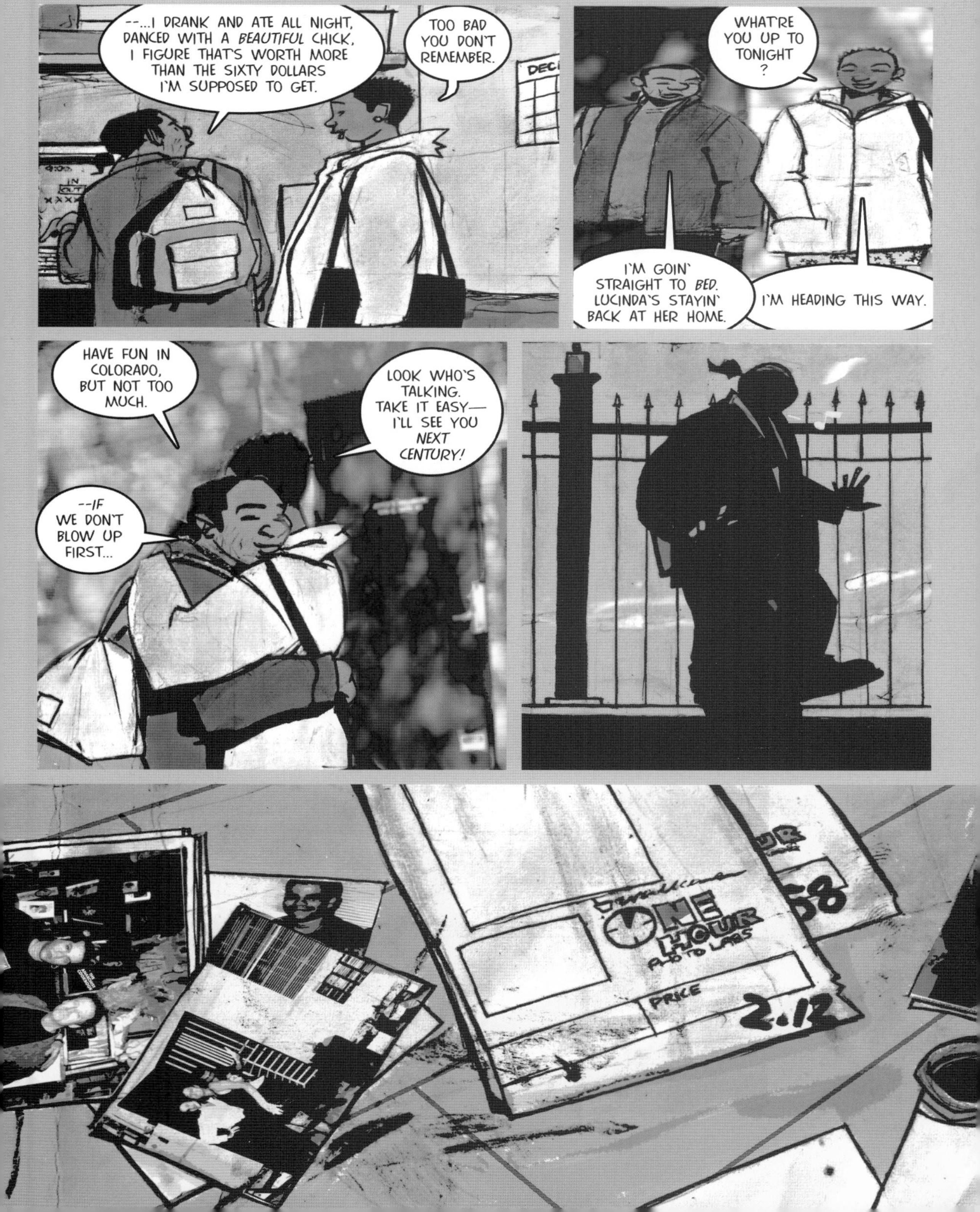
--...I DRANK AND ATE ALL NIGHT, DANCED WITH A *BEAUTIFUL* CHICK, I FIGURE THAT'S WORTH MORE THAN THE SIXTY DOLLARS I'M SUPPOSED TO GET.
TOO BAD YOU DON'T REMEMBER.
WHAT'RE YOU UP TO TONIGHT ?
I'M GOIN' STRAIGHT TO *BED*. LUCINDA'S STAYIN' BACK AT HER HOME.
I'M HEADING THIS WAY.
HAVE FUN IN COLORADO, BUT NOT TOO MUCH.
LOOK WHO'S TALKING. TAKE IT EASY— I'LL SEE YOU *NEXT CENTURY!*
--*IF* WE DON'T BLOW UP FIRST...
ONE HOUR PHOTO LABS
PRICE
2.12

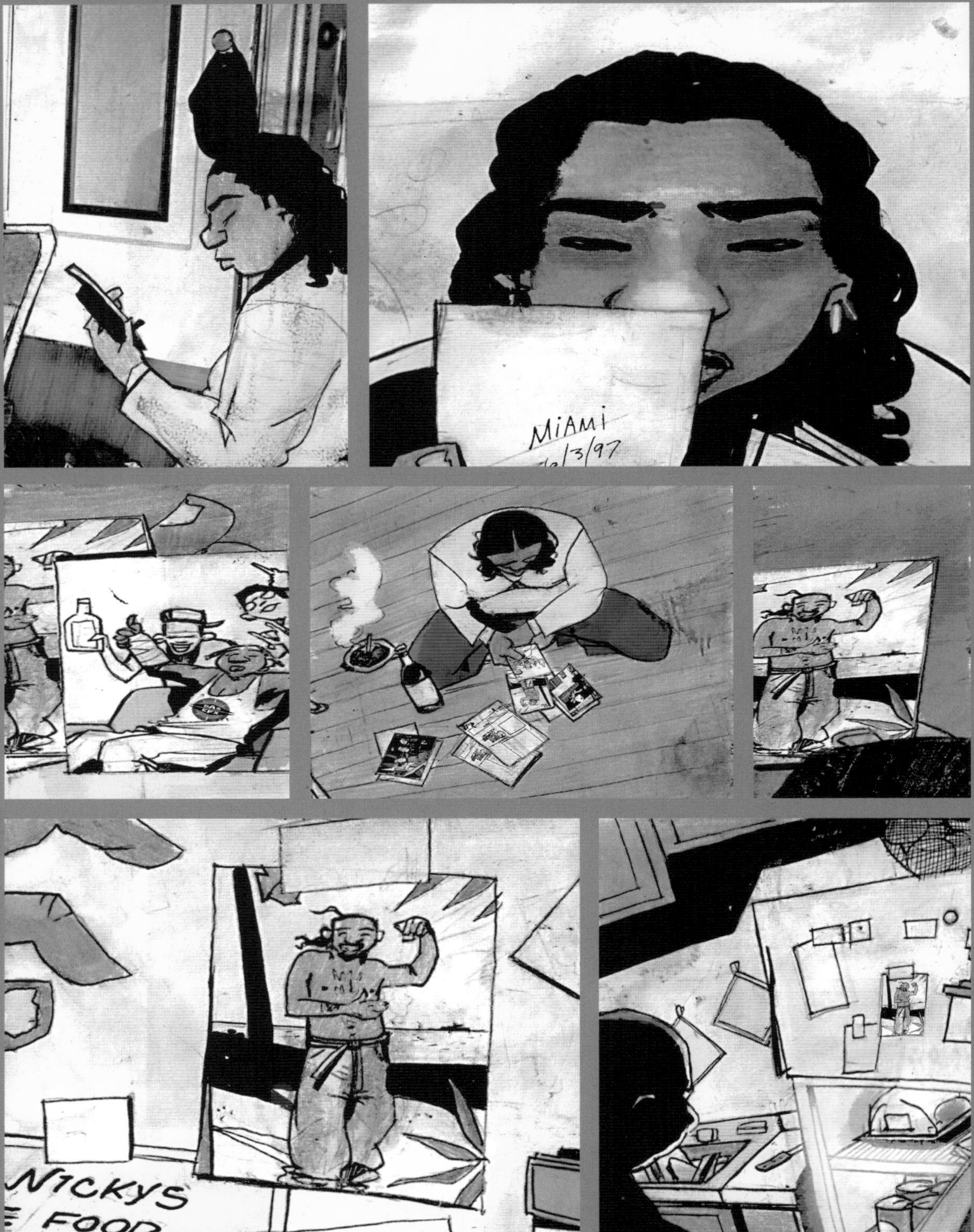
MIAMI
NICKYS
FOOD

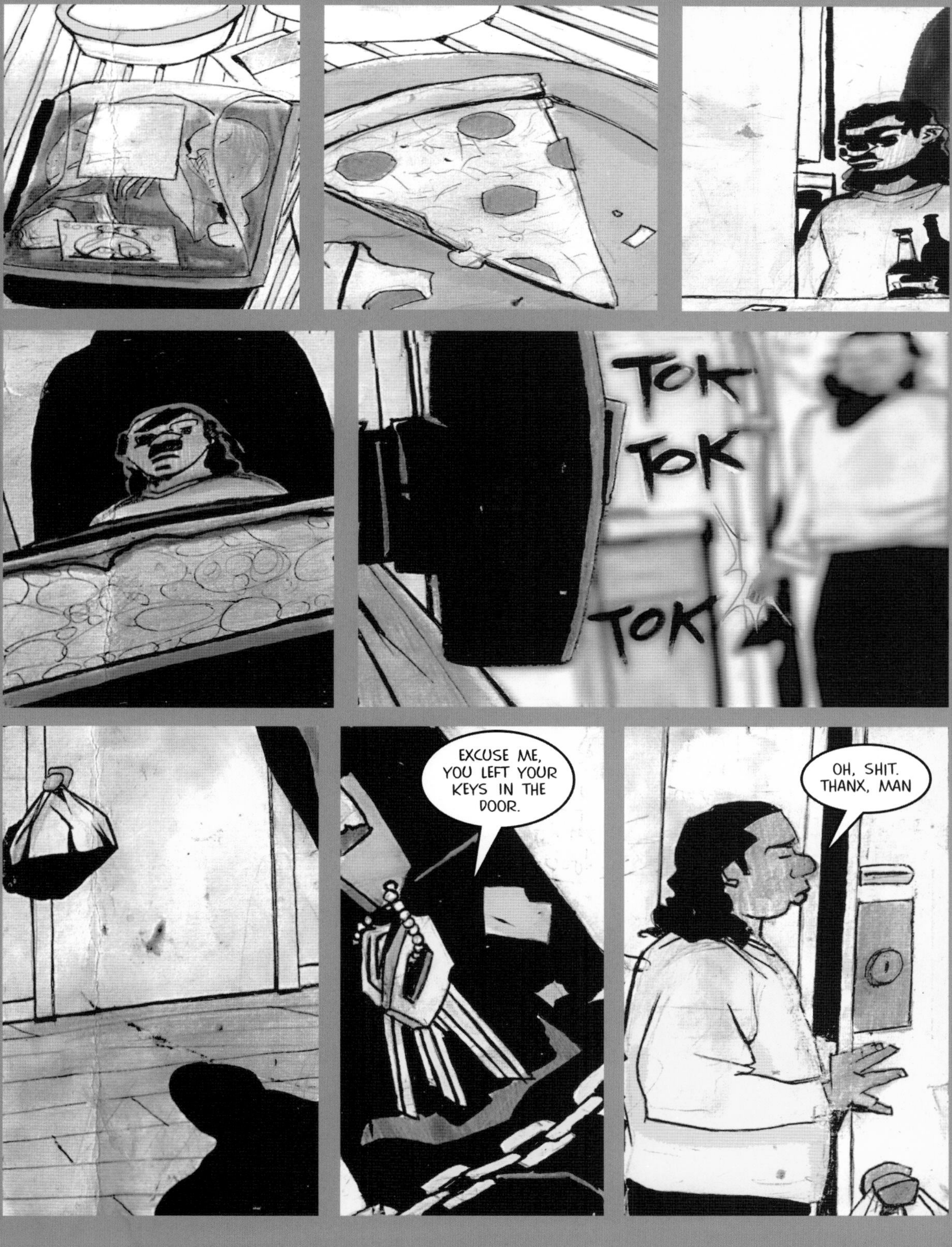
TOK
TOK
TOK
EXCUSE ME, YOU LEFT YOUR KEYS IN THE DOOR.
OH, SHIT. THANX, MAN

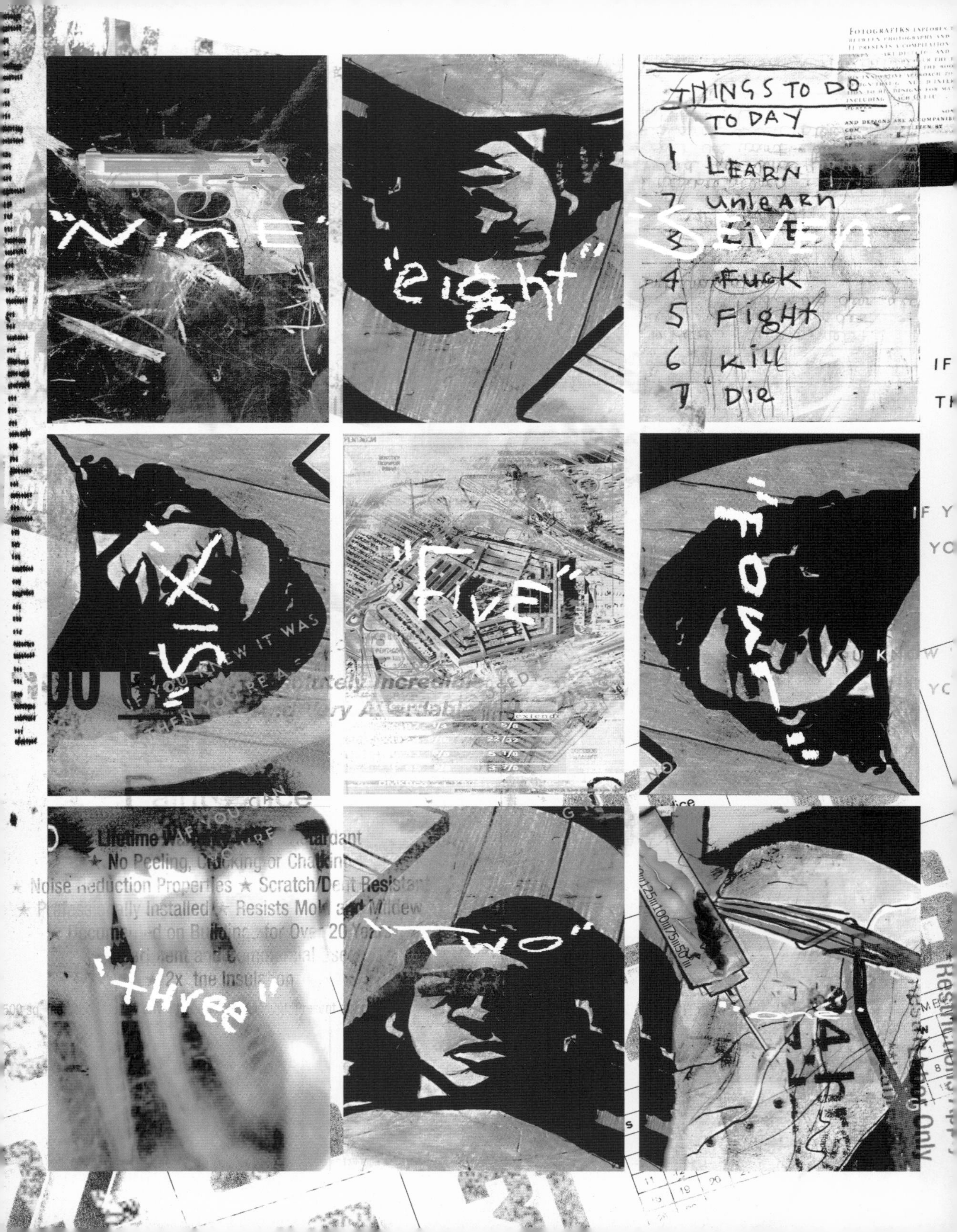
"Nine"
"eight"
THINGS TO DO TO DAY
1 LEARN
2 unlearn
3 LIVE
4 Fuck
5 Fight
6 kill
7 Die
"SEVEn"
"Six"
"Five"
"Four"
Lifetime Warranty
★ No Peeling, Cracking or Chalking
Noise Reduction Properties ★ Scratch/Dent Resistant
★ Resists Mold and Mildew
"tHree"
"Two"
"one"

YECAHH!! HERE IT IS FOLKS! THE BEGINNING OF A NEW EXCITING ERA.

A MOMENT OF REFLECTION, AS WE LOOK INTO THE PAST YEAR...

...A MOMENT OF HOPE AND DREAMS, AS WE GLIMPSE INTO THE FUTURE.

94.2 FM

YEAR 2 0 0 0! THE NEW MILLENNIUM! AS THE WORLD CELEBRATES...

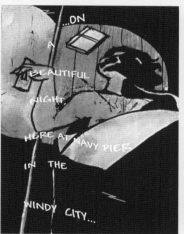

...ON A BEAUTIFUL NIGHT HERE AT NAVY PIER IN THE WINDY CITY...

HAPPY NEW YEAR KIX YOU AND YOUR FAMILY FROM D.J. G-NEWZ & OUR FAMILY AT KIX 94!

...THIS BROADCAST IS BROUGHT TO YOU BY TITAN COLA

NEW CENTURY? NEW COLA.

TITAN COLA!

--JOIN THE TITAN REVOLUTION..!

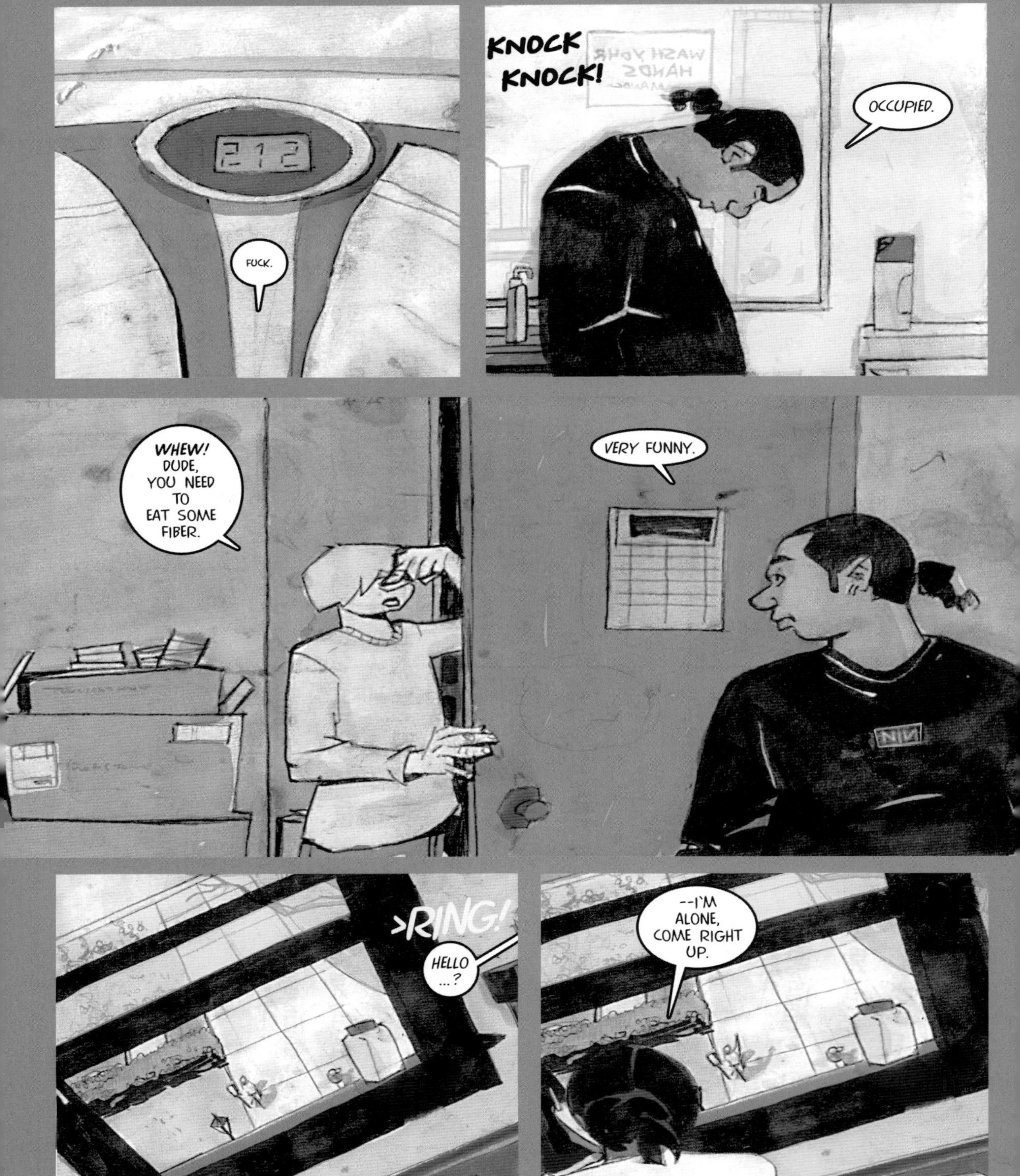
FUCK.
KNOCK KNOCK!
WASH YOUR HANDS
OCCUPIED.
WHEW! DUDE, YOU NEED TO EAT SOME FIBER.
VERY FUNNY.
NIN
RING!
HELLO ...?
--I'M ALONE, COME RIGHT UP.

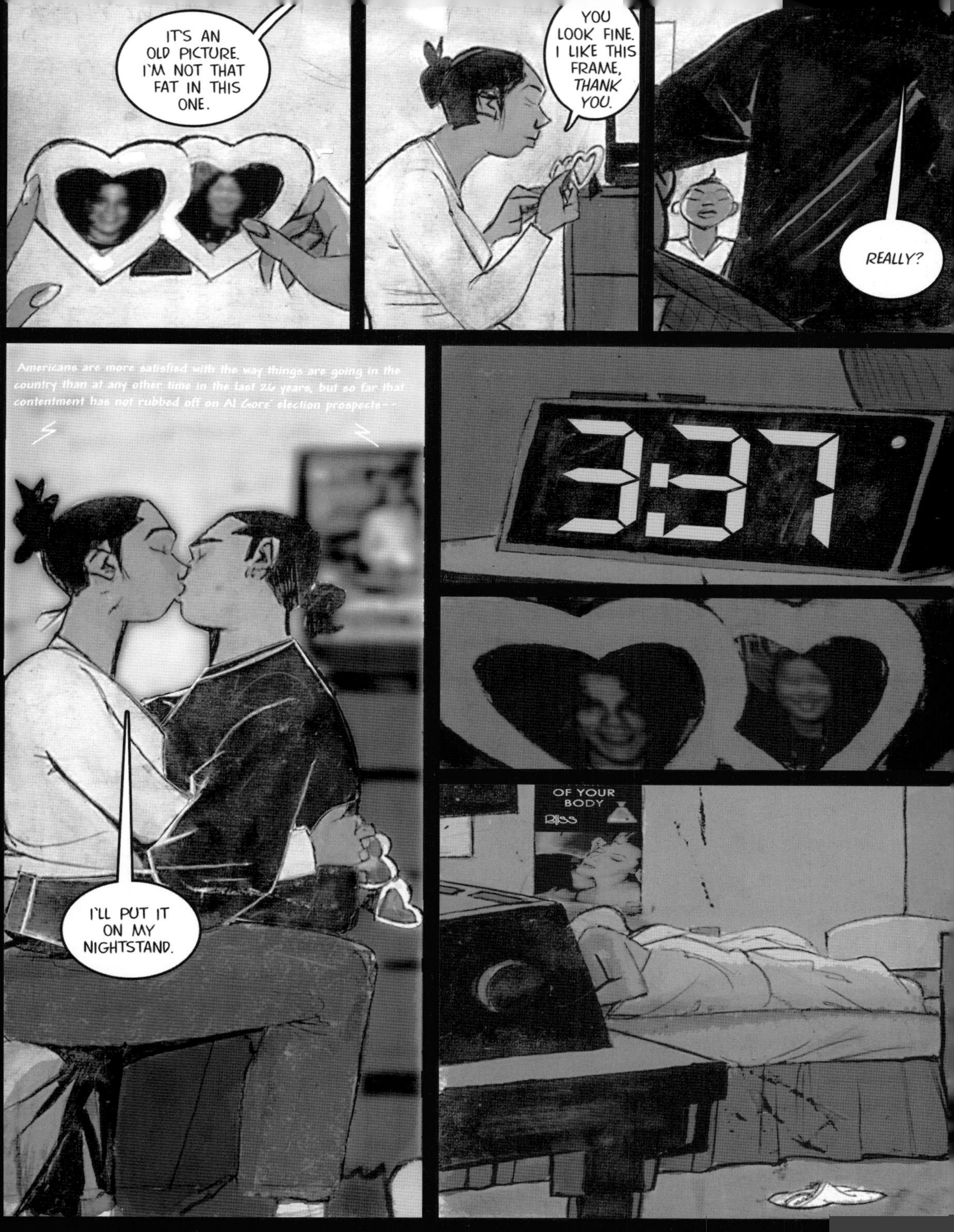
IT'S AN OLD PICTURE. I'M NOT THAT FAT IN THIS ONE.
YOU LOOK FINE. I LIKE THIS FRAME, *THANK YOU.*
REALLY?
Americans are more satisfied with the way things are going in the country than at any other time in the last 26 years, but so far that contentment has not rubbed off on Al Gore' election prospects--
I'LL PUT IT ON MY NIGHTSTAND.
3:37
OF YOUR BODY
BLISS

F YOUR
BODY
SS

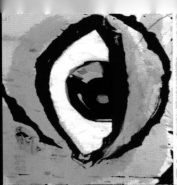

"Todo Poderso,

ROMPE SARAGUEY

descarga
toda
negatividad

y ve
la luz
del brillo
de tu
espada

Ding!

en el
nombre
de
Changó

Ding
Ding Di

San Lazaro
Y
Ochún

que ahora te invoco."

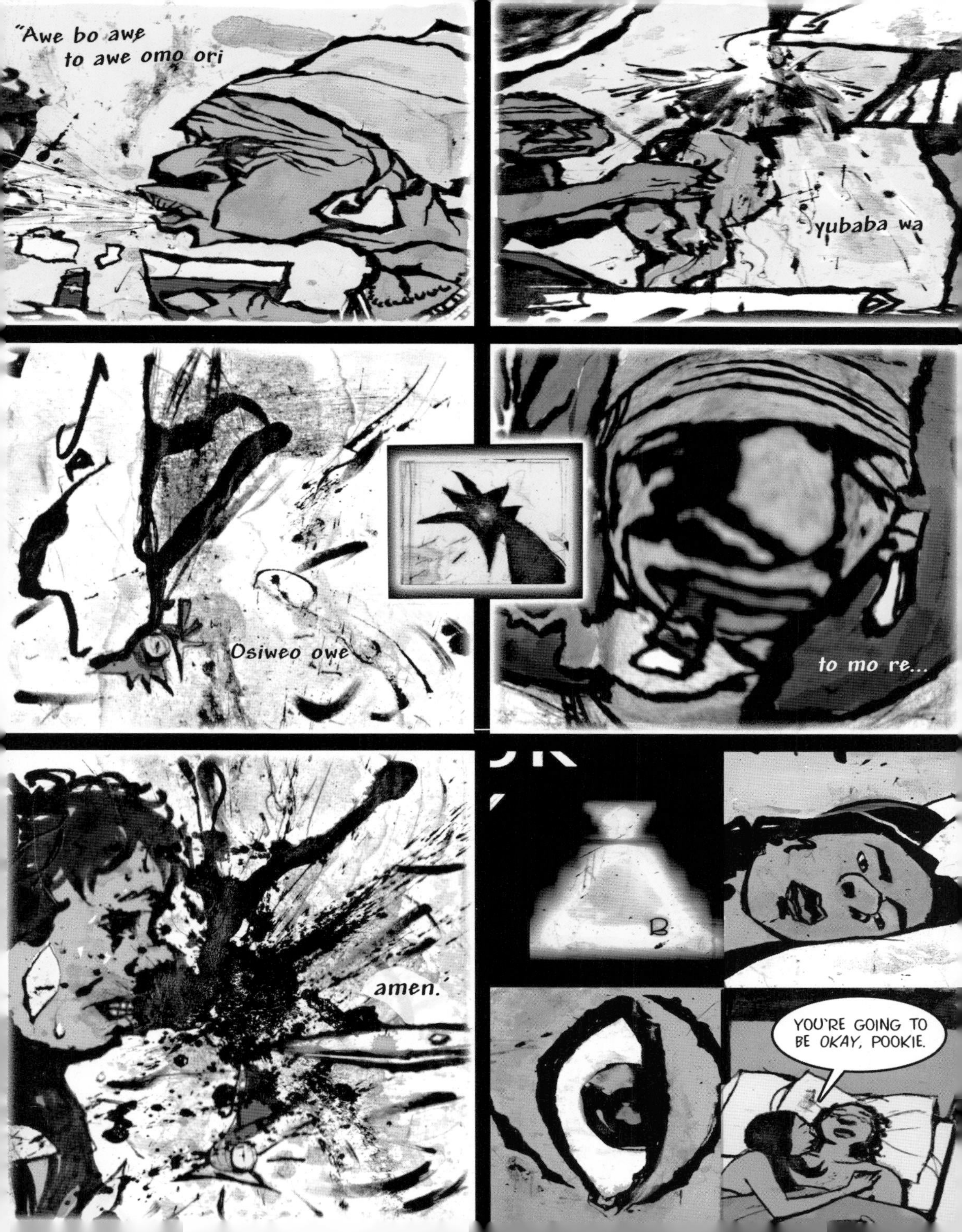
"Awe bo awe
to awe omo ori
yubaba wa
Osiweo owe
to mo re...
amen."
YOU'RE GOING TO BE *OKAY*, POOKIE.

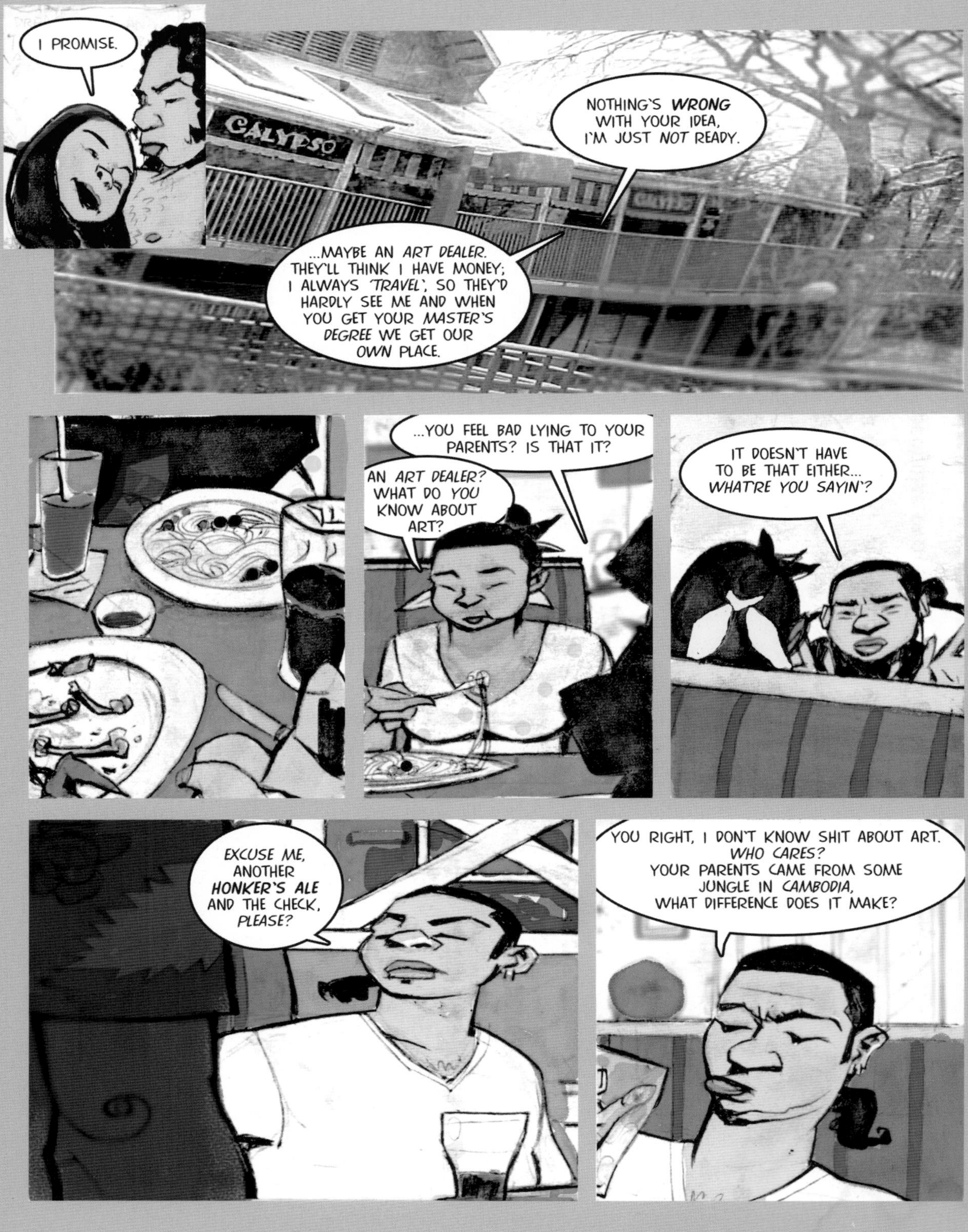
I PROMISE.
NOTHING'S WRONG WITH YOUR IDEA, I'M JUST NOT READY.
CALYPSO
...MAYBE AN ART DEALER. THEY'LL THINK I HAVE MONEY; I ALWAYS 'TRAVEL', SO THEY'D HARDLY SEE ME AND WHEN YOU GET YOUR MASTER'S DEGREE WE GET OUR OWN PLACE.
...YOU FEEL BAD LYING TO YOUR PARENTS? IS THAT IT?
AN ART DEALER? WHAT DO YOU KNOW ABOUT ART?
IT DOESN'T HAVE TO BE THAT EITHER... WHAT'RE YOU SAYIN'?
EXCUSE ME, ANOTHER HONKER'S ALE AND THE CHECK, PLEASE?
YOU RIGHT, I DON'T KNOW SHIT ABOUT ART. WHO CARES? YOUR PARENTS CAME FROM SOME JUNGLE IN CAMBODIA, WHAT DIFFERENCE DOES IT MAKE?

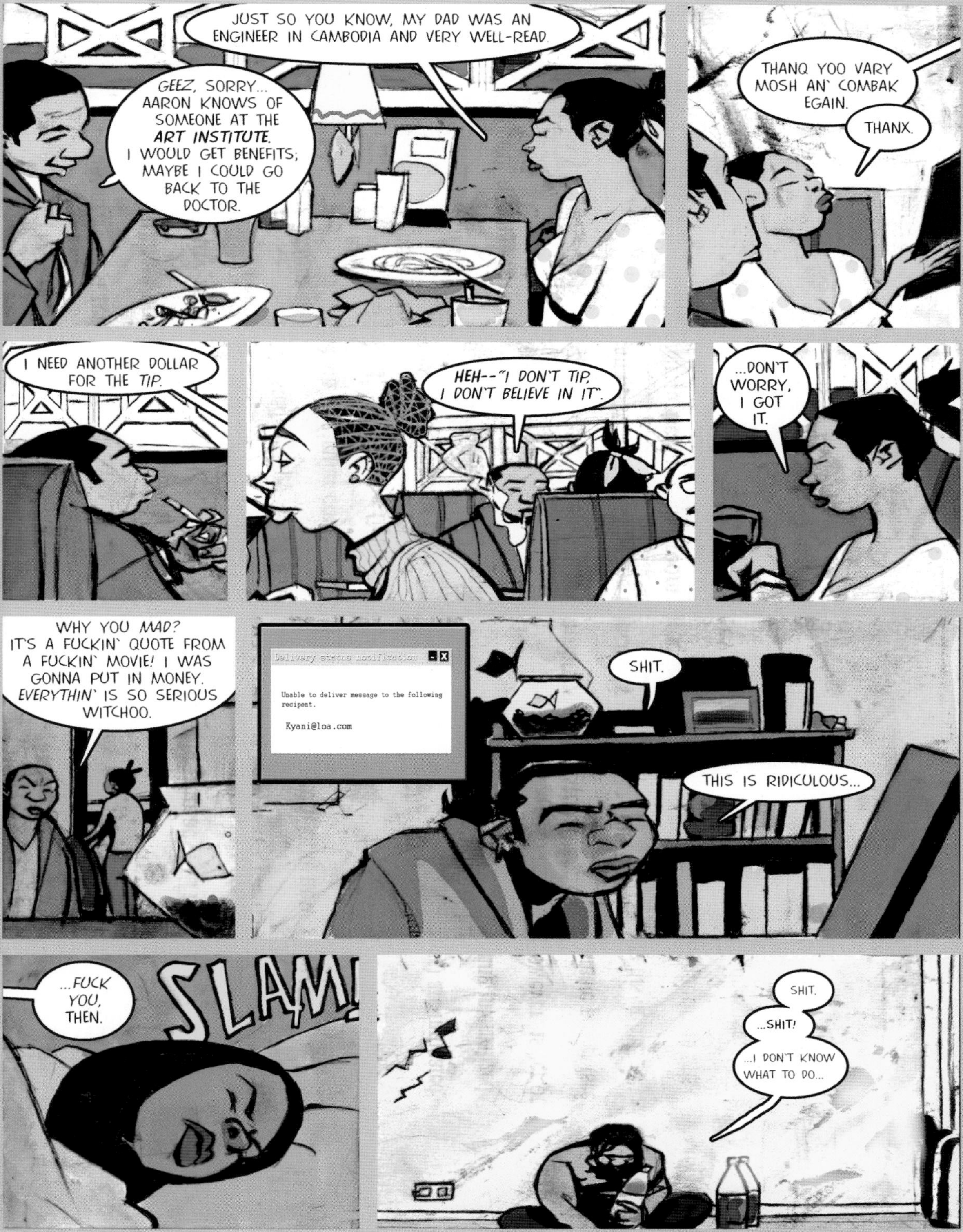
JUST SO YOU KNOW, MY DAD WAS AN ENGINEER IN CAMBODIA AND VERY WELL-READ.
GEEZ, SORRY... AARON KNOWS OF SOMEONE AT THE ART INSTITUTE. I WOULD GET BENEFITS; MAYBE I COULD GO BACK TO THE DOCTOR.
THANQ YOO VARY MOSH AN` COMBAK EGAIN.
THANX.
I NEED ANOTHER DOLLAR FOR THE TIP.
HEH--"I DON'T TIP, I DON'T BELIEVE IN IT".
...DON'T WORRY, I GOT IT.
WHY YOU MAD? IT'S A FUCKIN` QUOTE FROM A FUCKIN` MOVIE! I WAS GONNA PUT IN MONEY. EVERYTHIN` IS SO SERIOUS WITCHOO.
Delivery status notification
Unable to deliver message to the following recipent.
Kyani@loa.com
SHIT.
THIS IS RIDICULOUS...
...FUCK YOU, THEN.
SLAM!
SHIT.
...SHIT!
...I DON'T KNOW WHAT TO DO...

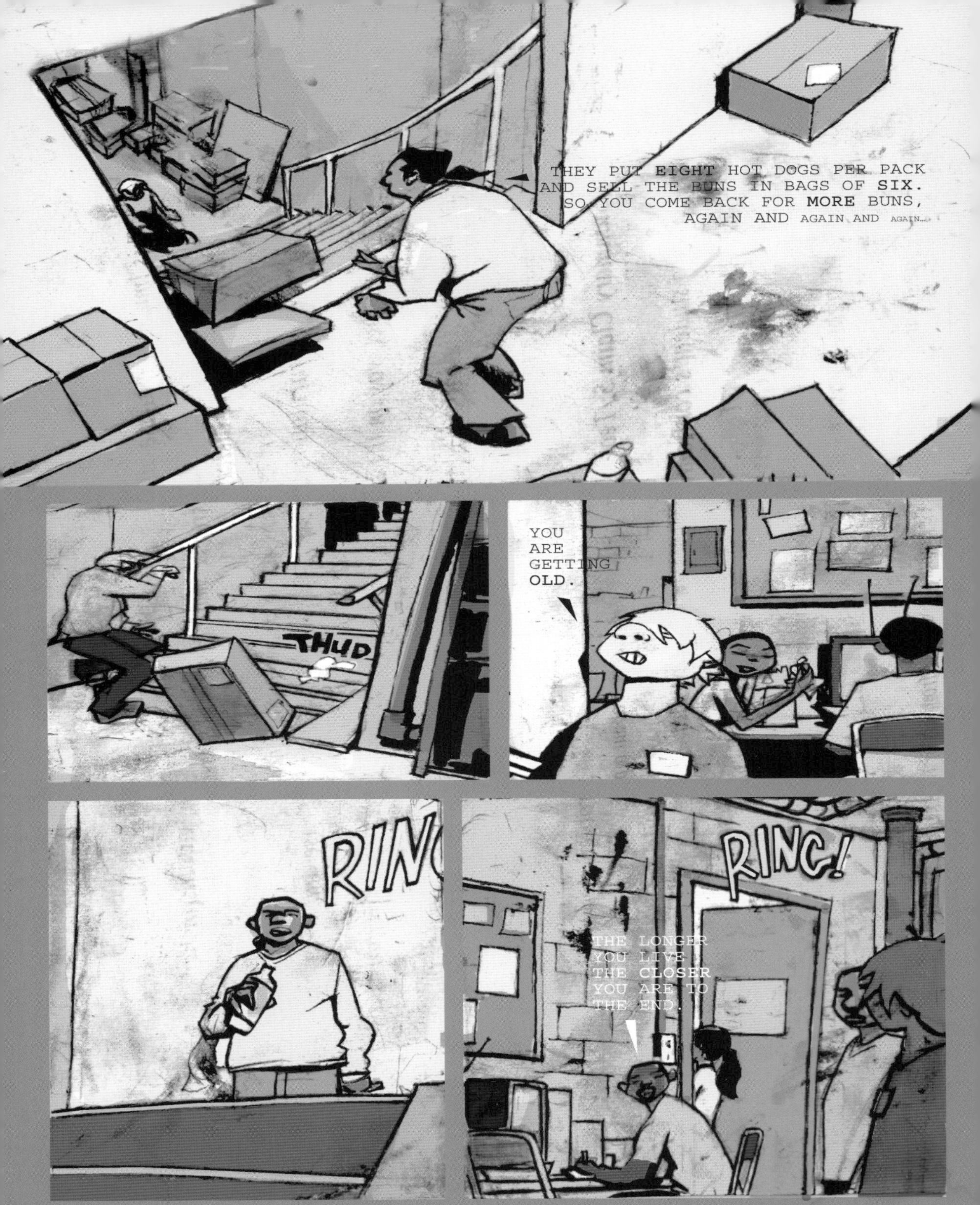
THEY PUT EIGHT HOT DOGS PER PACK AND SELL THE BUNS IN BAGS OF SIX. SO YOU COME BACK FOR MORE BUNS, AGAIN AND AGAIN AND AGAIN...
THUD
YOU ARE GETTING OLD.
RING
RING!
THE LONGER YOU LIVE THE CLOSER YOU ARE TO THE END.

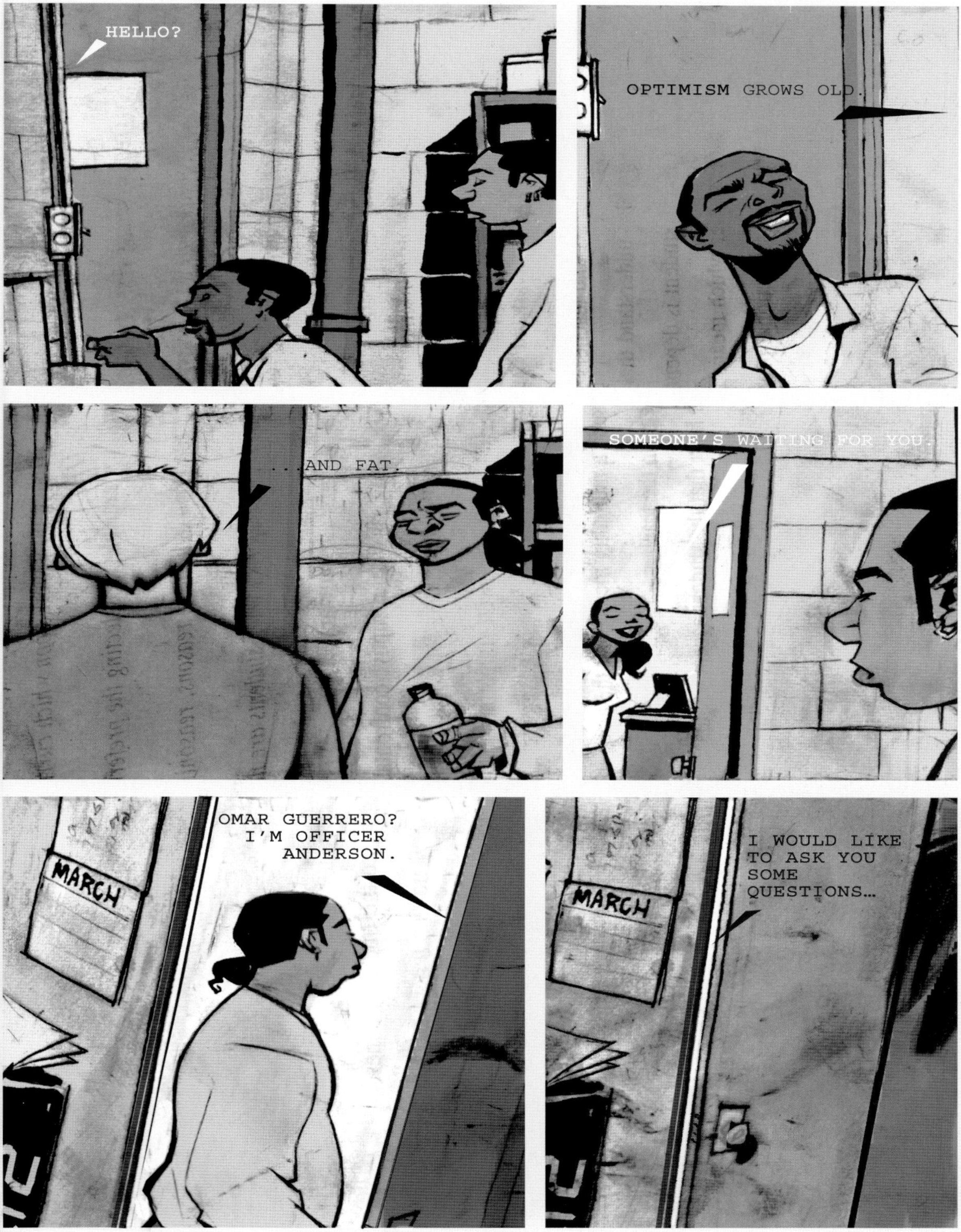
HELLO?
OPTIMISM GROWS OLD.
...AND FAT.
SOMEONE'S WAITING FOR YOU.
OMAR GUERRERO? I'M OFFICER ANDERSON.
I WOULD LIKE TO ASK YOU SOME QUESTIONS...

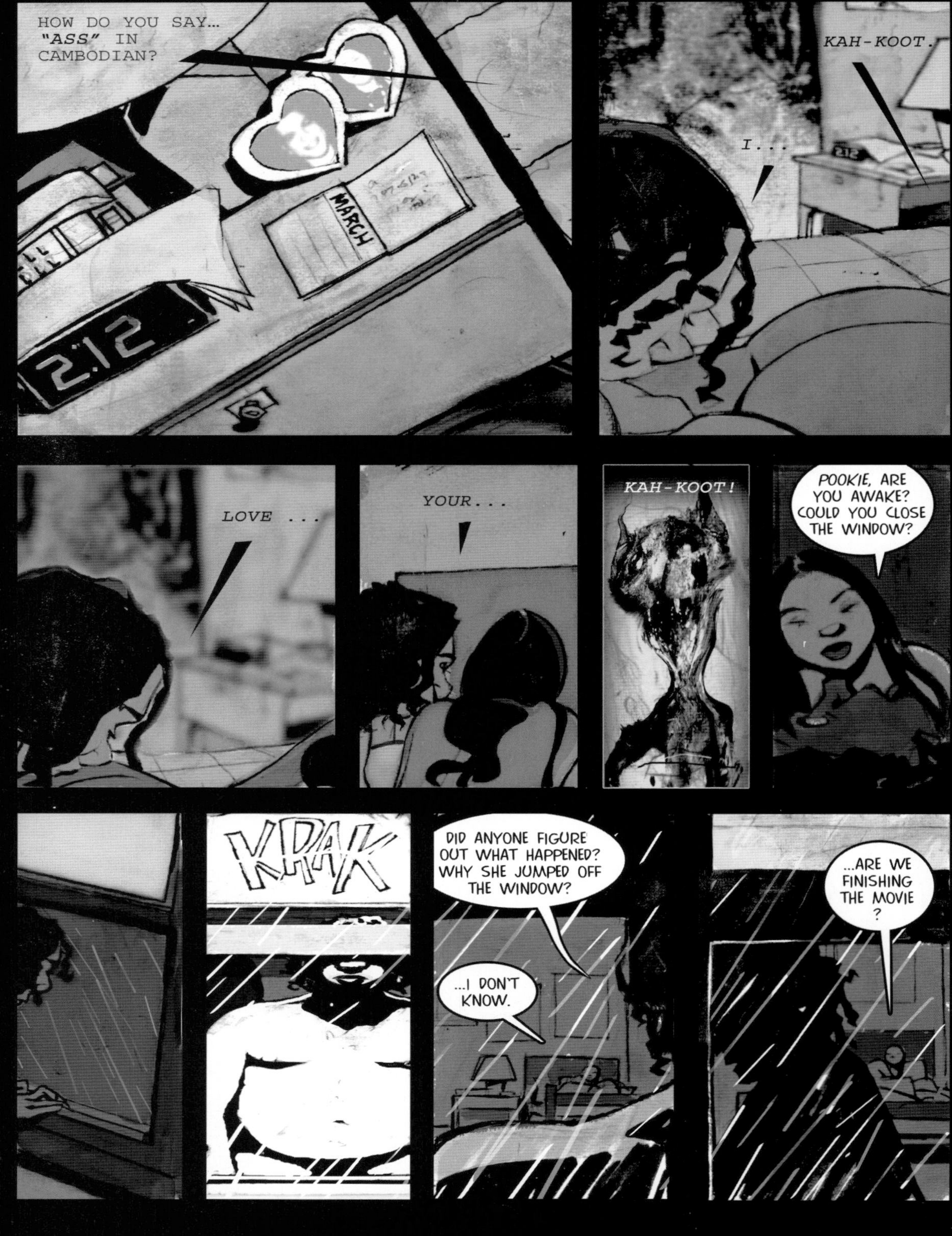
HOW DO YOU SAY... "ASS" IN CAMBODIAN?
KAH-KOOT.
I...
LOVE ...
YOUR...
KAH-KOOT!
POOKIE, ARE YOU AWAKE? COULD YOU CLOSE THE WINDOW?
KRAK
DID ANYONE FIGURE OUT WHAT HAPPENED? WHY SHE JUMPED OFF THE WINDOW?
...I DON'T KNOW.
...ARE WE FINISHING THE MOVIE ?

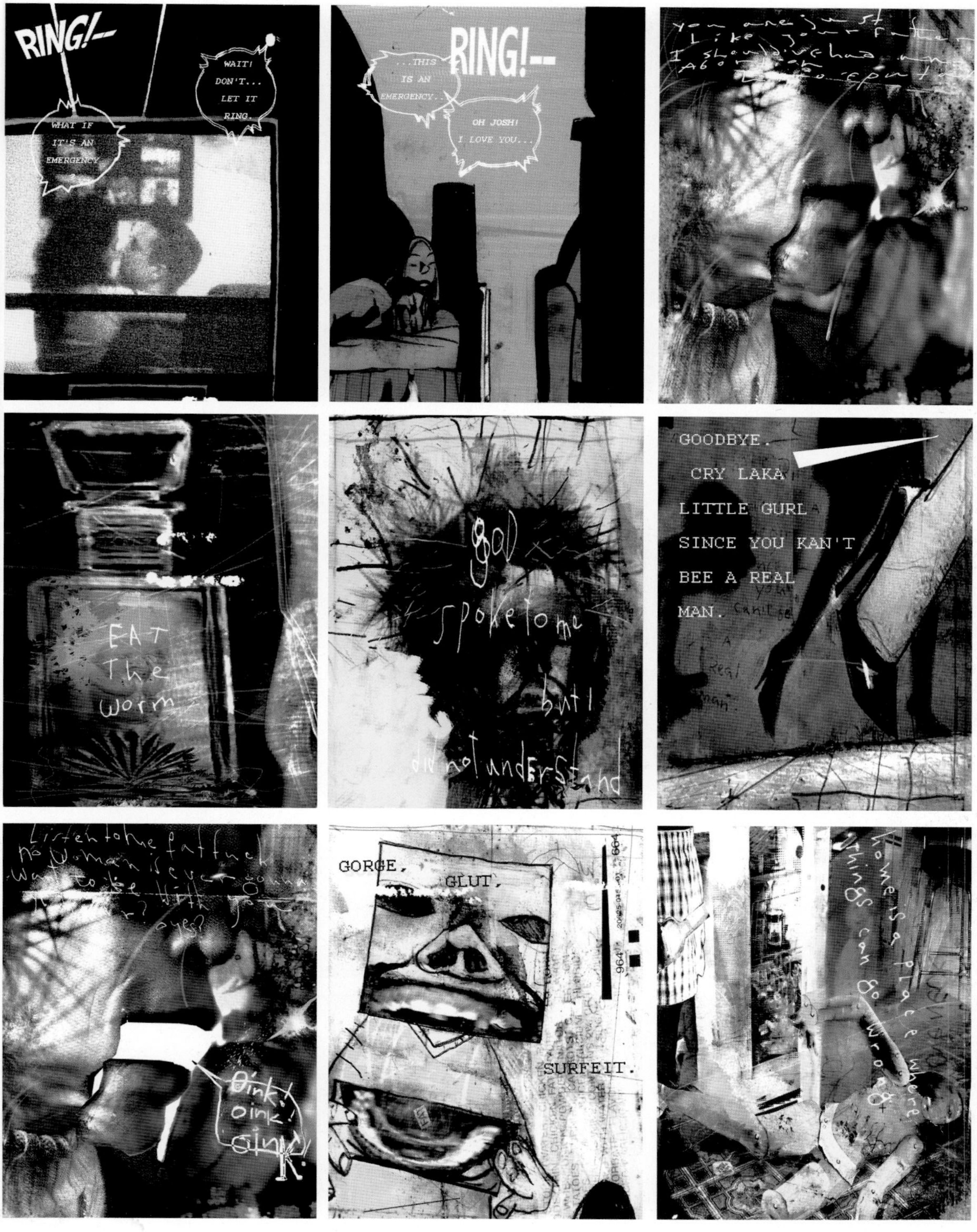
RING!--
WAIT! DON'T... LET IT RING.
WHAT IF IT'S AN EMERGENCY?
RING!--
...THIS IS AN EMERGENCY...
OH JOSH! I LOVE YOU...
you are just
Like your
EAT The worm
god spoke to me but I did not understand
GOODBYE.
CRY LAKA LITTLE GURL SINCE YOU KAN'T BEE A REAL MAN.
Listen to me fat fuck
no woman is ever gonna
Oink! oink! oink!
GORGE, GLUT, SURFEIT.
home is a place where
things can go wrong

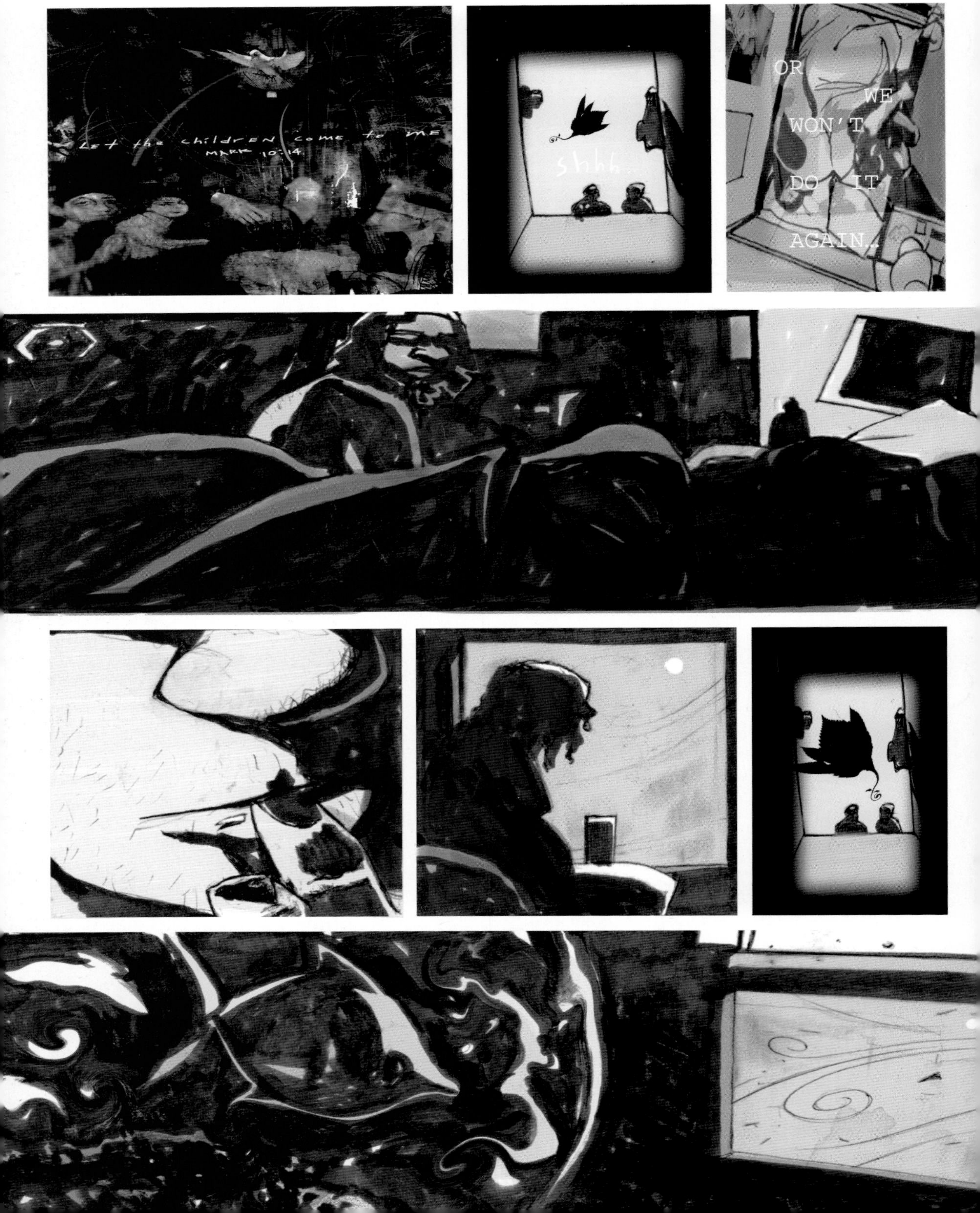
Let the children come to ME
MARK 10:14
shhh...
OR WE WON'T DO IT AGAIN...

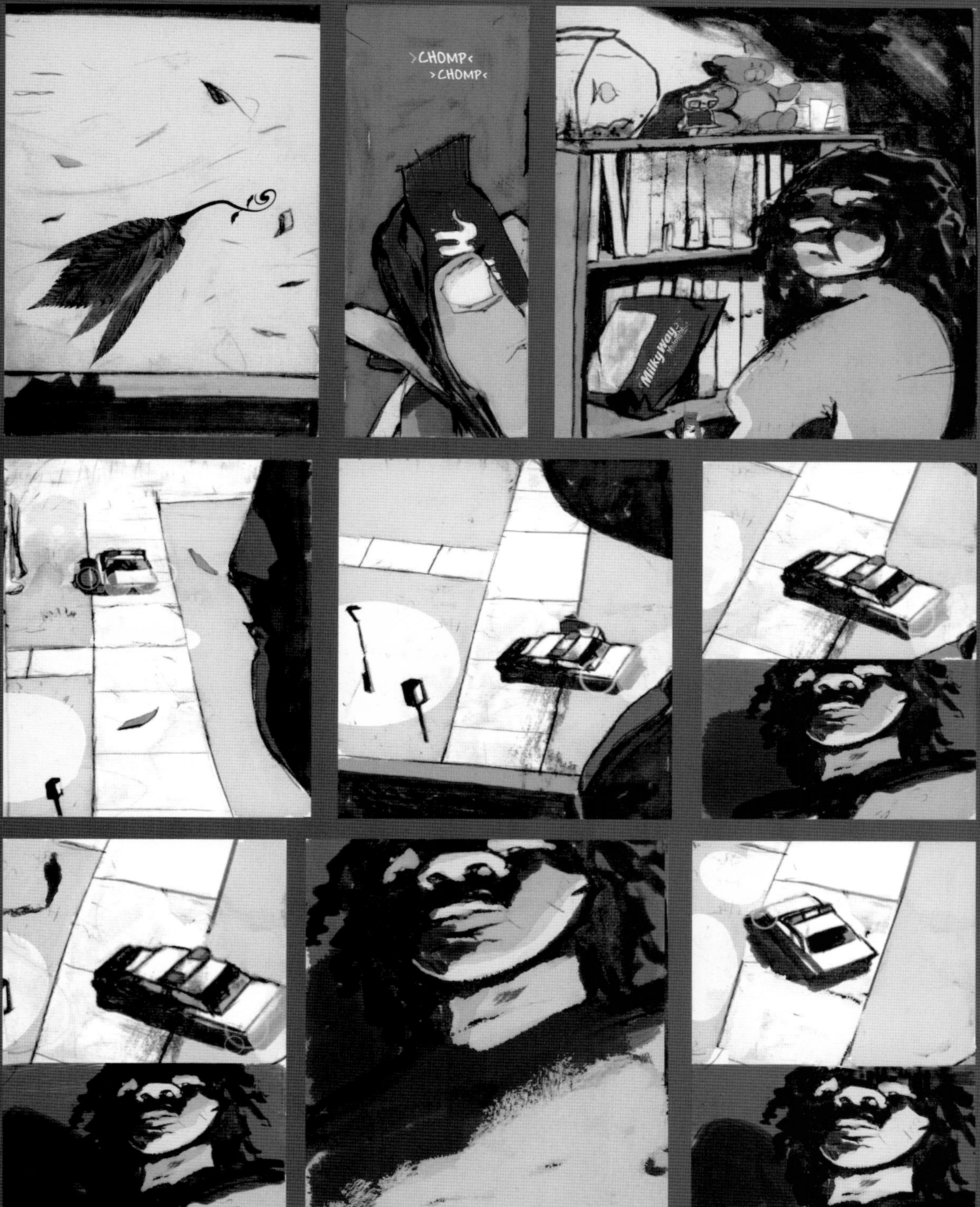
>CHOMP<
>CHOMP<
Milky Way

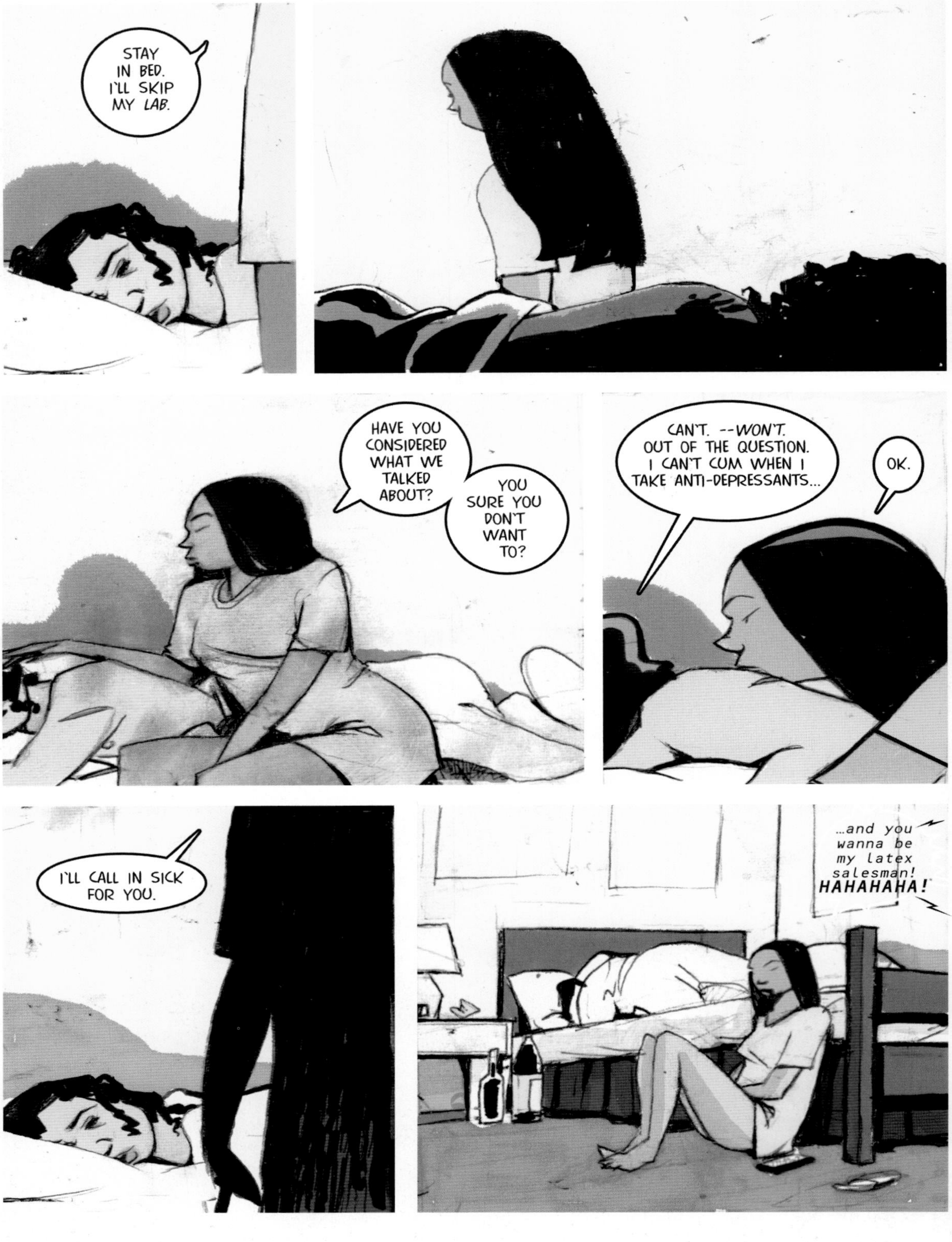
STAY IN BED. I'LL SKIP MY *LAB.*
HAVE YOU CONSIDERED WHAT WE TALKED ABOUT?
YOU SURE YOU DON'T WANT TO?
CAN'T. --*WON'T.* OUT OF THE QUESTION. I CAN'T CUM WHEN I TAKE ANTI-DEPRESSANTS...
OK.
I'LL CALL IN SICK FOR YOU.
...and you wanna be my latex salesman! **HAHAHAHA!**

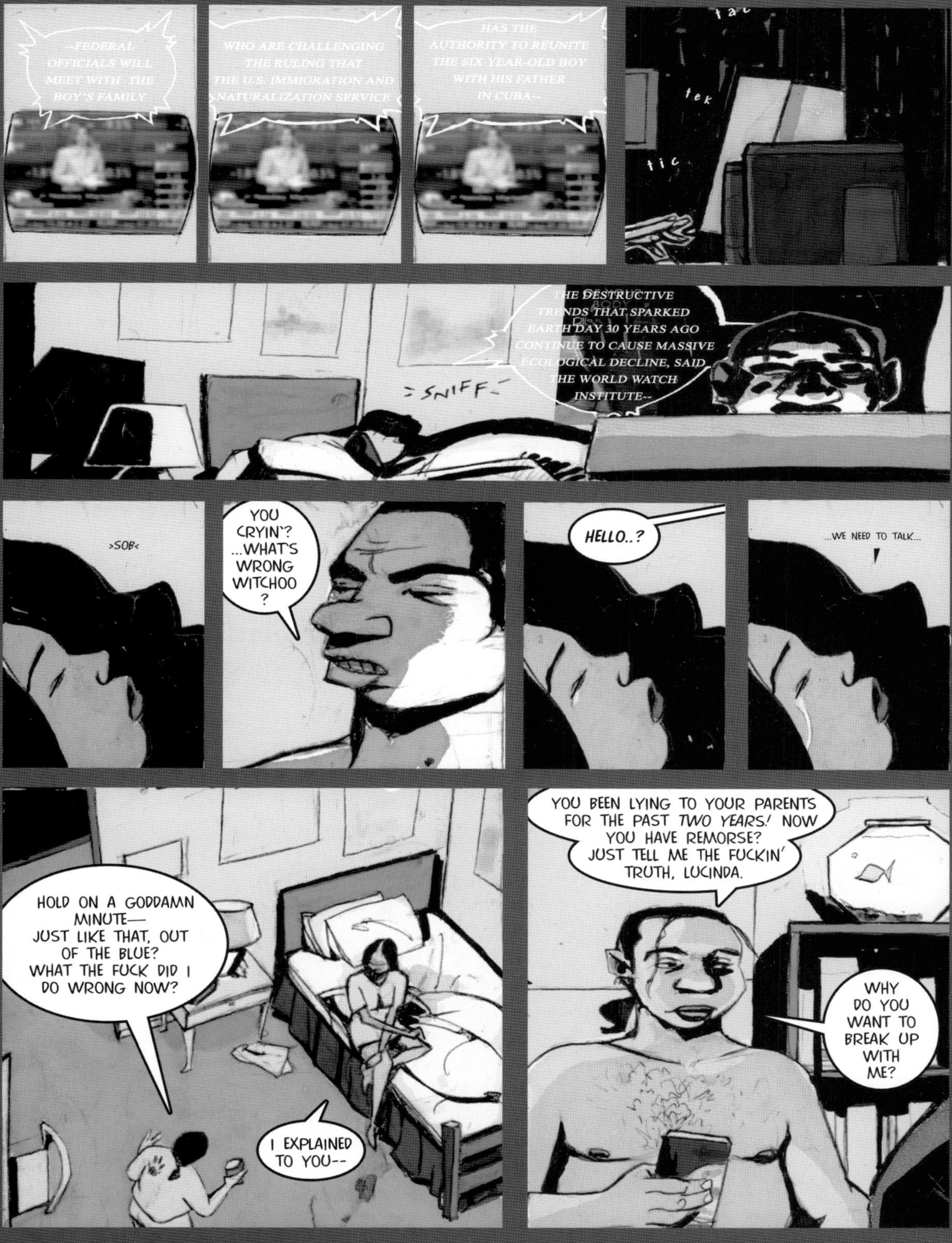
--FEDERAL OFFICIALS WILL MEET WITH THE BOY'S FAMILY
WHO ARE CHALLENGING THE RULING THAT THE U.S. IMMIGRATION AND NATURALIZATION SERVICE
HAS THE AUTHORITY TO REUNITE THE SIX YEAR-OLD BOY WITH HIS FATHER IN CUBA--
tac
tek
tic
THE DESTRUCTIVE TRENDS THAT SPARKED EARTH DAY 30 YEARS AGO CONTINUE TO CAUSE MASSIVE ECOLOGICAL DECLINE, SAID THE WORLD WATCH INSTITUTE--
>SNIFF<
>SOB<
YOU CRYIN'? ...WHAT'S WRONG WITCHOO?
HELLO..?
...WE NEED TO TALK...
HOLD ON A GODDAMN MINUTE— JUST LIKE THAT, OUT OF THE BLUE? WHAT THE FUCK DID I DO WRONG NOW?
I EXPLAINED TO YOU--
YOU BEEN LYING TO YOUR PARENTS FOR THE PAST TWO YEARS! NOW YOU HAVE REMORSE? JUST TELL ME THE FUCKIN' TRUTH, LUCINDA.
WHY DO YOU WANT TO BREAK UP WITH ME?

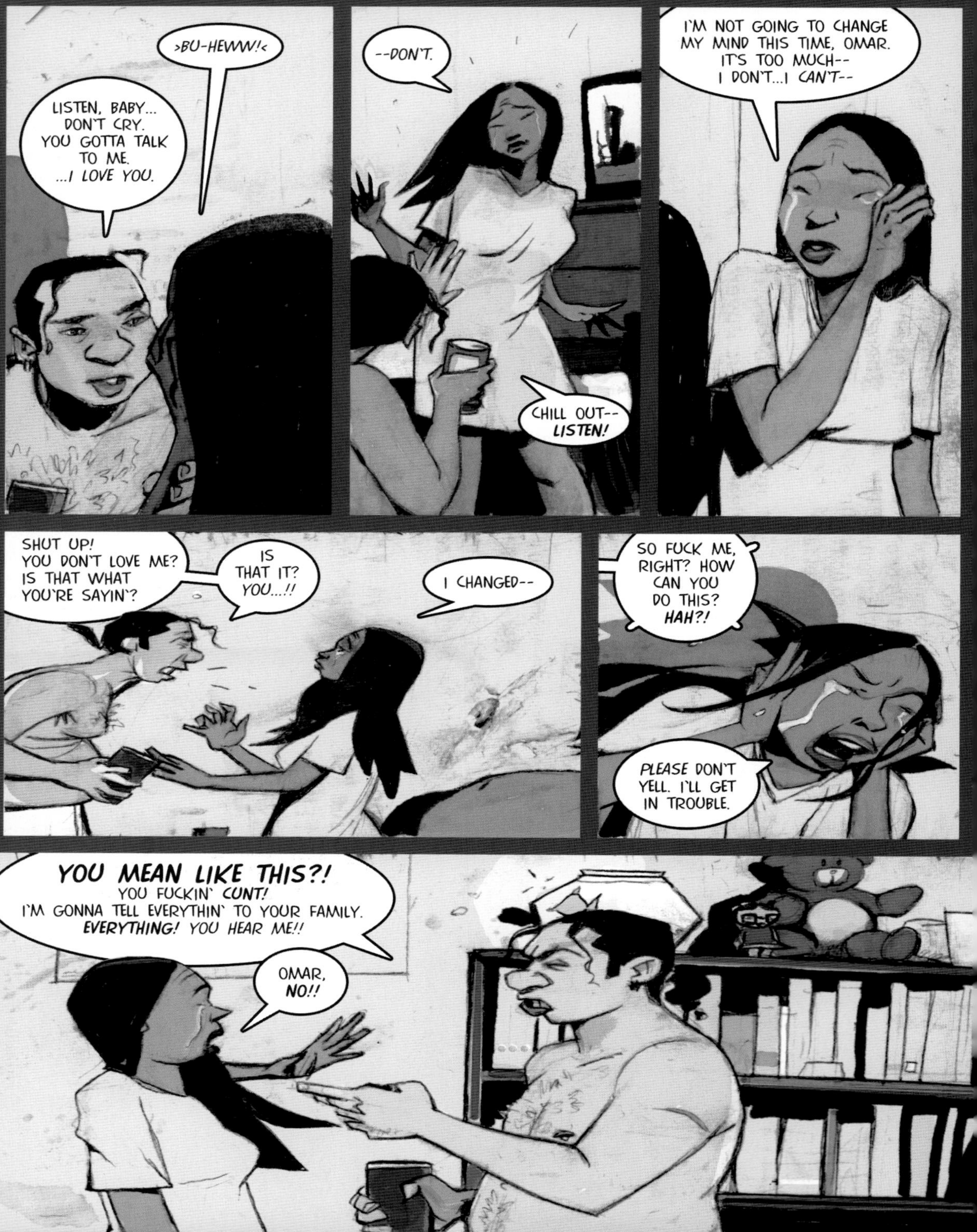

LISTEN, BABY... DON'T CRY. YOU GOTTA TALK TO ME. ...I LOVE YOU.
>BU-HEWW!<
--DON'T.
CHILL OUT-- LISTEN!
I'M NOT GOING TO CHANGE MY MIND THIS TIME, OMAR. IT'S TOO MUCH-- I DON'T...I CAN'T--
SHUT UP! YOU DON'T LOVE ME? IS THAT WHAT YOU'RE SAYIN'?
IS THAT IT? YOU...!!
I CHANGED--
SO FUCK ME, RIGHT? HOW CAN YOU DO THIS? HAH?!
PLEASE DON'T YELL. I'LL GET IN TROUBLE.
YOU MEAN LIKE THIS?! YOU FUCKIN' CUNT! I'M GONNA TELL EVERYTHIN' TO YOUR FAMILY. EVERYTHING! YOU HEAR ME!!
OMAR, NO!!

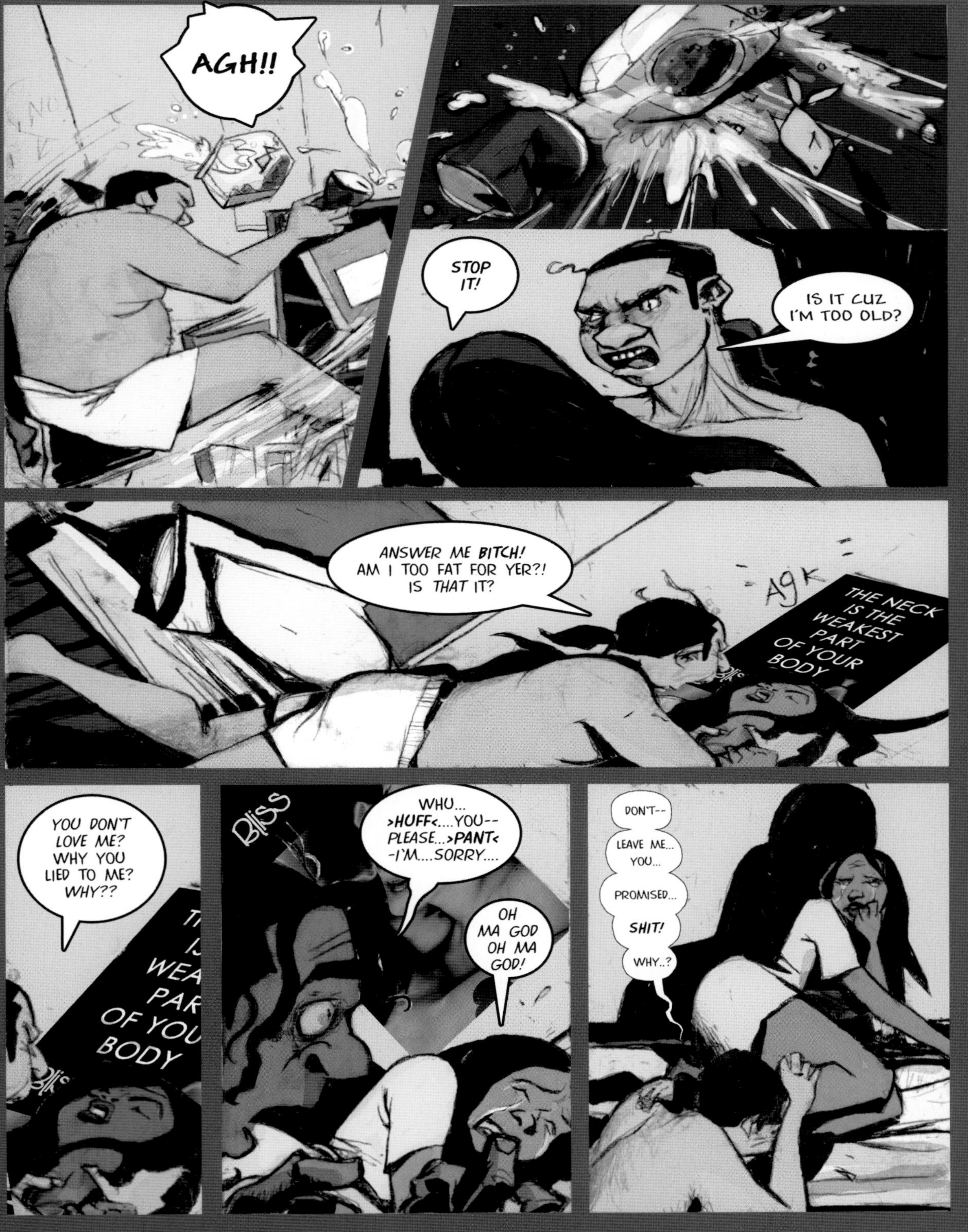

AGH!!
STOP IT!
IS IT CUZ I'M TOO OLD?
ANSWER ME BITCH! AM I TOO FAT FOR YER?! IS THAT IT?
AGK
THE NECK IS THE WEAKEST PART OF YOUR BODY
BLISS
YOU DON'T LOVE ME? WHY YOU LIED TO ME? WHY??
BLISS
WHU... >HUFF<....YOU-- PLEASE...>PANT< -I'M....SORRY....
OH MA GOD OH MA GOD!
DON'T--
LEAVE ME... YOU...
PROMISED...
SHIT!
WHY..?

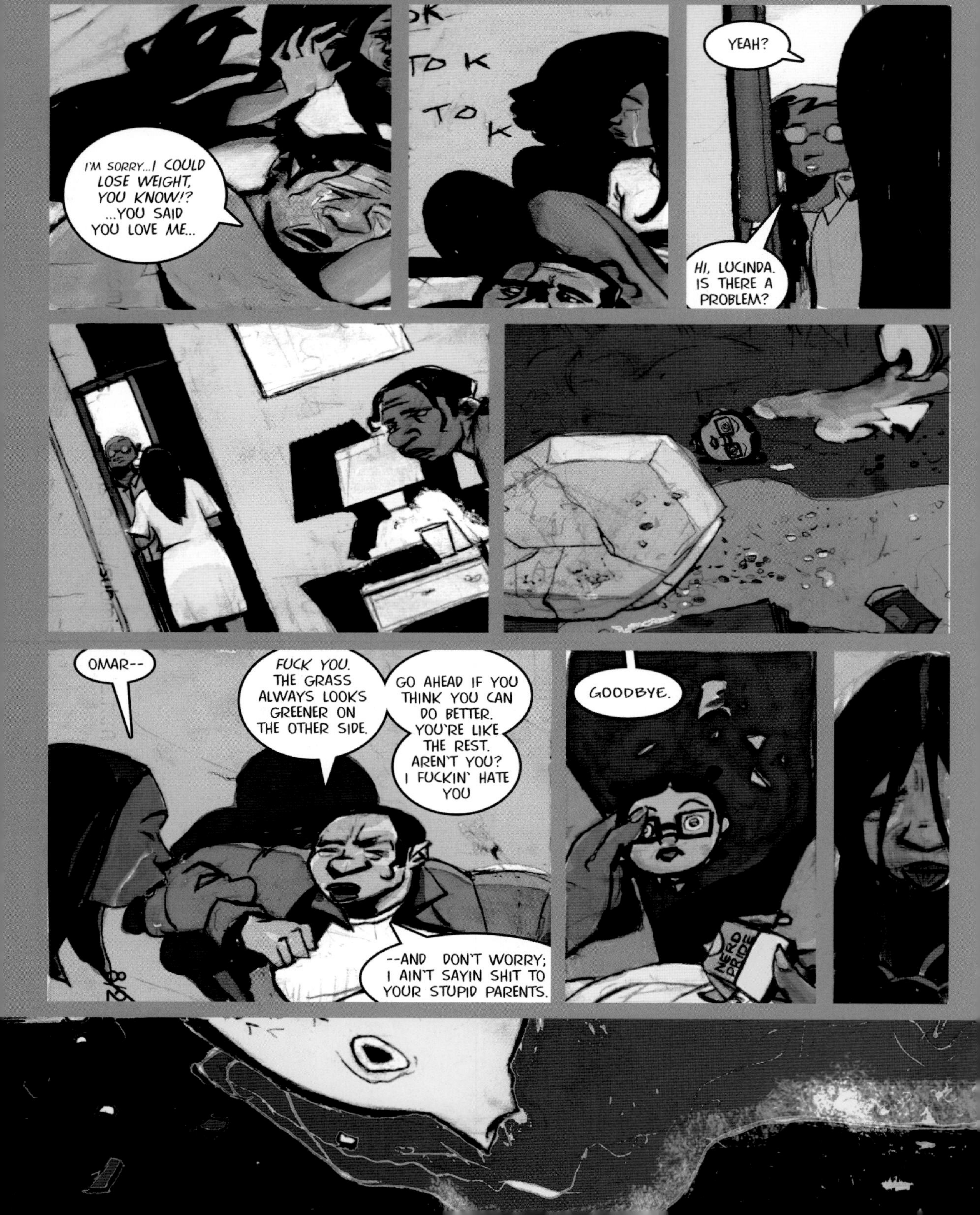
I'M SORRY...I COULD LOSE WEIGHT, YOU KNOW!? ...YOU SAID YOU LOVE ME...
TOK
TOK
YEAH?
HI, LUCINDA. IS THERE A PROBLEM?
OMAR--
FUCK YOU. THE GRASS ALWAYS LOOKS GREENER ON THE OTHER SIDE.
GO AHEAD IF YOU THINK YOU CAN DO BETTER. YOU'RE LIKE THE REST. AREN'T YOU? I FUCKIN' HATE YOU
--AND DON'T WORRY; I AIN'T SAYIN SHIT TO YOUR STUPID PARENTS.
GOODBYE.
NERD PRIDE

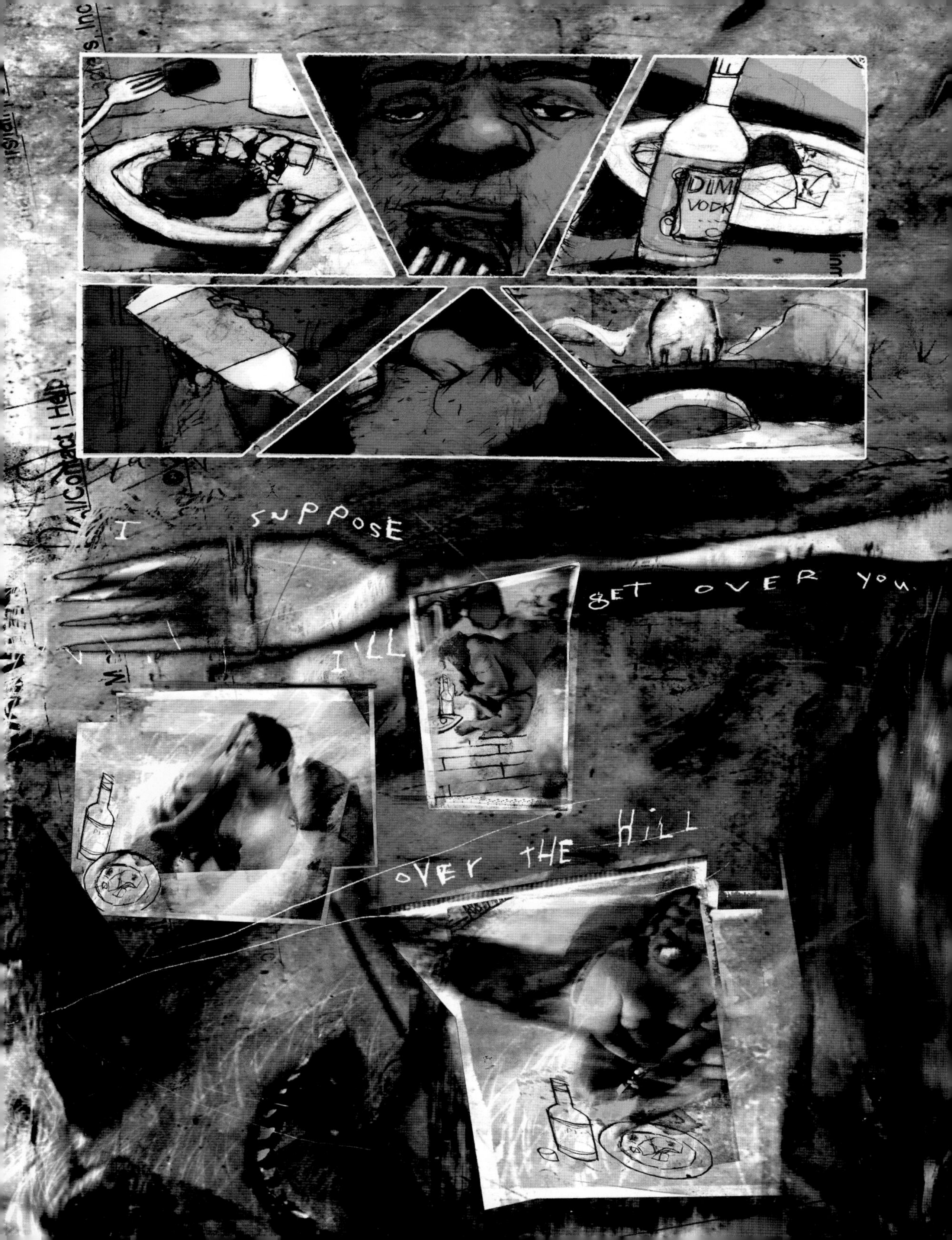
I SUPPOSE
I'LL
GET OVER YOU.
OVER THE HILL

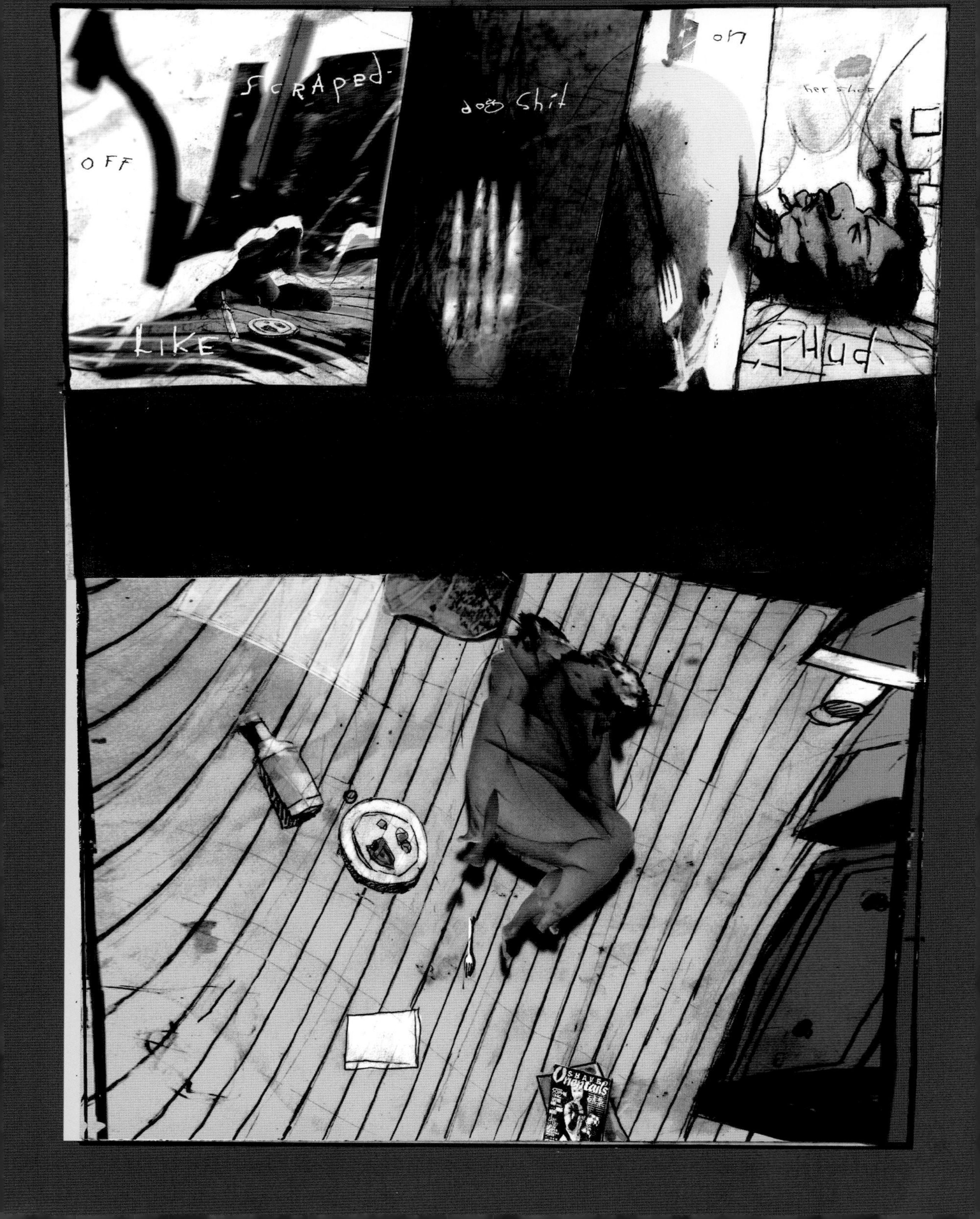
SCRAPED-
OFF
LIKE
dog shit
on
her shoe
THud

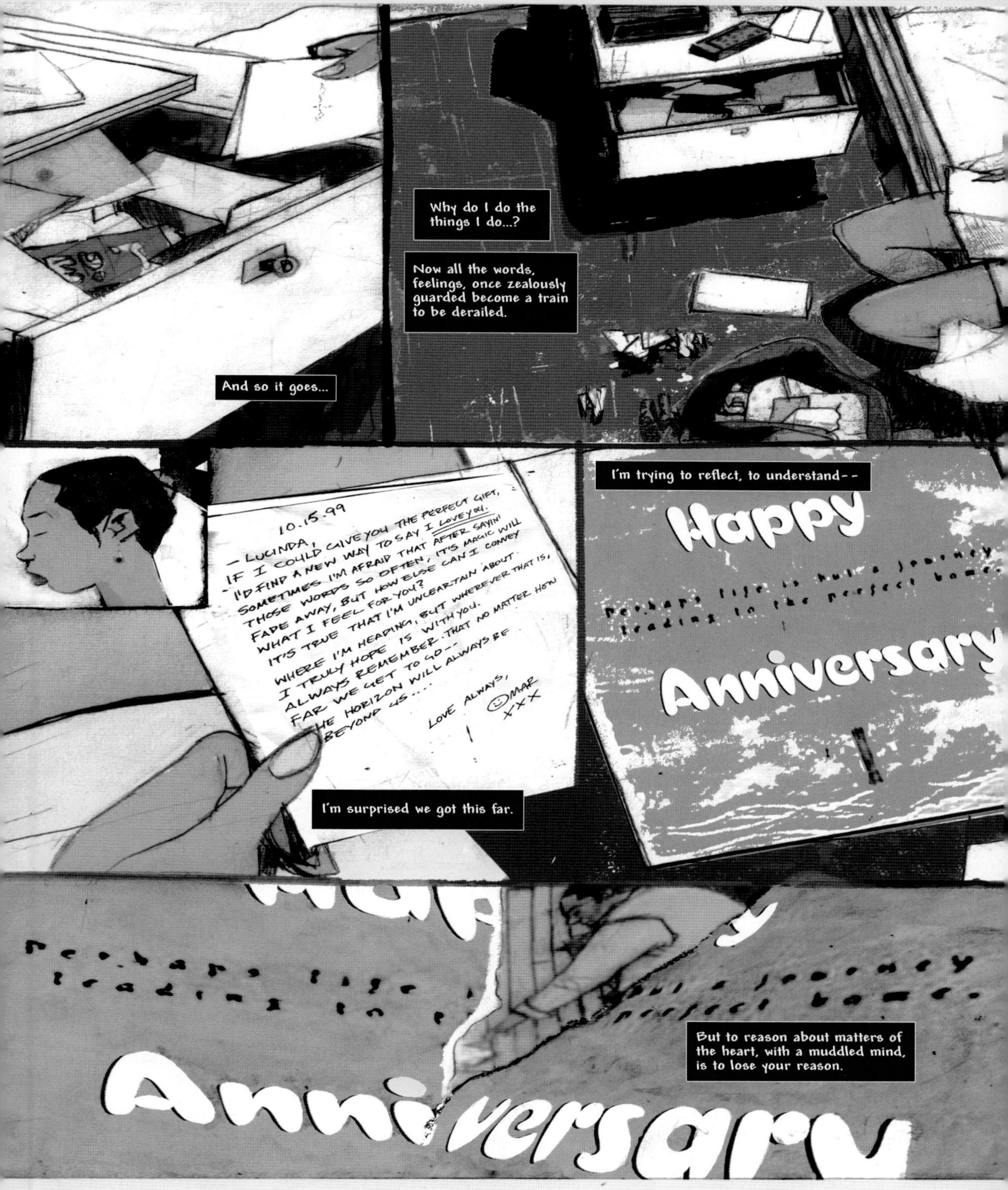

And so it goes...
Why do I do the things I do...?
Now all the words, feelings, once zealously guarded become a train to be derailed.
10.15.99
— LUCINDA,
IF I COULD GIVE YOU THE PERFECT GIFT, I'D FIND A NEW WAY TO SAY I LOVE YOU.
SOMETIMES I'M AFRAID THAT AFTER SAYIN' THOSE WORDS SO OFTEN, IT'S MAGIC WILL FADE AWAY, BUT HOW ELSE CAN I CONVEY WHAT I FEEL FOR YOU?
IT'S TRUE THAT I'M UNCERTAIN ABOUT WHERE I'M HEADING, BUT WHEREVER THAT IS, I TRULY HOPE IS WITH YOU.
ALWAYS REMEMBER THAT NO MATTER HOW FAR WE GET TO GO-- THE HORIZON WILL ALWAYS BE BEYOND US....
LOVE ALWAYS, OMAR XXX
I'm surprised we got this far.
I'm trying to reflect, to understand--
Happy
Anniversary
But to reason about matters of the heart, with a muddled mind, is to lose your reason.

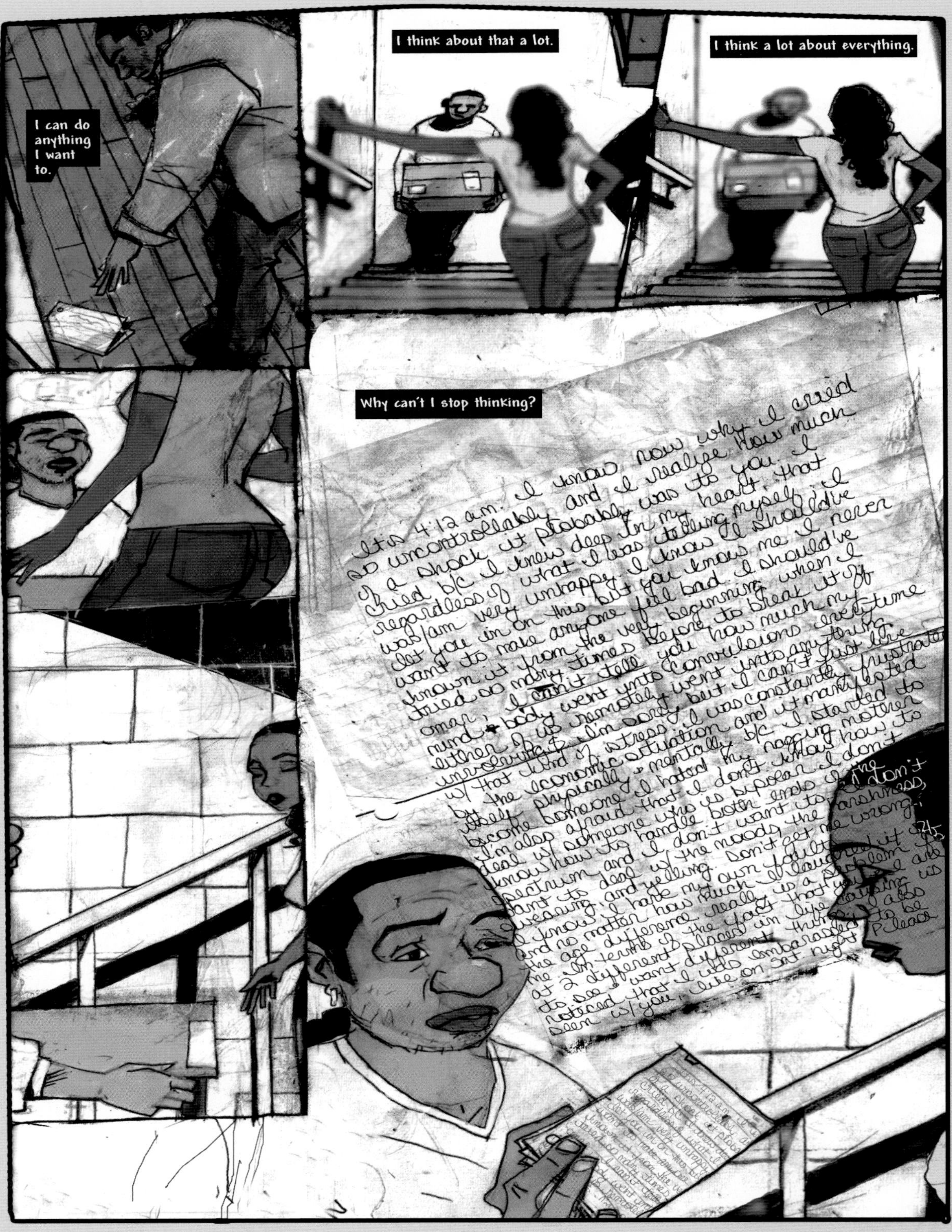
I can do anything I want to.
I think about that a lot.
I think a lot about everything.
Why can't I stop thinking?

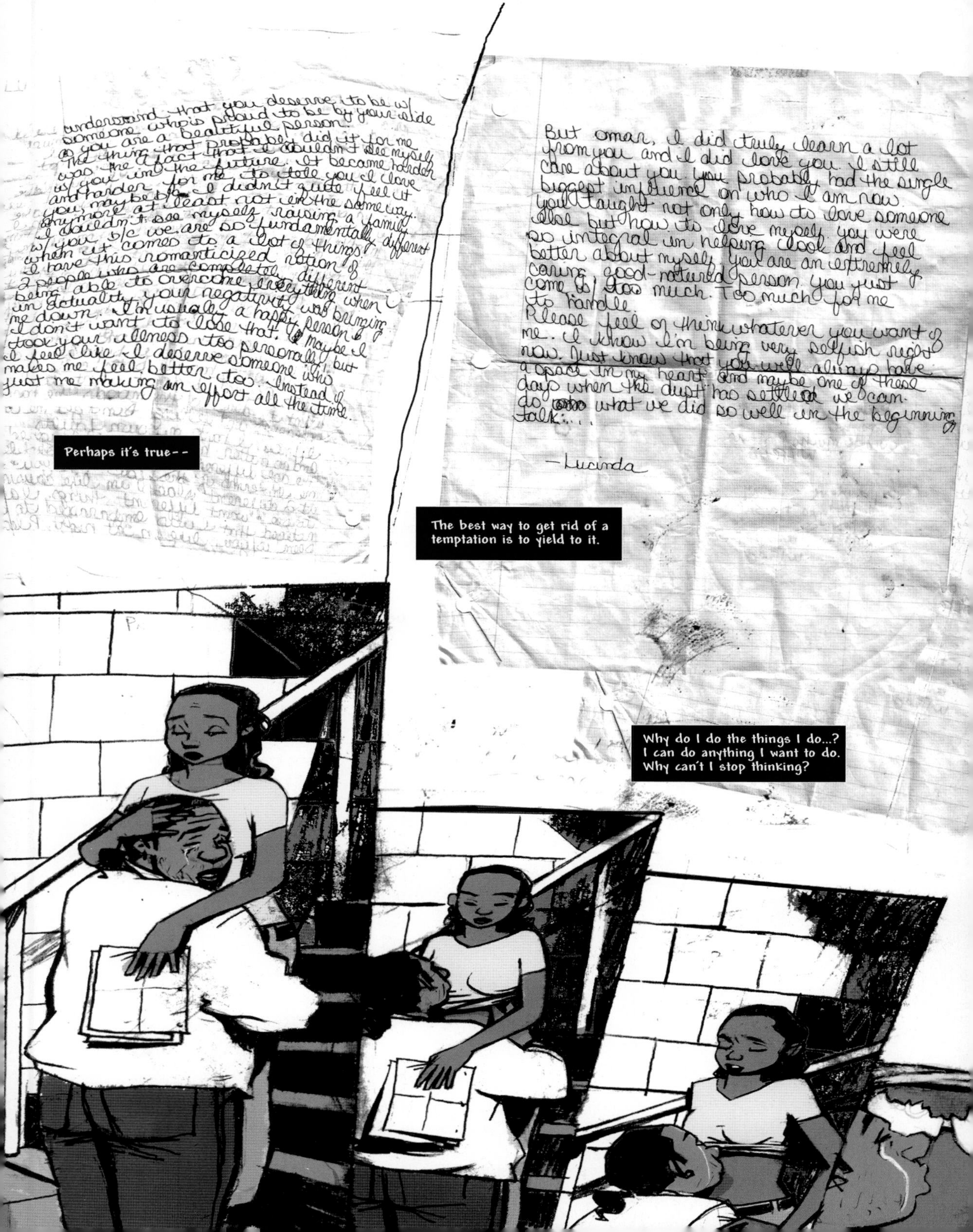
understand that you deserve to be w/
someone who is proud to be by your side
as you are a beautiful person.
The thing that probably did it for me
was the fact that I couldn't see myself
w/ you in the future. It became harder
and harder for me to tell you I love
you, maybe b/c I didn't quite feel it
anymore at least not in the same way.
I couldn't see myself raising a family
w/ you b/c we are so fundamentally different
when it comes to a lot of things.
I have this romanticized notion of
2 people who are completely different
being able to overcome everything when
in actuality your negativity was bringing
me down. I'm usually a happy person &
I don't want to lose that. & maybe I
took your illness too personally, but
I feel like I deserve someone who
makes me feel better too. Instead of
just me making an effort all the time.
Perhaps it's true--
But Omar, I did truly learn a lot
from you and I did love you. I still
care about you. You probably had the single
biggest influence on who I am now.
You taught not only how to love someone
else but how to love myself. You were
so integral in helping look and feel
better about myself. You are an extremely
caring, good-natured person. You just
come w/ too much. Too much for me
to handle.
Please feel or think whatever you want of
me. I know I'm being very selfish right
now. Just know that you will always have
a space in my heart and maybe one of these
days when the dust has settled we can
do what we did so well in the beginning
Talk....
—Lucinda
The best way to get rid of a temptation is to yield to it.
Why do I do the things I do...?
I can do anything I want to do.
Why can't I stop thinking?

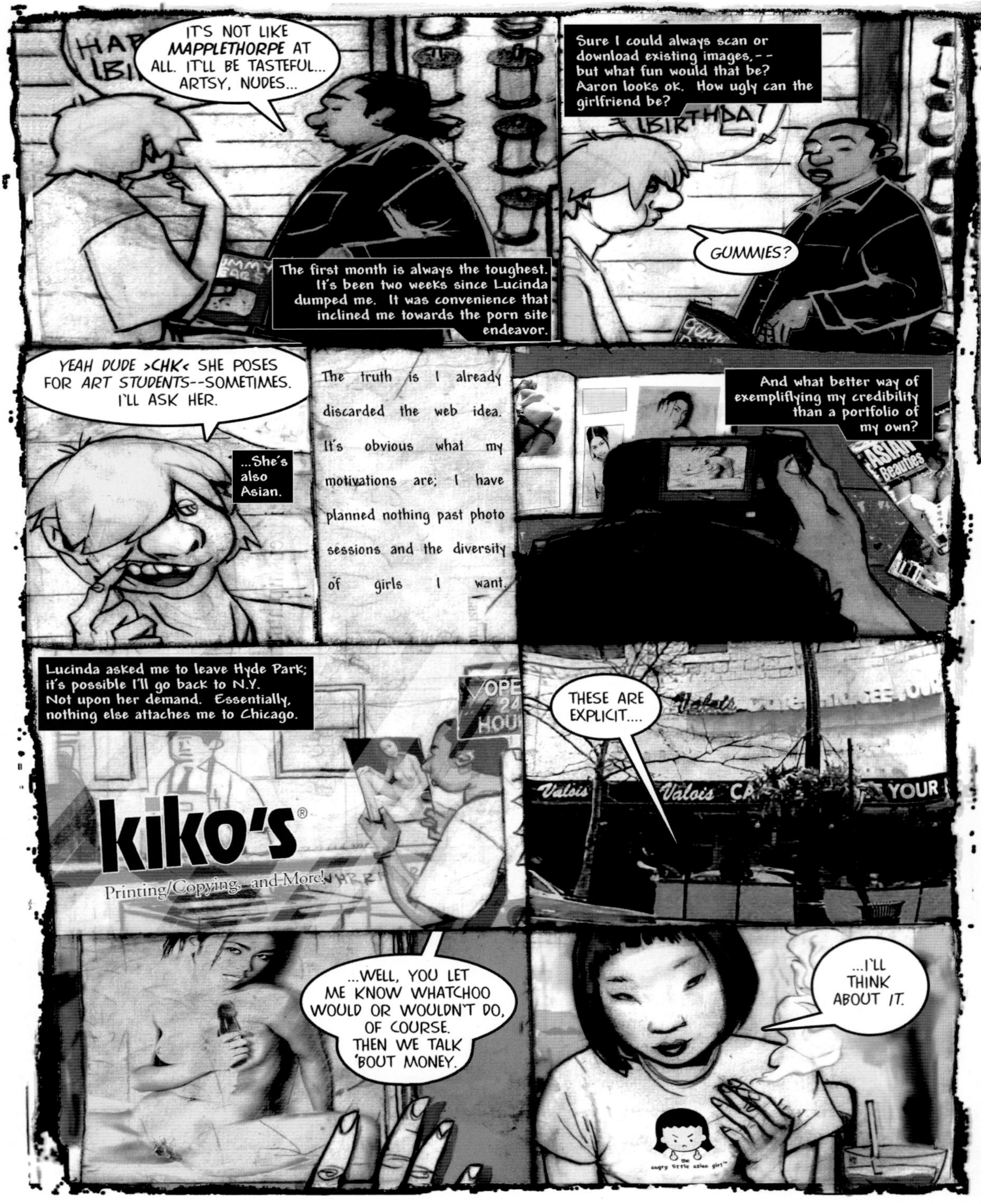
IT'S NOT LIKE MAPPLETHORPE AT ALL. IT'LL BE TASTEFUL... ARTSY, NUDES...
The first month is always the toughest. It's been two weeks since Lucinda dumped me. It was convenience that inclined me towards the porn site endeavor.
Sure I could always scan or download existing images,- - but what fun would that be? Aaron looks ok. How ugly can the girlfriend be?
GUMMIES?
YEAH DUDE >CHK< SHE POSES FOR ART STUDENTS--SOMETIMES. I'LL ASK HER.
...She's also Asian.
The truth is I already discarded the web idea. It's obvious what my motivations are; I have planned nothing past photo sessions and the diversity of girls I want.
And what better way of exemplifiying my credibility than a portfolio of my own?
Lucinda asked me to leave Hyde Park; it's possible I'll go back to N.Y. Not upon her demand. Essentially, nothing else attaches me to Chicago.
kiko's®
Printing/Copying, and More!
THESE ARE EXPLICIT....
...WELL, YOU LET ME KNOW WHATCHOO WOULD OR WOULDN'T DO, OF COURSE. THEN WE TALK 'BOUT MONEY.
...I'LL THINK ABOUT IT.

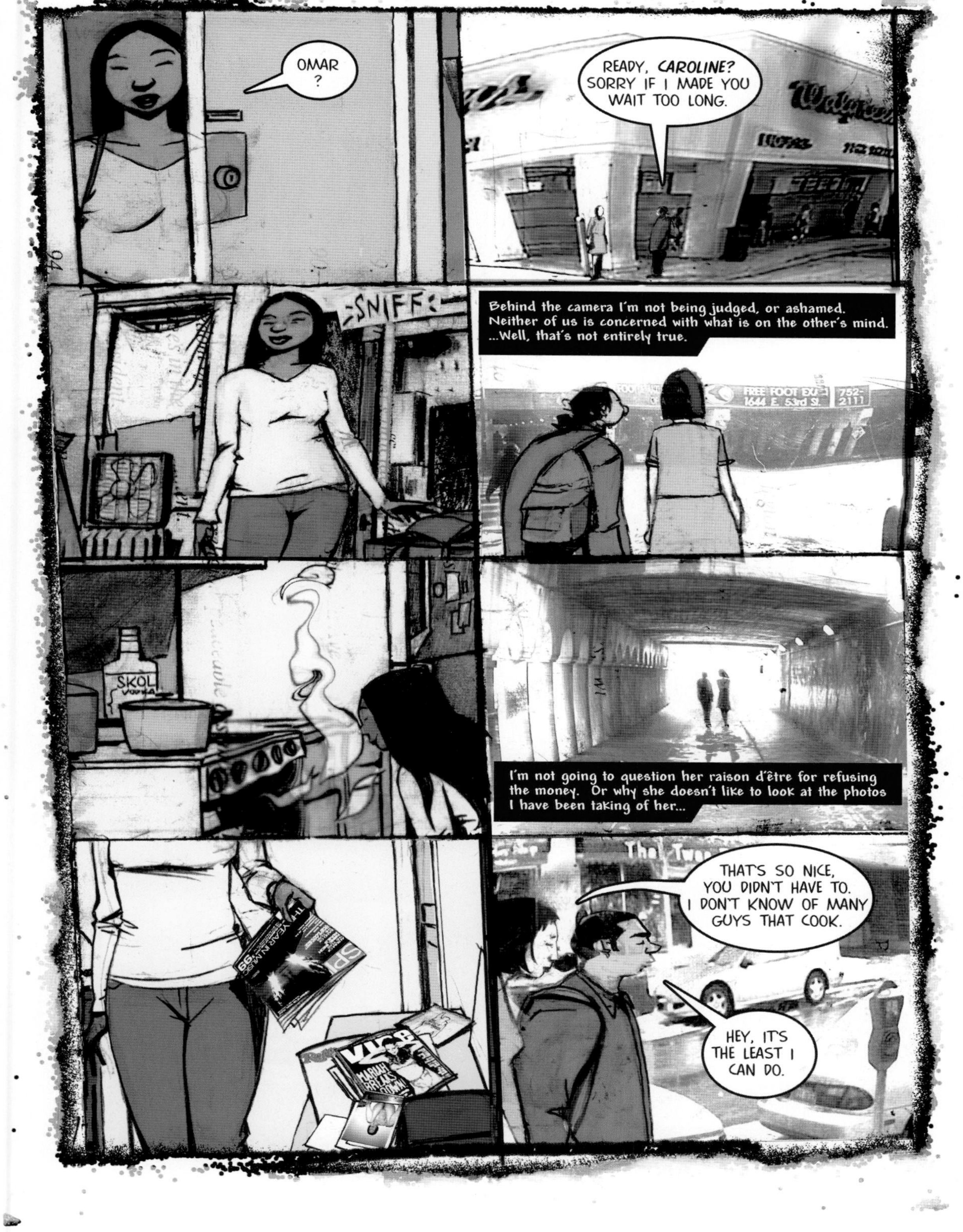

OMAR ?
READY, CAROLINE? SORRY IF I MADE YOU WAIT TOO LONG.
SNIFF
Behind the camera I'm not being judged, or ashamed. Neither of us is concerned with what is on the other's mind. ...Well, that's not entirely true.
FREE FOOT EXA
1644 E. 53rd St.
752-2111
SKOL VODKA
I'm not going to question her raison d'être for refusing the money. Or why she doesn't like to look at the photos I have been taking of her...
THAT'S SO NICE, YOU DIDN'T HAVE TO. I DON'T KNOW OF MANY GUYS THAT COOK.
HEY, IT'S THE LEAST I CAN DO.

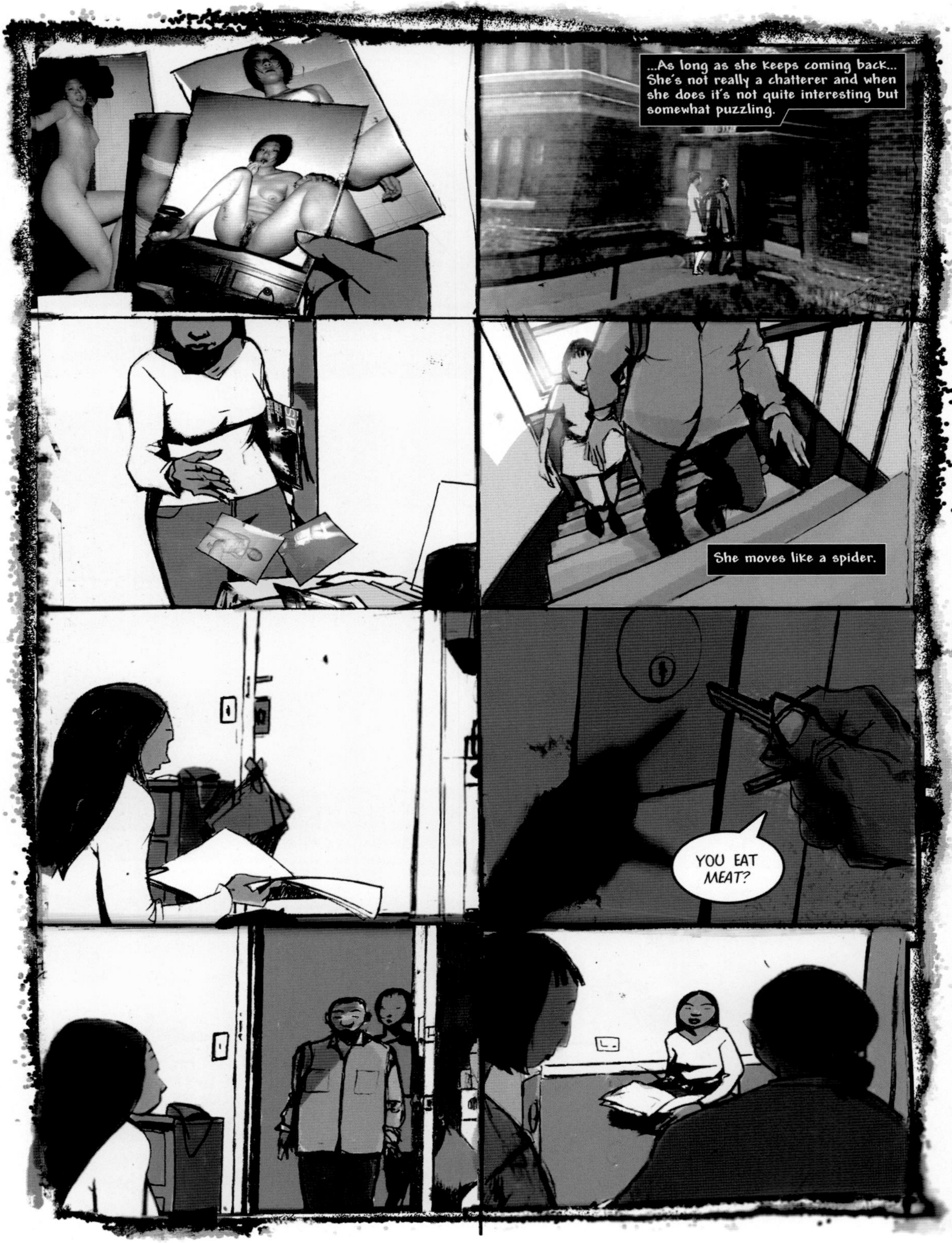
...As long as she keeps coming back... She's not really a chatterer and when she does it's not quite interesting but somewhat puzzling.
She moves like a spider.
YOU EAT MEAT?

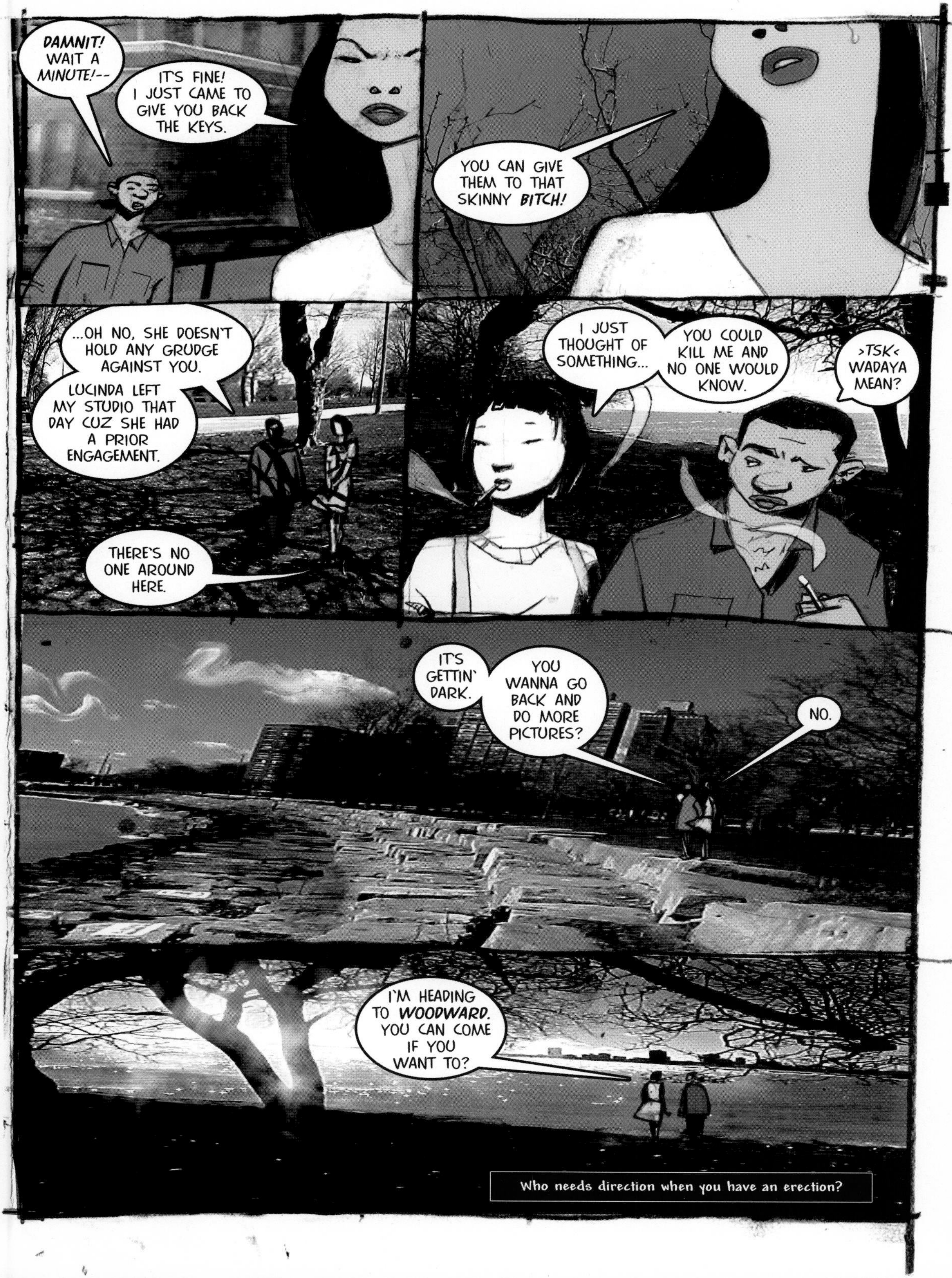
DAMNIT! WAIT A MINUTE!--
IT'S FINE! I JUST CAME TO GIVE YOU BACK THE KEYS.
YOU CAN GIVE THEM TO THAT SKINNY BITCH!
...OH NO, SHE DOESN'T HOLD ANY GRUDGE AGAINST YOU.
LUCINDA LEFT MY STUDIO THAT DAY CUZ SHE HAD A PRIOR ENGAGEMENT.
THERE'S NO ONE AROUND HERE.
I JUST THOUGHT OF SOMETHING...
YOU COULD KILL ME AND NO ONE WOULD KNOW.
>TSK< WADAYA MEAN?
IT'S GETTIN' DARK.
YOU WANNA GO BACK AND DO MORE PICTURES?
NO.
I'M HEADING TO WOODWARD. YOU CAN COME IF YOU WANT TO?
Who needs direction when you have an erection?

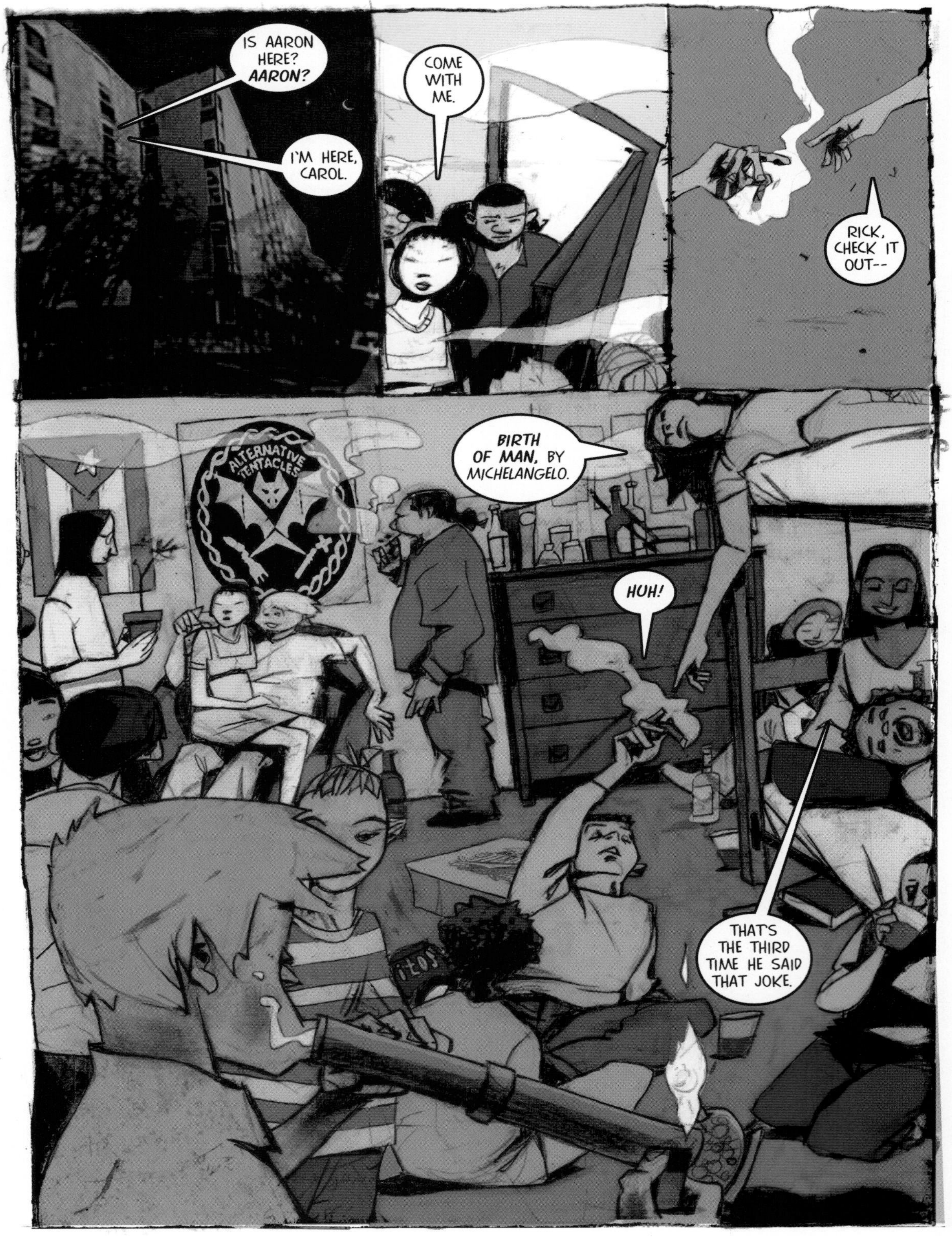
IS AARON HERE? AARON?
I'M HERE, CAROL.
COME WITH ME.
RICK, CHECK IT OUT--
ALTERNATIVE TENTACLES
BIRTH OF MAN, BY MICHELANGELO.
HUH!
THAT'S THE THIRD TIME HE SAID THAT JOKE.

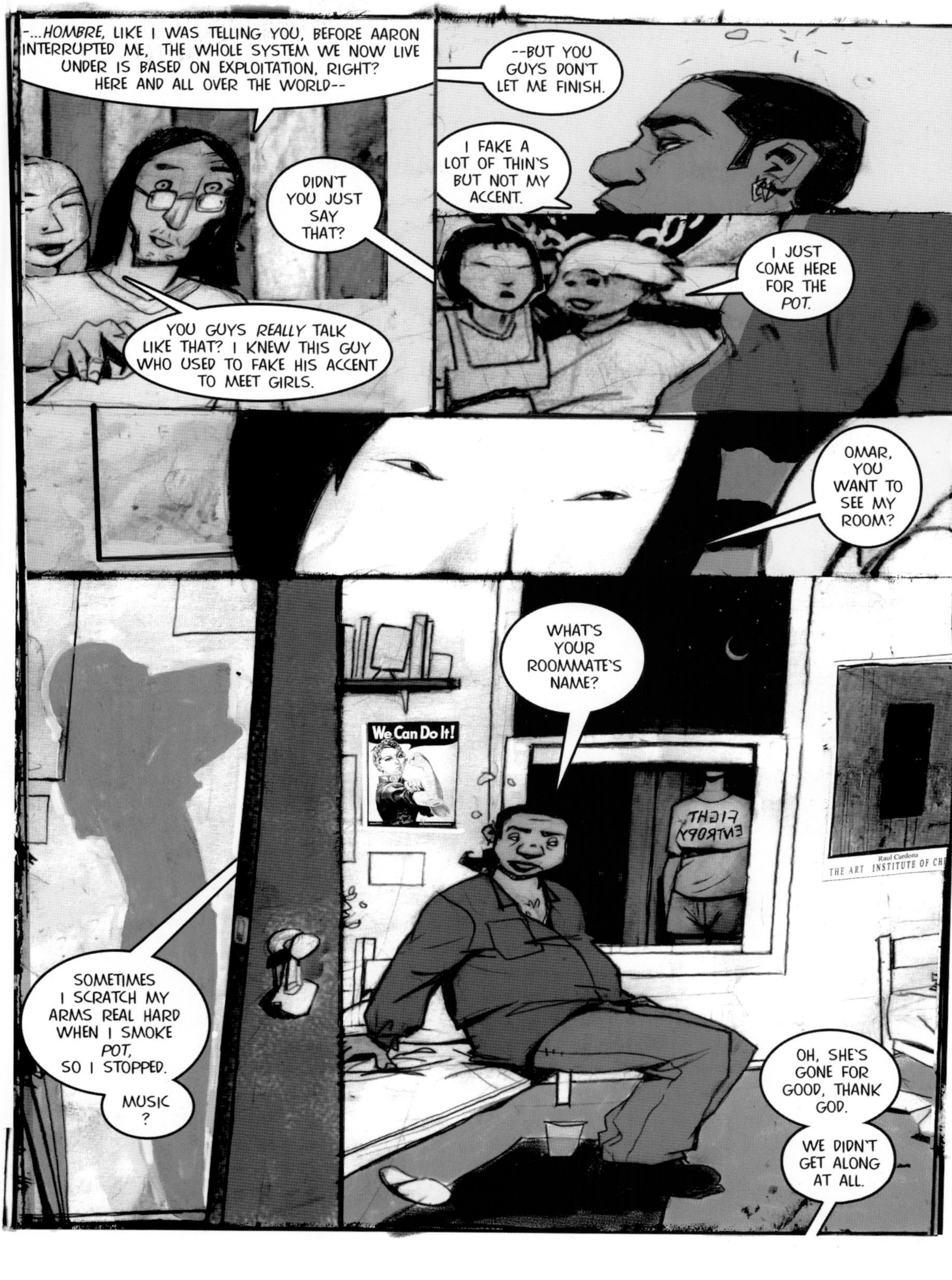
-...HOMBRE, LIKE I WAS TELLING YOU, BEFORE AARON INTERRUPTED ME, THE WHOLE SYSTEM WE NOW LIVE UNDER IS BASED ON EXPLOITATION, RIGHT? HERE AND ALL OVER THE WORLD--
--BUT YOU GUYS DON'T LET ME FINISH.
DIDN'T YOU JUST SAY THAT?
YOU GUYS REALLY TALK LIKE THAT? I KNEW THIS GUY WHO USED TO FAKE HIS ACCENT TO MEET GIRLS.
I FAKE A LOT OF THIN'S BUT NOT MY ACCENT.
I JUST COME HERE FOR THE POT.
OMAR, YOU WANT TO SEE MY ROOM?
We Can Do It!
FIGHT ENTROPY
Raul Cardona
THE ART INSTITUTE OF CH
WHAT'S YOUR ROOMMATE'S NAME?
SOMETIMES I SCRATCH MY ARMS REAL HARD WHEN I SMOKE POT, SO I STOPPED.
MUSIC ?
OH, SHE'S GONE FOR GOOD, THANK GOD.
WE DIDN'T GET ALONG AT ALL.

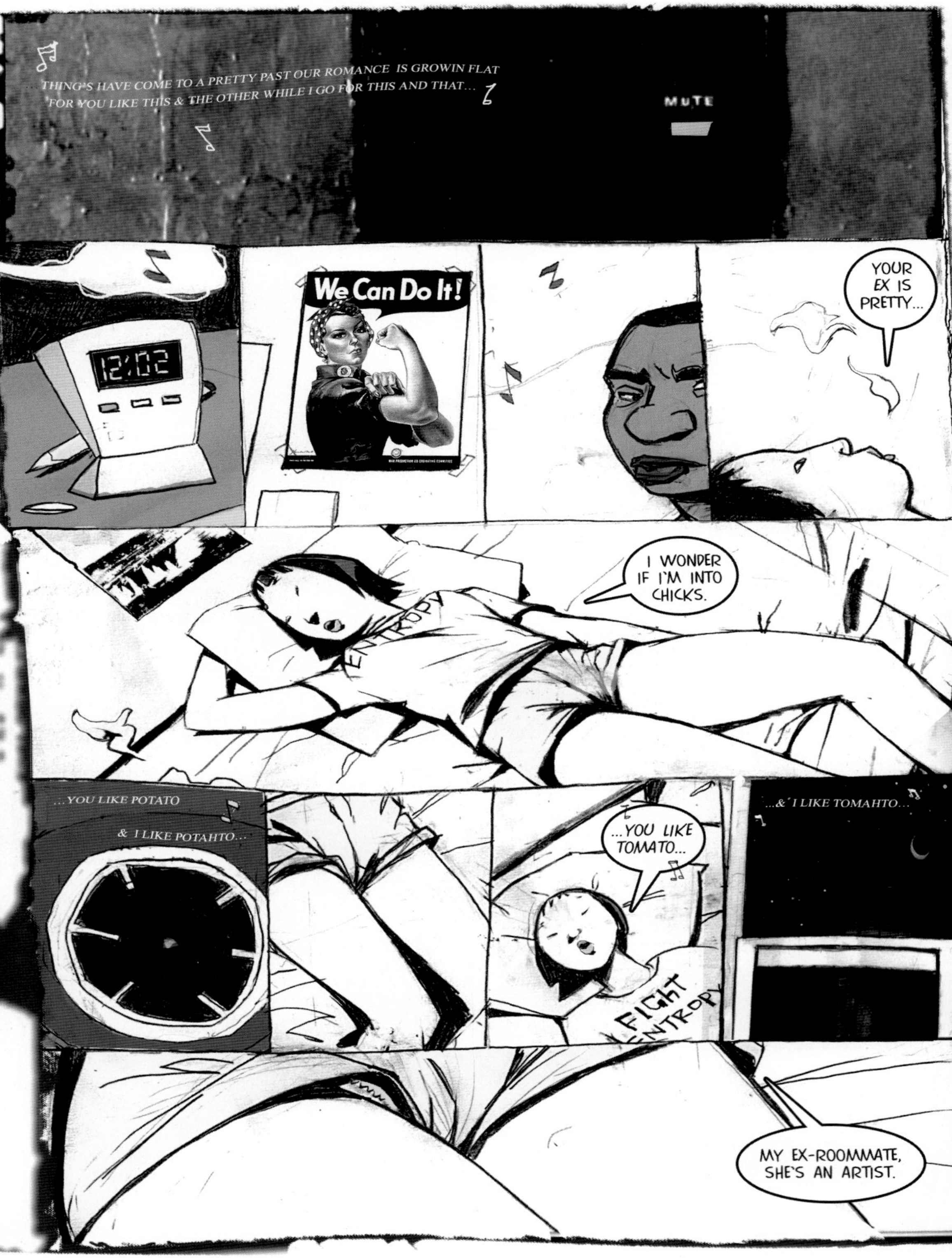
THING'S HAVE COME TO A PRETTY PAST OUR ROMANCE IS GROWIN FLAT
FOR YOU LIKE THIS & THE OTHER WHILE I GO FOR THIS AND THAT…
MUTE
12:02
We Can Do It!
YOUR EX IS PRETTY…
I WONDER IF I'M INTO CHICKS.
ENTROPY
…YOU LIKE POTATO
& I LIKE POTAHTO…
…YOU LIKE TOMATO…
FIGHT ENTROPY
…& I LIKE TOMAHTO…
MY EX-ROOMMATE, SHE'S AN ARTIST.

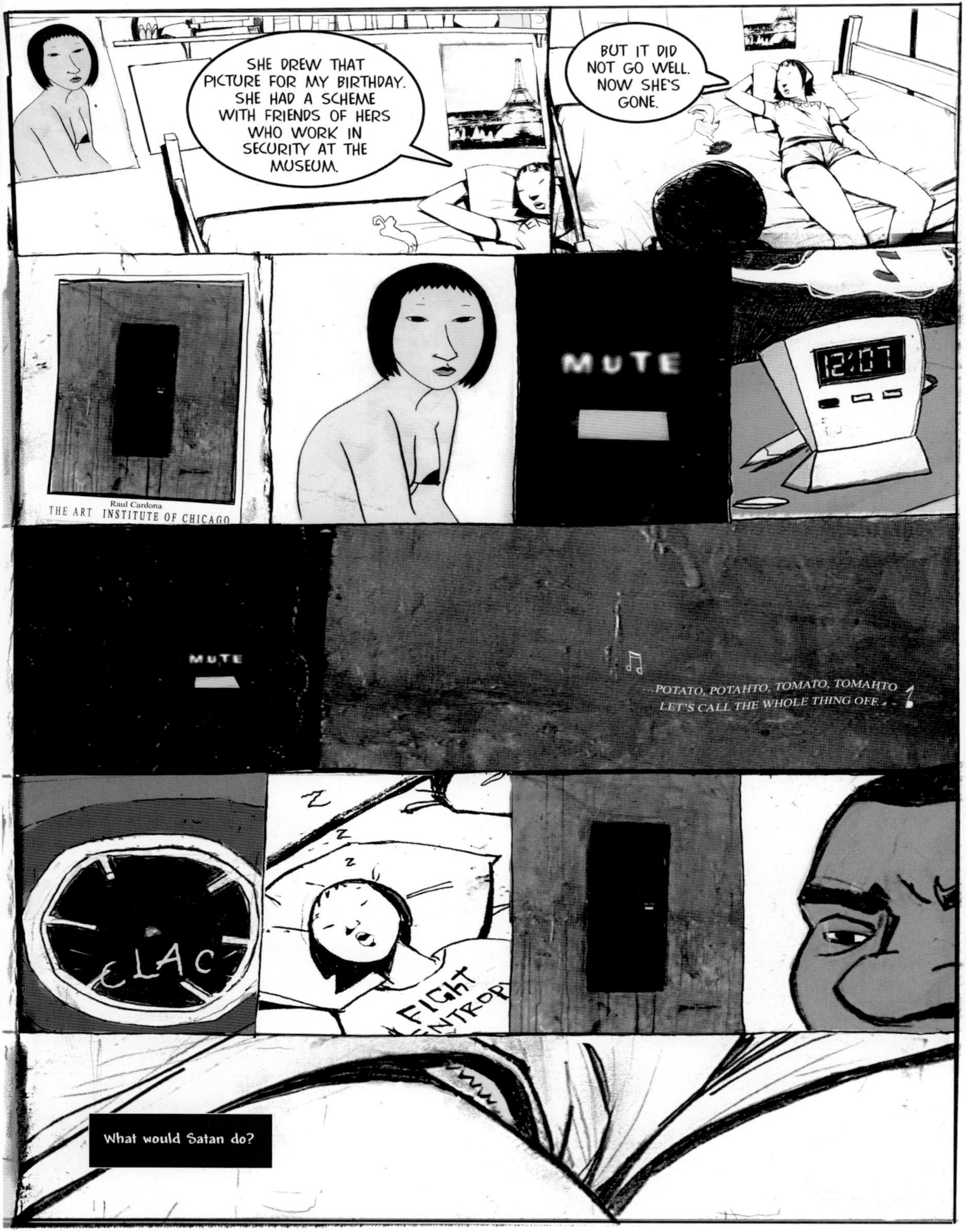
SHE DREW THAT PICTURE FOR MY BIRTHDAY. SHE HAD A SCHEME WITH FRIENDS OF HERS WHO WORK IN SECURITY AT THE MUSEUM.
BUT IT DID NOT GO WELL. NOW SHE'S GONE.
Raul Cardona
THE ART INSTITUTE OF CHICAGO
MUTE
12:07
MUTE
...POTATO, POTAHTO, TOMATO, TOMAHTO
LET'S CALL THE WHOLE THING OFF. . .
CLAC
Z
Z
Z
FIGHT ENTROP
What would Satan do?

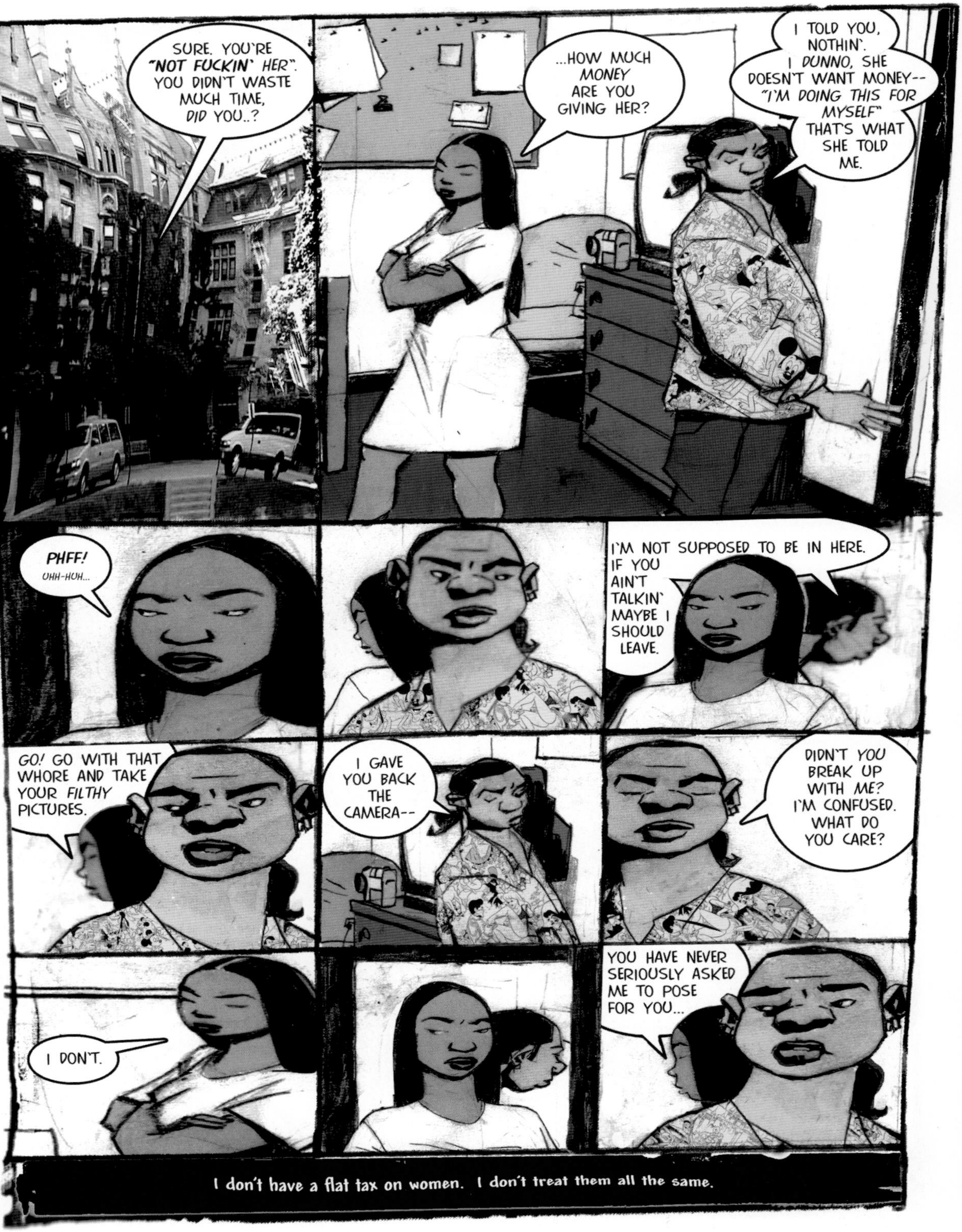
SURE. YOU'RE "NOT FUCKIN' HER". YOU DIDN'T WASTE MUCH TIME, DID YOU..?
...HOW MUCH MONEY ARE YOU GIVING HER?
I TOLD YOU, NOTHIN'. I DUNNO, SHE DOESN'T WANT MONEY-- "I'M DOING THIS FOR MYSELF" THAT'S WHAT SHE TOLD ME.
PHFF! UHH-HUH...
I'M NOT SUPPOSED TO BE IN HERE. IF YOU AIN'T TALKIN' MAYBE I SHOULD LEAVE.
GO! GO WITH THAT WHORE AND TAKE YOUR FILTHY PICTURES.
I GAVE YOU BACK THE CAMERA--
DIDN'T YOU BREAK UP WITH ME? I'M CONFUSED. WHAT DO YOU CARE?
I DON'T.
YOU HAVE NEVER SERIOUSLY ASKED ME TO POSE FOR YOU...
I don't have a flat tax on women. I don't treat them all the same.

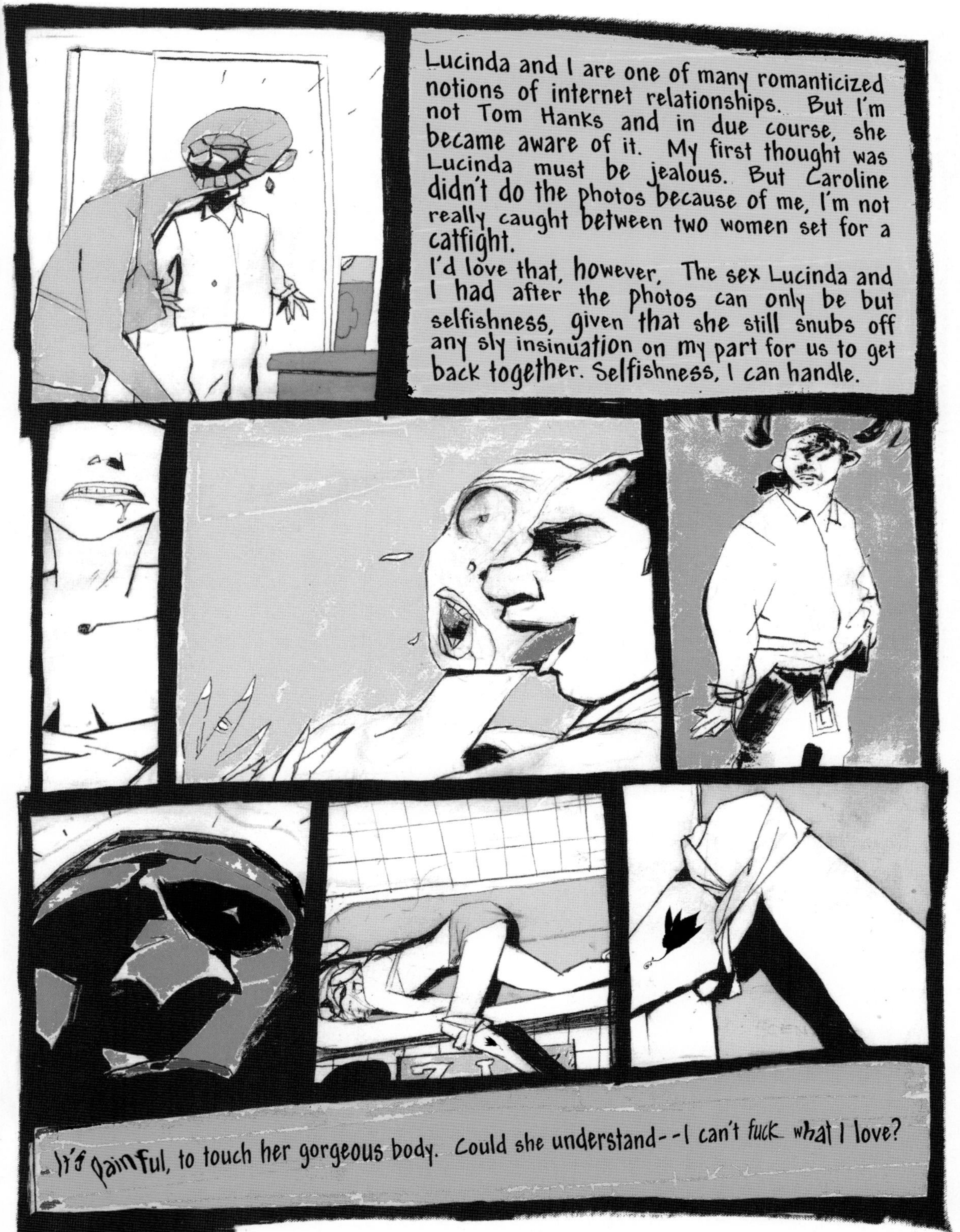
Lucinda and I are one of many romanticized notions of internet relationships. But I'm not Tom Hanks and in due course, she became aware of it. My first thought was Lucinda must be jealous. But Caroline didn't do the photos because of me, I'm not really caught between two women set for a catfight.
I'd love that, however. The sex Lucinda and I had after the photos can only be but selfishness, given that she still snubs off any sly insinuation on my part for us to get back together. Selfishness, I can handle.
It's painful, to touch her gorgeous body. Could she understand--I can't fuck what I love?

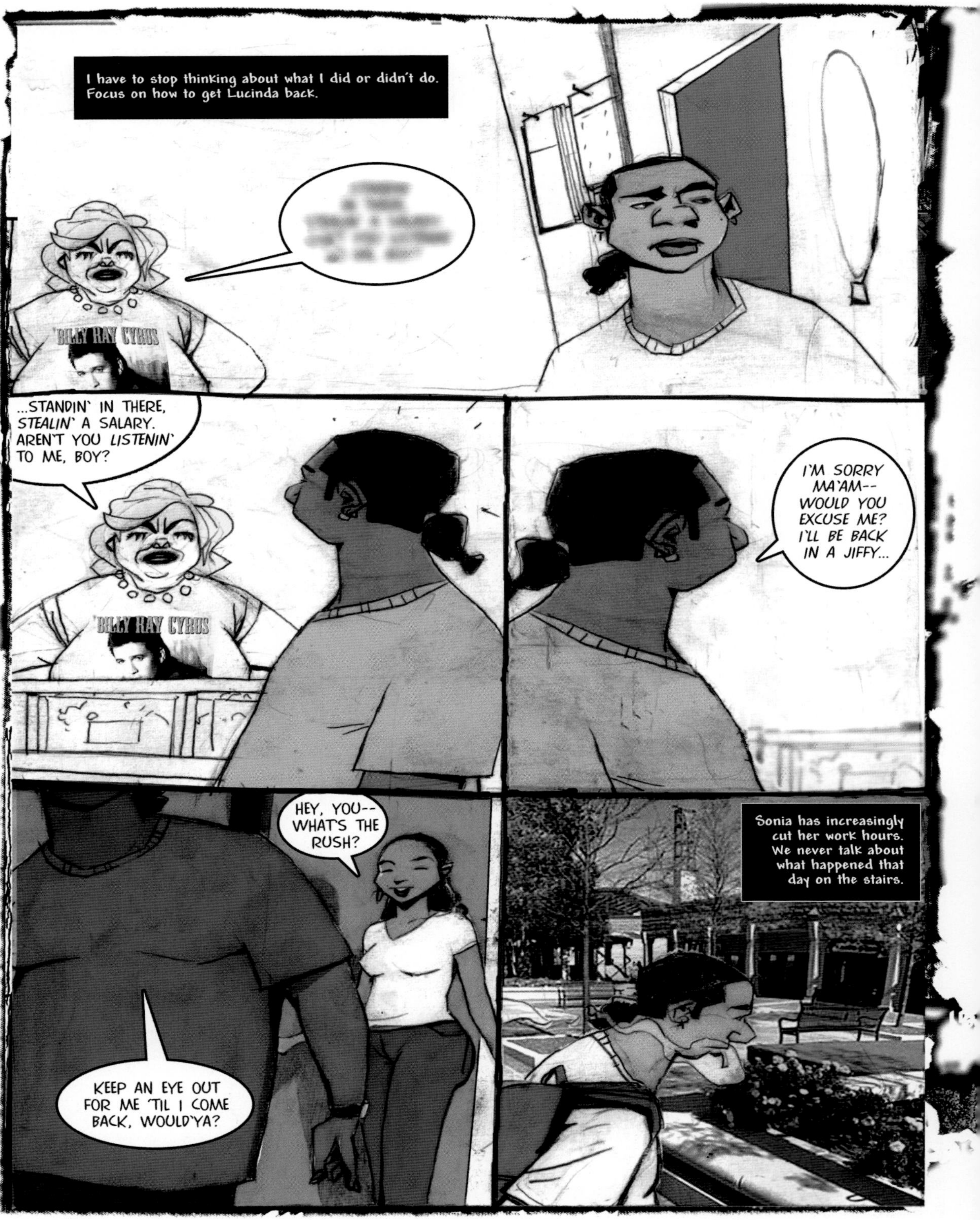
I have to stop thinking about what I did or didn't do. Focus on how to get Lucinda back.
BILLY RAY CYRUS
...STANDIN' IN THERE, STEALIN' A SALARY. AREN'T YOU LISTENIN' TO ME, BOY?
BILLY RAY CYRUS
I'M SORRY MA'AM-- WOULD YOU EXCUSE ME? I'LL BE BACK IN A JIFFY...
HEY, YOU-- WHAT'S THE RUSH?
KEEP AN EYE OUT FOR ME 'TIL I COME BACK, WOULD'YA?
Sonia has increasingly cut her work hours. We never talk about what happened that day on the stairs.

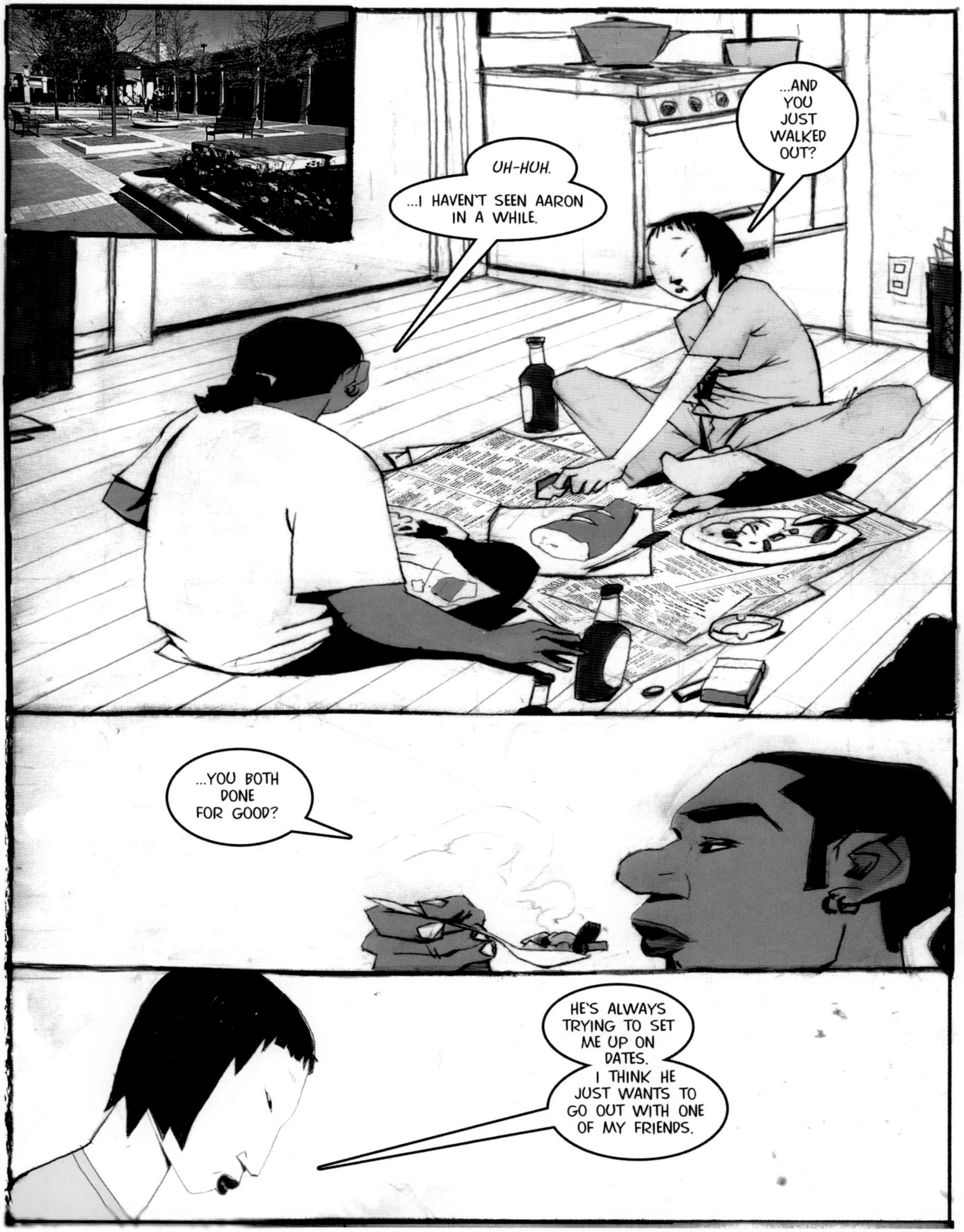
UH-HUH.
...I HAVEN'T SEEN AARON IN A WHILE.
...AND YOU JUST WALKED OUT?
...YOU BOTH DONE FOR GOOD?
HE'S ALWAYS TRYING TO SET ME UP ON DATES.
I THINK HE JUST WANTS TO GO OUT WITH ONE OF MY FRIENDS.

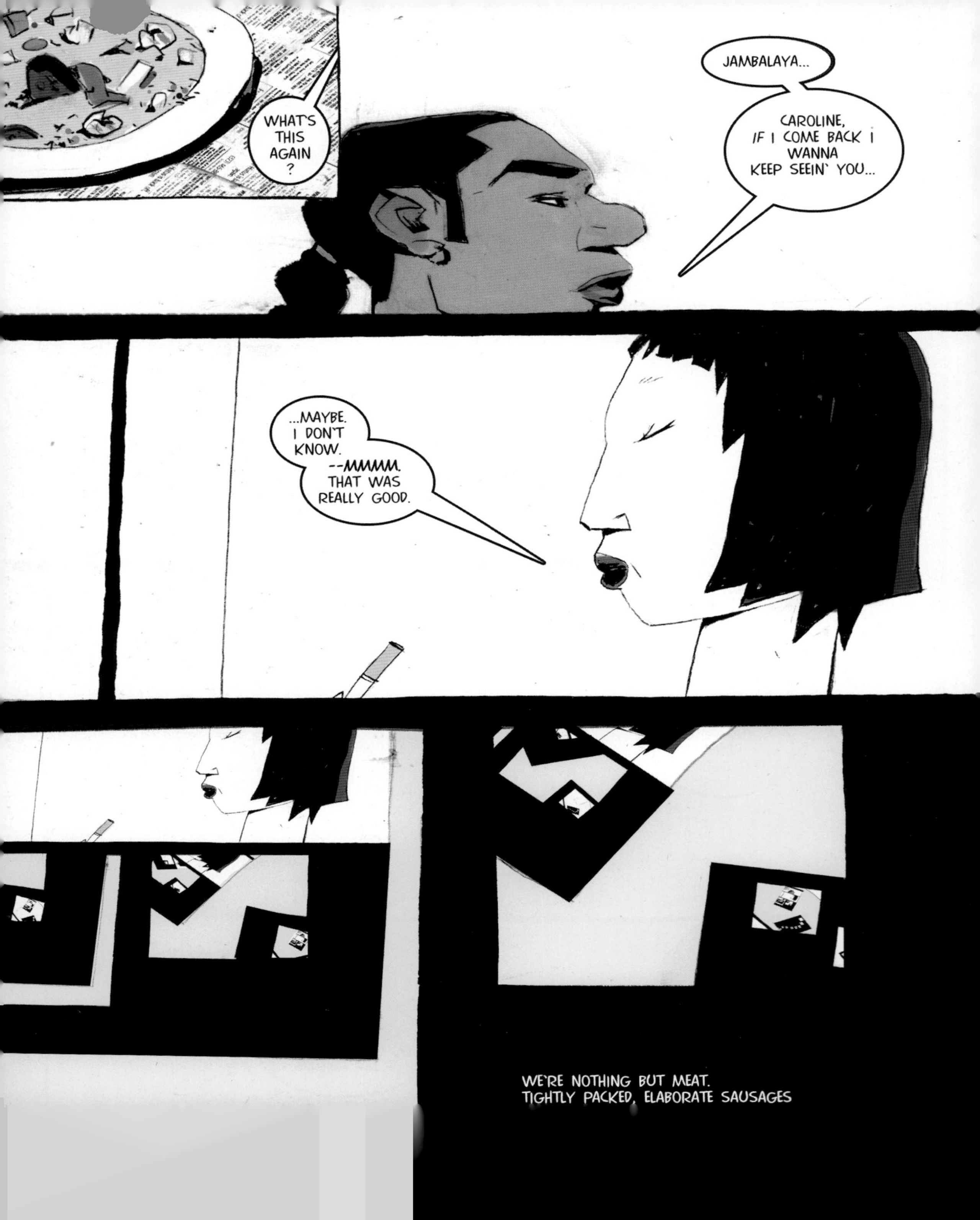
WHAT'S THIS AGAIN ?
JAMBALAYA...
CAROLINE, IF I COME BACK I WANNA KEEP SEEIN' YOU...
...MAYBE. I DON'T KNOW.
--MMMM. THAT WAS REALLY GOOD.
WE'RE NOTHING BUT MEAT.
TIGHTLY PACKED, ELABORATE SAUSAGES

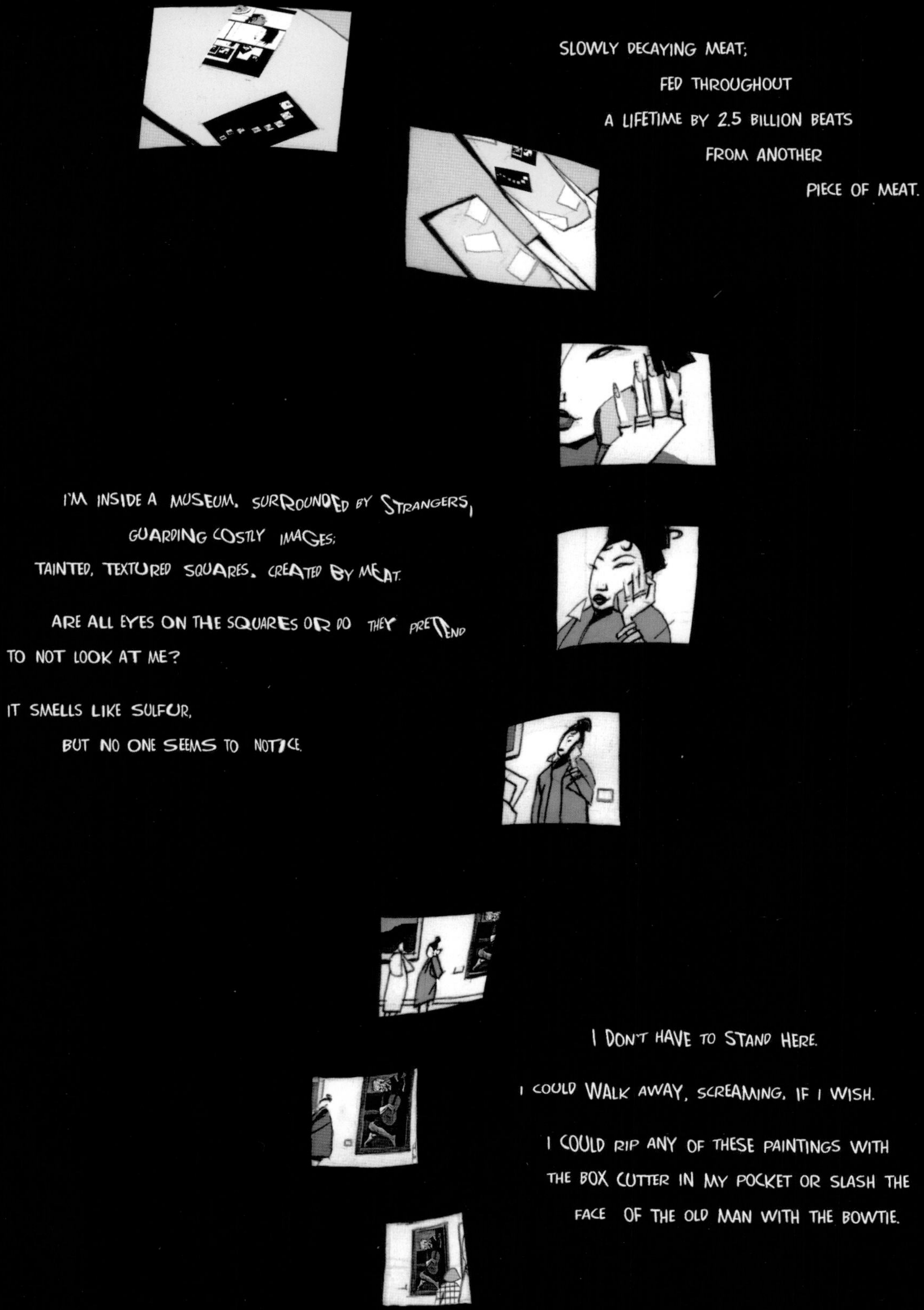
SLOWLY DECAYING MEAT;
FED THROUGHOUT
A LIFETIME BY 2.5 BILLION BEATS
FROM ANOTHER
PIECE OF MEAT.
I'M INSIDE A MUSEUM. SURROUNDED BY STRANGERS,
GUARDING COSTLY IMAGES;
TAINTED, TEXTURED SQUARES. CREATED BY MEAT.
ARE ALL EYES ON THE SQUARES OR DO THEY PRETEND
TO NOT LOOK AT ME?
IT SMELLS LIKE SULFUR,
BUT NO ONE SEEMS TO NOTICE.
I DON'T HAVE TO STAND HERE.
I COULD WALK AWAY, SCREAMING, IF I WISH.
I COULD RIP ANY OF THESE PAINTINGS WITH
THE BOX CUTTER IN MY POCKET OR SLASH THE
FACE OF THE OLD MAN WITH THE BOWTIE.

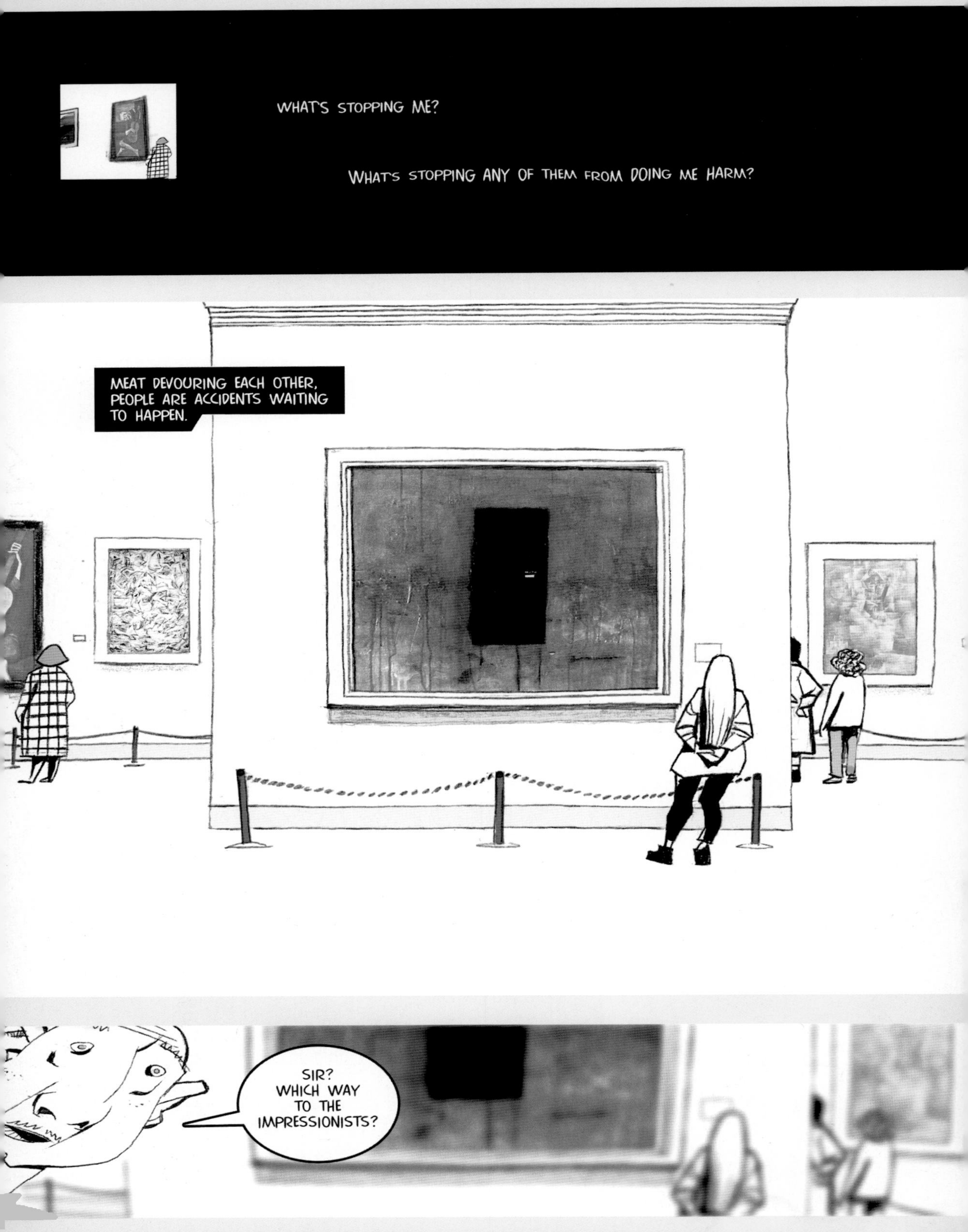
WHAT'S STOPPING ME?
WHAT'S STOPPING ANY OF THEM FROM DOING ME HARM?
MEAT DEVOURING EACH OTHER, PEOPLE ARE ACCIDENTS WAITING TO HAPPEN.
SIR? WHICH WAY TO THE IMPRESSIONISTS?

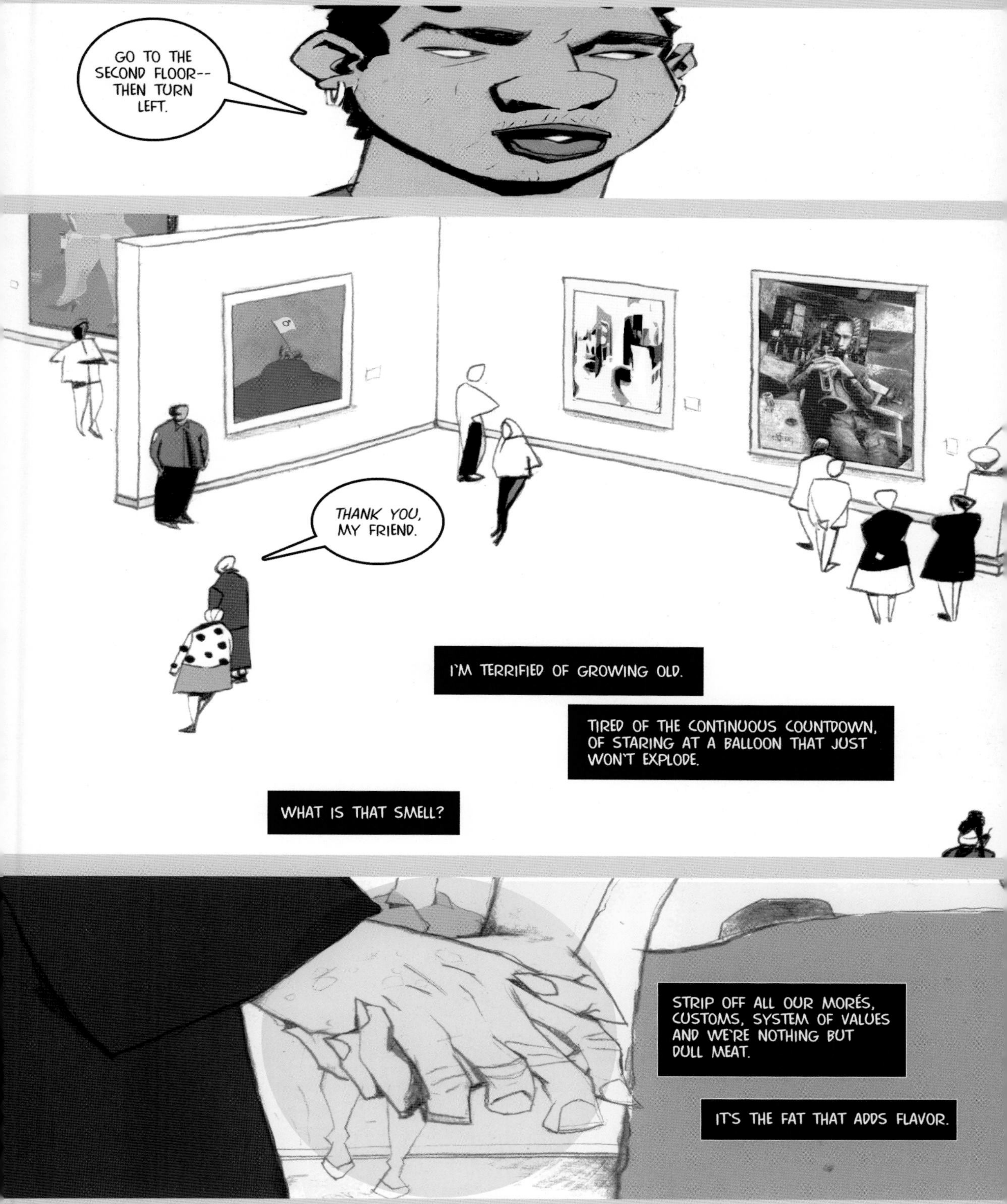

GO TO THE SECOND FLOOR-- THEN TURN LEFT.
THANK YOU, MY FRIEND.
I'M TERRIFIED OF GROWING OLD.
TIRED OF THE CONTINUOUS COUNTDOWN, OF STARING AT A BALLOON THAT JUST WON'T EXPLODE.
WHAT IS THAT SMELL?
STRIP OFF ALL OUR MORÉS, CUSTOMS, SYSTEM OF VALUES AND WE'RE NOTHING BUT DULL MEAT.
IT'S THE FAT THAT ADDS FLAVOR.

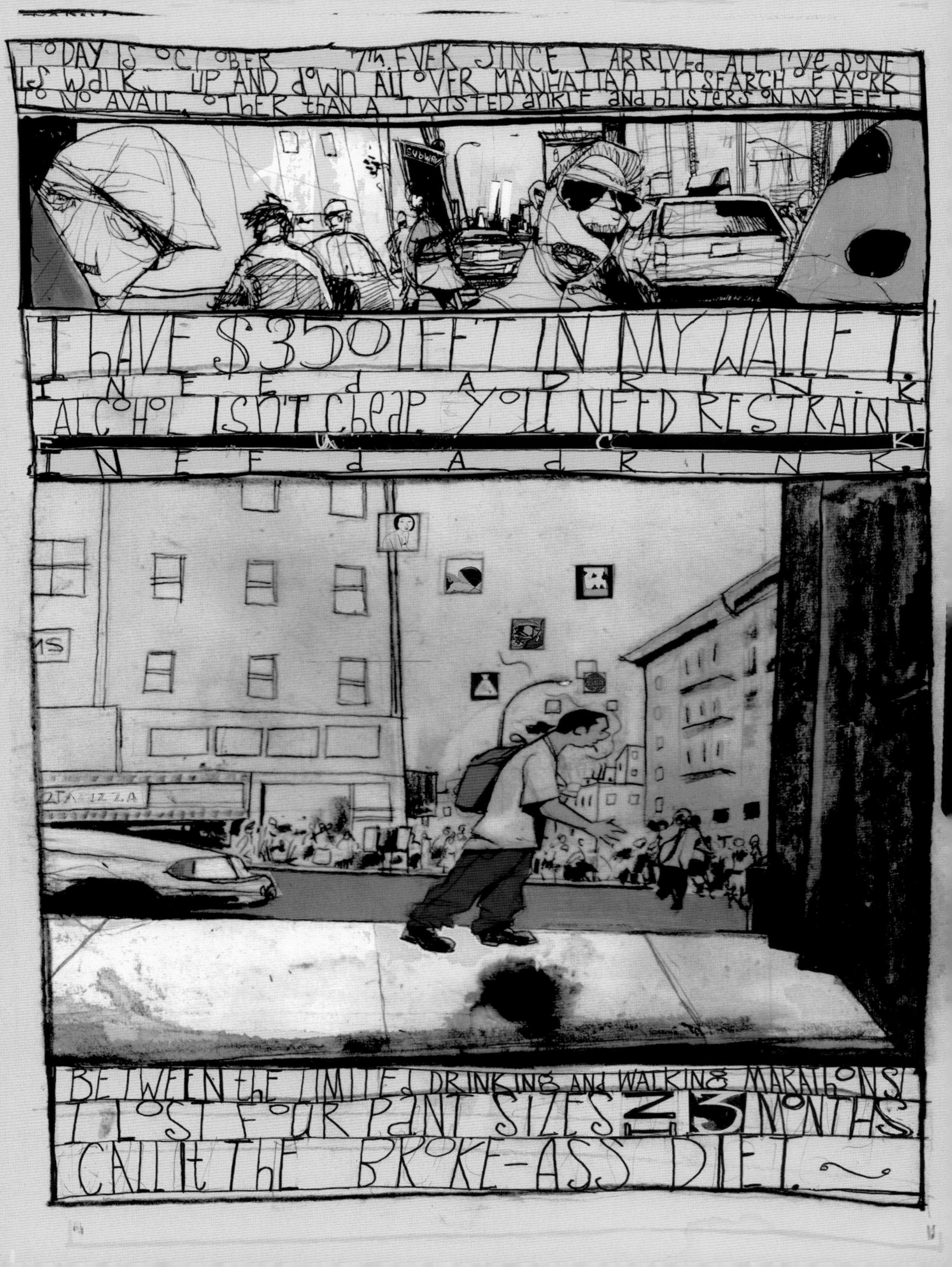
TODAY IS OCTOBER 7th. EVER SINCE I ARRIVED ALL I'VE DONE IS WALK... UP AND DOWN ALL OVER MANHATTAN IN SEARCH OF WORK TO NO AVAIL, OTHER THAN A TWISTED ANKLE AND BLISTERS ON MY FEET.
SUBWAY
I HAVE $350 LEFT IN MY WALLET.
I NEED A DRINK.
ALCOHOL ISN'T CHEAP. YOU NEED RESTRAINT.
I NEED A DRINK.
BETWEEN THE LIMITED DRINKING AND WALKING MARATHONS, I LOST FOUR PANT SIZES IN 3 MONTHS.
CALL IT THE BROKE-ASS DIET.

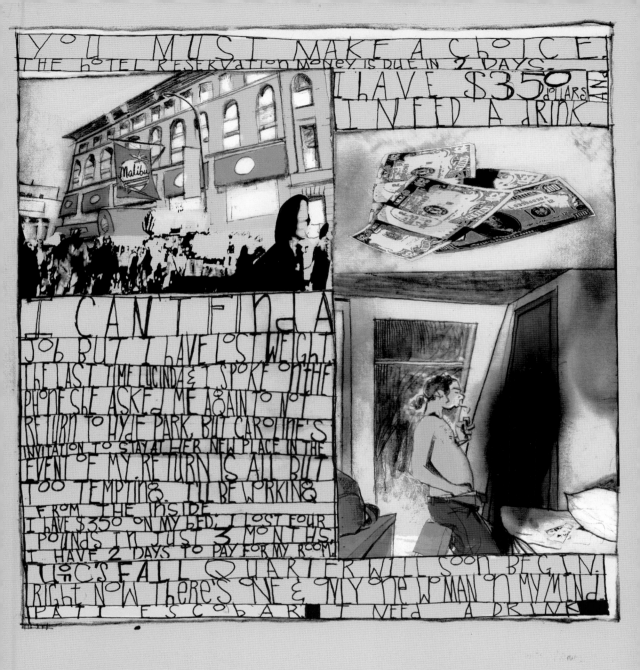

YOU MUST MAKE A CHOICE!
THE HOTEL RESERVATION MONEY IS DUE IN 2 DAYS.
I HAVE $350 dollars
I NEED A DRINK.

I CAN'T FIND A
JOB BUT I HAVE LOST WEIGHT
THE LAST TIME LUCINDA & I SPOKE ON THE
PHONE SHE ASKED ME AGAIN TO NOT
RETURN TO HYDE PARK, BUT CAROLINE'S
INVITATION TO STAY AT HER NEW PLACE IN THE
EVENT OF MY RETURN IS ALL BUT
TOO TEMPTING. I'LL BE WORKING
FROM THE INSIDE
I HAVE $350 ON MY BED, I LOST FOUR
POUNDS IN JUST 3 MONTHS.
I HAVE 2 DAYS TO PAY FOR MY ROOM
U OF C'S FALL QUARTER WILL SOON BEGIN.
RIGHT NOW THERE'S ONE & MY NEW MAN ON MY MIND.
PATTI ESCOBAR. I NEED A DRINK.

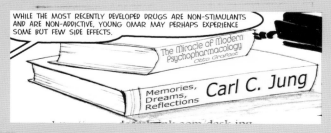

WHILE THE MOST RECENTLY DEVELOPED DRUGS ARE NON-STIMULANTS
AND ARE NON-ADDICTIVE, YOUNG OMAR MAY PERHAPS EXPERIENCE
SOME BUT FEW SIDE EFFECTS.

The Miracle of Modern
Psychopharmacology
Otto GraPont

Memories,
Dreams,
Reflections   Carl C. Jung

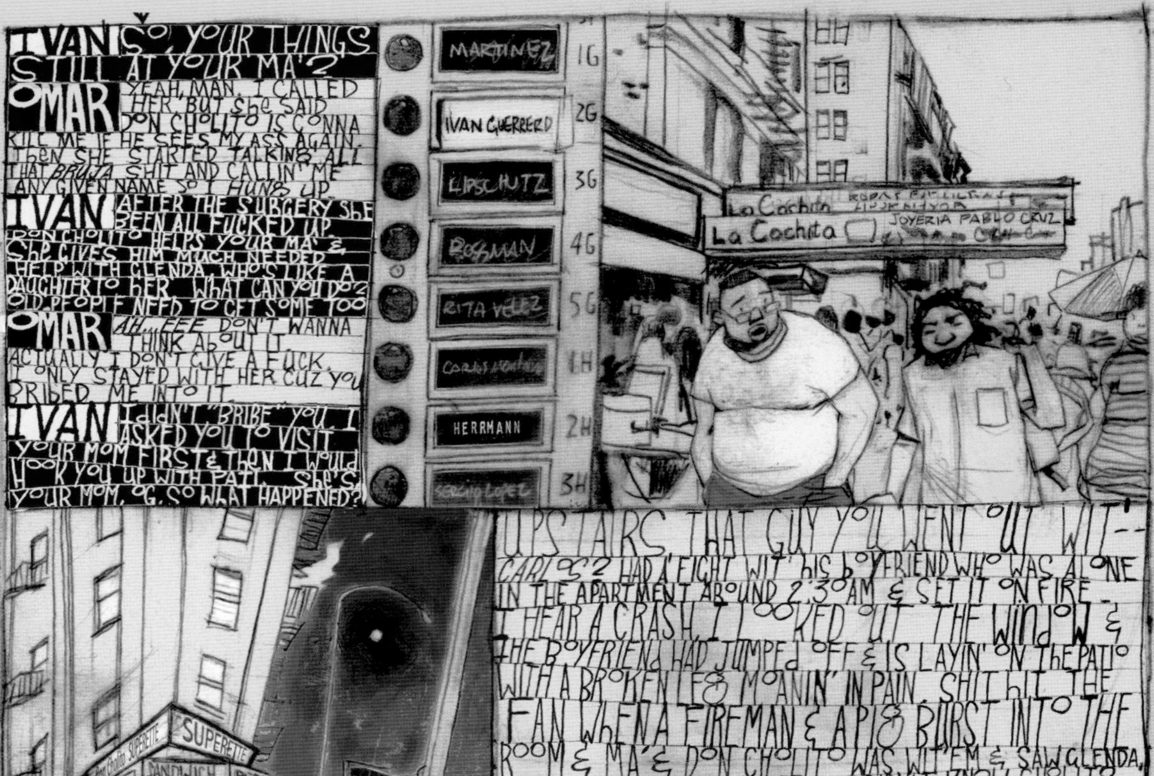
IVAN SO, YOUR THINGS STILL AT YOUR MA'?
OMAR YEAH, MAN. I CALLED HER, BUT SHE SAID DON CHOLITO IS GONNA KILL ME IF HE SEES MY ASS AGAIN. THEN SHE STARTED TALKING ALL THAT BRUJA SHIT AND CALLIN' ME ANY GIVEN NAME SO I HUNG UP.
IVAN AFTER THE SURGERY SHE BEEN ALL FUCKED UP. DON CHOLITO HELPS YOUR MA' & SHE GIVES HIM MUCH NEEDED HELP WITH GLENDA, WHO'S LIKE A DAUGHTER TO HER. WHAT CAN YOU DO? OLD PEOPLE NEED TO GET SOME TOO
OMAR AH... EEE DON'T WANNA THINK ABOUT IT. ACTUALLY I DON'T GIVE A FUCK. I ONLY STAYED WITH HER CUZ YOU BRIBED ME INTO IT.
IVAN I DIDN'T "BRIBE" YOU. I ASKED YOU TO VISIT YOUR MOM FIRST & THEN I WOULD HOOK YOU UP WITH PATI. SHE'S YOUR MOM, OG. SO WHAT HAPPENED?
MARTINEZ 1G
IVAN GUERRERO 2G
LIPSCHUTZ 3G
ROSSMAN 4G
RITA VELEZ 5G
1H
HERRMANN 2H
SERGIO LOPEZ 3H
La Cochita
La Cochita
JOYERIA PABLO CRUZ
UPSTAIRS, THAT GUY YOU WENT OUT WIT'-- CARLOS? HAD A FIGHT WIT' HIS BOYFRIEND WHO WAS ALONE IN THE APARTMENT AROUND 2:30 AM & SET IT ON FIRE. I HEAR A CRASH, I LOOKED OUT THE WINDOW & THE BOYFRIEND HAD JUMPED OFF & IS LAYIN' ON THE PATIO WITH A BROKEN LEG MOANIN' IN PAIN. SHIT HIT THE FAN WHEN A FIREMAN & A PIG BURST INTO THE ROOM & MA' & DON CHOLITO WAS WIT' EM & SAW GLENDA, NAKED WIT' ME ON THE BED-- I DIDN'T KNOW CHOLITO HAD A DAUGTHER. I GRABBED WHAT I COULD & GOT THE FUCK OUTTA THERE.
SUPERETTE
SUPERETTE
SANDWICH
BEER
WALK

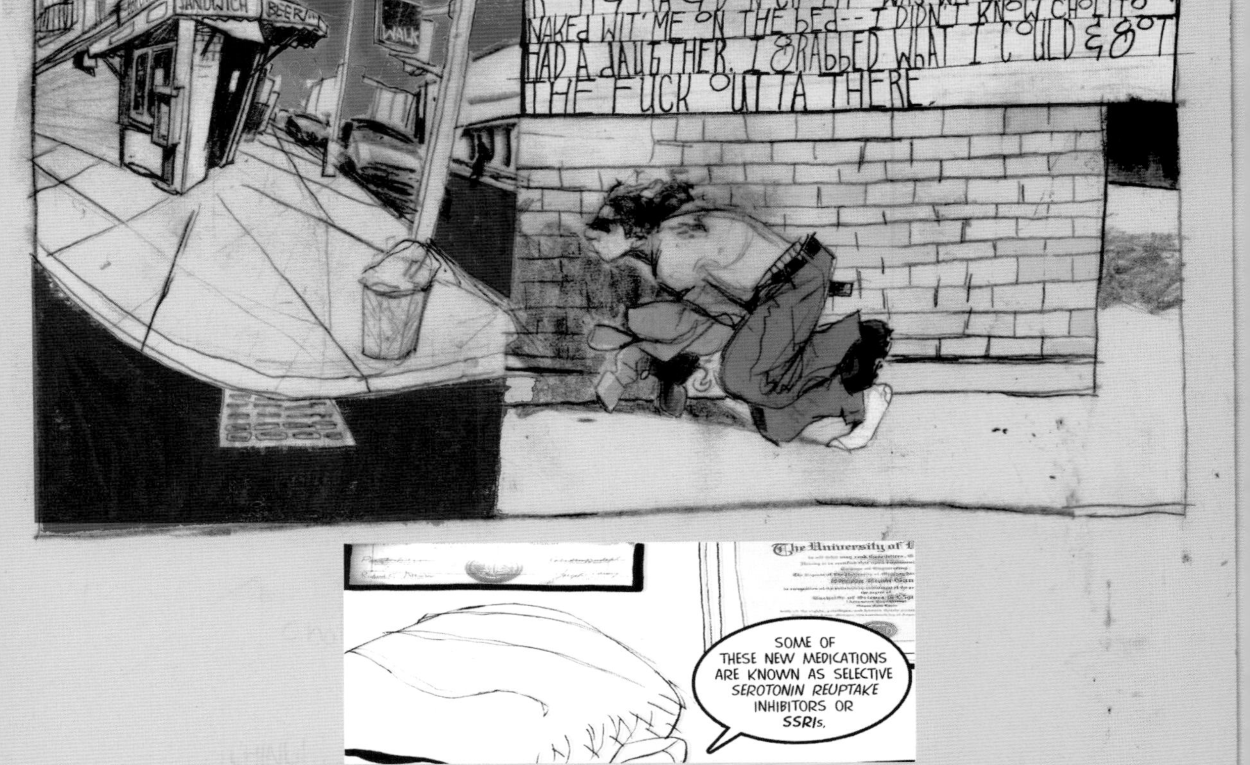
SOME OF THESE NEW MEDICATIONS ARE KNOWN AS SELECTIVE SEROTONIN REUPTAKE INHIBITORS OR SSRIs.

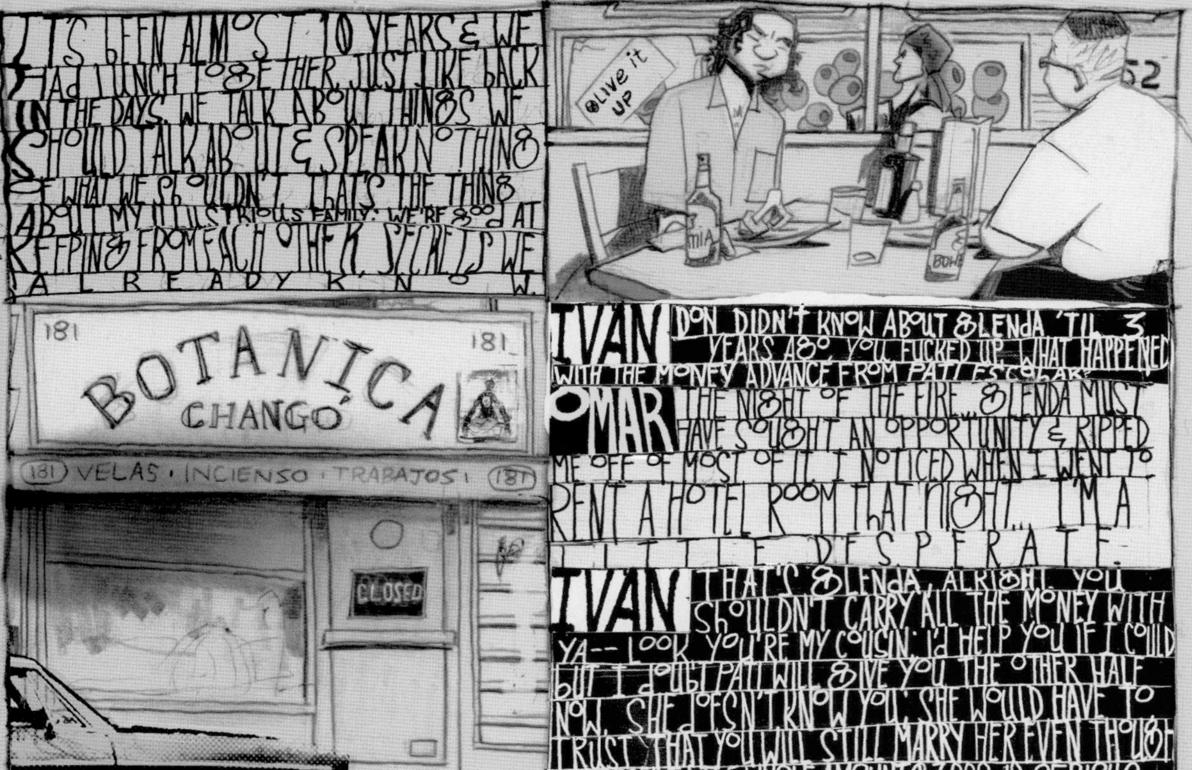
IT'S BEEN ALMOST 10 YEARS & WE HAD LUNCH TOGETHER, JUST LIKE BACK IN THE DAYS. WE TALK ABOUT THINGS WE SHOULD TALK ABOUT & SPEAK NOTHING OF WHAT WE SHOULDN'T. THAT'S THE THING ABOUT MY ILLUSTRIOUS FAMILY: WE'RE GOOD AT KEEPING FROM EACH OTHER, SECRETS WE ALREADY KNOW.
OLIVE IT UP
52
181 BOTANICA CHANGÓ 181
181 VELAS · INCIENSO · TRABAJOS 181
CLOSED
IVAN DON DIDN'T KNOW ABOUT GLENDA 'TIL 3 YEARS AGO. YOU FUCKED UP. WHAT HAPPENED WITH THE MONEY ADVANCE FROM PATI ESCOBAR?
OMAR THE NIGHT OF THE FIRE... GLENDA MUST HAVE SOUGHT AN OPPORTUNITY & RIPPED ME OFF OF MOST OF IT. I NOTICED WHEN I WENT TO RENT A HOTEL ROOM THAT NIGHT... I'M A LITTLE DESPERATE.
IVAN THAT'S GLENDA, ALRIGHT. YOU SHOULDN'T CARRY ALL THE MONEY WITH YA-- LOOK YOU'RE MY COUSIN; I'D HELP YOU IF I COULD BUT I DOUBT PATI WILL GIVE YOU THE OTHER HALF NOW. SHE DOESN'T KNOW YOU; SHE WOULD HAVE TO TRUST THAT YOU WILL STILL MARRY HER EVEN THOUGH YOU RECEIVED THE WHOLE AMOUNT. $3,000 IS SERIOUS DOUGH.
I WAS PETRIFIED BY WHAT DALIA USED TO DO WITH ME AT THE BOTANICA'S BASEMENT BUT I KEPT QUIET BECAUSE I LIKED IT.
HOW IS YOUR SISTER ?
DALIA'S FINE, STILL LIVING IN MIAMI.

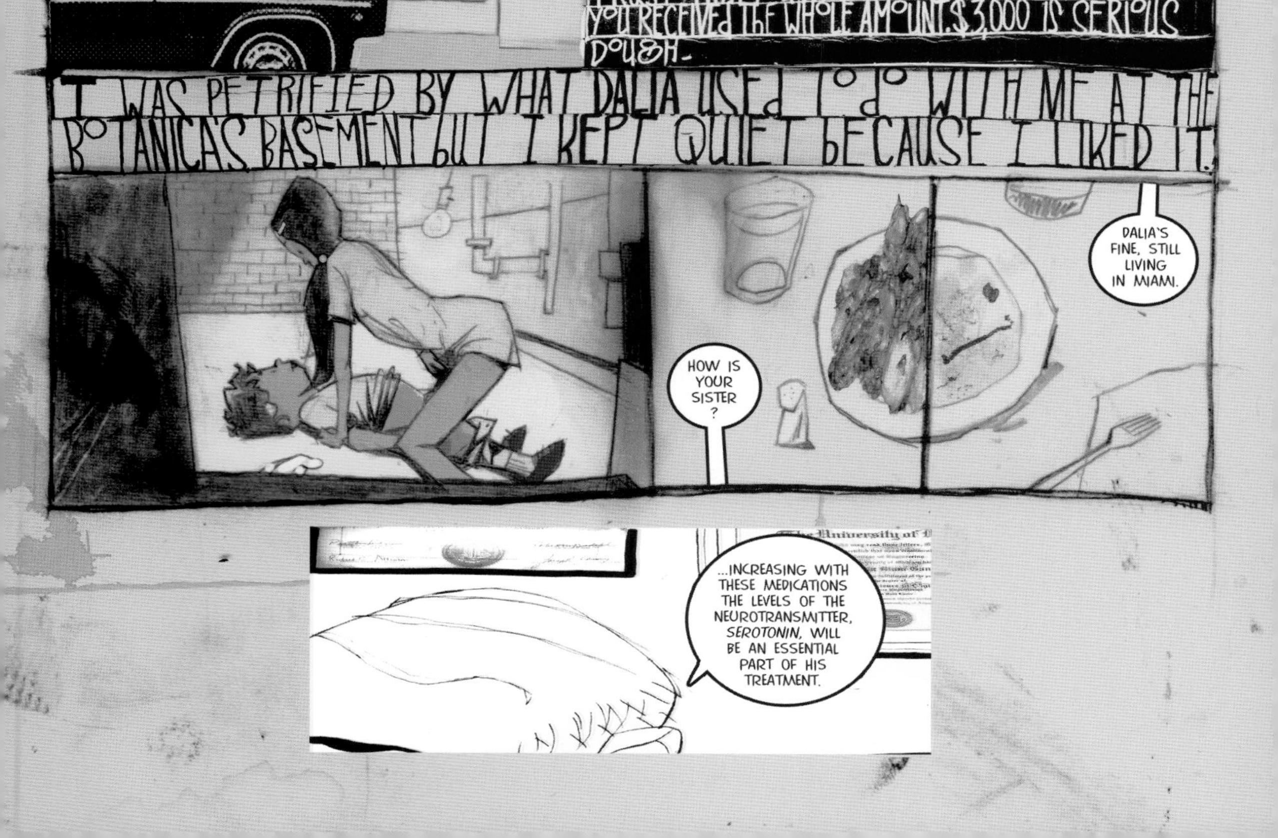
...INCREASING WITH THESE MEDICATIONS THE LEVELS OF THE NEUROTRANSMITTER, SEROTONIN, WILL BE AN ESSENTIAL PART OF HIS TREATMENT.

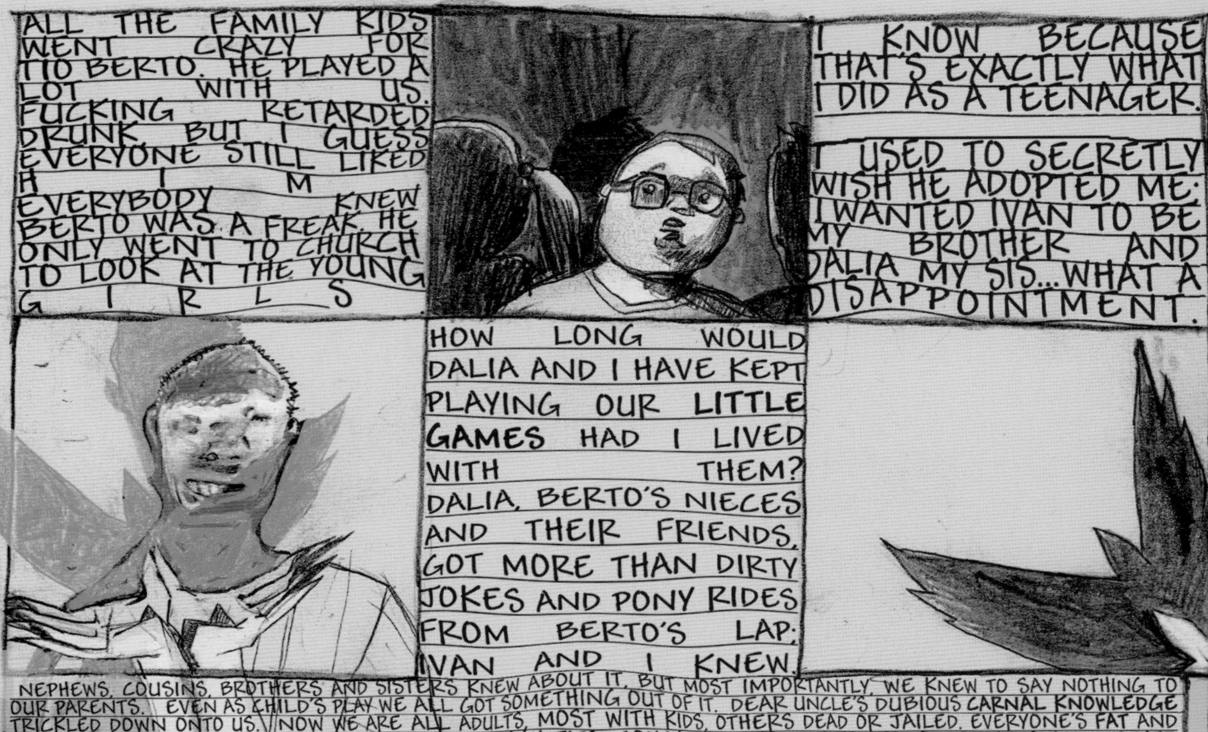
ALL THE FAMILY KIDS WENT CRAZY FOR TIO BERTO. HE PLAYED A LOT WITH US. FUCKING RETARDED DRUNK BUT I GUESS EVERYONE STILL LIKED H I M
EVERYBODY KNEW BERTO WAS A FREAK. HE ONLY WENT TO CHURCH TO LOOK AT THE YOUNG G I R L S.
I KNOW BECAUSE THAT'S EXACTLY WHAT I DID AS A TEENAGER.
I USED TO SECRETLY WISH HE ADOPTED ME. I WANTED IVAN TO BE MY BROTHER AND DALIA MY SIS...WHAT A DISAPPOINTMENT.
HOW LONG WOULD DALIA AND I HAVE KEPT PLAYING OUR LITTLE GAMES HAD I LIVED WITH THEM? DALIA, BERTO'S NIECES AND THEIR FRIENDS, GOT MORE THAN DIRTY JOKES AND PONY RIDES FROM BERTO'S LAP; IVAN AND I KNEW.
NEPHEWS, COUSINS, BROTHERS AND SISTERS KNEW ABOUT IT, BUT MOST IMPORTANTLY, WE KNEW TO SAY NOTHING TO OUR PARENTS. EVEN AS CHILD'S PLAY WE ALL GOT SOMETHING OUT OF IT. DEAR UNCLE'S DUBIOUS CARNAL KNOWLEDGE TRICKLED DOWN ONTO US. NOW WE ARE ALL ADULTS, MOST WITH KIDS, OTHERS DEAD OR JAILED. EVERYONE'S FAT AND STUPID, BALD OR SICK FUCKS, MISSING TEETH, SAGGY TITS, COUCH LEECHES, CRACK HEADS, PERVERTS AND MOTHER FUCKING THIEVES. CONVERSATIONS ABOUT CHILDHOOD ARE CAREFULLY EDITED. WE ARE GOOD AT KEEPING SECRETS, EVEN IF WE ALL ALREADY KNOW. WHAT AM I DOING HERE? I HAVE TO ESCAPE THESE PEOPLE. THEY'RE ALIEN TO ME. I NEED A DRINK. PATI ESCOBAR WILL HAND ME THE REMAINING HALF SOON AFTER WE SAY "I DO" AND HER CITIZENSHIP PROCESS BEGINS.
I CAN'T TAKE THAT LONG.

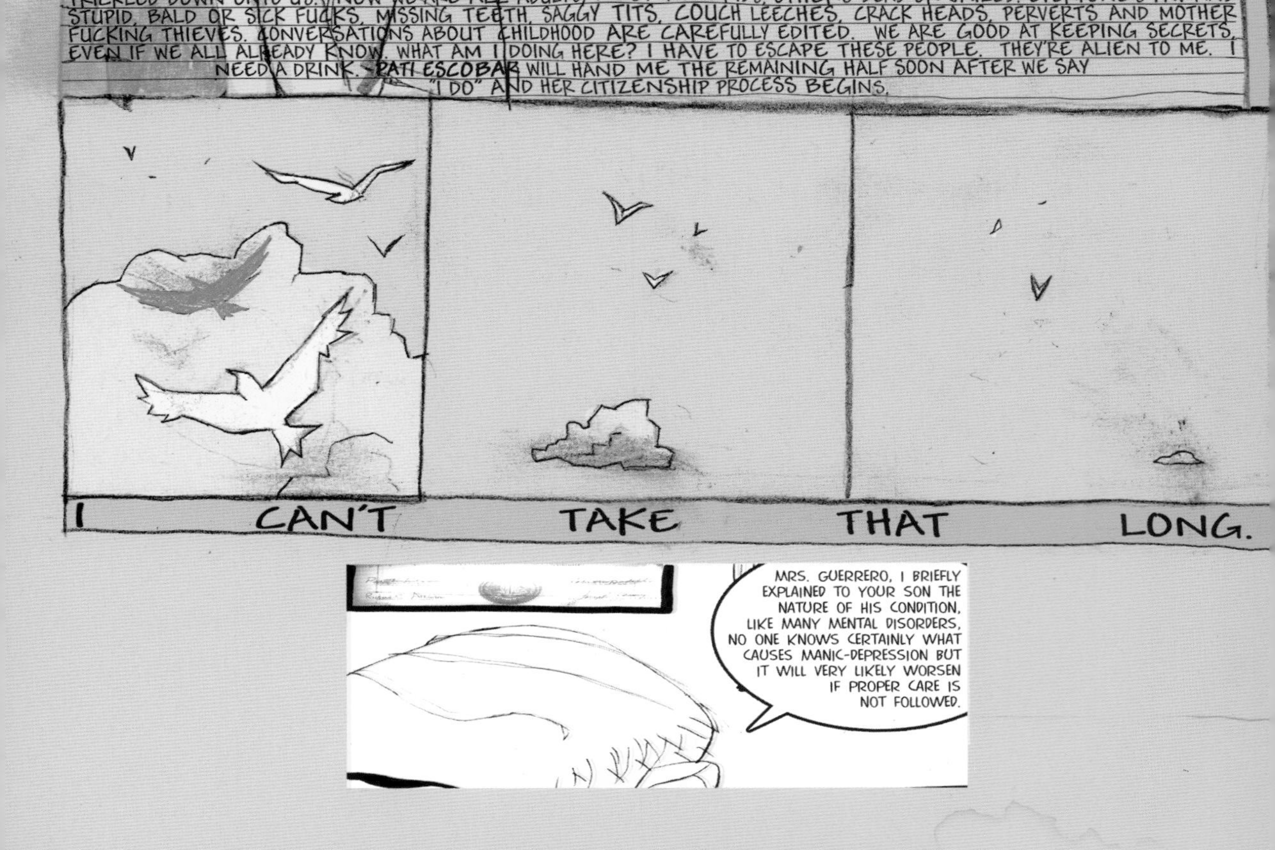
MRS. GUERRERO, I BRIEFLY EXPLAINED TO YOUR SON THE NATURE OF HIS CONDITION. LIKE MANY MENTAL DISORDERS, NO ONE KNOWS CERTAINLY WHAT CAUSES MANIC-DEPRESSION BUT IT WILL VERY LIKELY WORSEN IF PROPER CARE IS NOT FOLLOWED.

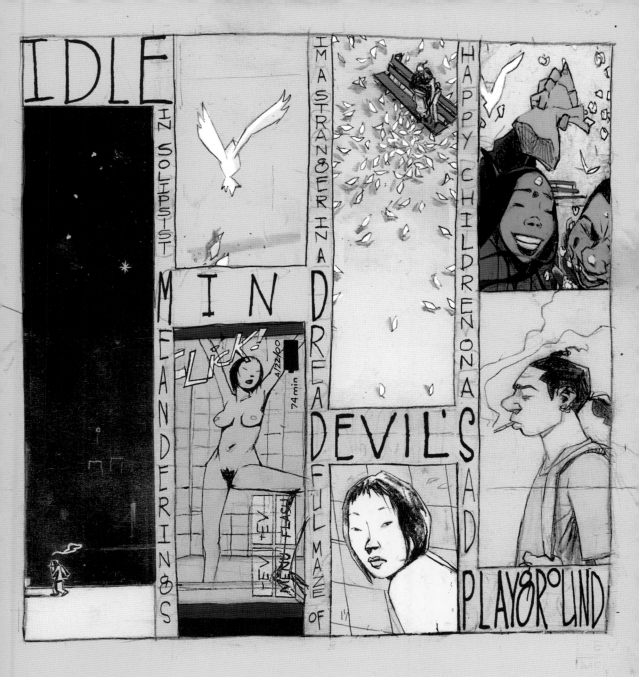

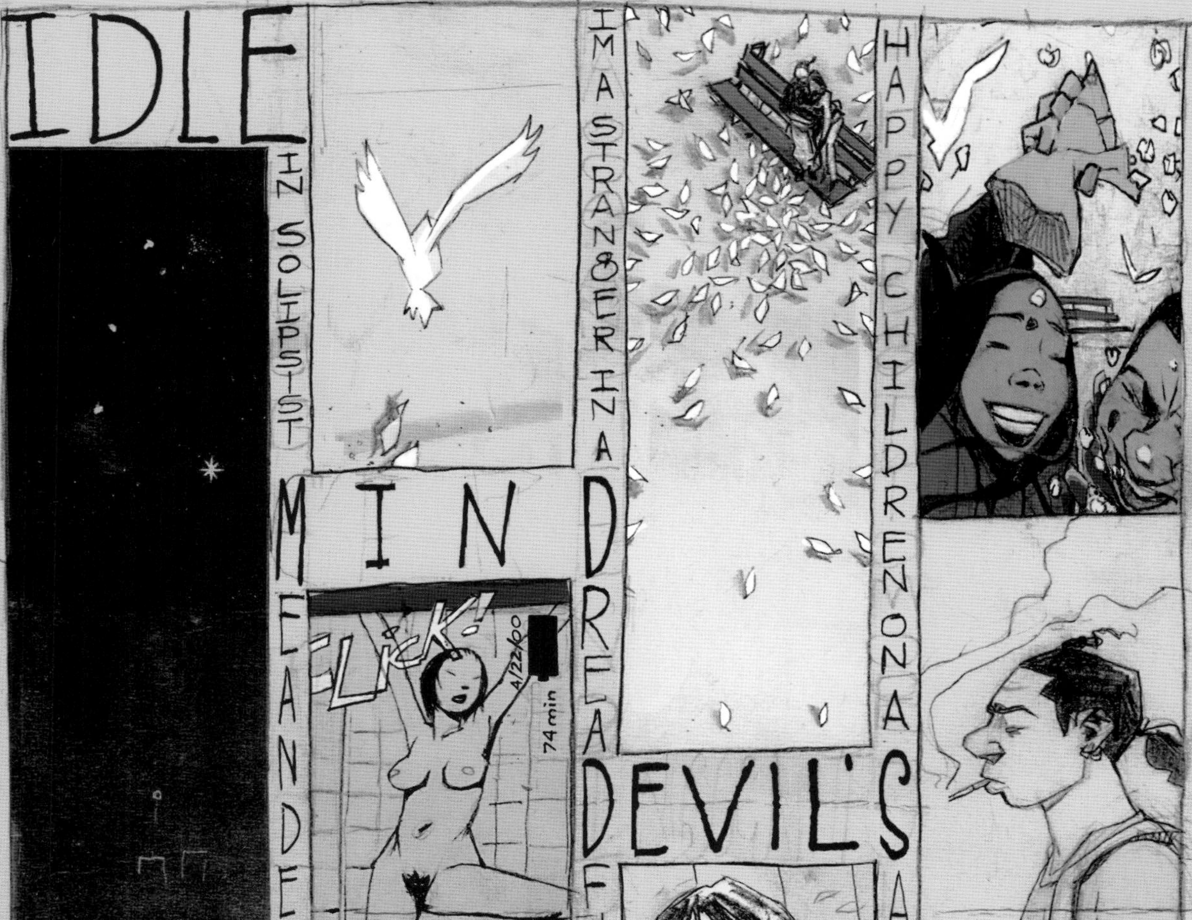
IDLE
IN SOLIPSIST
MIND
MEANDERINGS
CLICK!
4/22/00
74 min
-EV +EV
MENU FLASH
I'M A STRANGER IN A
DREADFUL MAZE
OF
DEVIL'S
HAPPY CHILDREN ON A SAD
PLAYGROUND

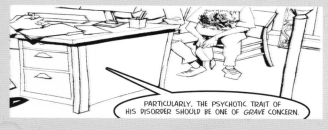

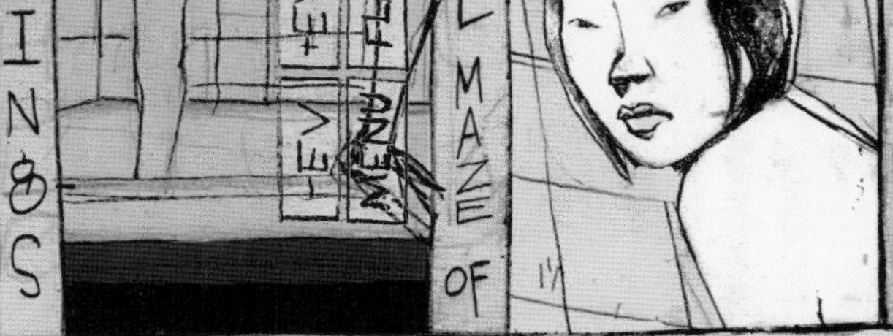
PARTICULARLY, THE PSYCHOTIC TRAIT OF HIS DISORDER SHOULD BE ONE OF *GRAVE* CONCERN.

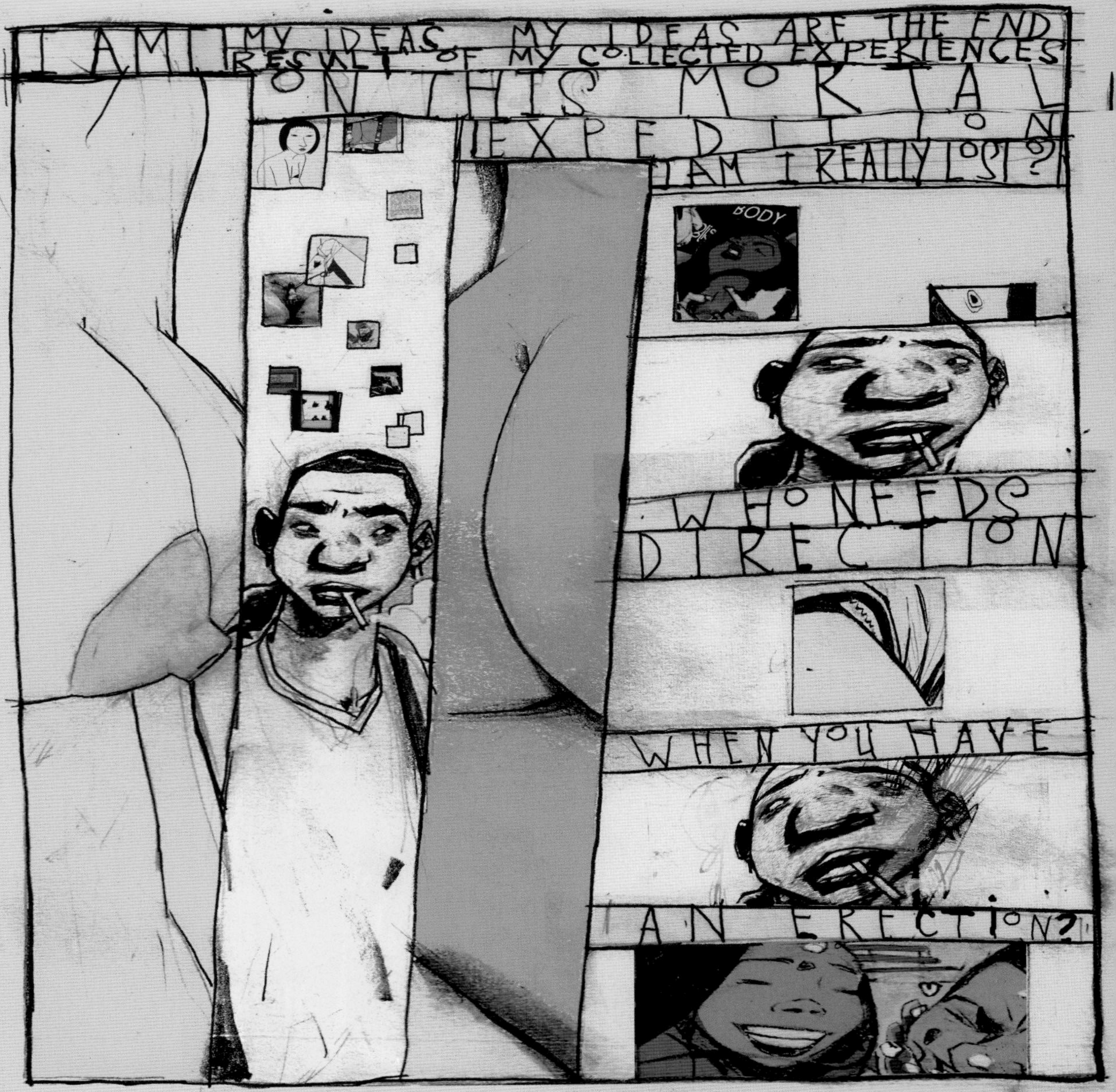
I AM I
MY IDEAS, MY IDEAS ARE THE END RESULT OF MY COLLECTED EXPERIENCES
ON THIS MORTAL EXPEDITION
AM I REALLY LOST?
BODY
WHO NEEDS DIRECTION
WHEN YOU HAVE
AN ERECTION?

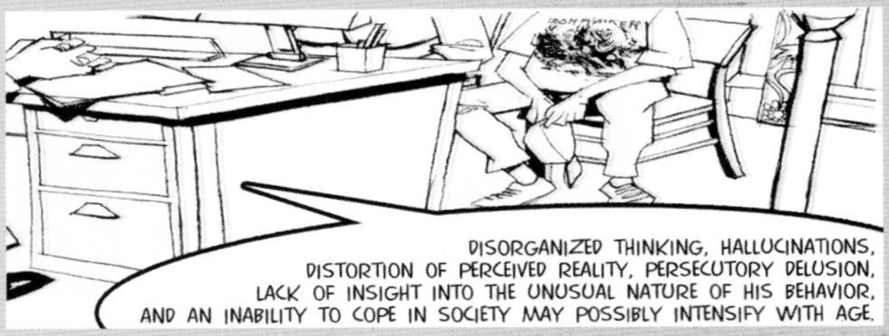
DISORGANIZED THINKING, HALLUCINATIONS, DISTORTION OF PERCEIVED REALITY, PERSECUTORY DELUSION, LACK OF INSIGHT INTO THE UNUSUAL NATURE OF HIS BEHAVIOR, AND AN INABILITY TO COPE IN SOCIETY MAY POSSIBLY INTENSIFY WITH AGE.

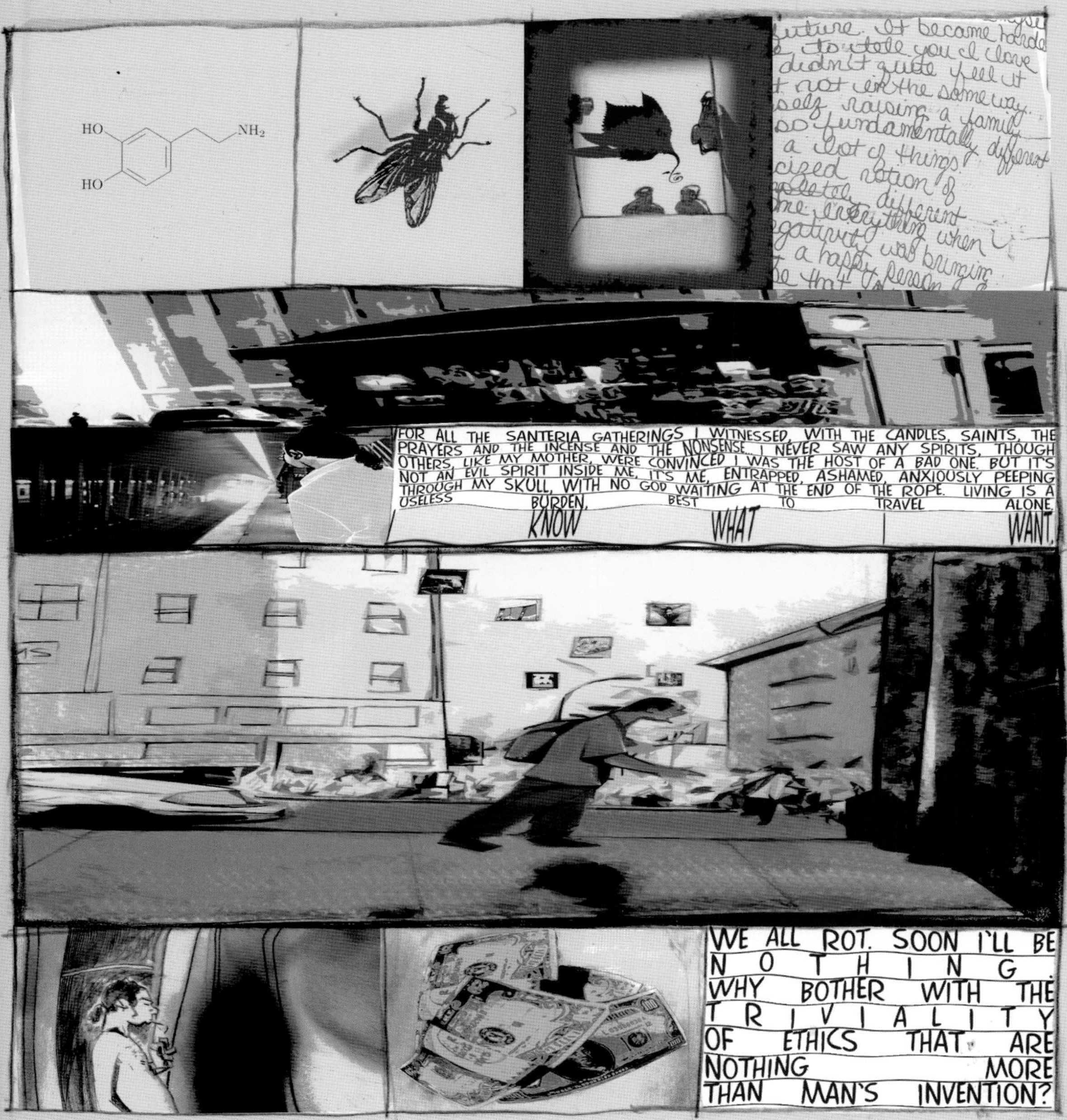
HO
HO
NH_2
FOR ALL THE SANTERIA GATHERINGS I WITNESSED, WITH THE CANDLES, SAINTS, THE PRAYERS AND THE INCENSE AND THE NONSENSE, I NEVER SAW ANY SPIRITS, THOUGH OTHERS, LIKE MY MOTHER, WERE CONVINCED I WAS THE HOST OF A BAD ONE. BUT IT'S NOT AN EVIL SPIRIT INSIDE ME, IT'S ME, ENTRAPPED, ASHAMED, ANXIOUSLY PEEPING THROUGH MY SKULL, WITH NO GOD WAITING AT THE END OF THE ROPE. LIVING IS A USELESS BURDEN, BEST TO TRAVEL ALONE.
KNOW WHAT WANT.
WE ALL ROT. SOON I'LL BE N O T H I N G. WHY BOTHER WITH THE T R I V I A L I T Y OF ETHICS THAT ARE NOTHING MORE THAN MAN'S INVENTION?

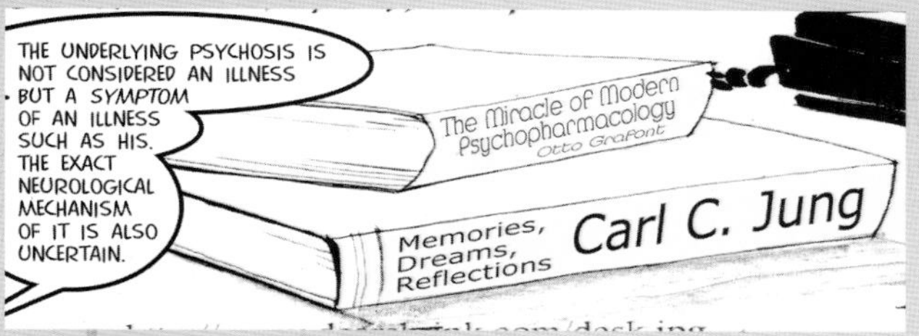
THE UNDERLYING PSYCHOSIS IS NOT CONSIDERED AN ILLNESS BUT A *SYMPTOM* OF AN ILLNESS SUCH AS HIS. THE EXACT NEUROLOGICAL MECHANISM OF IT IS ALSO UNCERTAIN.
The Miracle of Modern Psychopharmacology
Otto Grafont
Memories, Dreams, Reflections
Carl C. Jung

IAKCLAKCIAKCLAK CIAKCLAK CIAKCLAK CIAKCLAK CIAKCL

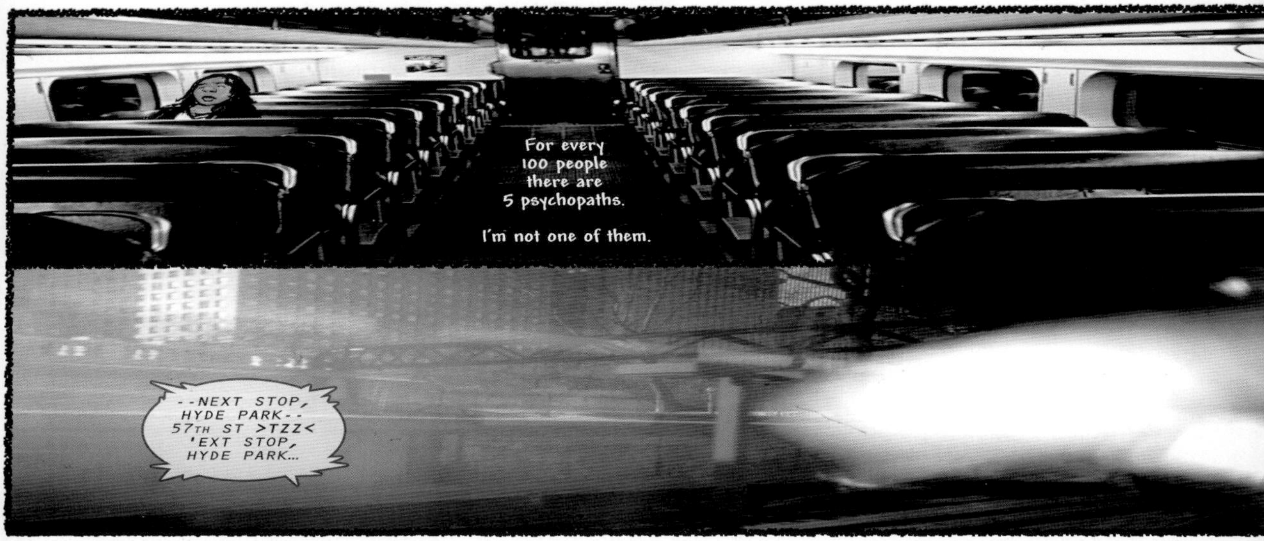
For every 100 people there are 5 psychopaths.
I'm not one of them.
--NEXT STOP, HYDE PARK-- 57TH ST >TZZ< 'EXT STOP, HYDE PARK...

An unjustly psychotic label for people with unconventional views of reality facilitates society's control over them. There's nothing wrong with me and I don't need to be molded with medications.

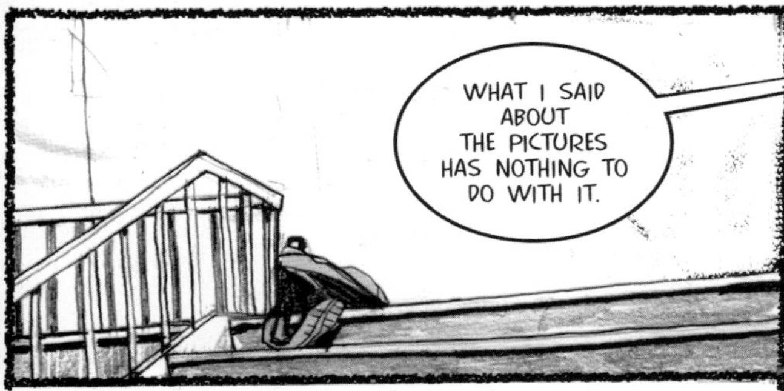
WHAT I SAID ABOUT THE PICTURES HAS NOTHING TO DO WITH IT.

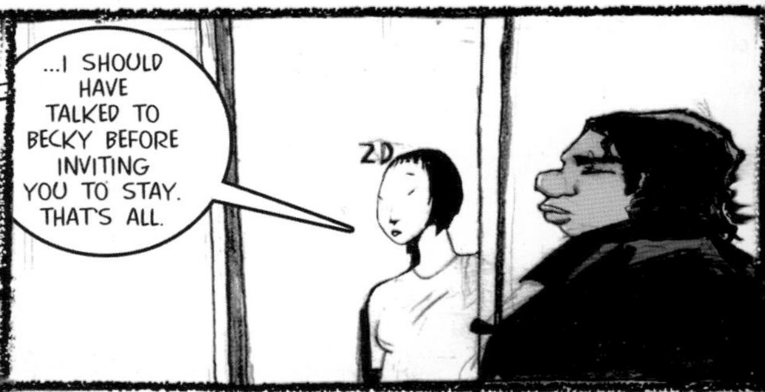
...I SHOULD HAVE TALKED TO BECKY BEFORE INVITING YOU TO STAY. THAT'S ALL.

I get depressed because life is pain.

We comply and then we die.

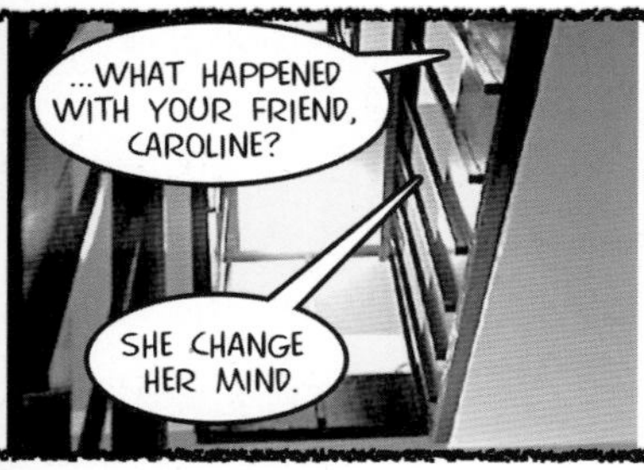
...WHAT HAPPENED WITH YOUR FRIEND, CAROLINE?
SHE CHANGE HER MIND.

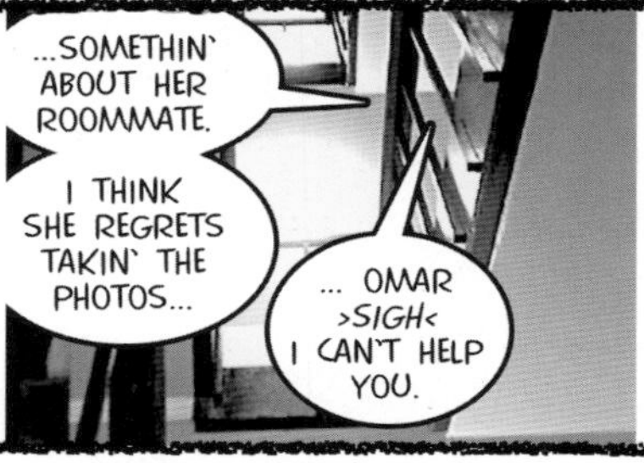
...SOMETHIN' ABOUT HER ROOMMATE.
I THINK SHE REGRETS TAKIN' THE PHOTOS...
... OMAR >SIGH< I CAN'T HELP YOU.

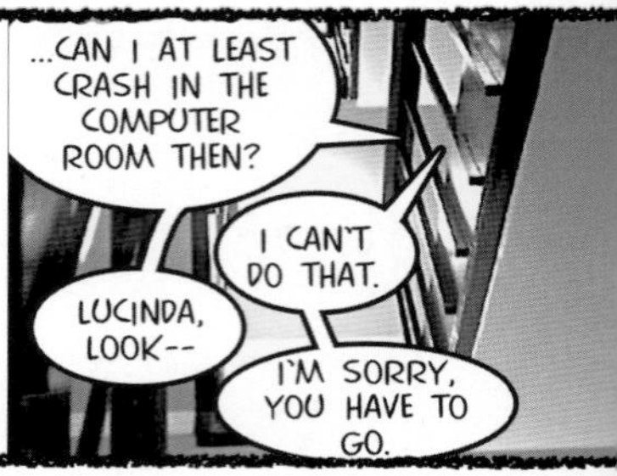
...CAN I AT LEAST CRASH IN THE COMPUTER ROOM THEN?
LUCINDA, LOOK--
I CAN'T DO THAT.
I'M SORRY, YOU HAVE TO GO.

I am manic because I love earthly delights, but I don't have time. I want it all at once or not at all, so as to drown the pain with pleasures, knowing that no matter how good a thing gets, it'll eventually end. My reality is what I see.

I don't believe in ghosts, good or evil, god, religion, governments.
I don't believe in anything. I'm weak and afraid; I can't even control my thoughts. I drink because there's no point to quitting.

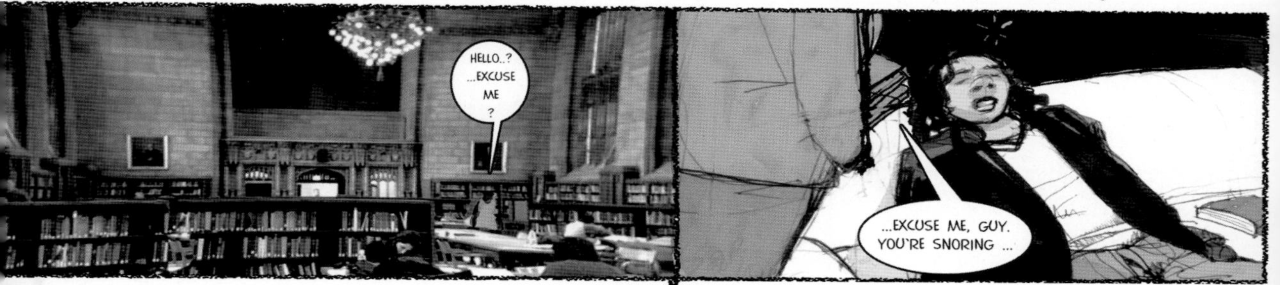
HELLO..? ...EXCUSE ME ?
...EXCUSE ME, GUY. YOU'RE SNORING ...

I'm no different from the rest. Excrement comes in all kinds of textures.

I'm a caged animal.
While abiding by an arbitrary system of values,
we're asked to remain calm, as we devour one another.

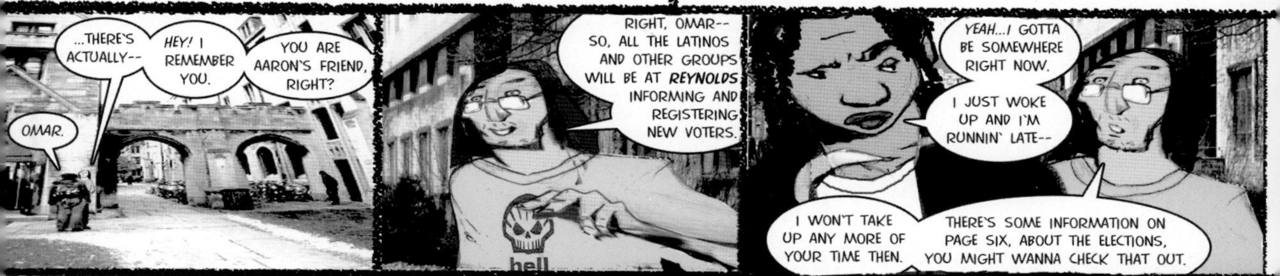
OMAR.
...THERE'S ACTUALLY--
HEY! I REMEMBER YOU.
YOU ARE AARON'S FRIEND, RIGHT?
RIGHT, OMAR-- SO, ALL THE LATINOS AND OTHER GROUPS WILL BE AT REYNOLDS INFORMING AND REGISTERING NEW VOTERS.
YEAH...I GOTTA BE SOMEWHERE RIGHT NOW.
I JUST WOKE UP AND I'M RUNNIN' LATE--
THERE'S SOME INFORMATION ON PAGE SIX, ABOUT THE ELECTIONS, YOU MIGHT WANNA CHECK THAT OUT.
I WON'T TAKE UP ANY MORE OF YOUR TIME THEN.

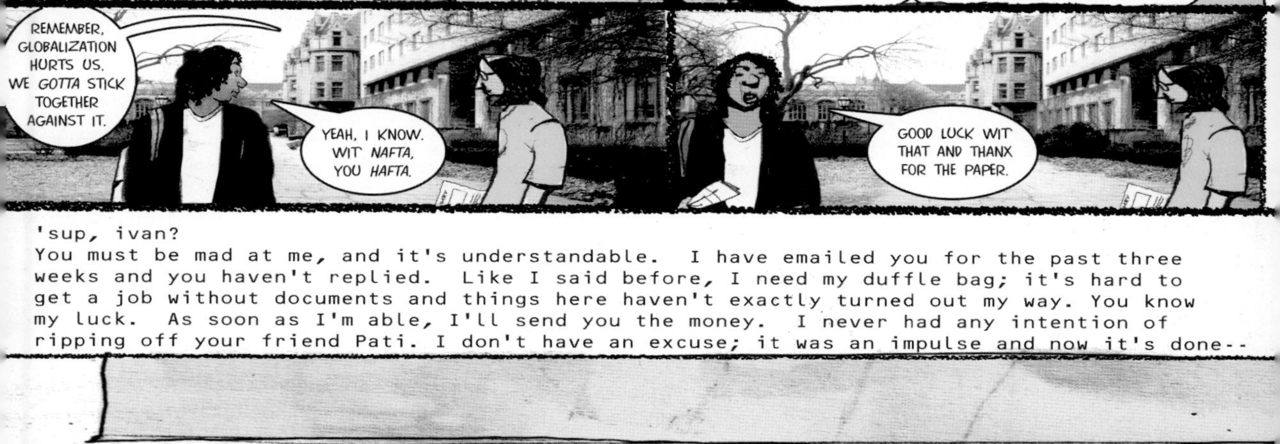
REMEMBER, GLOBALIZATION HURTS US. WE GOTTA STICK TOGETHER AGAINST IT.
YEAH, I KNOW. WIT' NAFTA, YOU HAFTA.
GOOD LUCK WIT' THAT AND THANX FOR THE PAPER.

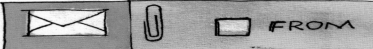

'sup, ivan?
You must be mad at me, and it's understandable. I have emailed you for the past three weeks and you haven't replied. Like I said before, I need my duffle bag; it's hard to get a job without documents and things here haven't exactly turned out my way. You know my luck. As soon as I'm able, I'll send you the money. I never had any intention of ripping off your friend Pati. I don't have an excuse; it was an impulse and now it's done--

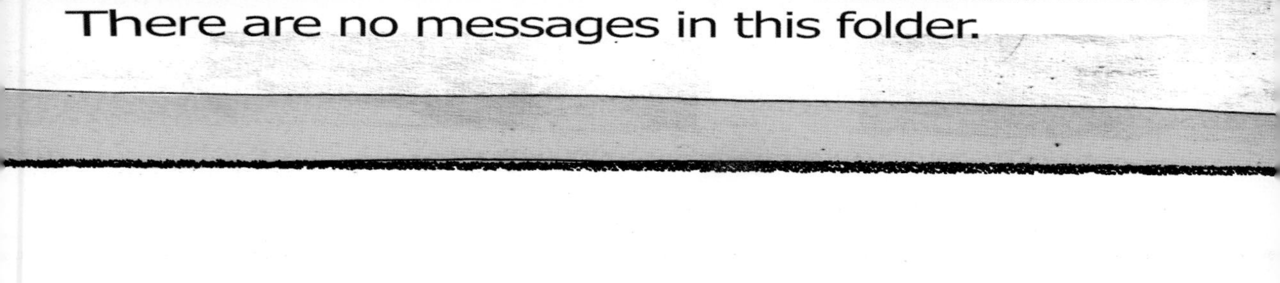
FROM
SU
There are no messages in this folder.

Anyway, I hope you can forgive me. I'm not doing great but it can always get worse.
When it comes down to it, all I need to survive is food and sleep, right?
--Again, my apologies. Take care,
Your cousin,
O. G.

☑ COPY MESSAGE TO SENT FOLDER

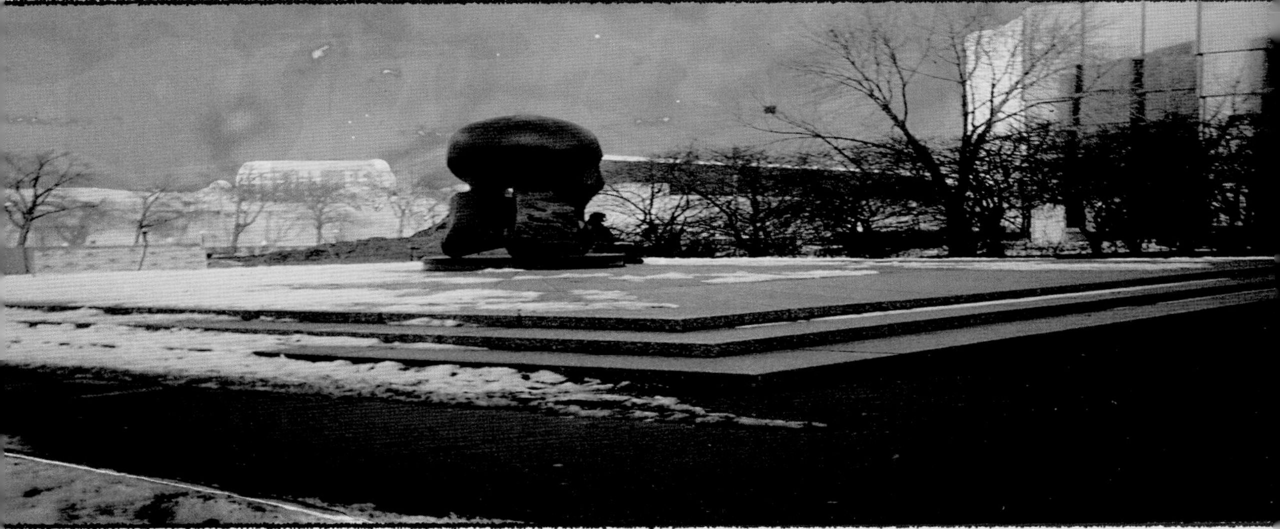

With such ease people come and go from our lives,
and memories are the only things that remain.
Memories, electric data stored in a mass of nerve tissue.
Just a mass of nerve tissue. Just a mass.

We never stood a chance, Lucinda.
No matter what your feelings for me were.
I rush after pleasure so fast that I might have rushed right past it.

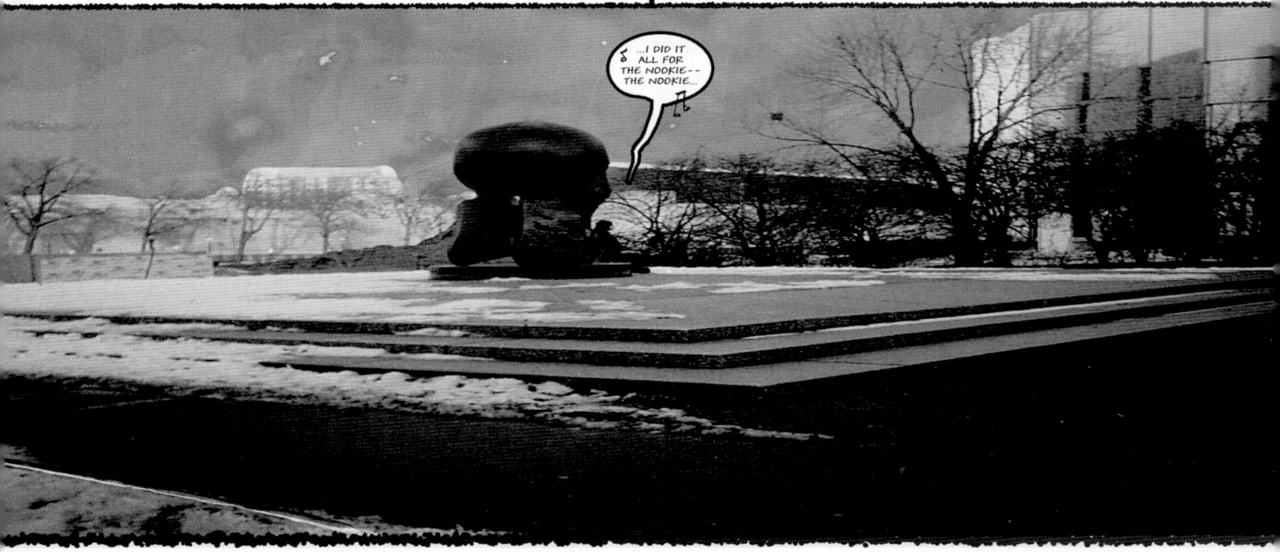
...I DID IT ALL FOR THE NOOKIE-- THE NOOKIE...

Something is missing in my life;
I don't know what I need to make life bearable other than lies and I don't look for what I need. I seek the things I want, things I desire.

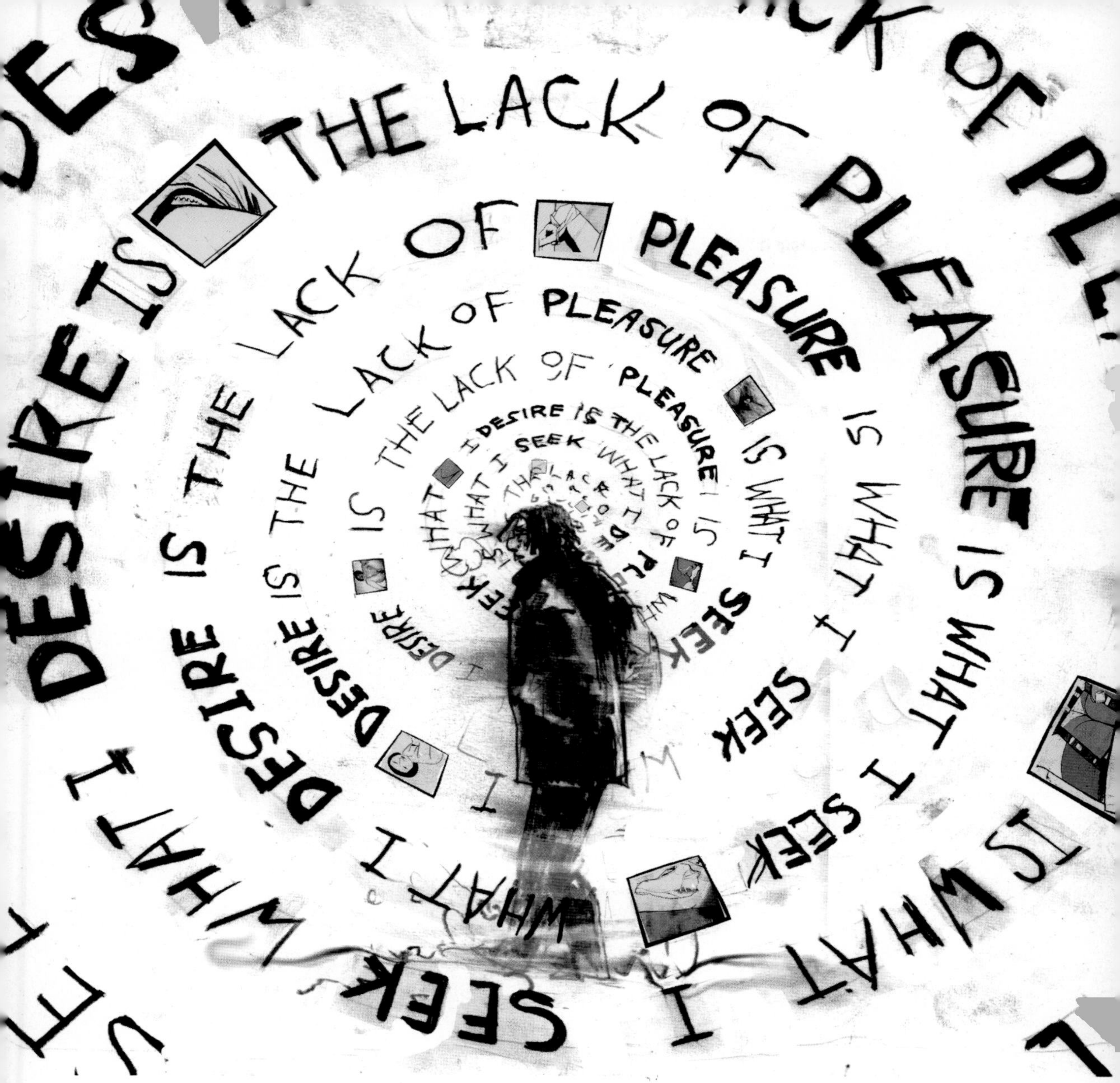
DESIRE IS THE LACK OF PLEASURE IS WHAT I SEEK
DESIRE IS THE LACK OF PLEASURE IS WHAT I SEEK
DESIRE IS THE LACK OF PLEASURE IS WHAT I SEEK
DESIRE IS THE LACK OF PLEASURE IS WHAT I SEEK
I DESIRE IS THE LACK OF PLEASURE IS WHAT I SEEK

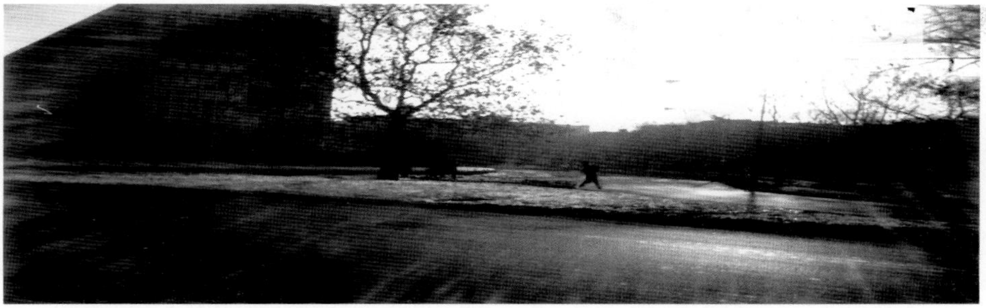

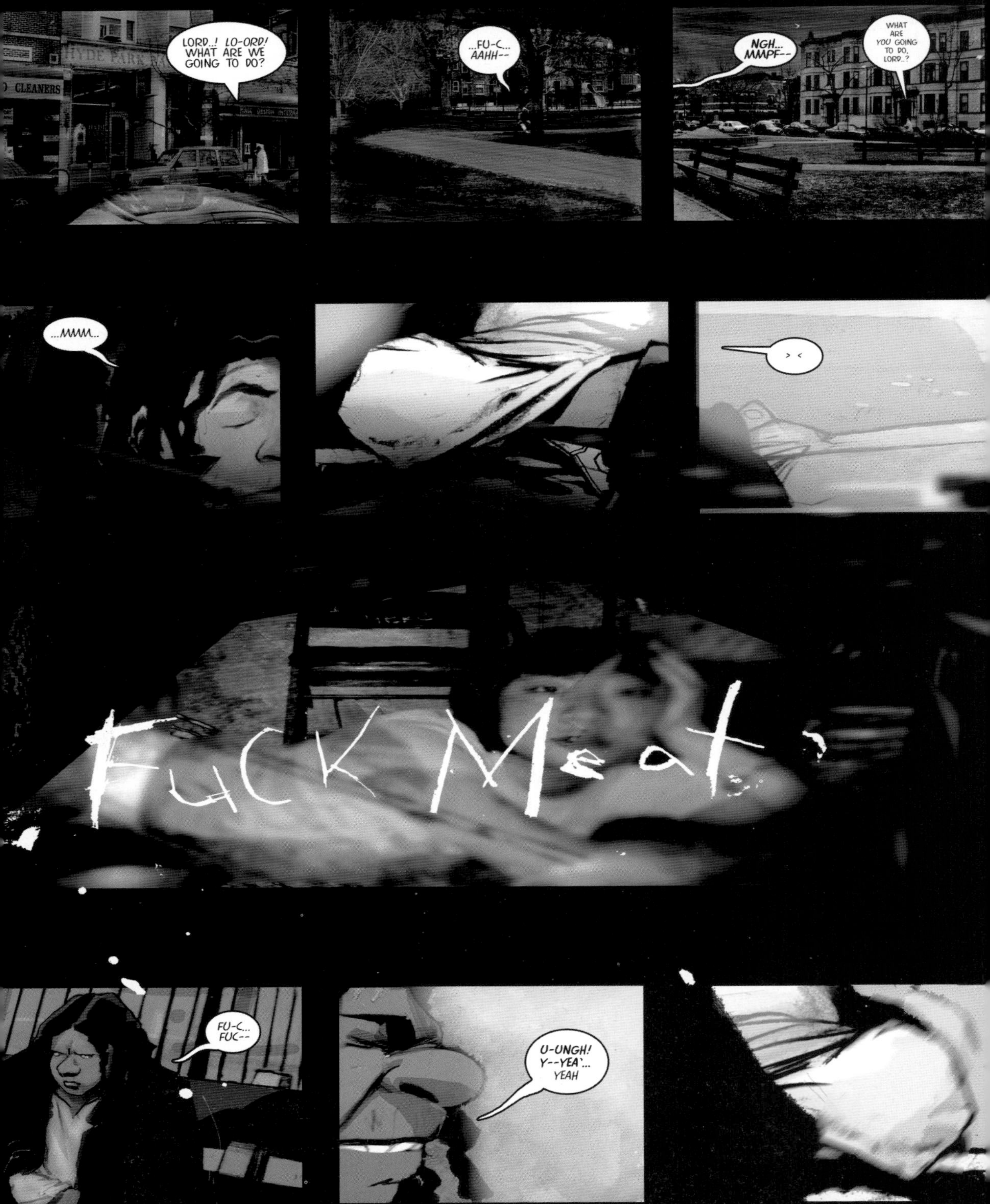
LORD..! LO-ORD! WHAT ARE WE GOING TO DO?
...FU-C... AAHH--
NGH... MMPF--
WHAT ARE YOU GOING TO DO, LORD..?
...MMM...
> <
FUCK Meat
FU-C... FUC--
U-UNGH! Y--YEA`... YEAH

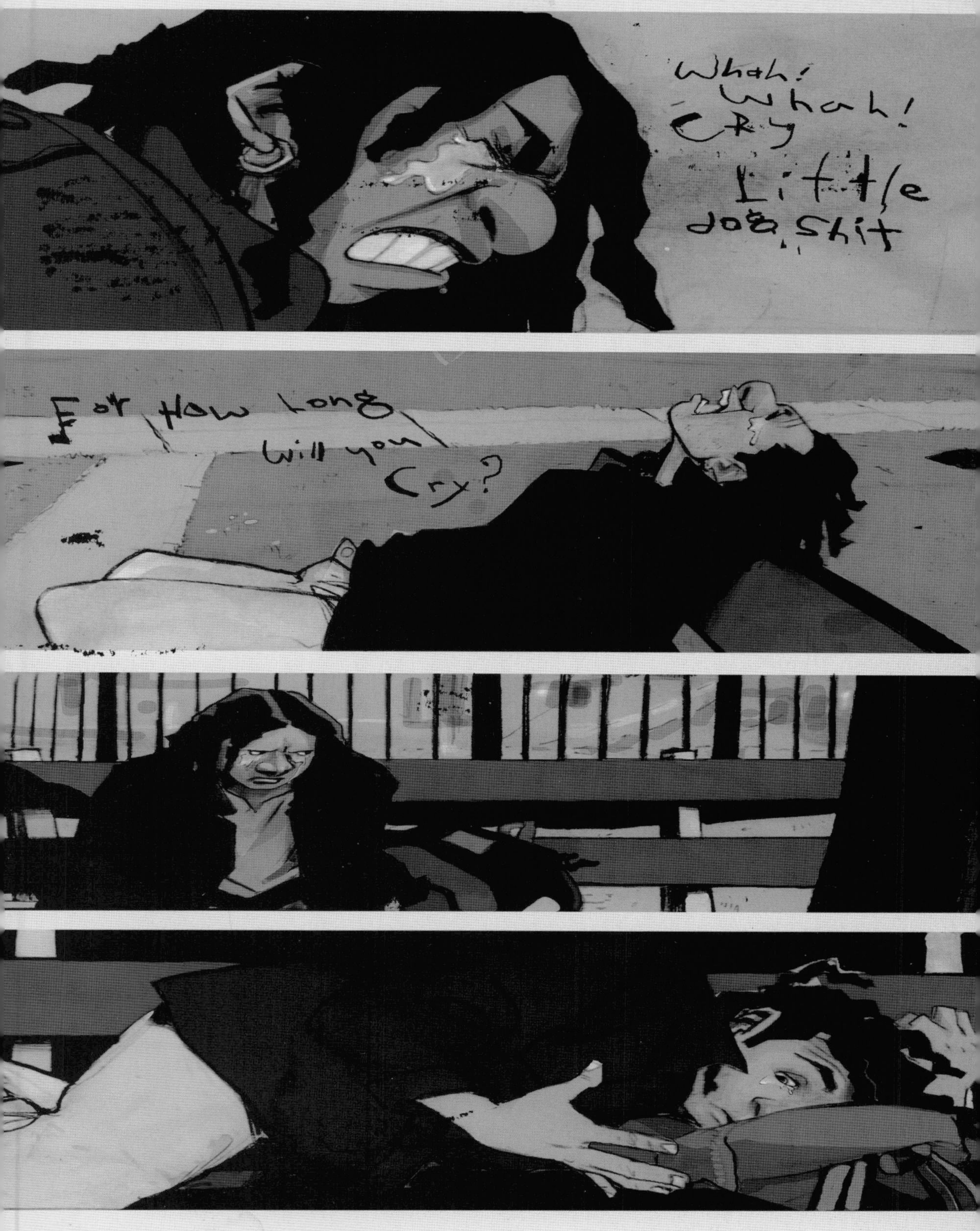
Whah! Whah! Cry Little dog shit
For How Long will you Cry?

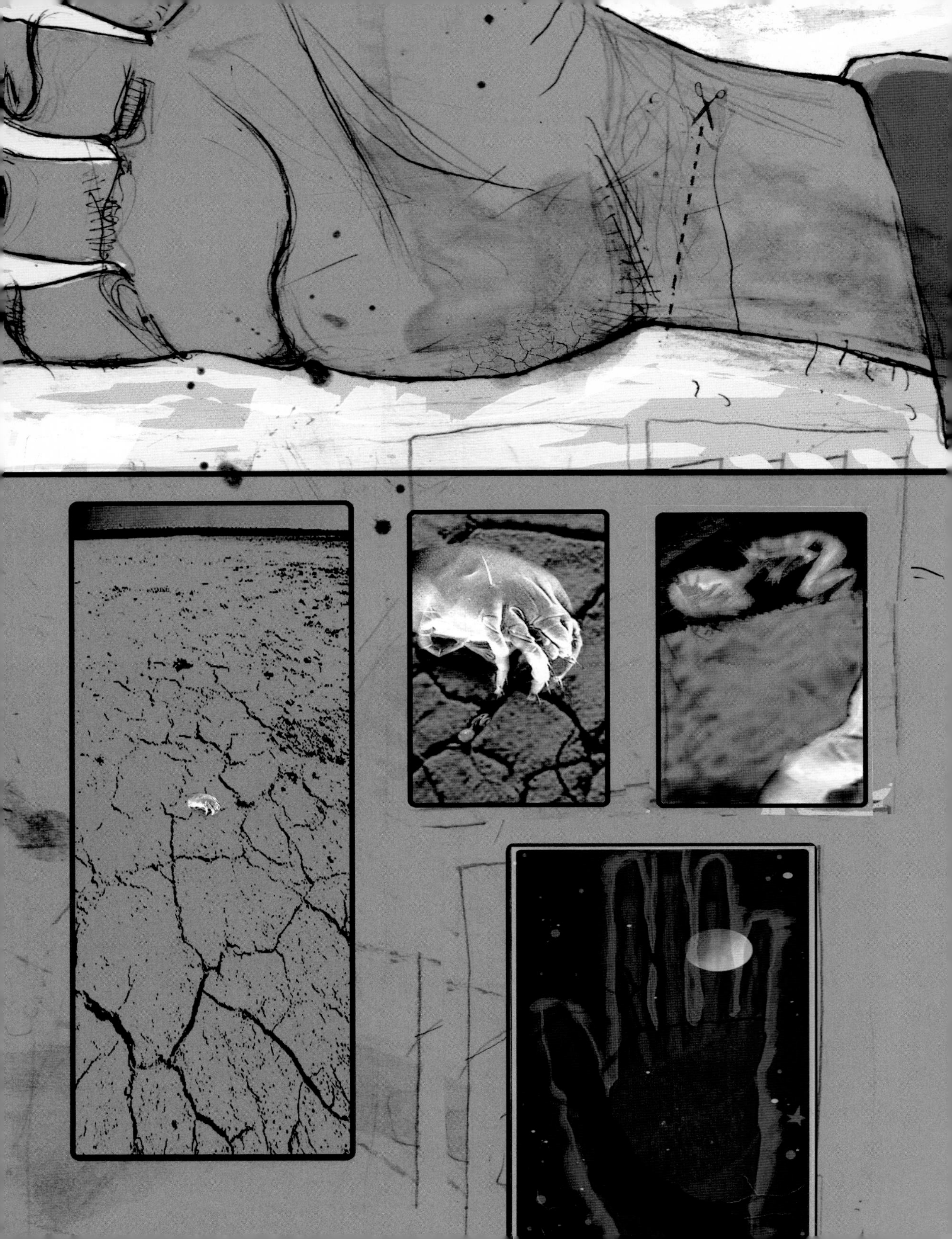

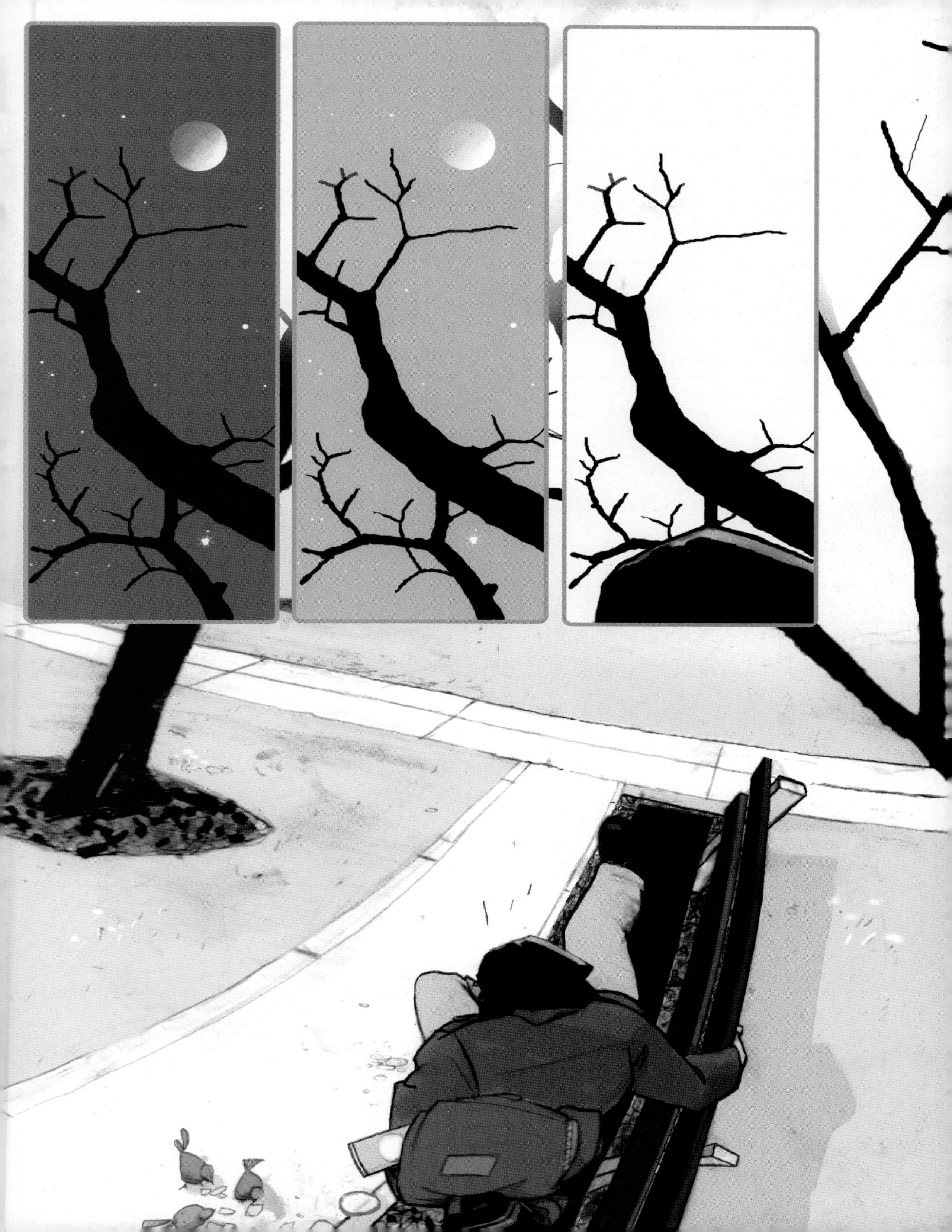

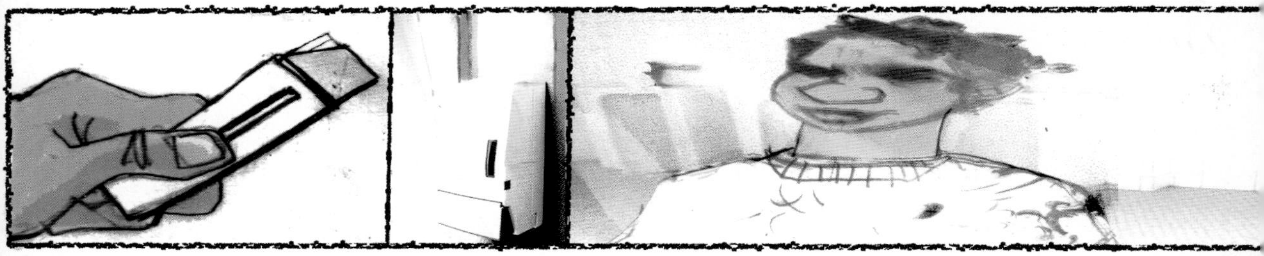

I think it's time for you to move on.

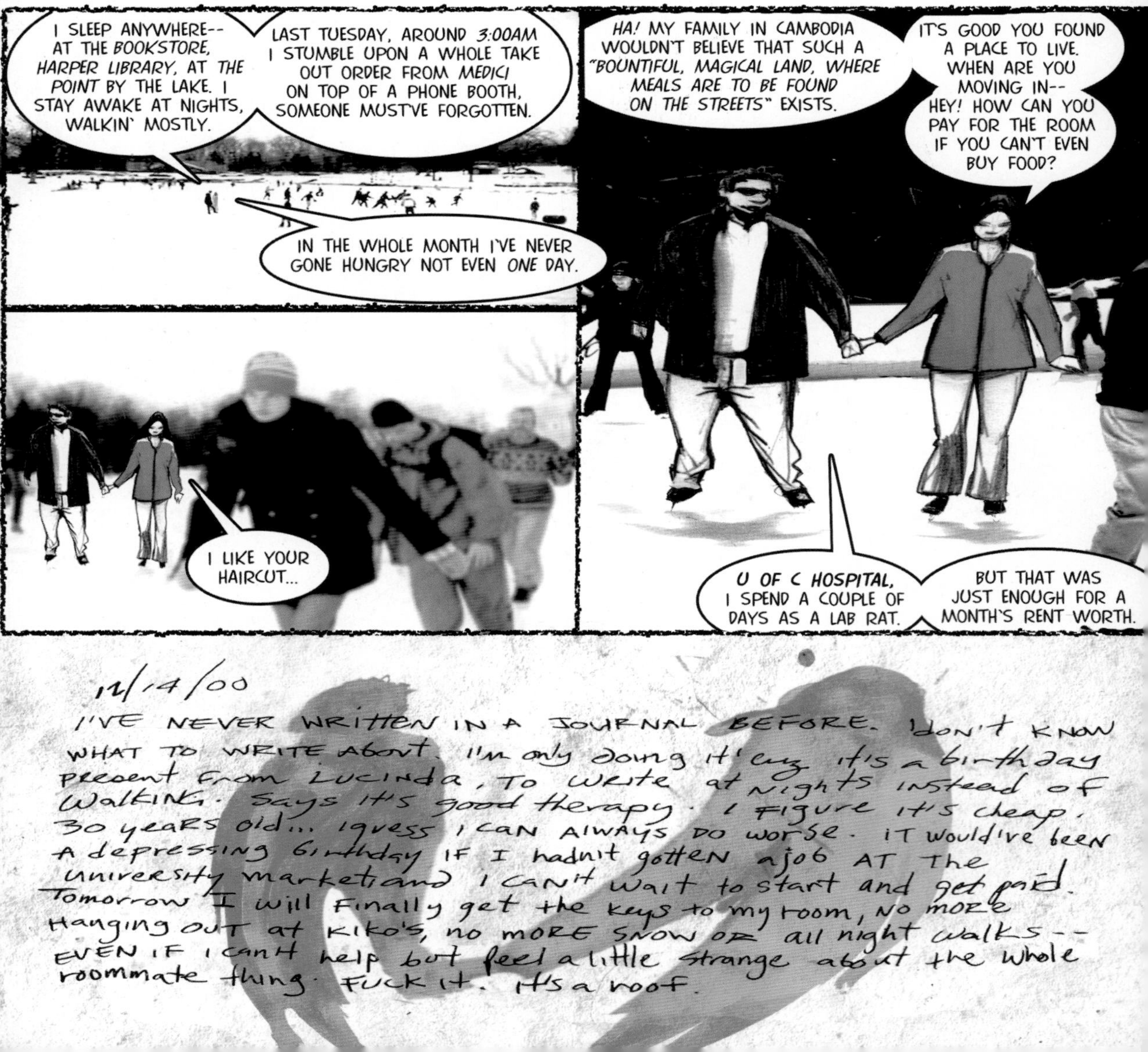

I SLEEP ANYWHERE-- AT THE BOOKSTORE, HARPER LIBRARY, AT THE POINT BY THE LAKE. I STAY AWAKE AT NIGHTS, WALKIN' MOSTLY.
LAST TUESDAY, AROUND 3:00AM I STUMBLE UPON A WHOLE TAKE OUT ORDER FROM MEDICI ON TOP OF A PHONE BOOTH, SOMEONE MUST'VE FORGOTTEN.
IN THE WHOLE MONTH I'VE NEVER GONE HUNGRY NOT EVEN ONE DAY.
HA! MY FAMILY IN CAMBODIA WOULDN'T BELIEVE THAT SUCH A "BOUNTIFUL, MAGICAL LAND, WHERE MEALS ARE TO BE FOUND ON THE STREETS" EXISTS.
IT'S GOOD YOU FOUND A PLACE TO LIVE. WHEN ARE YOU MOVING IN-- HEY! HOW CAN YOU PAY FOR THE ROOM IF YOU CAN'T EVEN BUY FOOD?
U OF C HOSPITAL, I SPEND A COUPLE OF DAYS AS A LAB RAT.
BUT THAT WAS JUST ENOUGH FOR A MONTH'S RENT WORTH.
I LIKE YOUR HAIRCUT...

11/14/00

I'VE NEVER WRITTEN IN A JOURNAL BEFORE. DON'T KNOW WHAT TO WRITE ABOUT. I'M ONLY DOING IT CUZ IT'S A BIRTHDAY PRESENT FROM LUCINDA, TO WRITE AT NIGHTS INSTEAD OF WALKING. SAYS IT'S GOOD THERAPY. I FIGURE IT'S CHEAP. 30 YEARS OLD... I GUESS I CAN ALWAYS DO WORSE. IT WOULD'VE BEEN A DEPRESSING BIRTHDAY IF I HADN'T GOTTEN A JOB AT THE UNIVERSITY MARKET AND I CAN'T WAIT TO START AND GET PAID. TOMORROW I WILL FINALLY GET THE KEYS TO MY ROOM, NO MORE HANGING OUT AT KIKO'S, NO MORE SNOW OR ALL NIGHT WALKS -- EVEN IF I CAN'T HELP BUT FEEL A LITTLE STRANGE ABOUT THE WHOLE ROOMMATE THING. FUCK IT. IT'S A ROOF.

Surprisingly, Lucinda and I are actually becoming friends. It [redacted] takes time to talk to get used to it. It feels good to talk to her without the demands of a relationship.

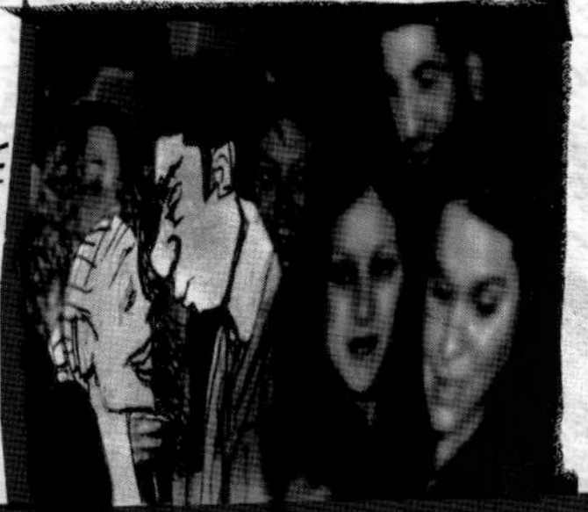

There's this dream I have never told her about where I'm walking down a street @ night and I sneak into some kinda frat party and the girl I'm trying to get it on with [redacted] is actually the suicide girl. She feels ill and I follow her to the washroom [redacted] ~~follow her to the washroom~~ and [redacted] I take advantage of her being fuck:d up.

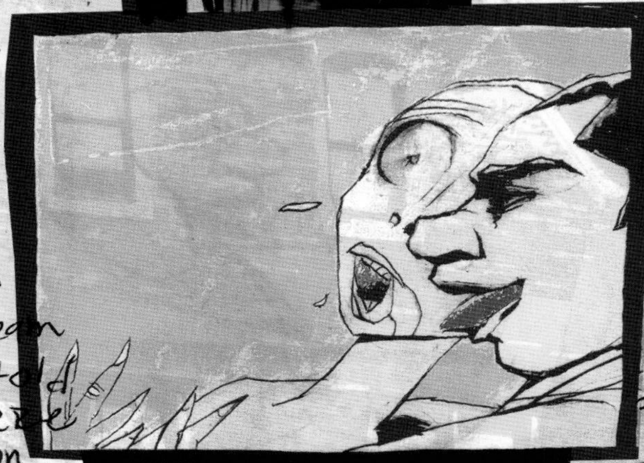

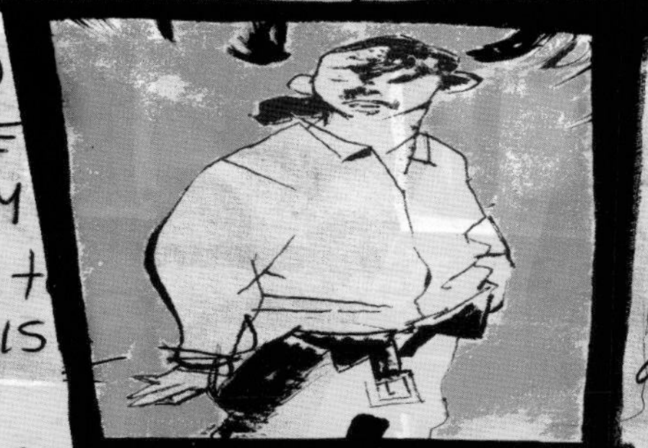

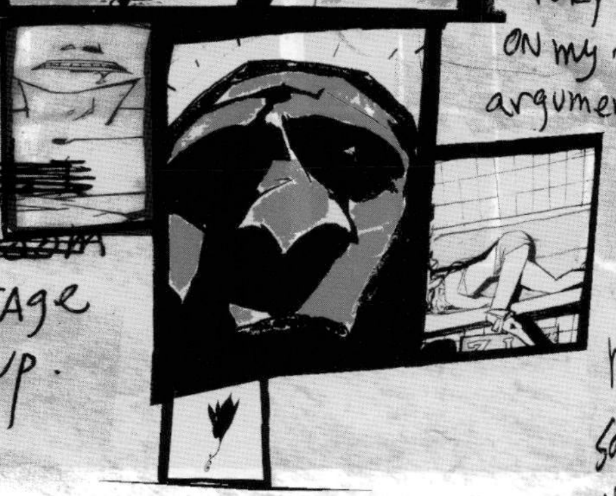

Then the bathtub slowly begins to descent into a hole, like a casket, as faceless figures observe. Then everything goes black.

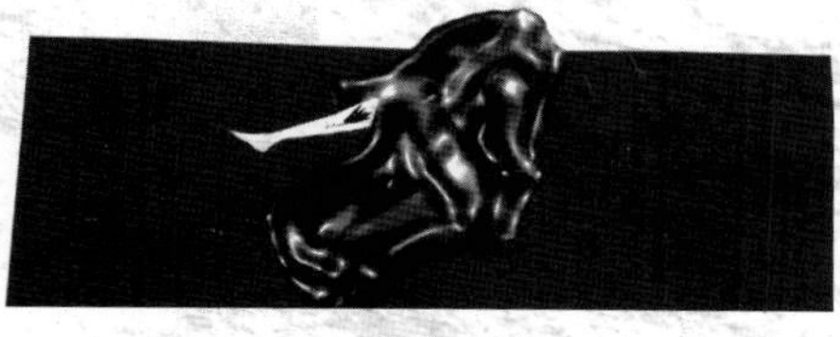

I don't even know what this girl Sara ~~really looks~~ really looks like, apart from the tatoo I saw on her that day, as Lucinda, I and other shaken Snell residents waited for her body to be taken away. Soon after that, I began to have this dream.

It's no surprise that no one knows much about it or why she did it? Suicides on campuses are always kept very low-key. It's not good PR.

On my 28th birthday I had an argument with Lucinda at Calypso café, I got up and left. I was really drunk, but I vaguely remember, later on, going inside the same frat house. My dream might not be a dream after all.

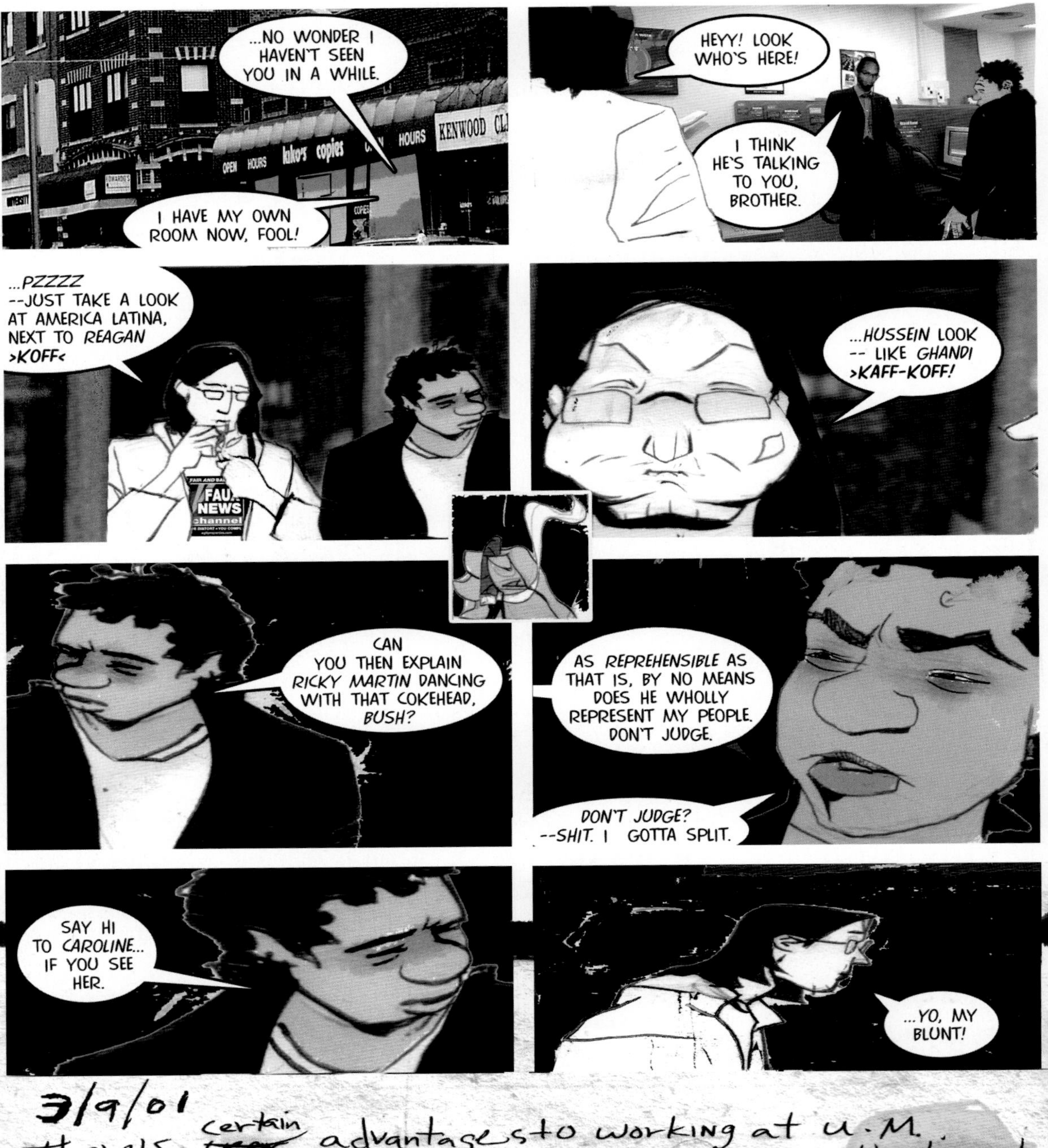

...NO WONDER I HAVEN'T SEEN YOU IN A WHILE.
I HAVE MY OWN ROOM NOW, FOOL!
KENWOOD CL
OPEN HOURS kiko's copies OPEN HOURS
HEYY! LOOK WHO'S HERE!
I THINK HE'S TALKING TO YOU, BROTHER.
...PZZZZ --JUST TAKE A LOOK AT AMERICA LATINA, NEXT TO *REAGAN* **>KOFF<**
FAUX NEWS channel
...HUSSEIN LOOK -- LIKE *GHANDI* **>KAFF-KOFF!**
CAN YOU THEN EXPLAIN *RICKY MARTIN* DANCING WITH THAT COKEHEAD, *BUSH?*
AS *REPREHENSIBLE* AS THAT IS, BY NO MEANS DOES HE WHOLLY REPRESENT MY PEOPLE. DON'T JUDGE.
DON'T JUDGE? --SHIT. I GOTTA SPLIT.
SAY HI TO *CAROLINE*... IF YOU SEE HER.
...YO, MY BLUNT!

3/9/01
there's ~~tear~~ certain advantages to working at U.M. Like free food and beautiful girls coming in all the time. I haven't gained any weight back, so I'm looking pretty good. [redacted] there's not a week that I don't get some digits. Funny how things work. Once I resigned to the idea of not being involved with Lucinda, she decided to get back together. We might even have a future.

Today is a very special day. We are moving in together. Lucinda has never had a pet, so I bought her a kitty. His name is Homer. After the writer. Not the cartoon character. There's a lot of skepticism in me about all this, but what are my options? I have to do something. I do feel a little intimideted, now that she is about to become a history professor. I decided I'm gonna get a diploma in culinary arts. I like cooking so what the hell. Lucinda seems pleased. No one knows me better than she does. Amaizingly she's fine with it this time, though I have never asked her why. She can keep that as her secret. I keep mine. For all the "Bad luck" I'm lucky to be with someone of her character... and such a fine ass too!

Even her optimism has start to rub off on me, but not too much. It's not all rosy particularly during my mood swings but I'm trying to get better. I'm not drinking as much as I used to, mainly because of the stomach pains. I can't say I'm Happy, but I'm content. I'm taking things in stride. There's a lot of work ahead and my brain needs constant vigilance. When Lucinda is around, everything is easier. I laugh more than usual. She's the best laughs I ever had, without having to HURT SOMEONE :)

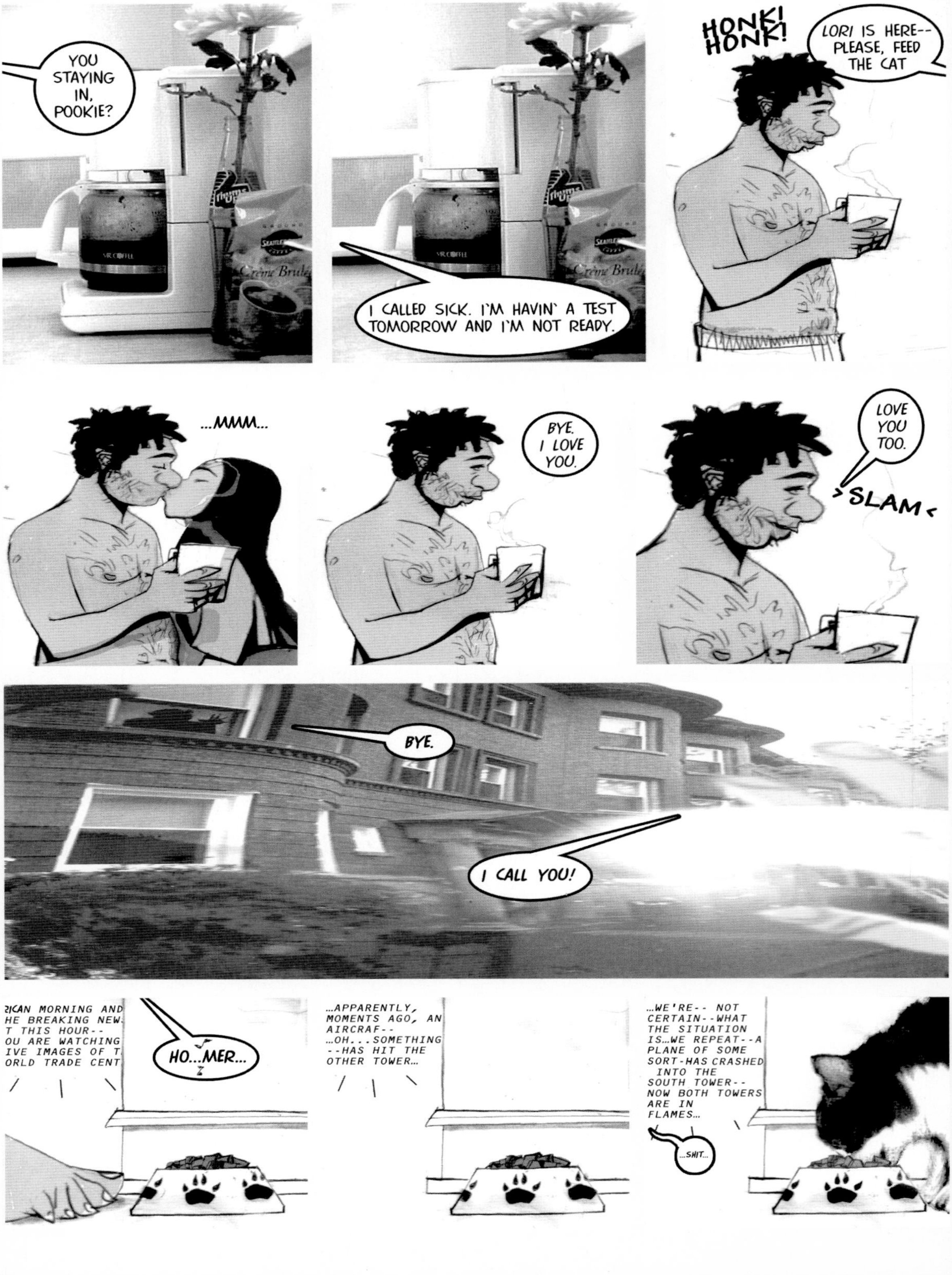
YOU STAYING IN, POOKIE?
I CALLED SICK. I'M HAVIN' A TEST TOMORROW AND I'M NOT READY.
HONK! HONK!
LORI IS HERE-- PLEASE, FEED THE CAT
...MMM...
BYE. I LOVE YOU.
LOVE YOU TOO.
>SLAM<
BYE.
I CALL YOU!
RICAN MORNING AND
HE BREAKING NEW
T THIS HOUR--
OU ARE WATCHING
IVE IMAGES OF T
ORLD TRADE CENT
HO...MER...
...APPARENTLY, MOMENTS AGO, AN AIRCRAF-- ...OH...SOMETHING --HAS HIT THE OTHER TOWER...
...WE'RE-- NOT CERTAIN--WHAT THE SITUATION IS...WE REPEAT--A PLANE OF SOME SORT-HAS CRASHED INTO THE SOUTH TOWER--NOW BOTH TOWERS ARE IN FLAMES...
...SHIT...

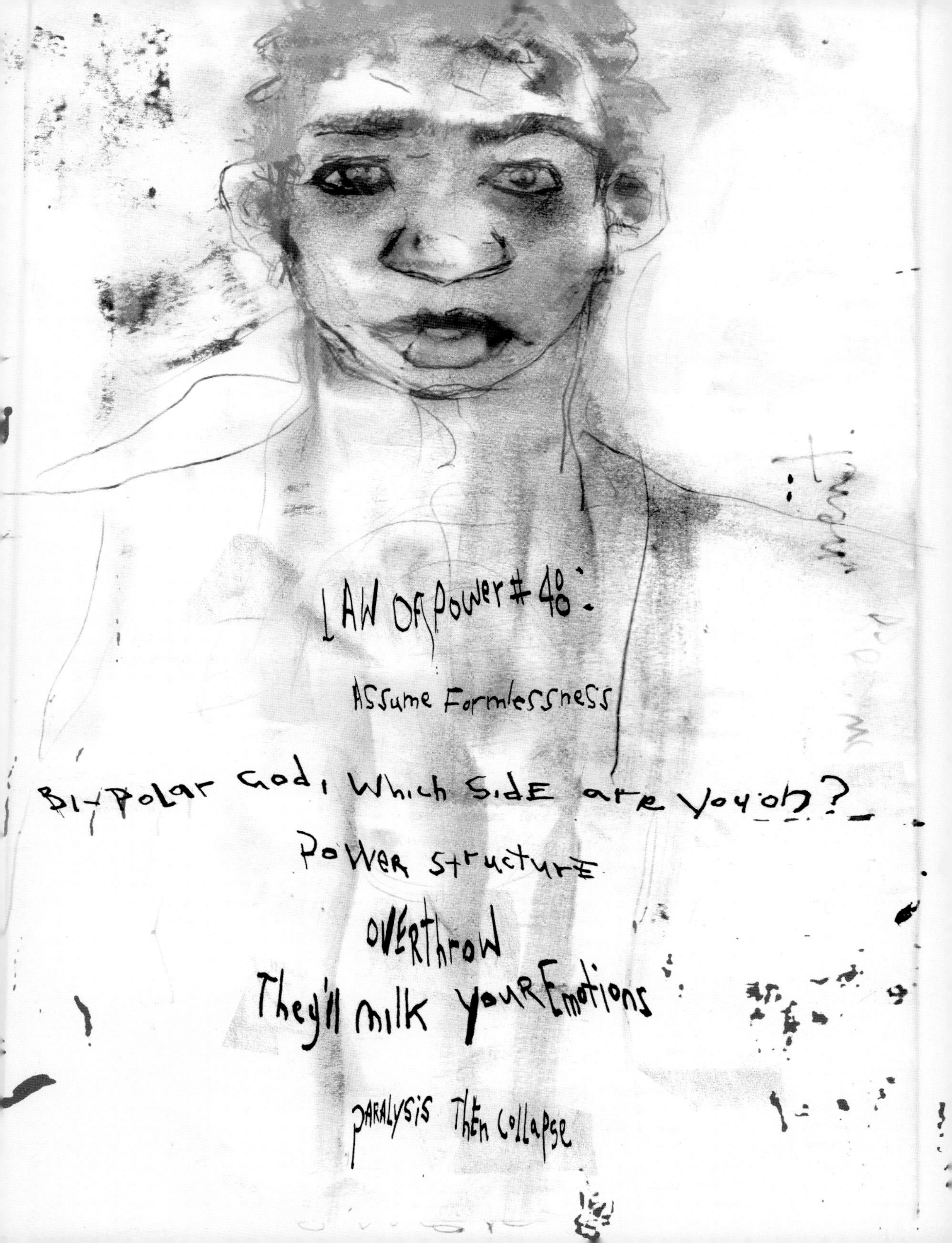
LAW OF POWER #48:
Assume Formlessness
Bi-Polar God, Which SidE are you on?
PoWER structurE
OVERthrow
They'll milk yourEmotions
paralysis Then collapse

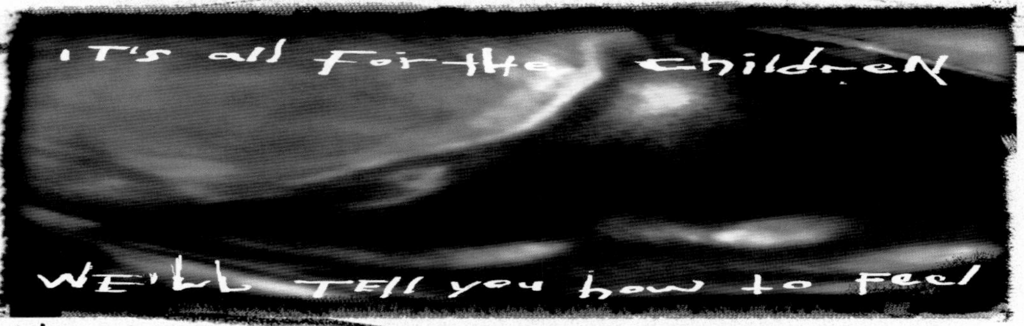
it's all for the children
WE'LL TELL you how to Feel

drink up, Fall down Drink up Fall down

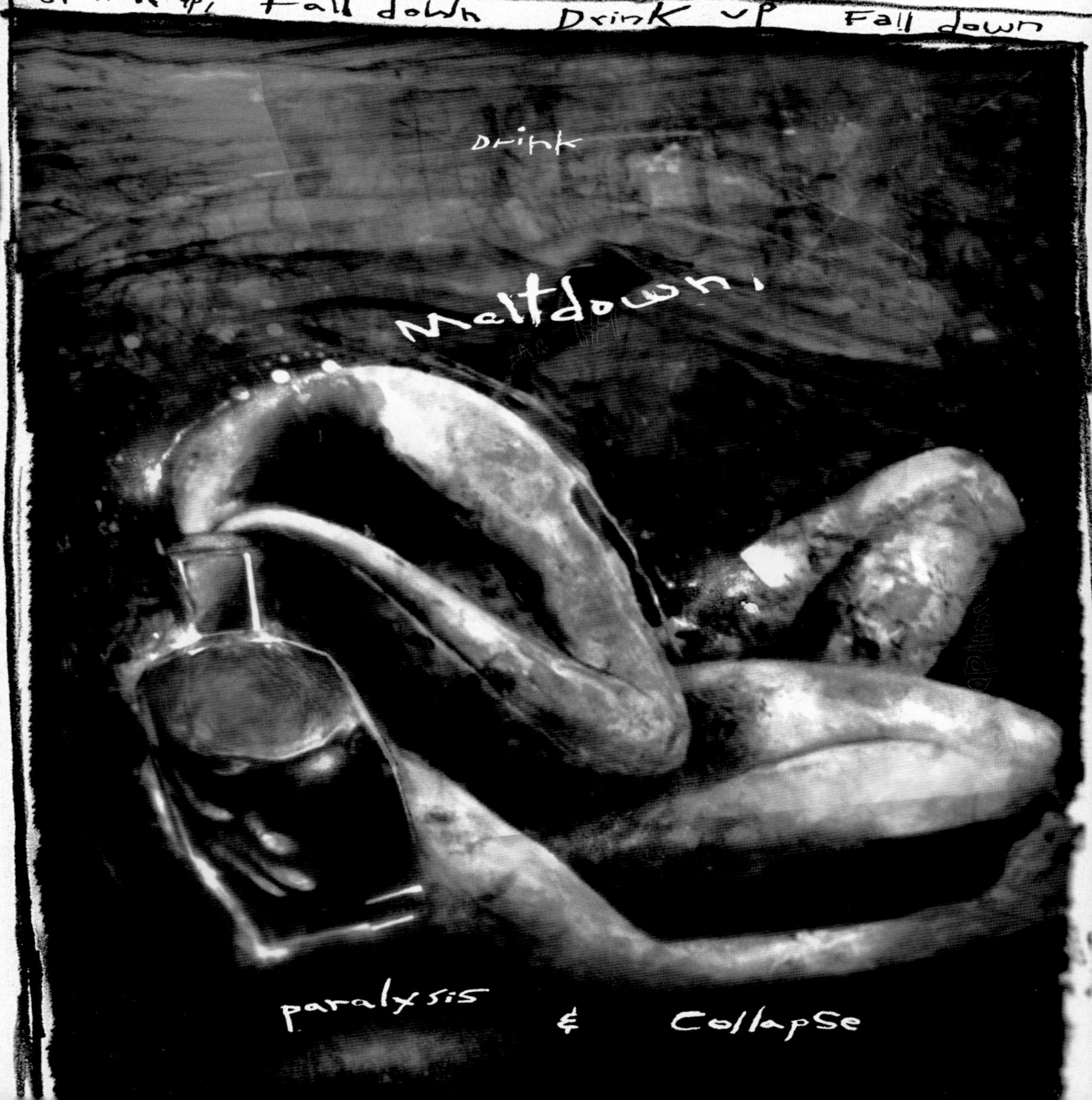
drink
Meltdown,
paralysis & Collapse

it will get bad before it gets worse

There's a Hero in all of us   Martyrs!

Let's Go, the kids are ready
have been trained for YEARS
on their old Nintendos

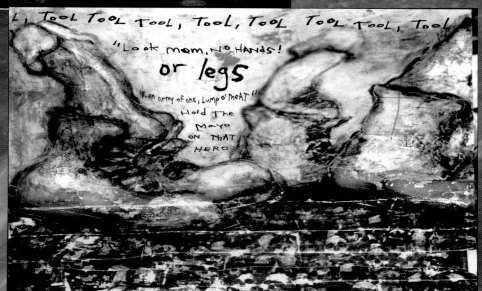

L, Tool Tool Tool, Tool, Tool Tool Tool, Tool

"Look mom, No Hands!
or legs

"An army of one, Lump o' meat"
Hold The
Mayo
on That
Hero

TOC TIC TOC TIC TOC TIC TOC TIC

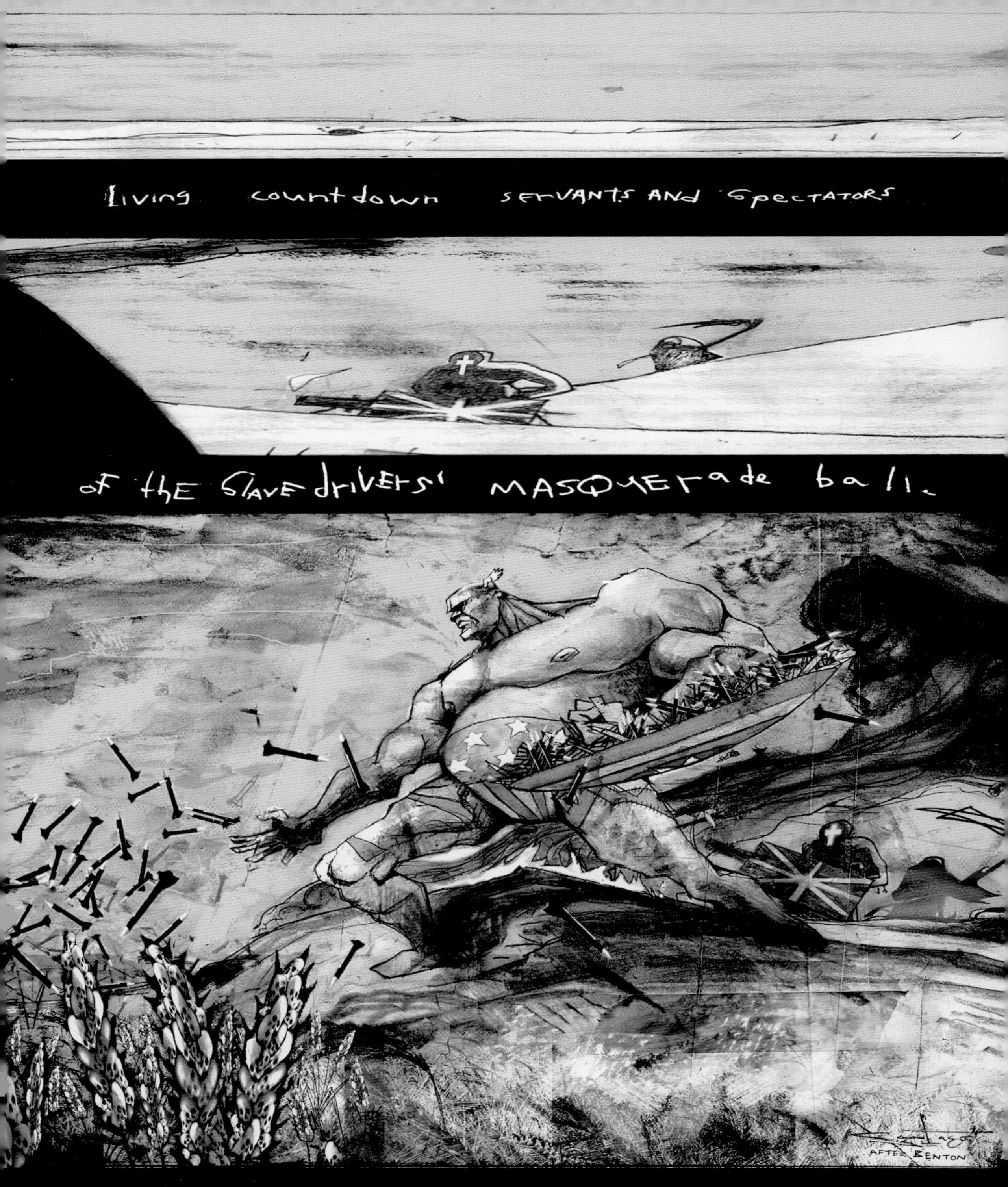
living countdown servants and spectators
of the slave drivers' masquerade ball.
AFTER BENTON

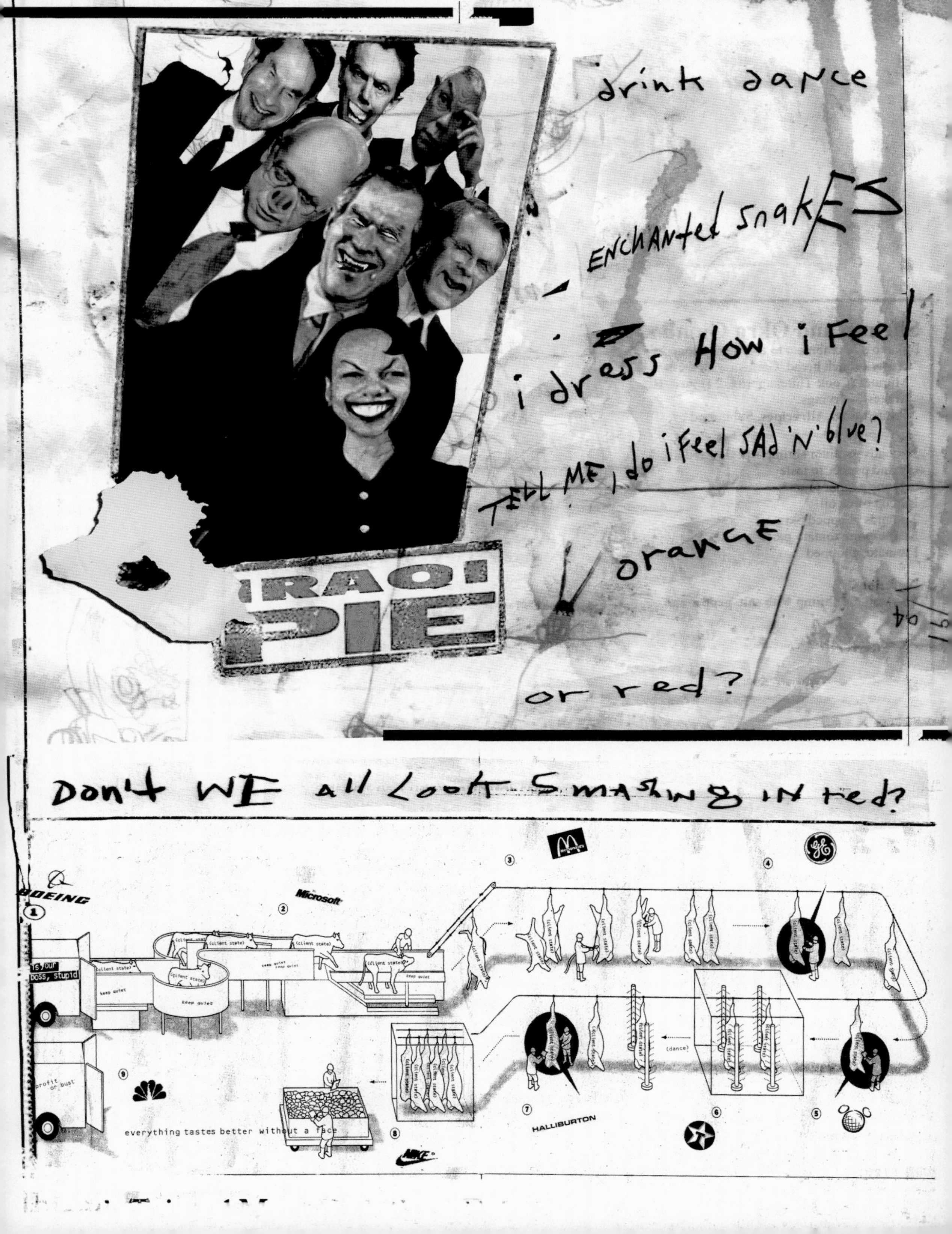

drink dance
ENCHANTED SNAKES
i dress How i Feel
TELL ME, do i Feel SAD 'N' blue?
orange
or red?
IRAQI PIE
Don't WE all Look Smashing in red?
BOEING
1
Is your boss, stupid
keep quiet
2
Microsoft
(client state)
3
4
(dance)
5
6
7
HALLIBURTON
8
9
profit or bust
everything tastes better without a face

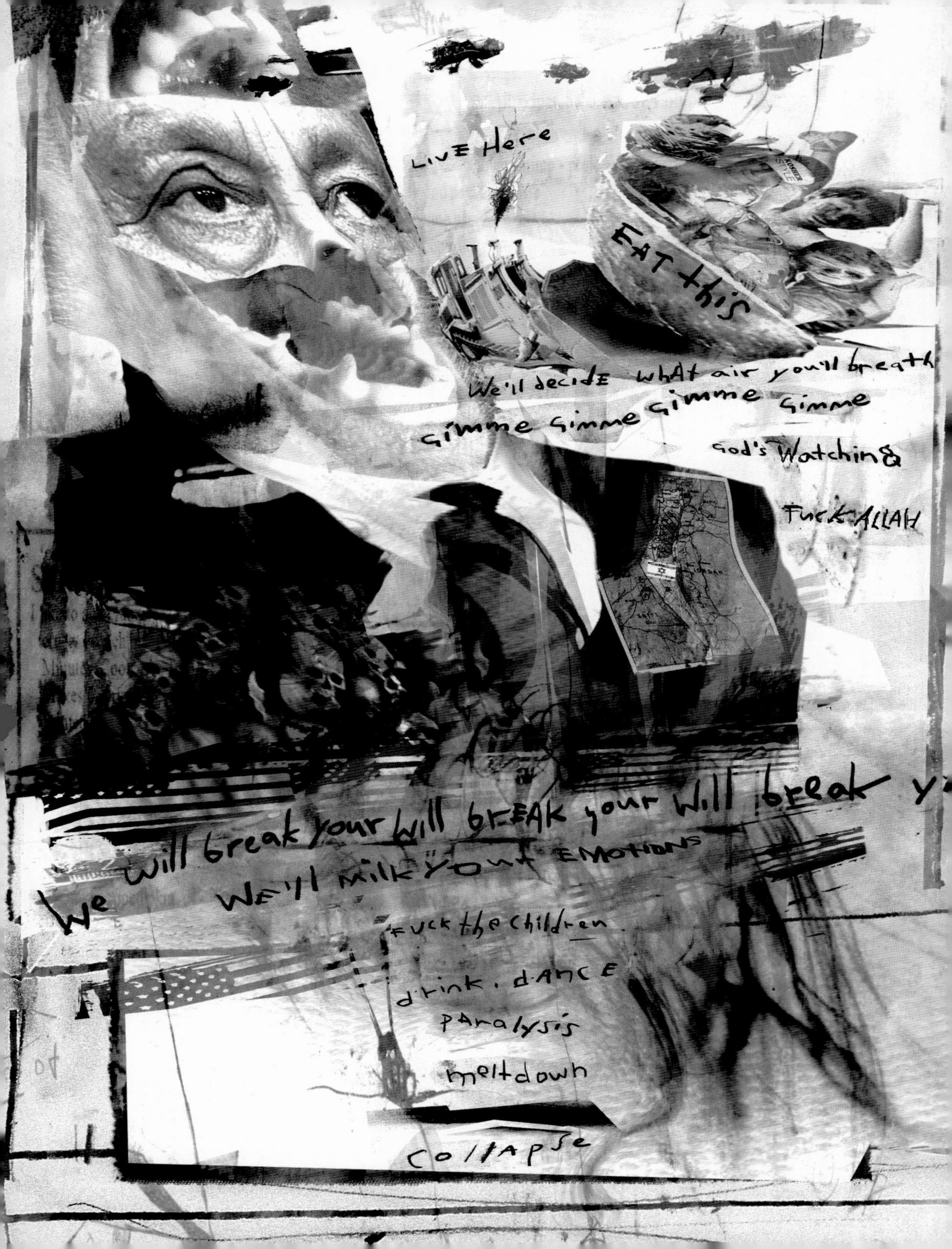
LIVE Here
KOSHER STYLE
EAT this
We'll decide WHAt air you'll breath
gimme gimme gimme gimme
God's Watching
Fuck ALLAH
We will break your will break your will break y
WE'll milk your EMOTIONS
Fuck the children
drink. dance
paralysis
meltdown
collapse

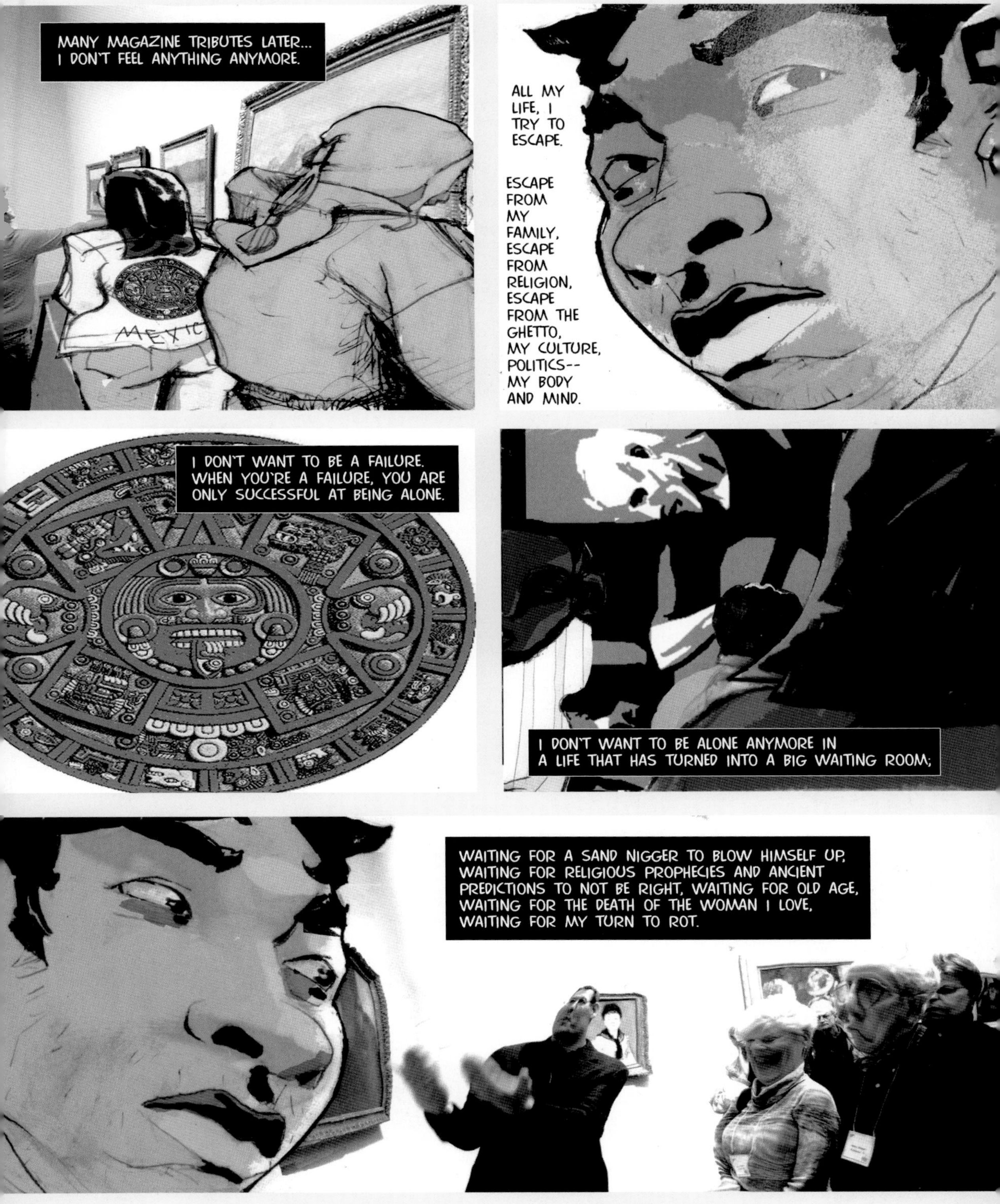
MANY MAGAZINE TRIBUTES LATER... I DON'T FEEL ANYTHING ANYMORE.
MEXIC
ALL MY LIFE, I TRY TO ESCAPE.
ESCAPE FROM MY FAMILY, ESCAPE FROM RELIGION, ESCAPE FROM THE GHETTO, MY CULTURE, POLITICS-- MY BODY AND MIND.
I DON'T WANT TO BE A FAILURE. WHEN YOU'RE A FAILURE, YOU ARE ONLY SUCCESSFUL AT BEING ALONE.
I DON'T WANT TO BE ALONE ANYMORE IN A LIFE THAT HAS TURNED INTO A BIG WAITING ROOM;
WAITING FOR A SAND NIGGER TO BLOW HIMSELF UP, WAITING FOR RELIGIOUS PROPHECIES AND ANCIENT PREDICTIONS TO NOT BE RIGHT, WAITING FOR OLD AGE, WAITING FOR THE DEATH OF THE WOMAN I LOVE, WAITING FOR MY TURN TO ROT.

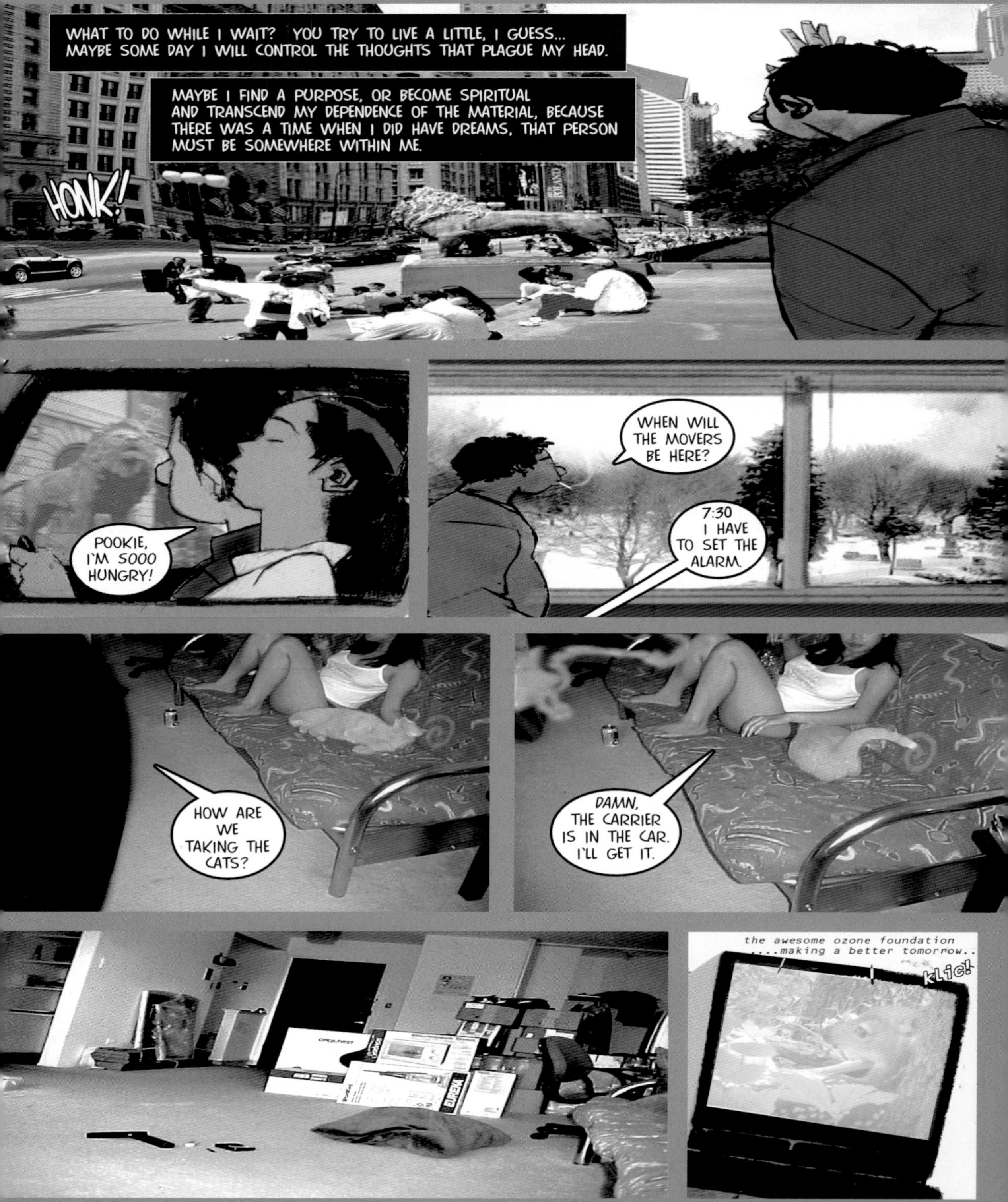
WHAT TO DO WHILE I WAIT? YOU TRY TO LIVE A LITTLE, I GUESS... MAYBE SOME DAY I WILL CONTROL THE THOUGHTS THAT PLAGUE MY HEAD.
MAYBE I FIND A PURPOSE, OR BECOME SPIRITUAL AND TRANSCEND MY DEPENDENCE OF THE MATERIAL, BECAUSE THERE WAS A TIME WHEN I DID HAVE DREAMS, THAT PERSON MUST BE SOMEWHERE WITHIN ME.
HONK!
POOKIE, I'M SOOO HUNGRY!
WHEN WILL THE MOVERS BE HERE?
7:30 I HAVE TO SET THE ALARM.
HOW ARE WE TAKING THE CATS?
DAMN, THE CARRIER IS IN THE CAR. I'LL GET IT.
the awesome ozone foundation
....making a better tomorrow..
kLic!

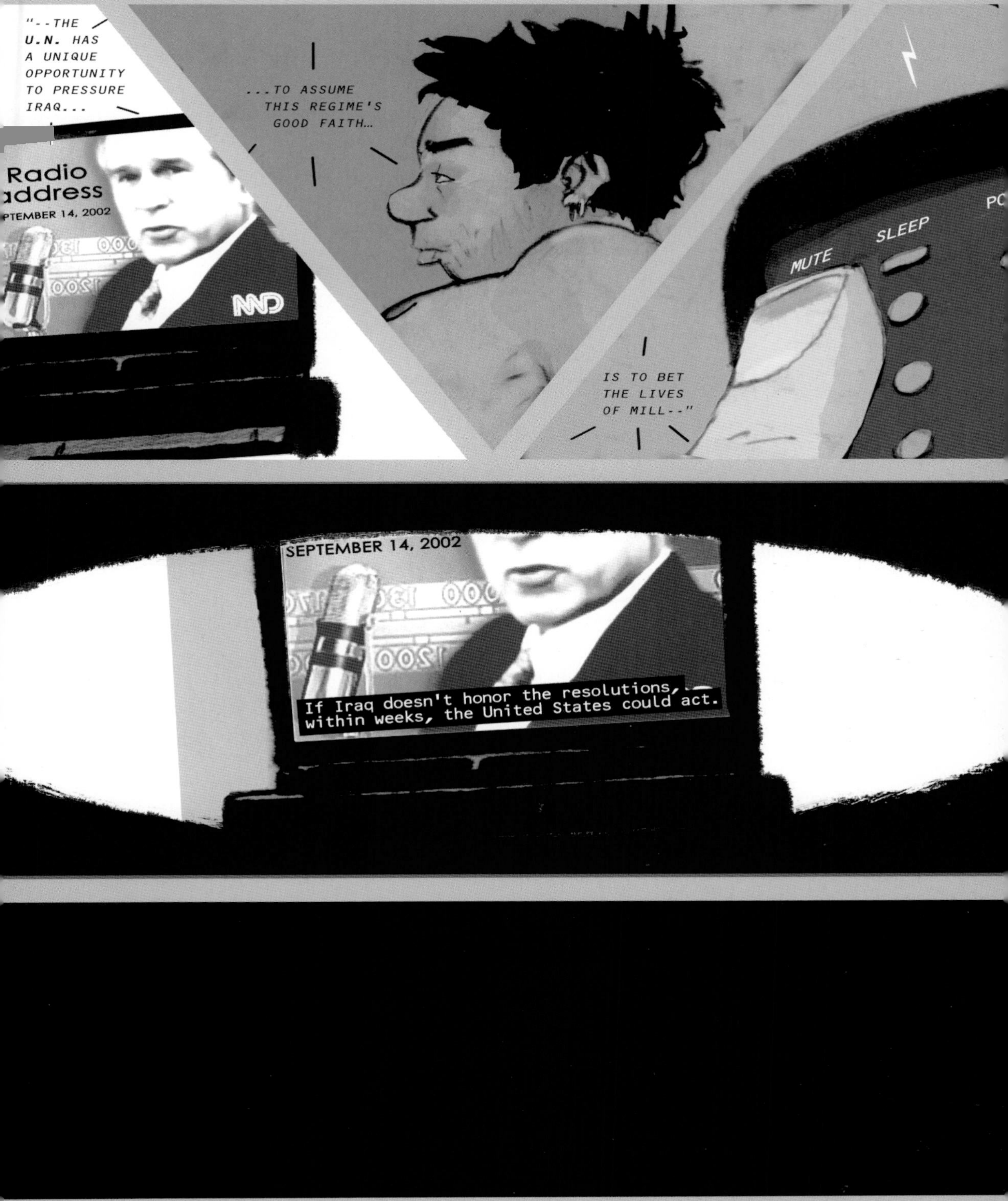
"--THE U.N. HAS A UNIQUE OPPORTUNITY TO PRESSURE IRAQ...
...TO ASSUME THIS REGIME'S GOOD FAITH...
IS TO BET THE LIVES OF MILL--"
Radio
MUTE
SLEEP
SEPTEMBER 14, 2002
If Iraq doesn't honor the resolutions, within weeks, the United States could act.

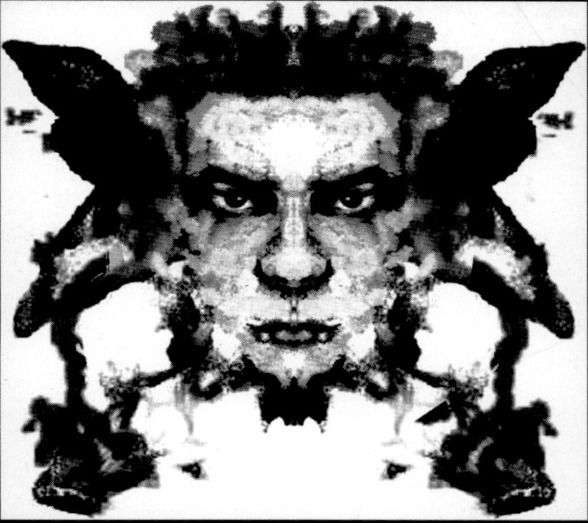

Photo by Frame 313 © 2004

Wilfred Santiago

painter of Shadow™

puertoRican, scorpio, 20th century, ♂, pagan

chicago, H_2O, A3, black&red, cat, wine, weed

△, ◐, 13

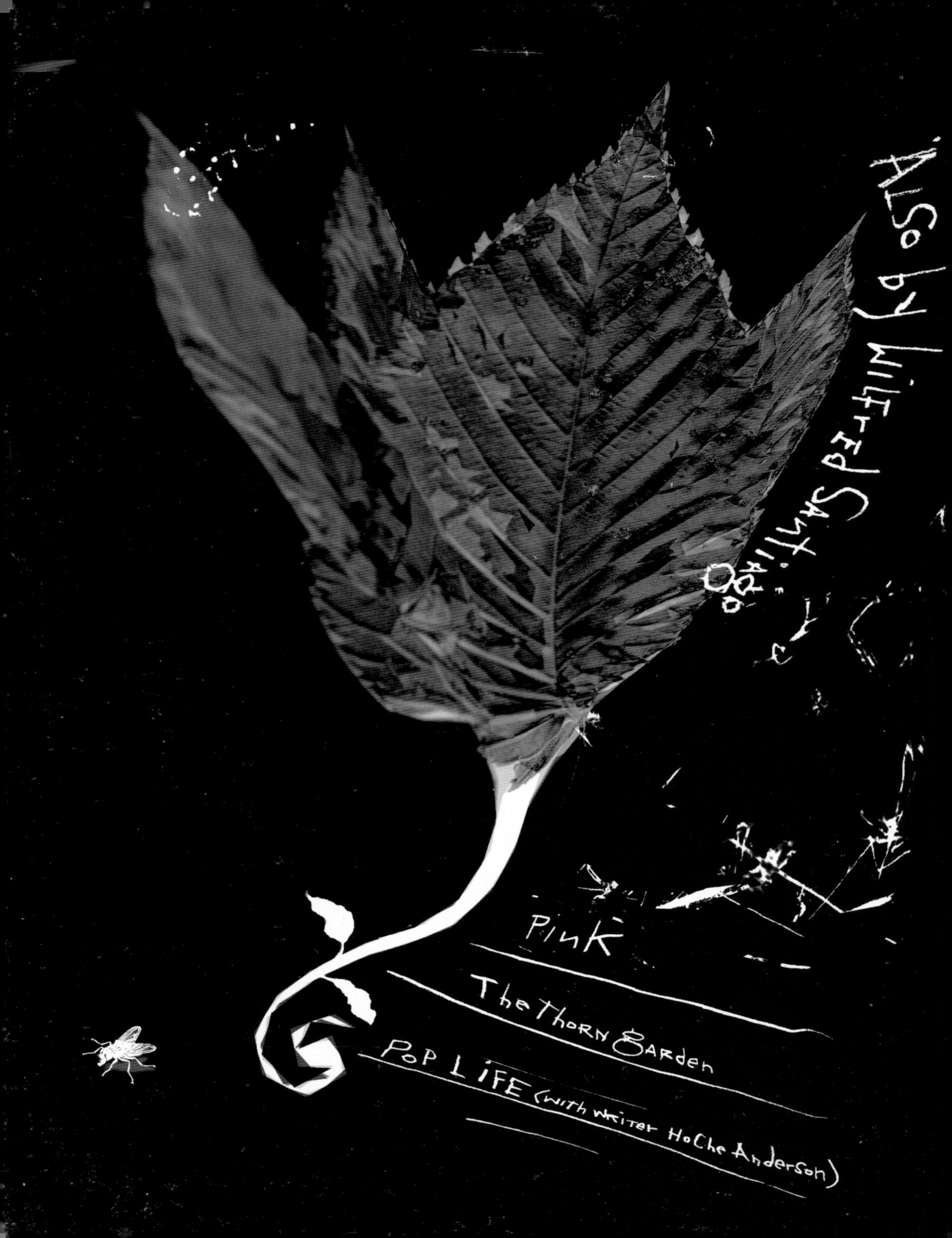
ALSO by Wilfred Santiago
Pink
The Thorn Garden
Pop Life (with writer HoChe Anderson)